Christmas Brides

Christmas Brides

Suzanne Enoch

Alexandra Hawkins

Elizabeth Essex

Valerie Bowman

St. Martin's Paperbacks

CHRISTMAS BRIDES

"One Hot Scot" copyright © 2013 by Suzanne Enoch.
"Once Upon a Christmas Scandal" copyright © 2014 by Alexandra Hawkins.
"The Scandal Before Christmas" copyright © 2013 by Elizabeth Essex.
"It Happened Under the Mistletoe" copyright © 2013 by Valerie Bowman.

All rights reserved.

For information address St. Martin's Press, 175 Fifth Avenue, New York, NY 10010.

ISBN: 978-1-250-06056-3

Printed in the United States of America

St. Martin's Paperbacks edition / October 2014

St. Martin's Paperbacks are published by St. Martin's Press, 175 Fifth Avenue, New York, NY 10010.

10 9 8 7 6 5 4 3 2 1

Table of Contents

One Hot Scot

Scot

❄

Suzanne Enoch

Chapter One

Julia Prentiss sat in the road as the tail of her mare vanished around a large pile of boulders. In other circumstances she likely would have thought the sight pretty—a black horse galloping, riderless, into the cloud-filled orange and purple sunset. It was precisely the sort of thing she'd imagined when she'd suggested that a summer visit to Scotland for her aunt's wedding would make for a perfect Christmas present. She fingered the ripped hem of her blue gown and scowled. This wasn't even remotely what she'd had in mind.

Nothing in the past five days, in fact, seemed like any sort of holiday gift she ever would have asked for. Not in a thousand years. So she supposed she shouldn't have been surprised at being flung to the ground now. It all went perfectly along with the horrid nightmare this so-called gift had become.

Once she had her breath back, she wiggled her fingers and her toes. Her backside would definitely be bruised tomorrow, but nothing seemed to be broken—which was also the first bit of good luck she'd managed in the past five days. It was also likely the last bit of luck she would see. She certainly couldn't risk waiting by the side of the road hoping for a friendly face. It was far more likely the next person she saw would be decidedly *un*friendly.

That thought sent a chill down her spine, and she carefully gathered her feet beneath her and stood. The long, narrow lake that had attracted her attention lay close by on her right, and though she should likely be spending her energy recovering that blasted horse, thirst had already turned her mouth to dust. With a quick look behind her at the empty rolling hills of rock and heather, Julia made her way to the water's edge, squatted down, and scooped up mouthfuls of blessedly cold water with both hands.

Whatever she thought of Hugh Fersen, Lord Bellamy, he'd chosen well when he'd dragged her off here. She'd been riding for two hours or so, and other than Bellamy Park and the scattering of cotters' shacks around it, she hadn't seen so much as a chimney. And now she couldn't see her horse either. In another twenty minutes, she wouldn't be able to see anything at all because it would be completely dark. Another thought occurred to her. Wolves had supposedly been killed off in the Highlands, but she wasn't as certain about bears. Or wildcats. And to think, she might have asked for a visit to Paris. Or a new gown.

"Damnation," she muttered. Would one bit of luck be too much to expect?

A splash of water out in the lake answered her. If she'd been hungry enough to consider raw fish, she would have been interested, but though breakfast had been hours and hours ago, she and her hunger hadn't yet reached the point of desperation. At the edge of the water she'd hoped reeds would offer her some sort of shelter from the view of the road, but evidently here either the weather wasn't temperate enough or the wind was too strong to allow any plants to grow above ankle height. A canyon would hide her, or a nice deep valley, but she didn't want to hide as much as she wanted to be gone from here entirely. Cowering under a tree wouldn't serve any purpose.

From somewhere in the distance a low sound rumbled across the craggy hills, and she shivered. Whether it was a gunshot or thunder, it reminded her how very exposed she was. Whatever her wishes, she would have to find somewhere to shelter and hope the night and the rain hid her trail. Julia straightened. As she turned, something caught her eye, and she bent down. A large swathe of checkered material had been folded and set across a low boulder. She snapped the cloth open to see black and white and gray squares with a thick red threading shot through them, almost like blood.

Bellamy's clan colors were blue and green and black; anything different was welcome. Had she finally gotten free of Fersen land? The low rumble repeated, and she wrapped the cloth around her shoulders. If rain came, she would have something beyond her once pretty blue ball gown to keep her warm at least.

Water splashed out in the lake again, and she looked back. And froze.

A figure rose from the ~~lake~~ water. A male figure, she noted, belatedly stepping backward as he moved directly toward her. Black hair, straight beneath the weight of the streaming water, brushed bare, broad shoulders. His well-muscled chest and abdomen came into view as the water fell away, and she took a heartbeat to wonder whether he wore anything at all before the up-sloping bank answered the question for her.

Oh, my. A thick cock rooted in dark, curling hair hung

between muscular thighs. She'd seen statues, of course, and the occasional naked toddler, but this was no toddler. And no statue. Taken altogether, he was . . . stunning.

She shook herself. He was also a stranger, and she was very much alone. "Stand back," she ordered, backing up another step.

He eyed her, wet black hair falling across one startlingly green eye as he tilted his head. "Ye seem to be wearing my kilt," he rumbled in a thick Highlands brogue.

Julia fingered the heavy material around her shoulders. "Oh. Oh!" Shrugging out of it, she flung the mass at him.

The large fellow caught the tartan as it slapped against his chest. Keeping his gaze squarely on her as if he thought she might vanish into thin air, he wrapped the long material twice about his waist and tucked the end away. "That'll do," he said a moment later. "Now. Ye're a Sasannach lass, are ye not? What are ye doing on my land?"

His land? Was he a Fersen, then, even with the different tartan colors? Or had she indeed found someone who might aid her? All the alliances and territories were terribly confusing, and now she wished she'd spent more time learning about them. Back before her Christmas gift had gone so horribly awry, she'd thought the idea of clans rather romantic. Oh, she should have begun running the moment this man's head emerged from the water. But if he didn't know who she was or why she was there, perhaps she did still have a chance to escape. "I was riding with friends," she ventured. "We were separated, and my horse spooked."

The green gaze trailed from her snarled red-brown hair half escaped from its pins to her equally disheveled blue gown. "Ye went riding in that?" he asked, producing a pair of boots from the other side of the boulder and stomping into them. "Unlikely." Abruptly he turned his back on her and began walking along a faint path in the heather.

"Wait!" Julia looked from the empty, dimming road behind her to the rapidly retreating half-naked man in front of her. The mare could be in York by now, for all she knew. Or worse, it might have returned to the stable from where Julia had procured her this afternoon. What mattered was that if Bellamy's men came across the horse, they would know she was on foot. And close by. *Drat.*

"Well, come along then," the large man said, not offering a backward glance. "I've nae got all night. And it'll be raining by suppertime."

When one was drowning, any bit of flotsam would do, she supposed. Gathering her skirts, she hurried after him. After ten minutes or so of walking to what looked like nowhere, a narrow valley opened up before her, the trail deepening into a surprisingly well-cut series of switchbacks leading down to the bottom. It was fairly easy to navigate but nearly impossible to see from above unless one knew where to look. She dearly hoped that Fersen didn't know where to look.

A waterfall to the left carried the runoff from the lake above into a narrow, fast-moving stream that cut through the middle of the valley in a series of cascading descents. Trees, elm and pine and sturdy oak, lined both sides of the water. If she'd been in a more expansive mood, she might have had a random thought or two about how it looked very like a hidden Eden below the stark hills and craggy peaks above.

"Where are we?" she ventured. According to the tale she'd spun, she was lost, after all. Therefore she'd asked a perfectly reasonable question.

"*Strath na saighead*," he rumbled.

Well, that wasn't at all helpful. "Beg pardon?"

"Valley of the Arrows," he said after a moment. "A great battle was fought here. A course, great battles were fought nearly everywhere in the Highlands." They rounded a stand of tumbled boulders, and a small stone house came into view tucked beneath the cliff. No, not a house. Not even a cottage. A tiny cotter's shack that hardly looked bigger than her bedchamber back at Sebree House in Wessex.

"That sounds exciting," Julia returned absently. So now she knew what the valley was called. That didn't answer the more pressing question. Was she still on Fersen land? Was he loyal to Fersen? She took a breath, trying to ignore the stiffness setting into her backside. "I hear that Clan Fersen has its seat nearby. Are you a part of Lord Bellamy's clan?"

"Is that where ye rode from?" the Highlander asked, stopping to turn around and look at her.

Escaping this afternoon had taken every bit of courage she possessed. If she had to do it again . . . "Please, just tell me if you're allied with the Fersens," she insisted, abruptly realizing that in a very isolated place she'd just taken herself even further from help in this hidden valley. She'd thought—hoped—this might be her chance. But if she was wrong, she'd just delivered herself back into Bellamy's hands, and he would make certain she never escaped again.

"Nae," he answered after a moment. "I answer to Clan MacLawry." He tilted his head, that stray strand of damp, raven black hair falling across one green eye again. "More or less."

She didn't know Clan MacLawry, but then most of the odd . . . antiquity of the Highlands had been a complete surprise. And where before it had seemed quaint, now it seemed distinctly dangerous. Rather like walking into a pit of vipers and not knowing which one was the most—or least—poisonous. "Oh," she ventured, deciding he expected some kind of reply.

"Oh," he repeated, a touch of humor brushing his gaze before he turned back to the cottage and continued forward.

"Is that MacLawry House, then? Who's the . . . clan leader? Might I speak with him?"

"Ye think that pile of rubble is the house of a clan chief? Ye're nae one of those Bedlamites escaped from the asylum, are ye?"

"No, of course not."

"Then, nae, that's an old cotter's shack I use from time to time when I go hunting. The chief of Clan MacLawry is Lord Glengask, who resides at Glengask Castle. And nae, ye cannae speak with him, as he's in London. His youngest brother Bear MacLawry is there, but it's near seven miles from here, and it's aboot to rain."

Seven miles? It might as well have been a hundred miles, since she had no horse and no idea which direction to travel. Thunder rumbled again, closer this time. "Is . . . is there anyone else here?"

"In the shack? Nae. Lenox House—where I live—is three or so miles from here. I can take ye there tomorrow when I've finished up here, or when the storm passes; whichever comes first." He pulled a rope latch and pushed open the heavy door. It opened with a squeak she couldn't describe as anything other than ominous.

"I . . . Perhaps you could tell me the direction to Lenox House? I'm certain I would be welcome there."

He folded his arms across his chest. "Aye? Do ye know Duncan Lenox and his kin, then?"

That would be quite a bluff, if she meant to attempt it. Those keen green eyes glinted at her, though, and she had the distinct feeling that he knew more than he was saying. About what, she had no idea. Julia forced a smile. "No, I don't."

Unfolding his muscular arms, he stuck out his right hand. "Well, now ye do. I'm Duncan Lenox. Come in, lass. I've hot water on fer tea and a rabbit stew on the fire. I'll nae harm ye. Ye have my word on that."

Duncan Lenox waited, his hand outstretched. If this woman had been out riding with friends and lost her way, he was a French poodle, but whatever lies she told, one thing was obvious—she was alone and in distress.

"You're—do you always go about naked, Mr. Lenox?" she asked, glancing from his hand to his face, her brown eyes wary.

"I needed a bath. I didnae expect to have a guest here." He lowered his hand again. "Are ye going to join me inside, or nae?"

"No. I feel more . . . It wouldn't be proper for me to be alone with a man inside his shack."

It wasn't precisely proper for him, either, but she didn't hear him complaining, did she? "Suit yerself, then." Hiding his amusement at her stunned expression, he walked into the shack and closed the door behind him.

He damned well couldn't rescue someone who didn't wish to be rescued. And he wasn't sending anyone on to Lenox House who could possibly bring trouble with her. And this woman was trouble. He could practically smell it in the air. Half-naked Highlander though he might be, he knew the rules of propriety. He had the feeling he was about to discover just how remote this valley was and just how far Society could reach.

Of course she could be some married lady off on an odd adventure. That would save him one set of problems but introduce a whole other one—namely, her husband and what that fellow would do if he discovered them sharing a rabbit stew in a tiny cotter's shack. He preferred to avoid *any* trouble, but that didn't seem likely today.

Above all that, he couldn't escape the sensation that he'd wandered into some faerie's trap. When he'd surfaced in the loch to see a lovely sprite wrapped in his clan colors, her auburn hair touched by the breeze and her brown eyes facing the setting sun, for a bare second he'd thought . . . Well, he wasn't certain what he'd thought, but it hadn't made any sense.

He did know what his body had thought, and it had taken a moment to let the cold water put everything back in place again. She'd have run for certain if she'd seen that bit leading the way. With a glance at the still-closed door he pulled on an old linen shirt, then walked over to throw another piece of wood on the fire and pull off the kettle to make himself a cup of tea. That done, he set the stew back over the fire; if that scent didn't tempt her to come inside, nothing would.

She seemed to think him part of the Fersen clan—or at least she had at first—and that idea had made her nervous. If she was tangled up with Bellamy, that made *him* nervous. But still, she clearly didn't belong here in the Highlands, and if she was desperate enough to follow a nearly naked man to his doorstep, he couldn't abandon her. Not even if leaving her standing there like Boadicea in the heather might have been the wiser decision.

All he'd wanted was to stop a few beasts from killing his calves, for the devil's sake, and perhaps to do a bit of fishing. To be certain he'd never caught a Sasannach woman in Loch Shinaig before. Duncan glanced toward the door again. Perhaps she'd gone, after all. That would take care of a substantial number of troubles. And all he would have to do was not go looking for her.

The door rattled and opened. "You would truly have left me out there in the dark and the rain, wouldn't you?"

So, the more difficult route, it was. He should have been dismayed and annoyed, but Duncan found himself smiling as he pulled down another teacup and set it on the plank table. "I had a hunch ye'd come inside if ye wanted to. I wasnae going to drag ye in. Have a seat."

Instead of doing that, she spent a moment looking around the small shack. A bed in the corner up against the side of the fireplace, the table, three chairs, two cupboards, and the corner by the door piled with gear for stripping and stretching deer hides during hunting season. Two windows, one looking north and the other west, were shuttered against the weather, and the single door stood opposite the hearth. There was nothing else inside except for a few bits and bobs that former residents had left behind and no one had bothered to dispose of.

"This is . . . small," she said. "If you own Lenox House, what are you doing out here?"

"We've had some wolves chasing after our cattle. I've been tracking after them." And he'd wanted a few days of quiet, but until he knew who she was and what she was doing in the Highlands, the details of his life at Lenox House could wait.

"You aren't bamming me, are you?" she asked, worry crossing her features. "I read that there are no wolves left in Scotland."

"Aye, I've heard that, as well. Old MacQueen of Findhorn claimed he killed the last of 'em near seventy-five years ago. Call them feral dogs if ye like, then, but someaught's killing my cattle, and it isnae rabbits. I'm keener on stopping it than on naming the beasts that're doing it."

She took a breath, offering him a small nod. "So you truly are Duncan Lenox? And you're only here to protect your cattle?"

"Aye. And this is my land. I'm here after wolves or dogs or rabid rabbits, and I'll nae harm ye, lass." Whatever had her so skittish, he could only reassure her with the truth. He sat in one of the chairs pulled up to the table. "But that's all ye'll get from me until ye tell me someaught aboot yerself."

He poured himself some more tea, which he decided was the most nonthreatening thing he could do. But he didn't need to be looking at his guest to know she still hesitated. Whatever had happened to bring her here likely wasn't pleasant. Finally, she sat in the chair across from him. "I don't know what I would have done if I hadn't come across you, then. I'm quite . . . lost, really. So thank you."

"Ye're welcome." Duncan nudged the pot of tea in her direction. "That's nae much information, though. I'll start for ye, shall I? Ye've a fear of the Fersens. Bellamy in particular. I've a keen suspicion ye were nae oot riding with friends. Nae in that dress. In fact, I think the only truth ye've spoken is that ye're lost."

Pretty brown eyes, almost black in the dimmer light of the shack, widened. "You're . . . more observant than I realized," she said after a moment.

"Ye mean I'm less stupid than ye hoped. Do ye care to tell me what's happened to ye then, lass?"

"I'm afraid I don't trust you enough for that, Mr. Lenox." Her hand shaking a little, she poured herself a cup of tea and dumped two lumps of sugar into the brew.

Wealthy, then, though he'd thought so from both her gown and her manner of speech. A poor lass would have been excited to see the sugar and used too much. This one used it without even thinking about it. "Call me Duncan," he said, and reached down to pull the knife from his boot. Before she could do more than gasp, he set it down on the table and pushed it toward her, hilt first. "Does that help yer trust?"

She ran her finger across the flat, carved hilt of whalebone then pulled it into onto her lap. "Prentiss," she supplied with a hesitation so slight he almost didn't notice it. The way she kept her gaze directly on his face the entire time didn't help his concentration, either. "Julia Prentiss."

The name meant nothing to him. He didn't spend much time reading the London newspapers, though, and even less perusing the Society pages, so she might have been the Prince Regent's cousin and he'd never have known it. "Well, Miss Prentiss, would ye care for some rabbit stew?"

"I am a bit hungry," she conceded. "You do your own cooking?"

"Here, I do. At Lenox House I have a cook. Mrs. Mac-Davitt," he replied. "But I've yet to poison myself."

"It's just you at Lenox House, then? No . . . wife or family?"

"I answered yer question," he countered, rising to find two bowls and ladle a generous serving of stew into each of them. "Ye tell me someaught aboot yerself."

"I didn't agree to this game."

Water began tap-tapping at the windows. "Fine. I'm accustomed to solitude here, anyway." Handing over a bowl, he seated himself again and dug into his supper.

A moment later she picked up her spoon and began eating. She had long, delicate fingers, he noticed, pretty, well-manicured hands despite the dirt currently under the nails. A proper lady's hands. So what the devil was she doing alone in the middle of the Highlands? He could order her to talk, he supposed, but handing her a fright wouldn't help either of them. No, she wanted to feel safe. And so he would be patient. To a point.

For several minutes they ate in relative silence while the storm came closer, the rain heavier and the thunder approaching like a giant's footfalls. "If I needed to send a letter to Aberdeen, could you assist me with that?" she finally asked.

Duncan kept eating.

"I asked you a question, Mr. Lenox."

"Duncan," he corrected, and shoveled in another mouthful.

She gave an annoyed-sounding sigh. "Could you help me get a letter to Aberdeen, Duncan?"

Pushing back in his chair, he reached for a bowl of salt and then scooted up to the table again. "This isnae a soft summer shower," he observed. "A good thing ye're here tonight and nae ootside."

Miss Prentiss set down her spoon, none-too-gently. "Are you going to answer my question?"

"Ye didnae answer mine. I told ye the rules. Ye're the one didnae wish to abide by them."

Her brown eyes narrowed. "And I told you that I'm not playing."

He couldn't help the smile that curved his lips. "Then I suppose we're at an impasse, Miss Prentiss."

Chapter Two

Duncan Lenox was quite possibly the most stubborn man alive. Surely any true gentleman would immediately offer aid to a young lady as completely alone as she was. And yet there he sat, devouring his third bowl of rabbit stew and eyeing her with a damnable twinkle in his eye, as if he had nothing better to do than aggravate her.

Perhaps he didn't have anything better to do, but she certainly did. Julia took a deliberate swallow of tea. "Mr. Lenox, I require your assistance. That should be all you—"

"Duncan," he interrupted.

"Duncan, then, for heaven's sake. I need to get word to Aberdeen, as soon as possible."

"And I can see that ye do so, once we get to Lenox House. After the storm passes."

"I'm willing to get wet in order to reach civilization." In her world, civilization meant safety—or at least a place where people knew the rules and minded them.

He snorted. "'Civilization'," he repeated. "At Lenox House? Ye definitely arenae from around here."

"Which means I have even more urgency to get word to Aberdeen." For God's sake, if he'd realized she hadn't been out riding, that she had nowhere else to go, that she wasn't dressed for the Highlands, why didn't he also see that she needed his assistance?

Duncan eyed her, light green eyes speculative. "Have ye ever played a game called 'questions'?" he asked.

"The children's game where someone thinks of a thing and the others guess what it is? Yes, of course. But I'm not playing it with you if that's what you're suggesting."

"I'll just guess some things anyway, and if ye like, ye can tell me if I'm correct or nae."

"I'm not playing," she repeated, turning her gaze back to her rather delicious stew.

"Ye were in Aberdeen to meet yer future husband," he said anyway.

"No."

"Ye were in Aberdeen," he amended, "on holiday."

"You're wasting time. If you want to be rid of me, it's as simple as escorting me to Lenox House, giving me a pen and some paper, and sending out my message."

"Ye were at a soiree," he went on, clearly intending to ignore her interruption. "A fancy one, with dancing. I can tell that because ye're nae wearing riding boots or walking shoes."

"Hurray for you, Mr. M– Duncan."

"Ye met Lord Bellamy at this party. Ye thought him a handsome lad, and so ye went off to kiss him, and then he promised ye a fine life if only ye'd come away with him to Bellamy Park, and ye—"

"I did no such thing!" *Of all the nerve.* "Stop talking, will you?"

Abruptly he sat forward, all trace of humor gone from his eyes. "Very well, lass. Since ye willnae give me yer circumstances, I'll give ye mine. I'm allied with the Mac-Lawrys. Most of them—the clan chief and his family—arenae here at the moment. My property edges onto Fersen land. We dunnae like each other, the Fersens and me. I stay oot of all the clan politics and rivalries as best I can, though, because Glengask and my nearest kinfolk are aboot seven miles away. And because I have nae brothers or cousins or uncles beneath my roof to take a stand with me. I *do* have beneath my roof three younger sisters and a grandmother I'll nae allow to be harmed or bartered for anyone's favor." He leaned closer still, pinning her with his direct, forest-tinted gaze. "So now I'll ask ye again, Julia Prentiss. What sort of trouble are ye bringing to my door?"

Oh, dear. She should have kept walking. She should have kept a tighter hold of her horse and kept riding to . . . wherever it was she'd been heading. And she should have asked for a new hat for Christmas. Then none of this would be happening. "I didn't mean to bring you trouble," she said quietly, the quaking that had been unsettling her insides for the past hours and days finally pushing her toward tears. "It found me. And maybe it was my own stupid fault, but—"

He reached out, grabbing her hand. The spoon she held clattered to the tabletop. "What happened?" he repeated, his voice quieter.

She had to tell him. However reluctant a hero he might be, her need for assistance remained. And she simply wasn't daft enough to go out into the storm in the middle of the night and hope for a more enthusiastic rescue. "I was in Aberdeen," she conceded, "with my mother and my sister. We were there for my aunt's wedding. We weren't going to attend, because it's the Season in London and because it's so far from home, but I told my parents that all I wanted for Christmas was a holiday in Scotland. I very much enjoy the writings of Walter Scott." She blinked, realizing she was blabbering.

His expression, though, didn't alter. "And?" he prompted, still holding her hand.

After what she'd been through, his grip should have dismayed or frightened her, but it didn't. His fingers were gentle, and she knew she could pull away if she chose to do so. A comforting touch . . . Perhaps she was being a ninny, but it was welcome.

"After the wedding my aunt's husband's parents held a large party. Lord Bellamy and a great many other peers were there. I knew Lord Bellamy from London, and so when he asked me to dance, I agreed. He was always very pleasant and even if he had something of a reputation for being a fortune hunter, he seemed . . . harmless enough." She frowned. "I didn't even think about that. It was simply nice to see someone I knew."

Julia cleared her throat. Whatever stupidity had gotten her here, it was far too late to do anything about that. Now she needed to get out of this situation. "We danced, and he said how pleasant it was to see me there and wasn't the weather lovely. Then he stumbled, and said he felt light-headed. I—stupid thing that I am—I helped him out to the balcony. The next thing I knew someone had put a cloth over my face. I awoke in a carriage with my hands and feet bound, and Bellamy sitting across from me asking just how much money I would be worth upon my marriage."

Duncan muttered something beneath his breath. She couldn't quite make it out, and she wasn't even certain it had been in English, but it sounded rather deadly. His hand tugged her closer, and then he pushed her sleeve up a bit. After three days of being unbound the bruises and scratches had begun to fade, but they were still there. "Did he hurt ye?" he asked, very quietly.

"No. When we arrived at Bellamy Park, he untied me, showed me to a very nice room, and told me that I was now utterly ruined and that he'd left behind a note saying we'd eloped. He would give me a day or two to decide to behave, and then he would have us married." She gave a bitter chuckle. "Evidently he didn't want an unwilling bride at the church. Just one who'd realized that she had no alternative if she ever wanted to show her face in public again."

"Bastard."

Julia slammed her free fist against the table. "And it would have worked, because I flirted with him, and people saw it. And because I put my arm around him while we walked to the balcony."

"But ye're nae married to him, I assume."

She lifted her head again, meeting his gaze. "No, I am not. I decided I would rather be ruined than married to that man and allow him to get a penny of my money."

"Well. Good fer ye, Julia. Ye showed a pound of spleen, running oot into the Highlands with nowhere to go and nae idea where ye were."

"I don't know whether it was spleen or idiocy, but at least it was *my* choice."

"Aye. Nae a pleasant Christmas gift at all, though."

"Not particularly." So now he knew her story. She watched his face carefully, looking for any sign that he would help her, or put her out in the rain, or worse, see her as an opportunity for himself. After all, while she hadn't said just how wealthy she was, she had told him that an aristocrat had been willing to kidnap her to claim her money. Unless he'd missed that bit—an act of providence about which she wasn't willing to wager.

Abruptly he pushed to his feet. "Do ye play chess?" he asked, walking over to one of the cupboards and pulling open a door.

"What?"

"Chess. Do ye play it?" As she watched, he pulled down a wooden board and a small box and returned to the table.

"I . . . A little, I suppose. I haven't played in years. Why are we going to play chess? I told you my story, and you said you would help me if I did."

He grinned as he resumed his seat. "Well, we're nae going anywhere tonight. We'll head for Lenox Hoose in the morning, if the rain lets up, and then we'll figure oot a plan."

Duncan could tell from her expression that she would rather they came up with a plan tonight, but for the devil's sake, he needed a moment or two to consider what she'd told him. Whatever dastardly thing Bellamy had done, the earl was not a man to be taken lightly. This was the sort of thing that began clan wars, one man taking in another's woman—whether the woman in question had any wish to be where she was, or not. And of course beneath all of that logic, he very much wanted to hunt down Bellamy and put a hole or two through him.

She kept looking at him with those pretty brown eyes of hers. "What?" he finally asked, pausing as he set up the chessboard.

"We're going to stay here tonight? The two of us?"

"Aye." He grimaced. "I take yer meaning, lass. Ye've naught to fear. Ye can have the bed. I'll be sitting up, just in case."

"You mean in case Bellamy comes looking for me here." Her expression didn't alter; the thought had already occurred to her, then. "Just how likely is that to happen?"

"I've nae idea. There's a great deal of land between Bellamy and here, but I reckon he'd prefer to look in more obvious places, because it's easier. And because it's storming outside."

She nodded, and another lock of her auburn hair came down from the disheveled bun at her crown. "And a man who kidnaps a woman rather than actually attempting to woo her would prefer the easier way."

"Precisely." He liked that she had a logical bent to her thinking; most other lasses would either be in a fair way to panicking all over again or would have given up when they lost the horse. If they'd had the courage to run at all.

"What if he does come?"

Duncan drew a breath. What he wished to do wasn't even close to being the wiser course of action, but he needed to use his brain rather than his fists. "Honestly, I'd prefer if I didnae have to fight him," he said aloud. "When two men from . . . unfriendly clans get into a brawl here, it can have ramifications."

"So you'll simply hand me back to him?" She stood, her chair falling over backward behind her and the knife he'd given her in her right hand. "I won't allow that!"

"Perhaps ye'll let me finish what I was saying before ye stick me, Julia. If ye dunnae mind."

"I wouldn't stick you. I would stab *him*."

He couldn't help grinning at that. "I'm all reassured, then." Moving slowly on the chance that she would forget what she'd just said and stab him anyway, he stood up and walked toward the bed. Taking the short footboard in his hands, he shoved the thing sideways.

Straw covered the floor there, as it did everywhere else. Brushing a bit of it aside, he found the indentation in the floor, dug his fingers into it, and lifted. "If he does come calling, ye'll hide in here. I'll nae suggest ye spend the night in here, though, because it's a wee bit cramped. And dark."

She walked up to where he crouched and bent forward to peer into the dark, wood-lined hole about the size of the bed that hid it. "Why do you have a priesthole in your floor?"

"My great-grandfather and most of his cotters were Jacobites. So I suppose it's a Jacobite hole. If any Sasannach soldiers came 'round, most cotters had a place to hide bonny Prince Charlie's followers, if need be."

She nodded, putting a hand on his shoulder as she leaned closer. "Would Bellamy know about it?"

"I doubt it. The hole's been there a hundred years, nearly. I've kept it repaired because . . . Well, because I'm a cautious lad, and I have sisters." He could feel her chuckle through her hand. It sent an interesting warmth running beneath his skin. Sternly he pushed the sensation away. She was likely to be enough trouble without adding lust into the mix.

"Is the hole to hide you, or them?"

He dropped the wood cover back over, scattered the loose straw to show her how well hidden it lay, and pulled the bed back in place over it. "They know aboot it, so it wouldnae do me much good. I have been tempted though, on occasion."

"How old are they? Your sisters, I mean," she asked, following him back to the table.

"Sorcha's sixteen, Bethia's thirteen, and Keavy's just nine. Sorcha turned into a banshee aboot a year ago, so I reckon I've got a year or two of sense left from Bethia, and hopefully half a decade from Keavy."

When he finished setting up the chess pieces and looked up at his guest, the lass was smiling at him. "You're very fond of them, aren't you?" she said.

"They're my sisters. I love them. They'll have me mad as a hatter and white-haired as a winter rabbit, but they and Grandmama Maevis are my only family."

"I think I was luckier today than I ever realized," she said after a moment, her smile fading. "I am quite aware that I might just as easily have stumbled across another Hugh Fersen or his ilk. Thank you, Duncan Lenox."

"Dunnae thank me til ye're safe with yer family." He realized he was staring at her mouth, and cleared his throat, shoving the board in her direction. "White or black?"

"Black," she answered, turning the chessboard so the white-painted wood pieces were aligned in front of him and the black ones toward her.

He shifted a pawn out and sat back to watch her. What was he going to do with her? The easiest, safest thing for him and his sisters would be to return Julia Prentiss to Bellamy. A man with sisters would have to be damned to ever do such a thing, though. Just the idea of someone dragging off one of his bonny girls made him ill and angry. No, not angry. Blood-boilingly furious, more like. And surprising or not, it was an easy thing to muster the same emotion when he imagined this lass in Bellamy's grasp.

The next best option would be for him to put her up on another horse and escort her back to Aberdeen immediately. That, though, would leave Lenox House vulnerable should Bellamy come looking for her—or for a substitute bride, if he was frustrated enough. Lord Glengask would have been a help, if he hadn't been in London chasing after his younger sister. Bear MacLawry was a possibility, but Glengask's youngest brother was as likely to start a fight with Bellamy as to resolve the situation.

No, having her send her letter asking for her kin to come and fetch her and keeping her hidden in the meantime was the only solution that made any sense. And it had nothing to do with the fact that she was pretty as summer and brave to boot. It had nothing to with the fact that she was more than likely ruined, and that he wasn't . . . content with the idea of sending so unexpected a female away. It was, quite simply, the correct thing to do.

"I believe it's your move, Duncan," she said, shaking him out of his thoughts.

That it was. He shifted another pawn, making a wall,

and for a time they sat and played and talked about nothing more pressing than the weather and Scottish weddings. She could likely use the time to gather her own thoughts, and the devil knew he had some things to consider, as well. She was a piss-poor player, but he didn't much mind that. When he played against Keavy, he made certain she won often enough to keep her from getting discouraged.

"Ye said ye were here with yer mother and sister," he finally asked. "What of yer father?"

"He stayed in London for the Season. He's . . . a viscount. Lord Prentiss. So he has to attend Parliament. And he said that while Scotland might be my idea of a gift, he would prefer a quiet household for a few weeks." She looked from the chessboard to him. "What of your parents? You said you had a grandmother."

"Aye. Grandmama Maevis. She's my father's mother. Both my parents died aboot seven years ago, when the fever came through one winter."

"Oh, my goodness. I'm so sorry."

Duncan shrugged, watching her fingers fiddle with a rook. "They went together, as they would have wished it. And I was already two-and-twenty, so the lasses had someone to look after 'em." At the time he hadn't been nearly as circumspect, but she didn't need to know that. When she moved a pawn to block his knight, he countered with a bishop. "How old is yer sister?"

"Elizabeth? She's sixteen. That's the one thing I'm grateful for—that Bellamy snatched me rather than her. She'll still be able to have her debut and dance and flirt, as any young lady wants to do."

"But none of that's left for ye? Ye're what, nineteen? Hardly on the shelf, lass."

"I'm one-and-twenty, and I've been missing for five days. And I was last seen in the unchaperoned company of an unmarried man. There was also the elopement letter he left on my behalf. We cannot forget that." Her fingers curled around the rook as if she wanted to choke the life out of it.

He could hardly blame her for that. "But if ye yell to the world that ye were taken against yer will, willnae that make a difference?"

Julia grimaced, releasing the rook in favor of a knight. "Some, perhaps. I'm still marriageable because of my dowry. But I'll be looked at askance and whispered about, and other ladies won't invite me over for tea." A tear ran down one cheek, and she brushed it away. "I can manage the gossip, as long as it doesn't hurt Elizabeth."

"Ye shouldnae have to manage it at all. None of this was yer doing, for St. Bridget's sake."

"That, Duncan, doesn't really matter. Thank you for saying it, though." She picked up a black knight and showed it to him. "Did you think this would be you today?"

He chuckled. "A black knight? Nae a white knight?"

She grinned back at him. "Well, you were naked."

"Aye. That I was." Meeting her gaze, he shifted another chess piece. In all honesty, he wasn't certain which one it was or if the move was even legal.

The door behind him rattled, the entire wall shuddering beneath a hard fist.

Christ in heaven. He jumped, and Julia sucked in a breath as though she thought it might be her last. "It's barred," he reminded her, scooping the chess pieces up and tossing them back into their box. Grabbing both them and the board he strode to the bed and pushed it aside, then lifted the trapdoor and tossed the game pieces into the hole. "In with ye," he whispered, taking her fingers to help her down. They shook in his big paw, and he squeezed a little. He handed down her nearly empty bowl of stew and her teacup, then smiled encouragingly at her.

The sight of large brown eyes gazing up at him as he

closed her into the darkness would stay with him forever, he thought, scattering straw and moving the bed back. As a louder, more insistent pounding began at the door, he shoved back the bedcovers, stripped out of his shirt, and dumped it into the chair Julia had occupied a moment ago. Then he pulled off one boot, ruffled his hair, and stomped to the door.

"Dooley, I told ye to . . ." He trailed off as Hugh Fersen, the Earl of Bellamy, glared at him. "Bellamy? What the devil are ye doing here?"

"We saw your light," the earl stated, swiping rain from his face. "May we come in?"

Duncan frowned. "Who's 'we'?" he asked, moving a step to the right so he blocked the entrance completely with his body. The figure behind Bellamy stepped forward, and a whisper of uneasiness curled down Duncan's spine. "Orville," he said, nodding.

Orville Fersen, Bellamy's cousin, smiled coolly, the expression fractured by a nose that had been broken at least twice. "We passed by Lenox House a bit ago," he said in his low, scratched voice. "They said ye were out here."

They'd been by Lenox House. Where his sisters would be sleeping. And he'd been here, three miles away. "Why are ye looking for me?" he asked, not budging from his place. "It must be near midnight."

"It's raining, Lenox. May we come in?" Bellamy repeated.

"I'm nae a friend of yers, Bellamy. Either of ye. And as I'm here hunting after someaught that's killing my animals, and I've half a suspicion it's ye and yer dogs, Orville, ye can damned well stand oot in the rain until lightning strikes ye dead."

"Care to wager on that, Duncan?" Orville moved in closer, his hand going to his waist. A dagger, no doubt. And his own was in the hole with Julia.

"That's enough, cousin. We're here for Lenox's aid, after all."

"Is that so?" Duncan retorted. "How might that be?"

"It's a bit embarrassing, actually," Bellamy said, his faded accent telling Duncan the earl had only recently returned from England—even if he hadn't been fairly aware of Hugh's comings and goings. "I seem to have misplaced something of mine."

"Aye? I may have a stray sheep or two of yourn, but I dunnae think that would bring ye here. Orville could see to yer sheep. And in the daylight."

"Seems that sheep would be *yer* interest, Lenox," Orville Fersen retorted, snickering.

"Never mind that," his cousin cut in. "I . . . Well, I'm married. And the young lady is—"

"Ye're married? My congratulations, Bellamy. I'd no idea."

"Yes, well, it was arranged, and I'm afraid my bride is quite . . . sheltered. Shy. She fled Bellamy Park this afternoon, and I'm afraid something ill has befallen her."

Duncan lifted an eyebrow. "She ran away? Did ye show her yer cock and the massive thing frightened her?"

Bellamy chuckled, the sound forced. "Something like that. Regardless, I'm worried, and I need to find her. Have you seen an English lady over the past few hours?"

"Nae. And I think that'd be someaught I'd remember. Do ye want me to ride oot with some of my lads and help ye look? Ye say she's a Sasannach? The Highlands is no place fer a stranger to be lost."

"I can manage the search. I do want permission to search the valley here. And your shack."

Duncan didn't bother hiding his frown. "Ye're welcome to search the valley. If I hear ye went through Lenox House while I was nae there, though, we're going to have a disagreement. I'll nae have Orville gawping at my sisters."

"Ye worried ye'll nae find another man to match me?"

"I'm worried ye'll give 'em nightmares, and I'll nae manage to marry them off at all." Duncan put a finger against Bellamy's wet chest. "Did ye search my home withoot me there?" he asked, very evenly.

"I took a quick look through your vacant rooms," the earl returned, "in the company of your butler. Orville waited outside with the horses. I know that you and he are . . . at odds."

"That's someaught, then," Duncan conceded begrudgingly, and he stepped to one side, allowing them into the cottage. "I've an objection to ye calling me a liar when I say yer lass is nae here. But I ken ye judge a man by yer own character, so I'll allow ye to look aboot. This once."

"Careful, Lenox. That almost sounded like an insult."

"It was meant to."

The two men stepped inside, shaking rain onto the dirt floor as they both shed their greatcoats and hats. Bellamy handed his garments to Orville, who sent his titled cousin a glare and then hung the dripping things on the wooden pegs driven into the wall beside the door.

"Dunnae think ye're staying here, Bellamy. Ye said ye were here to find yer lass. Have yer look, and be gone. I'll nae put ye up for the night."

"Why in such a hurry to be rid of us?" Orville asked.

"Because ye've already called me a liar once, and I dunnae like either of ye. And because I've work to do in the morning, and ye're keeping me awake."

The earl's cousin sent an assessing look about the single room, then back at Duncan. "So ye sleep in yer kilt, do ye?"

"Nae. I sleep naked. But then someone pounded on my door and woke me up. Any other stupid questions ye wish to ask?"

While he kept Orville glaring angrily at him, the earl

made a show of pulling open cupboards and looking through blankets and under the bed. "Could someone have come in here while you were out hunting?"

"And they've hidden in the cupboard? Are ye looking fer a woman or a mouse?"

"This isn't amusing. And I'd rather stay out of the rain tonight," Bellamy said absently, digging the spoon through the remains of the kettle of stew. "We could scour the valley at dawn."

"And I dunnae care what ye prefer," Duncan retorted. They could spend the night on the floor, but that would mean Julia would have to stay in the pitch-black hole for another four hours, with Bellamy snoring cozily only a few feet away. After what she'd already been through, he wasn't willing to subject the lass to that. "Ye can see she's nae here." He put a concerned look on his face. "Ye truly think she's oot in that weather? She could catch her death. What the devil made her run from ye, anyway?"

"That's my affair, Lenox. And for your own sake you'd best not be lying to me."

With a great deal of effort Duncan kept his expression even. "I dunnae ken why ye keep flinging threats in my direction, Bellamy. I've nae given ye so much as a cross look."

"Yes, you excel at diplomacy, Lenox. If your great-grandmother had been a Campbell rather than a Mac-Lawry, I imagine we'd be friends."

Duncan didn't imagine any such thing. He knew Bellamy to be high-handed and arrogant, and if not for the consequences, he might have told him so on several occasions. If there was ever a man who needed a good punch to the snout, it was Hugh Fersen. "As we're so near to friendship," he said aloud, "mayhap ye might tell me why ye think yer bride is hiding in one of my houses."

"The horse she stole returned to my stable two hours

ago, without her aboard. She's somewhere close by, and you're somewhere close by."

Moment by moment Duncan found himself more impressed by Julia Prentiss. However Bellamy had managed to prey on her kindness in order to get his hands on her, she'd gotten away on her own and with enough of the earl's pride that he'd come to a rival clan to find her. That, though, was neither here nor there. "Ye say she stole a horse from ye? That must have been quite the fright ye gave her."

"A simple misunderstanding, and none of your concern." Bellamy sank down on the edge of the bed. "How old is that pretty, black-haired sister of yours? Sorcha, I believe?"

"Didnae ye just say ye were married?"

"I am, yes. But Orville isn't."

"If Orville so much as winks at Sorcha, I'll put his eye oot. And then I'll put oot the other one, so he doesnae do it again."

The earl sent a glance over at Duncan where he still stood by the open door. "What's become of that diplomacy of yours?" he asked, a cynical smile touching his thin lips.

Duncan tilted his head. "Ask me more aboot my sisters and find oot." That was where he drew the line. And if Bellamy hadn't realized that by now, it was past time he did so.

"That stew smells mighty fine, Lenox," Orville commented. "I could stand a bowl of it before we go out into that storm again."

"A bard has to sing for his supper," Duncan returned, "Ye tell me why yer cousin married a lass, got her to Bellamy, and then had her flee, and I might consider that worth a stew."

"She came here first, and then I had Father Duggan marry us," Bellamy snapped. "She's dim-witted and flighty, but as I said, it was arranged. I'll have her back, and in my bed, and she won't flee again."

Now that was the Bellamy with whom Duncan was

better acquainted. And he decided that by now he would be feeling annoyed and put-upon. "Sounds like the two of ye'll have a grand time together. But barking at me aboot yer own shortcomings doesnae earn ye even a radish. Yer timid bride is nae here, and ye're beginning to stink up my cottage. Get oot. Now."

"And if we decide to stay?" Orville asked, stirring at the stew.

Duncan took a single step sideways and retrieved his rifle from behind the cupboard. "I'd say that would be a mistake."

Bellamy narrowed his eyes. "There's no call for violence, Lenox."

"I'm being cautious, Bellamy. And I'll nae have ye in here eating my breakfast while yer wife is oot in the rain waiting fer a rescue."

"Miss—My wife is the one who fled. She can spend a night wet and hungry if it makes her see sense," the earl retorted, backing toward the door. "And I'll expect you to keep an eye out for her, and inform me immediately if you see her."

"Aye, I'll inform ye, just so ye'll have no cause to come and interrupt my sleep again," Duncan agreed, refraining from commenting on Bellamy's slip of the tongue.

The two men pulled their wet coats back on. Orville yanked his soaked, drooping hat over his ears but stopped in the doorway to face Duncan again. "Aren't ye going to ask what she looks like?"

"I imagine if I see a strange lass fleeing on foot through the heather it would be her, but ye can tell me if ye'd like." Duncan took hold of the door, ready to slam it the moment they crossed the threshold.

"She has brown hair and . . . green eyes, I think. Or perhaps brown." The earl, already scowling at the rain, frowned. "And no, I don't remember. It was an—"

"An arranged marriage. I recall ye said that a time or two." No, she didn't have brown hair or green eyes. Duncan might only have been in her company for a short time, but he knew that. Miss Prentiss' hair had more sunset to it, a trace of auburn that turned to polished brass in the twilight. And her eyes were a sweet, rich brown.

"And she had on a blue gown," Bellamy added.

"If I see her, I'll send ye word. Or do ye want me to tie her over a horse and bring her to ye myself?"

"There's no need to frighten her further. Just send me word if you see her," the earl said, a touch too quickly. As if he didn't want anyone talking to his so-called bride.

Duncan wasn't about to comment on that subject any further, though. "I will." *Ye damned, lying bastard*, he added silently, and shut the door on the intruders and the wild storm outside.

Chapter Three

Julia wondered how long a person could survive without breathing. Her elbow itched, a stray hair tickled her nose, and yet she lay where she was, unmoving, her fingers clutching the box of chess pieces like it was armor.

The voices above her were only a little muffled; she could hear every word the three men spoke. She could imagine their expressions as easily as if she stood among them; Bellamy would be red-faced, his chin in the air because someone had dared to interfere with his perfect little plan. Orville Fersen, his narrowed eyes cynical, would be searching for her with the keen senses of a hound. And Duncan Lenox would be impassive, annoyed at the intrusion, and not giving any sign at all that he'd stashed her literally under the other men's feet.

When he insulted Bellamy, she actually smiled; she'd wanted so badly to tell the earl precisely what she thought of him and his dealings, and only the realization that she would fare better if she behaved had kept her from doing so. She liked the way Duncan defended his sisters, as well. It certainly spoke well of him. In fact, she found herself listening mostly to his voice, to his quick, measured responses and the way he used every opportunity to point out the difference between a true gentleman and what Bellamy clearly was.

After the door closed, the shack fell very quiet. Was Duncan belatedly wishing he'd chosen a different course of action? She knew as well as he that the longer she remained in his company, the more likely his part in all this was to be discovered. Then the bed above her shifted, the plank creaked, and firelight flooded into her black hole.

"I'm sorry I had to keep ye in there fer so long," he said, kneeling at the edge and holding out both hands for her. "If I'd shot 'em, more folk would have come by to ask questions."

She took his hands, his warm fingers curling around hers, and let him help her out of her hiding place. "I don't know if it's a compliment, Duncan," she returned, smiling, "but you are a splendid liar."

He inclined his head, standing up beside her. He was bare-chested again, his hair disheveled and one boot missing. Utterly delicious, the baser part of her decided. And utterly desirable.

"I'd nae lie to anyone with an ounce of honor," he said. "So compliment me all ye like."

His green eyes, darker in the firelight, met her gaze squarely. And there she stood, in a ruined dress, a disaster of a knot left in her hair, and straw in her shoes. An utterly ruined woman who'd, by some blind stroke of luck, lost her horse in front of quite possibly the one man in the Highlands who not only could help her, but had agreed to do so. At great peril to himself.

Before she could lose her nerve, Julia put a hand on his bare shoulder, leaned up, and kissed him on the mouth. She felt his surprise, and for a second she worried that he would push her away. Would she lose her rescuer? Would he think that she was purchasing his protection with her body?

His arms slid around her waist, pulling her up along his chest. His lips teased back at hers, warm and inviting. A foreign land, a near stranger, a tumbledown shack, a warm fire, and a thunderous storm outside. Perhaps none of this was real. Perhaps she was truly back in her own bed in Wessex, dreaming the very best Christmas dream of her life. Perhaps she didn't want to wake up. Not for a while, anyway.

"Lass, ye dunnae need to—"

"I want to," she returned, tangling her fingers into his black hair and pulling his face closer for another kiss. "I'm ruined, whatever story I choose to tell. And you . . . I want you, Duncan. We met when we shouldn't have. And tonight I . . . I feel like such a precious piece of luck shouldn't be disregarded."

"Ye dunnae know me, Julia," he returned, sitting on the askew bed with her gathered in his lap. And despite his words, he leaned in to take her mouth again.

He stirred beneath her bottom, and she took a quick, aroused breath. "I know you're honorable. I know you love your family. I know you're willing to go to a great deal of trouble to help a stranger."

"Nae fer a stranger," he said roughly, pulling the few remaining pins from her hair and dropping them onto the hearth—still mindful that he might have to hide her again. "Fer Julia Prentiss. I do it fer ye. Ye're a remarkable lass, ye know."

"I never thought so." Shivers going down her spine, she ran her fingers softly across his bare chest. His skin was warm, velvet above iron muscles. The body of a man who didn't sit in clubs all day ordering pheasant and talking about cravats.

"I've a belief that most people who think themselves amazing generally are nae so." He shifted, running his mouth along her throat and nipping at her ear. "Ye're the last thing I ever expected in my life, Julia. When I close my eyes, I'm nae even certain this isnae a dream. I mean to have ye. If ye have a different idea, ye'd best tell me before I shed my kilt again."

She chuckled, feeling breathless again, but excitement speeding through her like the cascading river outside. "I have the very same idea you have, Duncan." But dream or not, there was still Lord Bellamy outside. She glanced toward the door. It was latched again, with a sturdy bar holding back the world outside. Good. She wanted nothing from out there to make its way in here. Not tonight. Not ever, truly.

Duncan followed her gaze. "Take off that dress of yers, lass," he said, lifting her off his lap. "No one's getting in here again tonight."

Standing, he first threw another log on the fire, then walked to the door and jammed one of the chairs under the latch for good measure.

"The last time this door was barred was against the Sasannach army," he said, facing her again. "Now I do it to keep an English lass safe from Highlanders." With a grin he pulled the end of his kilt free and slowly unwrapped it from around his waist, letting it fall in a long, plaid tail to the floor.

"Not all Highlanders," she murmured, standing up to unbutton the back of her dress. Coming out of the lake he'd been impressive. Now, warm and aroused, he was simply . . . magnificent.

"Let me help ye with that." He moved up behind her, unfastening the last of the buttons. Slowly he tugged the sleeves down her shoulders, kissing her bared skin as he went.

Julia shut her eyes, moaning at the delight of the sensation. For a heartbeat she wondered what would have happened if she hadn't escaped Bellamy, but just as swiftly she shoved that thought aside. This wasn't Hugh Fersen. This was Duncan Lenox, and he was invited. He was welcome.

His fingers brushed across her bared breasts, and she snapped her eyes open again, startled. Lowering her gaze she watched him do it again, felt his palms close over her nipples. "Oh, my," she breathed.

"Ye like that, lass?" he whispered, kissing the nape of her neck.

"Yes. Aye."

Duncan chuckled, the sound rumbling into her own chest. "Ye're nae making fun of me, are ye, Julia Prentiss?" he asked, dipping one hand down inside her dress where it sagged at her waist and touching her . . . there.

She squeaked, jumping. No one had ever caressed her so intimately. And she couldn't escape the feeling that she would never want anyone else to do so. Ever. For heaven's sake, they'd barely met, but, this . . . he . . . it felt like it was supposed to be. Her, the last person to ever believe in love at first sight, yet here she was. With Duncan Lenox. Naked.

"If ye're getting skittish, ye need to tell me, lass."

"I'm not skittish. I just don't want to wake up."

His fingers stilled, and he moved around in front of her again. "I dunnae know what this is," he murmured, trailing a finger down her breastbone, "but I do like it. Faerie magic, or some such thing. That's what my sisters would say. Or perhaps this isnae yer Christmas gift, but mine." Shrugging, he leaned in to capture her mouth again, putting his hands on her waist and pushing her gown down to the floor.

Faerie magic. She liked the sound of that. In his company the Highlands didn't seem so far from home. Since she'd met him—heavens, had it only been eight hours ago?—her fall into despair and chaos and ruin had stopped dead. And whatever happened tomorrow, tonight she wanted to know what it was like to be in his arms. Faerie magic or not. If he was part of her Christmas gift, well, perhaps Scotland wasn't as much of a disaster as she'd begun to think.

Julia put her hands on his chest and shoved. She imagined she could more easily move a wall, but with a grin, he stepped backward and sank onto the bed, drawing her down over him. *"Neo-àbhaistiche bean-uasal,"* he said, chuckling as he ran his hands down her back to her arse, pulling her up against him.

"What does that mean?" She wanted to hold him and touch him and move against him all at the same time, but she settled for nibbling at the hard line of his jaw.

"I said ye were an unusual lady," he returned, his pulse speeding beneath her lips.

"Just one who's glad to be alive. And free."

Duncan smiled up at her, and the next moment she was wrapped in his arms and pinned beneath him. The reasons she could give him for wanting to be here perhaps didn't make much sense or sounded like she was merely grateful to him. Inside, though, the wish to be with him felt more like . . . need than it did gratitude. If she said something so absurd aloud, though, he'd likely flee shrieking into the night. And she did not want that.

As he kissed her, his hand moved between them again. One finger curled deliciously inside her, and she bucked, moaning again. "Auburn-haired lass," he breathed, teasing at her with two fingers now, kissing her in time with the motion of his hand, "come fer me."

She wasn't precisely certain what that meant, but the

sweet, breath-stealing tension running through her abdomen tightened until she couldn't do anything but hold onto his shoulders and arch against him. That must be what he'd been talking about, the small working part of her mind said. And then with a pulsing riot of sensation, she shattered.

"Oh, oh," she shivered, digging her fingers into him. "Oh, my. Was that what you meant?"

Duncan chuckled again. "Aye. And I'd like to play now, as well, if ye dunnae mind."

Nodding, she settled onto her back again as he nudged her knees apart. Then he replaced his fingers with his cock, sliding slowly, deeply inside her until with a quick, sharp pain, he'd buried himself completely.

"Are ye well?" he murmured, leaning sideways to take her left breast in his mouth and flick her nipple with his tongue.

It took her a moment to find her breath again. She nodded up at him, shivering deliciously once more. He began to move, sliding with exquisite slowness out and in again. The heat of him enveloped her, outside and in, warm and safe and very, very arousing. She wanted to memorize all of him—the play of muscles beneath his skin, the weight of him on her, the curve of his mouth when he smiled down at her, the flecks of amber in his deep green eyes when they met her gaze. And the way they fit, perfectly, together.

His pace increased, and she tightened inside again, digging her fingers into his shoulders as that rush flooded through her, deeper and longer than it had before. With a groan he held himself against her, then kissed her hot and open-mouthed before he leaned his forehead against her shoulder.

"Well," he murmured, kissing her soft skin and waiting

for whatever it was—reality, guilt, dismay—to creep into his heart.

Instead, Duncan wanted to repeat the experience at the earliest possible moment. He shifted off of her, turning onto his back and sitting up to pull the heavy blankets up over them as she curled against his side.

"Well," she returned in the same tone. "You've given a ruined lady a very high measure for comparison."

Duncan frowned. "Ye want to go off and compare me, then?"

The muscles of her back tensed beneath his hand. "That's not what I meant." She lifted her head from his shoulder, her brown eyes serious. "This . . . I'm not asking anything from you, Duncan. I'm not going to weep and declare that you've despoiled me, because Bellamy saw to that when he dragged me off into the Highlands. I said it poorly, clearly, but—"

"I take yer meaning, lass," he interrupted. "I just didnae expect it." Though from her, as extraordinary as she'd been up to this point, he likely should have expected just that sort of declaration. "It was a 'thank ye fer a fine evening, but I dunnae expect anything else of ye.' "

"Yes. Precisely." With a satisfied smile that made him stir again, she sank back against him.

"Tell me someaught, Julia Prentiss. Did ye have a beau back in London?"

"Not as such, no," she answered, her voice slowing as she relaxed. "Several gentlemen have—had—offered for me, but I didn't . . . Well, I never felt the desire to be with them as I did with you. As I do with you." Her fingers ran idle circles around his chest, the sensation intimate and surprisingly arousing. "What about you? You're a heroic sort of fellow, and not entirely displeasing to the eyes. Do you have a particular lady?"

That he did, though he hadn't until a few hours ago. Would that idea frighten her all over again? Would she think he was after her fortune just as Bellamy had been, except that he was more clever about it? The last thing he wanted to do was send her running into a rainstorm at night with Bellamy likely close enough to sneeze on. "Most ladies I meet cannae withstand my sisters," he said aloud, wondering if he'd ever been as careful about anything as he was being about this conversation. "She'd have to be brave and extraordinary to even wish to meet them. And if they liked her, well, how could I do any differently?"

"I'd like to meet your sisters," she muttered sleepily. "You make them sound very grand."

"Aye, that they are," he whispered back, idly twining his fingers through the straying ends of her disheveled auburn hair. Had she realized what she'd said? That she wanted to meet them because the equation ended with him? Or was he being too clever for a young lady who'd spent five days being frightened and who finally felt safe for a moment or two?

After a moment she stilled, her breath slow and light across his chest. Beside them the fire in the hearth crackled, while the tapping of the rain at the windows danced across his hearing like the fingers of a dream. Further away now thunder rumbled, passing through the deep dark of everywhere outside this tiny cottage.

Could he imagine a lifetime with this Englishwoman he'd only known a few hours? Was it odder that he was already asking himself that question, or that he already could imagine her by his side? That he wondered if their children would have her wild auburn hair? That he wanted his sisters to meet her, because he already knew they would adore her? None of it made any sense at all, but he'd never known anything with such certainty in his life. Him, the cautious man who weighed every action against the possible consequences to his family and to himself, so mad for a stranger that he felt willing to risk . . . everything for her.

"Duncan?"

He blinked. "Aye?"

"What if he comes back?"

"I'll nae close my eyes, *leannan*. I promise."

She drifted off to sleep again, evidently reassured by his answer. And he meant it; if Bellamy knocked at his door again, the earl was a dead man.

"Is it still raining?"

Duncan turned from gazing out the western-facing window. Julia had sat up, the blankets draped deliciously around her waist. For a moment he wished he hadn't bothered to dress; not taking full advantage of the remaining moments of peace they had seemed like an ungodly sin. "Nae," he said aloud, pouring her a cup of tea, dropping two lumps of sugar into the strong brew, and bringing it over to the bed. "It stopped nearly an hour ago."

"What time is it?"

He shrugged, watching her drink. "Nearly seven o'clock, I would guess. I've nae a clock here."

She looked around, as if seeing the shack for the first time. "I can't even imagine a day without a clock or a pocket watch telling me when I'm to go out walking or when it's time to dress for the theater," she said with a grin. "It's actually rather heady."

"I'll be happy to take a hammer to every clock at Lenox House, then," he returned, sitting on the edge of the bed. "Do ye fancy some eggs fer breakfast?"

"We can't stay here, can we? Don't you think he'll be back?"

"I think he'll definitely be back when he cannae find ye anywhere else. We can take a damned minute to eat, though."

Julia nodded. "And then you'll take me to Lenox House?"

"I gave ye my word that I would, lass."

For a long moment her brown gaze searched his face. Then she nodded. "I don't suppose I could wash up somewhere. I likely look like one of those banshees you have here."

He grinned. "Aye, ye frighten me a bit. It's too muddy and too damned cold fer ye to go down to the river, but I'll bring ye up a bucket and put it over the fire." Standing, he went back over to the cupboard. "And I think ye'd be better served with a coat and some trousers. Ye'd be easier to miss that way, if anyone should see us walking." He pulled out a spare shirt and trousers he kept in the cottage and placed them across the foot of the bed.

"You're not wearing your kilt," she said belatedly, her cheeks darkening as she looked him up and down.

"I dunnae wear it that often, really. It's easier fer bathing, though. And a few other things." With that he leaned down and kissed her softly on the mouth. She wasn't allowed to pretend that last night hadn't happened.

Julia wrapped both hands into his hair, kissing him back. Evidently she didn't want to forget about last night. "I like those other things," she murmured against his mouth.

"Good." Reaching beneath the bed, he handed her the knife. "I'll be back in two minutes. Three at the most. If I'm longer, I loaded the rifle. It's behind the cupboard there. Ye know how to use it?"

She took a quick breath. "Yes. But just be back."

"I intend to be."

He might have told her the direction to Lenox House, he supposed, but in the Highlands finding anything was no easy task. She'd be better off trying to negotiate her way out of trouble with the help of the rifle.

Once he'd pulled the chair away from the door and set the plank that barred it aside, he picked up the bucket and slipped outside. Clouds hung low enough in the sky to obscure the top of the cliffs on either side of his valley, and spent rain ran in rivulets along the stone and mud to the river. He had a second pair of boots, but her feet were much smaller than his. Her own shoes were nearly useless, but perhaps he could wrap them with rabbit fur to at least keep her warmer. Yesterday had been balmy by Highland standards, but today the air had a considerable bite to it.

It took some effort not to glance back at the cottage every minute. If anyone was watching him, though, they would know he had something precious stashed there— and the longer he could keep that secret, the better. He did what he could to look for signs that Bellamy and his cousin or any of his men remained in the valley, at the same time trying to give the appearance that, other than a mild curiosity over a supposedly missing Sasannach woman, nothing in his life had altered.

Squatting atop a weather-flattened rock, he scooped up a bucket full of cold water and made his way back up the mild slope to the cotter's shack. Once he left here with a second person, he could only hope that Bellamy hadn't told anyone else he'd been staying here alone. Because while he could make Julia look unlike an English lady, he couldn't make her invisible.

On the chance that she already had the rifle pointed at the door, he knocked before he pulled down on the latch and shouldered the old oak open. "It's me."

She appeared from right behind the door, his knife in her hand and wearing nothing but his spare shirt, hanging down to her bare thighs, and his kilt across her shoulders. He hadn't expected her to be cowering somewhere, but he liked that she'd been ready to act. Bending down a little, he kissed her again.

"Ye do look bonny in MacLawry colors," he told her, as he hung the bucket over the fire to warm the water.

"Do the colors mean something?" she asked, running her hands down the heavy wool.

"White fer snow and pure intent, black fer determination, and red fer blood," he replied, digging back into the second cupboard for the boiled eggs he'd wrapped in a cloth when he'd hiked down here three days ago. "The grays are whatever ye like; they happen in the weaving."

"Clouds," she decided, looking down at her makeshift wrap.

He chuckled. "Clouds it is, then. Do ye care to have yer toast black or still showing its colors?"

"Still showing its colors," she said with a grin. "But I can help, you know. I may not know how to make rabbit stew, but I believe I can peel an egg."

"Nae. Ye take yer bath." He handed her a cloth, sliding the bucket out from the flames. "I intend to watch ye, though. I'm nae much of a gentleman."

"Hm." Holding his gaze with her own, Julia slipped out of the kilt and set it on the bed, then pulled the shirt off over her head. Then, naked and lovely as the day was new, she dunked the cloth in the water and began cleaning herself.

"Sweet Bridget," he murmured. "Keep that up, and I'll have ye back on the bed again."

She smiled. "You should see me in a bathtub."

"Oh, I intend to. I've a great brass one just off the master bedchamber at Lenox House. I'll give it ye, if ye'll let me share it with ye once in a while."

Her expression shifted a little. " 'Once in a while'? Am I staying?"

Damnation. "If ye'd like, Julia. I've nae chains in my house, but I'd nae have bedded ye here if I didnae . . . care fer ye."

"Haven't you had lovers before? I know you were no virgin, Duncan."

So now *he* was the moon-eyed simpleton. "The women I've been with—it's been on equal terms, with precautions taken. A mutually-agreed-on encounter."

Now she frowned. "That sounds very businesslike."

"I'm a very cautious man. Except fer last night. Except fer ye, Julia. Ye spin my head aroond, and God knows that's a rare thing fer me. Very rare." As he spoke he approached her, finally putting his hands on her warm, bare shoulders. "Am I the only one spinning?"

Brown eyes blazed into him. "I've been spinning for days, Duncan," she said slowly.

Keen . . . loss stabbed through him. Of course she had been. She barely knew where the ground was, and he'd . . . well, he'd taken advantage. "And I'm a stupid man. I apologize to ye, lass. Ye've nothing to fear from me. I—"

She put the damp cloth against his mouth. "You made me stop spinning," she whispered. "I don't know what we are, but I'm . . . I don't feel ready to give this up. To give you up. Because part of me believes I might have found something magical. And the other part of me wants to believe the first part."

"Is there a third part?" he asked, putting his hand over hers and lowering the damp cloth to his chest, over his heart.

"Yes. The part that worries I'm being a complete fool."

"If ye are, then we're both foolish." Keeping her fingers captured, he tilted her chin up with his free hand and kissed her again, slowly and deeply and thoroughly.

"Then I'm willing to risk another hour," she returned, pulling his shirt from his trousers. "Are you?"

"Aye. That I am." With a grin, he lifted her into his arms.

Chapter Four

The trousers felt scratchy against her thighs, but Julia tied the rope Duncan had given her around her waist and rolled up the bottoms of the legs until her feet stuck through. Even if he hadn't suggested she not wear her ball gown she was more than tired of it—not just because it was dirty and torn, but because of what it represented. She'd been stupid and naive that night, and she'd paid for it with her reputation. If her grandfather hadn't seen fit to gift her with forty thousand pounds upon her marriage, she would have lost her future, too.

She glanced across the room at Duncan, seated at the table with her shoes and trimming a pair of rabbit pelts to fit around them. At this time yesterday she'd been in a corner of a bedchamber that didn't belong to her, watching a man she thought she knew become more and more a stranger, and more and more frightening.

At the beginning Bellamy had been pleased with himself, but polite and even a touch apologetic. When she didn't swoon or fall to her knees and agree to marry him to save her reputation, his polite veneer had begun to melt away. By yesterday morning she'd begun to fear that he would resort to something physical—something like what she and Duncan had been up to last night and this morning. Except it wouldn't have been the same, because the idea of Bellamy touching her like that disgusted and horrified her.

When she'd found Duncan, after her initial aggravation—and in part because of it—she'd thought perhaps she was . . . infatuated. He'd saved her, after all, whether he'd set out to do so or not. But the more they spoke, the more she realized that she simply liked him. She liked his honest, straightforward manner; she liked the way he cared for his sisters, his sense of humor, the way he seemed to understand her and made her feel she'd been brave. Of course he couldn't be perfect—no man was. But for heaven's sake, he was gorgeous and compassionate and obviously seemed as stunned by the attraction between them as she was.

When he'd said he would give her a bathtub and share it with her, her first thought had been that she did want him to do so. She did want more time with him. A great deal more time. The only thought that troubled her was her blasted money. Duncan knew she was ruined, since he'd helped a great deal with that. He also knew she would receive a very large dowry upon her wedding. When her grandfather had written up his will, she'd only been seven. And he'd likely been thinking that he wanted to ensure she had a fine, comfortable life. Unfortunately, he'd also seen to it that nearly every man in England saw her as a walking bank account. But did Duncan see her that way?

"Put on yer shoes, lass, and I'll see if I can bind them up fer ye," he said, standing to bring her the light dancing slippers.

When he knelt at her feet a thrill ran down her spine.

Did it matter if he wanted her money or not? Certainly no one else had ever made her feel this way. And she had more than a suspicion that no one else ever would. "Perhaps I'll begin a new fashion," she said, putting a hand on his shoulder and placing her right shoe and foot atop the makeshift rabbit boot while he wound strips of leather around it.

"Oh, I doubt that," he returned, amusement in his voice. "But if it keeps yer feet warm and dry, I'll call myself satisfied."

Once he'd wrapped up both feet, she took an experimental stroll across the shack. "You could be a cobbler," she announced. It certainly was not high fashion, but with the fur on the inside her feet felt warm, and the hide on the outside should keep her feet from getting wet. It was very clever, really.

"Well, if I fail as a gentleman farmer, I'll set up a wee shop." Standing, he walked over, kissed her soundly on the mouth, then shrugged a satchel over his shoulder and handed her a heavy coat. "Ye'll nae look like Miss Julia Prentiss," he decided, watching her shrug into the dark brown coat. "And we've only three miles to cover. Ye have the knife?"

She lifted the back of the coat to show it to him, tucked into her waist against her spine. "I'd almost rather stay here."

"Aye. So would I." Stopping in front of her, he cupped both her cheeks in his broad, longer-fingered hands. "I'll nae let anyone harm ye, Julia. I promise ye that."

She lifted up on her toes and kissed him softly. "I know you won't. Now let's go, before I lose my nerve."

He'd already doused the fire, and when he blew out the last lantern they were left standing there in the quiet gloom. Then, before she could change her mind, he pulled open the door and walked outside. A heartbeat later he motioned for her to follow.

Bellamy and the awful Orville Fersen were somewhere about. For all she knew they could be just over the next rise or around a stand of boulders. With a shiver she hurried her step, keeping her eyes on Duncan's broad back. With a rifle over his shoulder and that determined look in his eyes, she certainly would have hesitated to accost him. She hoped anyone they wandered across would come to the same conclusion.

"Duncan?" she said, to keep her mind from jumping onto every possible thing that could go wrong.

"Aye?"

"I heard Bellamy say your great-grandmother was a MacLawry. Is that why you're a part of that clan?"

"Aye. I also have a great-uncle who's a Campbell, but we dunnae talk aboot him." He slowed a little, drawing even with her. "I like the MacLawrys. They've stood against the landowners trying to drive their own people out of the Highlands in favor of sheep and grazing land, fer one thing. They're good people, Glengask, his brothers and his sister, and their father before them."

"But you could have chosen to side with the Campbells, if you wanted to?"

He sent her a sideways glance. "I suppose, though I'd have to have a damned good reason to change my allegiance. And even if I had been a Campbell, I wouldnae have given ye over to Bellamy. There's allegiance, and there's what's right and true." Taking a short breath, he brushed his fingers against hers. "I have sisters, Julia. I hope any man with sisters would have come to yer aid."

"That's a nice thought, but not everyone values what's right over money and allegiance." And she'd been supremely lucky to find someone who did.

"I hope ye didnae share my bed because ye're grateful that I'm nae a dastard."

She shook her head, moving a half step closer so that their fingers touched with every step. "Every man *should* be a gentleman, but not many are. But I didn't share your bed because of that. I shared your bed because I wanted to." More than she'd ever wanted anything else in her life. Badly enough to risk whatever might come next.

His fingers curled around hers. "If yer family, when they get yer message, decides to return ye to London, do ye think ye'd mind having a Highlander and his three sisters come to call on ye there?"

Julia looked up at his profile, the black hair lifting from his forehead in the stiff breeze. "You would go all the way to London?"

"I'd go all the way to China, lass, if ye'd see me."

"I would see you." She ducked her head, knowing from the heat in her cheeks that she was blushing. "I'd be happy to see you."

"Well. I'm glad that's settled, then."

They walked through the rough countryside in silence for a short time, holding hands. The wind on her face was cold, but with the heavy coat and trousers and rabbit-reinforced shoes, Julia barely felt the chill. She'd thought going to Scotland would be a quaint adventure. She'd asked for the gift because it would take her away from the Season in London, from the parade of suitors who were far more interested in her income than her character. The gift of an escape from her future. When Bellamy had grabbed her, the gift had become a nightmare. Now, though . . . Now she would be perfectly happy never to return to London at all, if it meant she could see Duncan and hold his hand and kiss him whenever she chose.

"Are ye tired, lass?" he asked, glancing again over his shoulder.

"No. I go for walks all the time."

"Let's hurry a bit then, shall we?"

The outside chill abruptly found its way down her spine. "Is it Bellamy?" she asked stiffly.

"Two men on horseback. I dunnae if it's him or one of his, but we've only half a mile or so to go. I'd prefer to be indoors before they catch up."

"So would I."

He sent her a reassuring grin. "We'll nae run, because they'll chase us like hounds. But some haste wouldnae do us wrong."

Oh, she agreed with that. He helped her over a stone wall covered with moss that looked older than the Roman conquest, and they strode along a faint path worn in the grass and heather as trees blew wild around them. "Is another storm coming?" she asked.

"Another storm's always coming here," he returned with a quick grin. "Once we round the hill, ye'll be able to see Lenox House. I've men aboot, but the cotters are on the far side of the valley by the river."

"You have cotters?"

"Aye. Aboot a hundred or so. Nothing close to what Glengask has. Or Bellamy."

The trail curved around the green, sloping side of the hill, and if they hadn't been in such a hurry, she would have stopped in her tracks. Lenox "House" was something of a misnomer. It was nearly a castle by English standards, all tall stone walls of white and windows looking across the valley. It was at least the size of Bellamy Park, and much more . . . friendly looking, if she said so herself. But it did look welcoming, and warm—or perhaps that was because she knew its owner was much the same.

"It's lovely," she said aloud, panting.

A gun fired somewhere behind them, the sound echoing into the hills and mountains like high-pitched thunder. Julia flinched and nearly lost her footing. Swiftly

Duncan caught her up under the elbow, holding her close against him until she had her balance again.

"Nae need to worry, lass. They willnae shoot ye. They only want us to stop." He whistled loudly, and a trio of men appeared from the direction of the stable. "Lads, find yer muskets and get to the house!" he bellowed.

The men disappeared again. Julia risked a glance over her shoulder and nearly shrieked. Bellamy and his cousin were only a hundred or so yards behind them and riding at a full gallop. "Duncan!"

"I know." Turning around, he unslung his rifle and lowered it in their direction. "Go to the side door, lass," he said, backing in the same direction.

"Give me what's mine, you thief!" Bellamy yelled.

"Come and take her, then!" Duncan returned, "If ye can do it with yer head blown off!"

She reached a heavy oak door at the side of the house. Just as she had a heartbeat to wonder if it would be locked, it swung open, and a tall, redheaded man motioned her inside. "In with ye, lass. Where's Master Duncan? I heard him bellowin'."

"Right behind me."

She ducked behind the door so she could watch without being seen; as she was the bone of contention, staying out of Bellamy's view seemed the wisest thing she could do. Duncan stood a few feet before the open door, his rifle leveled in the earl's direction. Bellamy and Orville rode back and forth in front of him, clearly trying to see if they could make their way past his guard.

"This is trouble you don't want, Duncan!" Bellamy called out, scowling. "Whatever she's told you is a lie. She belongs to me, and you're only doing yourself and your sisters a disservice."

"If ye dunnae know what she's told me, how do ye know it's a lie?" he shot back.

"You're protecting her, so she's lying. Hand her over, and we'll forget this ever happened."

"Get off my land, and ye'll live to see sunset," Duncan replied, his voice as cool as if he was talking with Julia over their game of chess.

"Bah. We'll be back, with help. You have until three o'clock to come to your senses, Lenox!"

He stood there blocking the door until both men had ridden out of sight. Only then did he lower the rifle and walk into the house. "Murdoch," he said, "I want men with weapons at the windows."

"Aye, Master Duncan." The servant took Duncan's rifle and then their coats and hats. "Bellamy brought himself by here yesterday, asking after a brown-haired English lass. Insisted on looking through the house. I let him, but I kept that damned Orville Fersen ootside."

With a nod, Duncan took Julia's hand, leading the way into the bowels of the house. "Where are my sisters?"

"When the ruckus started, Sorcha herded the other two upstairs to yer grandmama's room."

"Good. Who else is here?"

"Just the usual lads, and Mr. Finchey and Father Ross come to ask for donations for rebuilding Mrs. MacGeath's house after her boy kicked over the lantern." The redheaded man kept pace behind them, as if he was accustomed to his employer dashing headlong through the large house. "This would be the brown-haired English lass, then?"

"Aye, though any man with eyes could see that her hair's auburn, nae brown."

As simple as it was, that seemed like a compliment. Heaven knew she hated it when people said her hair was brown. "Brown" sounded like such a dull color. "Auburn," though . . . Julia shook herself. Clearly she was exhausted if she could spend time worrying over how people described her hair. She half turned and waved a hand in the butler's direction. "Pleased to meet you, Murdoch."

"And ye, lass."

"Keep Finchey and Father Ross here, Murdoch," Duncan ordered. "If they'll nae help, they can at least be witnesses."

"They'll nae be leaving, then. I'll see to it now." As they started up the stairs, Murdoch veered away toward the rear of the house.

"Is he your butler?" she asked, winded and her fur-bound feet clumsy now on the precise stone stairs.

"He organizes the house, so I suppose so. Dunnae call him that, though, or he'll be putting on airs."

Duncan was glad that Julia could still take a moment here and there and notice what lay around her; most women in her position would likely be in a dead faint by now. But then he'd already realized that she wasn't like most women. Or any woman he'd ever met, truly.

With Bellamy giving them until three o'clock, he had somewhere around three hours to prepare for a fight. Until yesterday he would have spent a great deal of effort to avoid just this sort of conflict, because the last thing he wanted was to have neighbors who preferred him dead. Unfriendly was one thing, and the lot of them were accustomed to that. But this was different.

He stopped at the top of the stairs and turned to the right, heading for the westernmost bedchamber on the floor. Belatedly it dawned on him that perhaps his first priority shouldn't be introducing Julia Prentiss to his loved ones, but that was what he meant to do. He wasn't going to leave her sitting in the morning room while he made plans to protect her.

Aside from that, his lasses needed to like her—not because he would surrender her if they didn't, but because it felt . . . vital that they view her the same way he did. So he could know that this wasn't some faerie tale, but a real woman and a real . . . chance at something wondrous and unexpected.

"Grandmama Maevis?"

"Are ye alone, Duncan?"

"Nae. I've a lass with me."

"The Sasannach lass Bellamy's foaming over?"

He squeezed Julia's fingers in his. "Aye."

"Well, let's have a look at her, then. Open the door slow, lad."

Doing as she suggested, he lowered the handle and eased open the narrow door. His grandmother sat in the center of the room, her white hair piled high and a blunderbuss comfortably across her lap. He was well aware that she knew just how to use the big musket.

"Ye havenae stashed my sisters in the wardrobe, have ye?" he asked, drawing Julia in behind him.

"We're behind the sofa," his youngest sister, Keavy said, straightening.

The other two joined her in standing, then came around the furniture to hug him. All of them talking at once, they regaled him with the tale of how Bellamy had come calling and demanded to look through their house, and how Keavy had wanted to bloody his nose for being a Campbell and daring to set foot on Lenox property.

"Ye've had quite the adventure then, aye?" he broke in. "So have I. Ladies, this is Miss Julia Prentiss. Julia, Sorcha, Bethia, and Keavy. And Grandmama Maevis."

His sisters curtsied in a ragged wave then dragged Julia into the conversation. Duncan relinquished her, grinning at her expression, before he went to squat down beside his grandmother's chair.

"Bellamy means to come back for her at three o'clock," he said in a low voice. "He'll have more men and more weapons with him."

"Why did she run from him? He's no Adonis, but a marriage is a ma—"

"He didnae marry her. He dragged her oot of a ball in Aberdeen, intending to bully her into marriage to save her reputation. She's an heiress, with a cartful of money going to her husband on her marriage."

"And she ran oot from under Hugh Fersen's beady little eyes?"

Duncan grinned. "Aye. That she did. She stumbled across me, and I hid her in the old cottage."

His grandmother eyed him. "And?" she prompted.

"And what? We waited oot the rain and made our way here. Bellamy crossed our trail aboot half a mile from the house."

"Ye were holding her hand, lad," Maevis said in a lower voice.

He could dissemble, he supposed, but that would only make explaining things more difficult later. "Aye. That I was. She . . . It's odd, I suppose, since I've only known her one day, but she's . . . dear to me." Duncan sent a glance in Julia's direction, to find her seated on the couch, smiling, with Sorcha holding one of her hands, and Keavy the other.

"How dear?"

"Very dear."

"Enough fer ye to risk yer sisters and Lenox House?"

"I'll attempt to avoid that, but I'll nae hand her over. Bear MacLawry's still at Glengask. I'll send the four of ye there to keep ye safe."

"By the time we arrived and Bear decided to charge to yer rescue, it'd be too late, Duncan. Ye think Bellamy would lose a minute of sleep over burning this house to the ground because of pride and money?"

"I dunnae mean to lose, Grandmama." He took a breath. "Father Ross is here. I'll send him with y . . ." Duncan trailed off. *Father Ross was in the house.*

Maevis narrowed her eyes. "Duncan, what in St. Bridget's name are ye thinking?"

"Excuse me for a moment, Grandmama."

She grabbed his wrist as he stood. "Ye mean to *marry* her? Bellamy can make her a widow and still marry her."

"Aye," he whispered back. "But he wouldnae get her dowry. That would go to me and mine. And that might just stop him."

"Just to save her from a beau she doesnae favor? Ye're more cautious than that, lad."

He shook his arm free. "It's more than that, and ye know it. I . . . I know I'm a cautious man. But when I see her, I want to beat my chest and roar."

"Duncan . . ."

With a forced smile, he backed away. "She may say nae, and this will all be moot, *seanmhair*." Ignoring the scowl she sent after him, Duncan made his way to the sofa. "I need a word with ye, Julia," he said, holding out his right hand.

She curled her fingers into his and stood. "Your sister, Keavy, was just telling me that she can shoot a musket. She's volunteered to take a window in the attic and shoot any Fersens or Campbells who dare show their faces."

"Aye. She's bloodthirsty," he agreed, glancing at his nine-year-old sister. Still holding Julia's hand, he led the way out of the room and down the hallway to the north-facing conservatory, the one with a view overlooking the mountains and the endless rolling Highlands. His favorite view. "What did ye think of them? My sisters, I mean?"

"They're delightful. And I think they liked me."

"As do I. They generally dunnae hang onto guests. Especially a Sasannach." He took a moment to look out the window. She'd come here on a lark. Could she—would she—wish to remain?

"What is it?" she asked, furrowing her brow.

"I've an idea. If we spent the next six months as we intended, I'd call on ye in London, and I'd woo ye, and then I'd sink on one knee and ask ye to marry me."

Her eyes searched his. "I think you've already wooed me, Duncan. Unless you've decided this is too much of a risk. I can't—I won't—I won't go with him, but I can flee here. If you give me a horse, then perhaps I—"

"Do ye want to flee here? Because I dunnae want that."

"Well, I don't want it, either. But I'm trying to figure out what you're saying, and it's rather aggravating."

Taking her other hand as well, he sank down on one knee. "What I'm saying is, if I already know that I'll ask ye fer yer hand in six months, why cannae I ask fer it today? I've known ye fer a day, lass, and at the same time I feel like I've known ye forever."

Her face had grown pale, but her grip on his hands was hard and firm. "Duncan, you don't have to do this to protect me."

"Nae. It has the added benefit of protecting ye, but it's nae why I'm doing it."

"But Bellamy might murder you, just to get hold of me again. That won't help anything, and it would . . . it would kill me if something happened to you."

"I happen to have a priest under my roof today. And a cartful of witnesses. If I'm yer husband, then yer dowry is mine, isnae?"

She nodded, frowning. "Yes."

"And if he kills me, yer dowry goes to my heirs, doesnae? It would be oot of yer hands?"

"Yes."

"Then it would go to our child, if we made one last night," he murmured. "And if we didnae, my nearest male relation is Lord Glengask. He'd return the money to ye. I'll write it all oot, just to make it clear that Bellamy has nothing to gain here."

Now her hands were shaking in his. He hoped that was a good sign, and it didn't mean she was about to wallop him. Perhaps he was being mad, but once he had the thought, it made more sense than quite possibly anything he'd ever done before. All he needed was her agreement. If she wanted him.

"You think I might be with child?" she whispered.

"We didnae . . . That is to say, *I* didnae take precautions. I didnae expect to meet ye, Julia. I didnae think I'd want ye so. I—"

She pulled one of her hands free and put it gently over his lips. "Is this what you want, Duncan? Tell me you're not simply being the generous, heroic man I know you to be."

He smiled up at her. "Fer God's sake, lass, I feel like a scoundrel, using Bellamy to get ye bound to me. If it didnae sound foolish fer me to say it, I'd tell ye that I love ye. I *will* tell ye that this is the beginning of love, that what I feel fer ye will only become more and more. But ye should know, I mean to live here, with my sisters. Ye'll be far from London most of the year, and—"

"Yes."

He swallowed. "Yes, ye'll be far from London, or yes ye'll—"

"Yes, I will marry you. Today. Now. And I will hurt anyone who tries to come between us."

Slowly he stood again, pulling her into his arms and kissing her warm, soft mouth. "No one's allowed to come between us," he murmured.

When he considered all of the chance moments that might have gone differently, the number of things that had to go just as they did in order for them even to meet, he had to become a believer in . . . something. In God, in Providence, in Magic, in Love. Or all of them, just to be certain he gave the correct entity its due.

"Shall we tell my family then, lass?"

She grinned up at him. "This should be interesting."

A little better than two hours later, Julia Prentiss wasn't Julia Prentiss any longer. She was Julia Lenox. The priest had hesitated, but clearly he knew who buttered his bread. And just as plain was the respect he had for Duncan, the way he'd known that Mr. Lenox didn't do things frivolously.

Before she said her vows she'd attempted to trace the route of her money, tried to discern once and for all if this had somehow been Duncan's way of manipulating circumstances in order to gain her dowry. It wasn't logical, though. Aside from the grand state of Lenox House, his lands were green, his gardens well-kept—every sign that he had a fair amount of wealth all on his own. He hadn't known who she was in the world, and the papers he had written up by the solicitor Mr. Finchey, who'd accompanied Father Ross to the house, clearly stated that her income was to go to their mutual child. If that turned out to be impossible, it would be inherited by Lord Glengask, and no one there seemed to doubt for a second that the marquis would see the money returned to her—not as a conditional dowry, but as an actual cash sum *to* her and *for* her.

It was actually a better arrangement than she could have hoped for even in a love match. Because anyone who wooed her would do so knowing she had a purse worth forty thousand pounds attached to her wrist. She had hesitated to even believe any of the sweet words her potential beaux had spoken to her for that very reason. But Duncan . . . Duncan had found a way to give the money back to her, or at least for the benefit of her children.

She looked at him as he leaned over the table and signed the last of the hastily written agreements. Duncan. Her Duncan, now. It wasn't at all how she'd imagined her marriage, because her parents would have seen to it that she had a huge, grand cathedral wedding as befitted an heiress and daughter of a viscount. As he'd said, though, today or six months or a year from today, it would have been him and her. The setting was secondary.

As if sensing her gaze, Duncan glanced up at her and flashed a grin. "Ye'll have quite the note to send yer mother now, won't ye, lass?" he said, handing the pen back to Mr. Finchey.

"I imagine she'll be relieved, once I explain."

Walking up, he cupped her face in his broad hands and leaned down to kiss her. "Are ye certain ye won't stay inside with Grandmama and her blunderbuss?" he asked in his deep, rolling brogue.

She shook her head. "If you and Father Ross and Mr. Finchey are going to be standing there facing him, then so am I. Otherwise he might think it's a ruse, that I've escaped and you're trying to mislead him or something."

"Ye've already proven yerself, ye know. If ye dunnae wish to see him face-to-face, I'll nae ask it of ye."

"Master Duncan, they're coming up the road!"

He turned at Murdoch's bellow. "They're early. I'm nae surprised, but it's a wee bit rude, dunnae ye think?"

"Don't jest. He's a dangerous man." And she was very, very nervous. If any little thing went wrong, she could well lose Duncan. And she'd only just found him. She wanted a forever to get acquainted with her husband.

"I'm a dangerous man as well, *leannan*."

As she saw the expression in his light green eyes, she believed him. He'd already defied the earl twice, at gunpoint, and he'd stood practically on his own against Fersens and Campbells all around him for his entire life. Warmth flitted down her spine. When this was finished—and she had to believe that it would go as planned, because anything else was intolerable—it would be him, and it would be her. Together.

He held out his hand to her. "Let's get this over with, shall we?"

"I'm ready."

Outside the house five horsemen had arranged themselves in a semicircle facing the front door. Behind them another two or three dozen men on foot and on horseback trudged onto the wide, stone-covered drive. According to Father Ross' whispering, they were mostly Campbells.

"So you've decided to hand her over to me, then?" Bellamy asked, his steel-gray gaze pinning her in a way that made her feel like an insect beneath his heel. "It's almost a shame you've come to your senses."

"Why is that?" Duncan asked coolly, his face expressionless.

"Well, here you are, alone, and here I am, with nearly thirty men. And you can see who I happened across at my house." He gestured at the tall, lean man beside him. The fellow had reddish brown hair nearly as long as Duncan's and a faint scar that ran across the right side of his face from his chin up beneath his ear. "Or are you not acquainted with Mr. Gerdens-Daily?"

Duncan inclined his head, a muscle in his jaw clenching. "George."

"Lenox. I hear ye've stolen my cousin's wife."

"Nae. I aided a lady yer cousin kidnaped."

The scarred man tilted his head. "I havenae heard that version of the tale."

"Because it's a lie. Julia Prentiss agreed to marry me, and then she fled. I want her back. Now."

Light brown eyes, almost amber, turned to look at her. Dangerous eyes, in a different way than Bellamy was dangerous. The eyes of someone who might slip up behind a man in the night with a knife. She shuddered.

"Miss Prentiss," he said, his tone level, "why dunnae

ye tell us what happened to ye, and why ye fled my cousin on the day ye agreed to marry him?"

"I did no such thing!" she snapped.

"What do you care what she says, George? Duncan Lenox lied to me. He's been harboring my property, and he threatened to blow my head off. He's the MacLawrys' cousin. And we all know what you've said about the Mac-Lawrys, how they all belong in the ground."

Duncan took a step forward. "My argument's nae with ye, George."

Gerdens-Daily lifted a hand. "Tell me yer story, lass."

Taking a breath, her gaze never wavering from the scarred man's face, she told him. Everything from agreeing to dance with a familiar face to waking up in the carriage to stealing the horse from Bellamy Park and fleeing, to meeting Duncan—although she didn't mention that he'd been naked and hiding from Bellamy when the earl came to the shack looking for her.

"None of it matters now anyway," Duncan broke in. "I've taken steps to see that ye cannae get what ye want from her, Bellamy."

The earl's eyes narrowed. "What steps?" he asked succinctly.

"I've married her."

Bellamy's face turned a blotchy gray. "You *what*?"

"Aye. Father Ross married us. Mr. Finchey and a dozen of my men witnessed it. Her dowry is now mine. Ye'll never have it, no matter what ye do. So turn around and go home, and be grateful I don't pull ye off that horse and have ye arrested fer what ye did to my wife."

For several moments Bellamy sputtered and spat, until Julia thought he might suffer an apoplexy and drop dead on the Lenox House front drive. The thought didn't trouble her at all.

Finally, the earl jabbed his finger at Mr. Gerdens-Dailey.

"You're a Campbell, George, just as I am. I demand that you and Orville destroy Lenox for what he's done to me. Burn his damned house to the ground and all his family with it."

Gerdens-Dailey crossed his wrists over the cantle of his saddle. "Do ye, now, Hugh? Ye *demand* that I do yer dirty work?"

"He's a bloody MacLawry! Put him beneath the ground!"

Behind them the sound of muskets and rifles cocking in the windows was quite possibly the most frightening thing Julia had ever heard. Even though he'd told her to stay clear of him, she edged a step closer to Duncan. Her Duncan.

"Ah," George drawled. "Well, it just so happens that I stopped by yer house today on my way back from London. I had someaught to tell ye. While I was there staying with Berling, I had a wee conversation with Ranulf MacLawry." He glanced over at Julia. "That's Lord Glengask, if ye were wondering."

"You did? Is he dead?" Bellamy looked like a rat who'd just scented cheese.

Duncan, on the other hand, paled. "And how did this conversation end?" he asked slowly, taking a half step away from her, putting distance between them again.

"Most of it was private," Gerdens-Dailey went on easily, as if he was unaware of the roiling emotions all around him. "But it ended with us shaking hands and agreeing that fer a time, at least, we'd refrain from spilling each other's blood." Abruptly he reached up, doffed his hat, and bowed to Julia. "So my best wishes, Mrs. Lenox. Mr. Lenox. We'll be bidding ye good day."

"We—No, we will not!"

The scarred man wheeled his horse, cutting in front of Bellamy's mount and making the gelding hop backward nervously. "Aye, we will. And ye will leave them be, or

I'll hear aboot it. Ye'll not make me a liar because of yer own bloody greed, Hugh."

"I—"

"Tell me ye understand, Hugh," Gerdens-Daily insisted, pinning his cousin with that amber gaze.

"I . . . understand," Bellamy finally grunted, deflating.

"Good." Turning again, Gerdens-Daily replaced his hat and inclined his head at Duncan. "*Meala-naidheachd ort*," he said. "Consider this yer wedding gift from the Campbells."

"Aye. I will. Thank ye, George."

The men turned west, back the way they'd come, with George Gerdens-Daily bringing up the rear. In a few moments they were gone over the crest of the hill. Julia couldn't stop looking, though, waiting to see if they'd changed their minds, if they would turn back and ride her down and drag her away from her newfound paradise.

Duncan's arm slid gently across her shoulder. "Ye look rooted to the spot. Do ye regret marrying me, now that we're finished with that *amadan*?"

She didn't know what the word meant, but it didn't sound at all like a compliment. "What did Mr. Gerdens-Daily say to you?"

"He said, 'congratulations'." Slowly he turned her to face him, so she could gaze into his light green eyes. The serious determination she'd seen in them a few minutes ago was gone, replaced by a growing amusement and . . . affection. "Do ye regret it? I can have Father Ross here annul the whole thing, ye know."

Father Ross cleared his throat. "Actually, the Church has to—"

"What do ye say, Julia? Will ye stay a Lenox? Will ye stay with me and be my wife?" Duncan interrupted, clearly not interested in facts.

She held his gaze for a long minute, a slow smile curving her mouth. "How do you say 'wife'?"

"*Bean*. And husband is *céile*, if ye were wondering."

"Then I will stay and be your *bean*, Duncan Lenox, and you will be my *céile*."

He lifted her in his arms. "Forever?"

Now *this* was a Christmas gift, better than any she would have ever dared imagine. A gift, and even more. There was truly some sort of magic in the Highlands. She'd thought that might be so when she'd seen Duncan emerging, naked, from the lake. Now, as she looked down at his grinning face and his wild black hair, she knew it. "Forever."

Once Upon a Christmas Scandal

Christmas Scandal

❄

Alexandra Hawkins

Love sought is good, but given unsought, is better.

—William Shakespeare,
Twelfth Night, act 3, scene 1.

Chapter One

December 1826, London

"Bloody hell! What were you and Father thinking? You can't keep something like this from her. Ellen *must* be told."

It wasn't the anger she heard in her brother's voice that gave her pause. Lady Ellen Courtland was used to her older sibling's blustering. Nor was she surprised by Vane's unexpected presence. Squires, the family's butler, had revealed when she had encountered him downstairs that Lord and Lady Vanewright had been escorted upstairs. She assumed Vane and Isabel had also brought their infant daughter, which would have greatly pleased their mother.

"There is no reason for you to take that tone with me, Christopher," their mother, the Marchioness of Netherley said, sounding aggrieved.

It was the pain in Vane's voice that had Ellen silently debating if she should continue upstairs to deliver the book she had procured from the library on her father's behalf or linger near the threshold of the drawing room to glean the reason for her sibling's impassioned outburst.

Isabel murmured something, but her soothing tones were too soft to be discerned from a distance. Calm and sensible, the young countess had married into a family that often reminded Ellen of a bevy of colorful, highly excitable peacocks, but she was a welcome addition to the eccentric family.

Vane's response to his wife was an incomprehensible growl.

Her mother's heightening exasperation reached Ellen's keen hearing with startling clarity. "Do you ever spend time in your sister's company? No one simply *tells* Ellen anything. The girl has become increasingly stubborn and set in her ways. Besides, she and your father have grown quite close the past year. She has been faithfully by his side, each time my dear Lord Netherley was ordered by the physician to remain confined to his bed. When she learns . . ."

Ellen had heard enough. Stealthily, she turned her back and closed her ears to her mother's grim confession and continued up the staircase. She was mindful not to put pressure on the second step since it creaked, and the last thing she wanted to do was call attention to her presence.

Ellen's heart ached with the knowledge that her brain refused to address. In the last eight months, the family had summoned Dr. Ramsey to the house on seven occasions. Three of the instances had required her father to remain bedridden for more than a week. The last one had occurred only nine days earlier. It was her father's heart. Dr. Ramsey called the condition angina pectoris. It was a fancy medical term to describe a heart condition that was slowly robbing her father of strength and breath. Lord

Netherley was dying, and it broke her heart that she was witnessing her beloved sire's health steadily decline.

Ellen reached the next landing as her eyes burned with unshed tears that would only anger her father if she allowed herself to grieve. There would be plenty of time for that later. Christmastide was approaching. The busy household staff was already preparing for the upcoming festivities. Every day, her father could not resist grumbling about all of the clattering downstairs. Since they were remaining in London, he had told Lady Netherley that there was no need for days of grand celebrations, particularly on the final night—Twelfth Night. Her mother promptly agreed, however, the small army of servants cleaning the old house from top to bottom revealed that her mother would get her way in the end.

She paused in front of the door to her father's bedchamber and took a deep breath to steady her pulse. No tears. No high emotions. No surprises. Lord Netherley required calm, soothing surroundings in order for him to regain his strength. Over the past year, she had proven to be a competent nurse and companion.

Ellen knocked, and opened the door at her father's gruff consent to enter. "What are you doing out of bed?" she scolded at the sight of him standing at the end of the bed, using the bedpost to keep himself upright.

"What the devil do you think I'm doing?" her eighty-three-year-old father shouted back at her. "If Ramsey has his way, I'll die in that bed."

It was not the first time Lord Netherley had spoken those words. Ellen shook her head in exasperation as she seized the spare blanket folded on a nearby chair. "On your feet or toes up, you'll catch your death prancing about the house in your nightshirt," was her crisp reply. She wrapped the blanket around his shoulders. "Now don't give me any more trouble and settle back into bed."

His small act of defiance had already sapped his strength. He clutched the edges of the blanket to his chest as Ellen tidied his bedcovers. "Is that my book?" he asked, his gaze narrowing on the book she had tucked under her arm.

"It is," she confirmed. "If you behave, I might linger and read it to you."

Ellen grasped the corner of the linen sheet and lifted it, a silent invitation for the marquess to climb into bed. He complied, but he could not resist complaining. "I'm not some weak child who needs coddling."

She bit back a smile. "I know, Papa. It is just your misfortune to be burdened with a daughter who likes to spoil you."

Lord Netherley's eyes narrowed suspiciously at her bland tone. He was breathing heavily when she covered his bare legs with the sheet and blankets. "I can read my own damn book, if I please."

"Of course," she replied agreeably, handing him the book. "Vane and Isabel are visiting with Mama in the drawing room. I can always join them downstairs . . ."

"No." He freed the book from her loose grasp. "We have business to discuss."

Ellen crossed her arms over her breasts. "What business? As your younger daughter, anything related to your estates would fall on Vane's shoulders since he is your heir. Nor have you desired my assistance in the conservatory. You declared me too spirited and impulsive to look after your precious plants."

The marquess rubbed his balding head, causing the remaining hair to stick out in all directions. "If we are going to argue, I prefer not to have you towering over me like a sword-wielding Valkyrie."

"We are not going to argue. Dr. Ramsey does not approve."

"Ramsey is an old woman. He does not approve of

anything." He gestured at the walnut parcel-gilt bergère behind her. "If we're not going to argue, then do as you are told. Pull the chair closer and sit."

Ellen signaled her displeasure with an audible sigh, but she humored her father. Once she was seated, she gave him an expectant look. "So what is this business between us?"

Lord Netherley gave her a measured stare that would have made most individuals squirm in their chair. "The business I wish to discuss is what is missing in your life."

She frowned in genuine puzzlement. "I do not understand. Thanks to you and Mama, I lack for nothing."

"A husband, girl!" he snapped impatiently, ignoring her soft groan. "You should be preparing for an evening out that includes a dozen gentlemen vying for your attention, but I suspect you have already told your maid that you will be staying home."

"Mama told you that her attempt to match me with Lord Ely went awry."

"Awry?" His cheeks reddened as he dragged in air through his mouth. "You told the poor man that minutes in his presence made you ill. What do you have to say for yourself?"

Ellen bit her lower lip as she struggled not to laugh. Once she had herself under control, she said, "I was merely being honest, Papa. The afternoon I spoke to Lord Ely, it took seconds to realize the gentleman had been remiss in his morning ablution. I would wager it had been *days* since he had been reunited with his toothbrush."

"Enough." Her father raised the book in his hands as if he was fighting down the urge to fling it at the nearest wall. "And what of Mr. Neese? What was wrong with him?"

"His right leg is shorter than his left," she blurted out. "The difference sends him into tables, plants, and walls."

She had exaggerated a bit about Mr. Neese's clumsiness. However, she had sensed her mother's meddling the moment the gentleman had awkwardly asked her to dance. She had put them both out of misery as quickly as possible.

"And Lord Rouger?"

Ellen tried not to stare at the muscle twitching near her father's left eye. "What of him?"

"Did you truly liken his handsomeness to your favorite horse?"

She leaned forward, her face guileless. "It was a sincere compliment, Papa."

"The devil it is. How do you expect to marry if you keep insulting each prospective suitor?"

She shrugged carelessly as she leaned into the upholstered back of the chair. "Perhaps I won't marry. Between Vane and Susan, you and Mama have plenty of grandchildren."

Her father managed a soft sputtering sound of disbelief. "Not marry? You think I want you settled with a husband of your own because I require more grandchildren? Half the time, I cannot recall all the names of your sister's brood."

Ellen's lips twitched, but she offered no opinion about her older sister and her children. "If it is not more grandchildren, then I see no reason to rush into marriage just because you and Mama insist it is time. I understood the necessity of Vane marrying since he is your heir, but why must I?"

His bushy eyebrows shot upward in disbelief. "Why? You expect me to give you a reason for something that most daughters consider a duty to one's family?"

"Yes."

Lord Netherley's eyes flared with pain and fury, and belatedly Ellen knew she had gone too far. "Unfinished business."

"I do not understand."

"I am dying, Ellen." He held up a hand to silence her. "No arguments. Everyone prefers to ignore the truth, especially your mother. I may have lasted longer than Ramsey's dire predictions, but I can feel it, daughter. I don't have much time left."

Her eyes filled with tears, and she could not prevent them from slipping down her cheeks. "No," she said, her throat suddenly raw with emotion. Hearing her father confirm her unspoken fears made them all too real for her. "Perhaps Dr. Ramsey . . ."

The elderly marquess shook his head. "Ramsey has done all he can for me. After my last attack, he told me that I should get my affairs in order."

Wordlessly, she sprang from the chair and into her father's arms. Ellen felt his hesitation before he enfolded her into his embrace. She pressed the side of her face against his chest and cried as she listened to the thundering of the heart that would eventually fail her sire. Never comfortable with emotional females, he allowed her to indulge her tears for a few minutes before he grasped her by the arms and encouraged her to stand.

"Dry your tears, my girl. It wouldn't do for your mother to see them."

"Yes, Papa," she said, accepting the handkerchief he offered her. She dutifully wiped away the tears from her face.

"That's better." He scrutinized her efforts with a gleam of approval. "You are strong, and rarely allow your emotions to rule you. It's an admirable trait in a wife."

"Papa," she said, wearily.

"No arguments, Ellen. Your mother may have failed in finding you a husband, however, I will not."

Her eyes crinkled with reluctant humor. "So you have taken up matchmaking?"

"I have no time for such nonsense," he said, sounding offended by the suggestion. "There are other ways to attract an eager husband for you."

A trickle of unease moved down her spine. "What have you done?"

Lord Netherley held her gaze. "I've tripled your dowry."

Ellen gasped. "You had no right."

"As your father, I have every right."

Shaking her head, she backed away from the bed. "Do you know what you've done?"

Lord Netherley's eyes narrowed with a shrewdness that sent her heart racing. "I've taken the steps necessary to ensure that most men will overlook your sharp tongue."

"You have done more than that, Papa." She glowered at him. "You have placed a bounty on my head. Every fortune hunter in England will insist on an introduction!"

He was untroubled by her peevish conjecture. "I credit you with enough sense not to marry a penniless scoundrel."

Her laughter held a trace of bitterness. "I find little solace in the compliment. Especially since you are literally buying me a husband—a husband that I do not require or desire!"

"I am not buying anyone."

"Call it bribing, if you like," she shot back, furious at what her father had done. "How long do I have?"

Her father did not feign confusion at her question. "The decision was made more than a month ago."

Curse it all! This meant the news of her enticing dowry had reached well beyond London by this point. And yet, no one had warned her. Ellen wondered if the rest of the family knew of Lord Netherley's intentions.

"You should have told me."

"I just have," he said unsympathetically. "Since your mother is insisting on opening the house during Christmastide, I expect you to conduct yourself in a manner befitting a lady."

Understanding flooded through her. "We are staying in town because Mama is expecting to parade me in front of potential suitors."

And she had believed her father's health was so poor that he could not travel.

"Lady Netherley has never been able to resist a chance to fill this house to the rafters with guests," he hedged when he took note of her expression.

The tears glittering in her eyes had nothing to do with sorrow. She felt betrayed by her own father. Fury bubbled up from within her. Her lips parted, and she wanted to scream at him for his high-handedness, but managed to catch herself. Dr. Ramsey had strict orders about not upsetting his patient.

Ellen marched to the door and gave the knob a vicious twist.

"Where are you going?"

She stiffened at his question. "Sparing myself a scolding from Dr. Ramsey."

"We have not finished—"

"Oh, I believe you have said enough, Papa," she said over her shoulder as she opened the door and stepped across the threshold.

"Ellen . . . come back here!"

The door shut with a satisfying bang. She continued down the passageway until she reached the staircase. Blindly, Ellen gripped the railing for support as she struggled with the myriad of emotions vying for dominance.

How could her father have done this to her?

Too hurt to care about appearances, she released her pent-up feelings with a piercing scream.

Downstairs in the stately drawing room, Ellen's scream brought her brother to his feet. Vane exchanged a concerned look with Isabel before he met his mother's guilt-ridden gaze. "You should have warned her of Father's plans," he said, taking no satisfaction in being right.

Lodging in an inn, less than two hundred miles from London, a gentleman was rejoicing. The news of Lady Ellen Courtland's plump dowry had already reached the man's ears four days earlier. Seated at a narrow writing desk, he opened his journal with the intention of detailing the journey in which he was embarking to court his future bride. His earlier conquests had involved ladies much younger than the thirty-year-old Lady Ellen. However, he was prepared to make sacrifices. Such a large dowry implied a certain amount of desperation on Lord Netherley's part to unburden himself of his youngest daughter.

Fortunately for everyone, his interests aligned quite nicely with the elderly marquess's. By Twelfth Night, the lady and her dowry would be his.

Chapter Two

Derrick Martin Hunt, Earl of Swainsbury casually studied his three companions as he waited for the gentleman on his left to come to a decision about the cards in his hand. The hint of moisture dampening the man's forehead indicated that no amount of glaring would change his abysmal luck. A subtle movement from across the table caught his attention. Lord Ravens, his partner for the past two hours, smirked at the obvious distress emanating from their opponent. His partner, on the other hand, sat blissfully unaware of his friend's distress. His hands and eyes were full of the elegantly attired prostitute sitting on his lap. There was no doubt in Derrick's mind that the gentleman and the woman would quit the table soon to find a discreet room to finish their business.

He had visited London countless times, but this was the first time he had visited Nox. He had naturally heard wild tales of the establishment that was a notorious gambling hell to the public, but the private rooms required membership to an exclusive gentlemen's club. The *ton* referred to the seven founders as the Lords of Vice. From what he had gleaned from bits of gossip, Lord Ravens was not one of the original members, but his connection to them would suffice.

"Rouger, since the card you desire is not in your hand, I highly recommend displaying one that is," Lord Ravens said, clearly growing as bored as Derrick with the younger lord's hesitant play. "Besides, I doubt your partner will last much longer with the delightful Callie wiggling on his lap."

"Did you say something, Ravens?" Lord Mereworth murmured between kisses.

Ravens brushed back a lock of dark hair that tickled his cheek. "Just nudging Rouger so you can slip something other than your hand between her thighs." He winked, including Derrick in his obvious amusement at their predicament.

"You're a good host, Ravens," Mereworth said, chuckling.

Ravens captured the young prostitute's hand and chivalrously kissed it. Callie giggled. "I am the *best* in all things, my good man," he said without a trace of smugness. In the earl's opinion, he was simply stating a fact.

"Rouger?" Derrick pressed.

"Oh, very well," Lord Rouger muttered, surrendering to the gentle teasing from his companions. He played his card. "There . . . are you satisfied?"

Derrick and Ravens had won.

"Indeed, I am," Mereworth said, freeing the woman from his embrace. The viscount stood, but hastily positioned himself behind her so his arousal was not on prominent display. "Come along, m'dear. Let us find—uh, Ravens?"

The earl waved him off. "Berus will show you the way."

Derrick blinked, impressed with Nox's efficient steward's sudden appearance. The man had a quiet manner that allowed him to blend into the shadows when he wasn't needed.

Berus inclined his head to Lord Mereworth. "If you will follow me, milord."

With a farewell wave, the viscount and his female companion departed.

"An excellent trouncing, Ravens." Lord Rouger stood. He nodded at Derrick. "Swainsbury. A pleasure. All yours this night, but I warrant we shall meet again."

"I look forward to it," Derrick said politely. He did not bother pointing out that he had not traveled to London in December to spend it playing cards with such an incompetent cardplayer.

Ravens observed the brief exchange between Lord Rouger and Derrick with a speculative expression on his face. He did not speak until Derrick leaned forward with the intention of standing and saying farewell to his new friend.

"It's early yet. Stay, and have a drink with me."

Without waiting for a reply, Ravens walked away to speak to one of the members of Nox's staff. A minute later, he returned with a bottle of brandy and two glasses.

"You will discover that Nox's cellar is quite respectable." He laughed, and shook his head. He removed the cork from the bottle and filled both glasses. "Even if the same cannot be said about its club members."

"The Lords of Vice."

"Aye. Though I suspect what you know of the gents comes from the gossips."

The accusation offended Derrick. "Why do you say that?"

With glass in hand, Ravens waggled a chiding finger at him. "Berus told me this was your first visit to Nox. If you were acquainted with Frost and the others, you would have been a regular patron of the gambling hell or even a private member."

The earl was curious about him—that much was obvious. Derrick had inherited the Swainsbury title from his uncle years ago, so unlike many of his peers, he had not spent his life preparing for his future duties. The new obligations had not allowed him the luxury of enjoying the amusements in London. Every decision, journey, and task served a purpose, and that included his presence at Nox.

"You are correct. I have not had the pleasure of meeting your friends."

"Oh, I cannot claim that all seven of them view me as a friend." Ravens took a sip of brandy as his expression grew contemplative. "However, we have an amicable arrangement when it comes to Nox. So . . . what brought you to our doors this evening?"

He expected there would be questions since he was not viewed as a member of the *ton*. "Must there be a reason?"

"Have I mentioned that I have an enviable ability to measure a man's character at a glance?"

Derrick grinned at Ravens's boast. The man's arrogance was boundless. Although he conceded, the earl's casual delivery had a certain charm. Against his better judgment, he found himself liking the gentleman.

"No, I do not recall you mentioning this while we were playing. I assume you have come to a decision about me?"

The earl set down his glass of brandy. With clasped hands, he rested his elbows on the table and scrutinized Derrick as if he were a puzzle that needed to be solved. "Aye. While you are a competent cardplayer, you are not the sort of gentleman who tosses his fortune away in gaming hells. On three occasions, a female approached you and expressed an interest in seeking your favor. You turned them away."

Enjoying the game, he said, "Perhaps I have a wife at home."

Lord Ravens grinned. "I disagree. You might have rejected the women, but your expression revealed that you were not adverse to their attentions. To their misfortune, you were here for another purpose."

"I am impressed and flattered," he admitted, hoping the other man would take it as a compliment.

"You should be." Ravens leaned back in his chair. His posture appeared relaxed, but Derrick wasn't fooled. "I normally don't make a habit of interfering in another man's business. However, I have decided to make an exception with you."

Derrick snorted softly. A gentleman like the earl paid attention to everyone's business. It was one of the reasons why he had sought him out.

Lord Ravens picked up his glass of brandy. "So why don't you tell me the true reason you asked Berus for an introduction."

Derrick sampled his brandy as he silently debated over how much he should reveal. "I seek an introduction, and I was told that you were discreet and possessed the appropriate connections."

"My name opens many doors. Who do you wish to meet?"

"Rumor has it that Lord and Lady Netherley will be opening their manor house doors to friends and family in celebration of Christmastide."

"For a man unfamiliar with the family, you are very well informed." Ravens idly rolled his glass of brandy against his palms. "Aye, the Netherleys will hold several dinners and balls. An invitation to their Twelfth Night ball is highly coveted. I suppose you wish an introduction to Vane."

"Vane?"

"Lord Vanewright," Ravens said, not fooled by Derrick's feigned ignorance. "Not only is he a founding member of Nox, he is Lord Netherley's heir."

Derrick had considered approaching Vanewright directly, but discarded the idea almost immediately. He shook his head. "I doubt Lord Vanewright would approve if he learned why I have come to London."

Understanding flashed in Lord Ravens's eyes. "Ah, so you have heard about Lady Ellen's dowry, and have aspirations to claim it."

Derrick shrugged, unwilling to explain why the dowry was so important to him. "Perhaps I have come to meet the lady who has inspired such a fortune."

The earl chuckled. "Vane will not approve."

"I do not need Vanewright's approval," Derrick muttered, burying the unwelcomed sympathy he felt for the man who would consider it his duty to protect his sister. "Lord Netherley's will suffice, though even he might be reluctant to trust a gentleman who has no intimate connections to his friends or family. Hence my problem. You said that you can discern a man's character. Will you help me?"

Lord Ravens brought his hand to his face, and thoughtfully stroked his chin. His direct gaze did not falter as he studied Derrick in silence. Finally, he said, "Aye, I believe I shall."

Chapter Three

"Mama says you are still sulking about this dowry business."

Ellen scowled at her older sister's accusation. She did not bother denying the charge. Her fifty-two-year-old sibling often behaved like a second mother, but some things could not be helped. Married to Lord Russell Pypart since she was eighteen years old, Susan had an impressive brood of twelve children who ranged in ages from the five-year-old to the eldest one, who had recently turned thirty-three.

Ellen had managed to avoid her sister when she had arrived at Netherley House early that afternoon. Due to their large party, she had even escaped riding in the same coach with her inquisitive sibling as they traveled to Vane and Isabel's town house. It wasn't until she had offered to arrange the bouquet of flowers she had personally selected from her father's conservatory that Susan had cornered her.

"And pray, what does Papa have to say?"

Susan watched as Ellen fussed over the bouquet. "He does not care if you sulk. He knows you will do your duty as I did."

Her mouth flattened into a mutinous line. "He cannot marry me off if no gentleman offers for my hand."

"According to Mama, three gentlemen have privately declared their intentions."

Ellen accidentally crushed one of the lilies as her hands fisted at the news. "Why was I not told?" It was not as if one of these brave fellows had dared to approach *her*. If they had, she would have done her best to convince each one of them to reconsider. With a grimace, she bent the stem of the ruined flower in half and stuffed it into the porcelain vase until it was concealed.

Having noticed her sister's clever attempt to hide the damage, Susan laughed. "And give you the opportunity to reject all potential suitors out of hand? Oh, I think not. Besides, with many bachelors out of town this month, Papa is willing to wait for a suitable candidate."

"Have you not noticed there are more than a few unmarried gentlemen attending Vane and Isabel's rout?" Ellen asked plaintively. "Betrayed by my own brother. I never thought it possible."

Susan gently captured both of Ellen's wrists before she could decapitate another flower. "Darling sister, Vane would rather sever a limb than hurt you. If you were not avoiding him and the rest of the family, he would have told you that he is also concerned about this dowry business. You are a very wealthy heiress, and that always attracts unwanted attention."

"Is there any other sort?" she said, feeling bitter about the whole subject.

Her sister caressed Ellen's cheek affectionately. "You will never know unless you open your heart. 'Tis the season for miracles, after all." Susan glanced at the bouquet.

"Have you finished abusing those poor flowers? Mama is awaiting our return. She has a few gentlemen who would be honored to meet you," she said, the corners of her eyes crinkling with amusement.

"Run along. I will join you and Mama shortly," Ellen said, deliberately prolonging the inevitable.

"Yes . . . well, do hurry, or else she will send Vane to fetch you." Susan walked to the arched doorway of the antechamber and paused. "You have good reason to be upset with Papa. However, do not let your anger and fears ruin what little time we have left with him."

Ellen remained silent. Satisfied she had made her point, her sister left her alone in the small room. It vexed her that Susan was correct. Feeling vulnerable, she glanced sadly at the bruised bouquet on the table. Much like her life, she had made a mess of it.

"Are you lost, too?"

She lifted her head, and turned at the sound of the gentleman's voice. Her breath caught in her chest at the stranger's approach. A little taller than her brother, this was a gentleman who commanded attention whenever he entered a room. He was beautiful in the masculine sense. A well-proportioned body to gain an artist's and a lady's appreciation, dark brown hair that was lighter than her own and cut short to keep it from curling, and a strong chin and mouth. If she could find fault with his looks, it would be his ears. They stood out a little, but she found the subtle flaw rather endearing. His gray-colored eyes were fixed solely on her, which was slightly unsettling, due to their intensity. A tiny shiver of anticipation flitted through her. If he was one of Vane's friends, she did not recognize him.

In response to his question, she said, "Not at all. This is my brother's house."

On closer inspection, she noticed his gray eyes had flecks of gold within their depths.

"Excellent," he said, the corners of his mouth curling upward into a smile. Subtle dimples appeared on his cheeks, which only added to his charm. "Then it is providence that I have stumbled across you, for I am."

"I beg your pardon?" Ellen positioned her body so he could not see the mangled bouquet of flowers.

Her tongue felt thick and her mouth slightly parched. She wanted to groan aloud at her strange behavior. This was not the first time she had encountered a gentleman. In fact, growing up around Vane and the other Lords of Vice, she had considered herself quite immune to masculine charm and a handsome visage.

Who was he? Had he come this evening because he had heard the Marquess of Netherley was willing to give away a king's ransom to the gentleman who would marry his youngest daughter?

"Lost." His smile dimmed at her guarded expression. "I was supposed to join my friend in the library and I— Forgive me, I did not mean to intrude or frighten you. I thought I heard you speaking to someone and wondered if I had circled around back to the drawing room. I will leave you alone."

For a possible suitor, the gentleman was quite eager to flee her presence.

Whoever he was, there was no call for rudeness. "Wait." Ellen closed the distance between them and offered him a shy smile. "You were not mistaken. My sister and I were discussing . . ." She hastily swallowed her confession. There was no reason to bring up family business. "You must have passed her on the stairs. I was planning to join her in the drawing room. However, I would be happy to show you to the library."

"You are too generous, Miss . . . ?"

"Lady Ellen . . . Lady Ellen Courtland." She inclined

her head as she curtsied. "I am Lord and Lady Netherley's youngest daughter, and Lord Vanewright's sister."

Their gazes locked. "You honor me, Lady Ellen. Permit me to return the courtesy. My name is Derrick Hunt, Earl of Swainsbury." He bowed.

"A pleasure, Lord Swainsbury. Now, with your permission, I will direct you to the library. It isn't far. In fact, I am confident you would have discovered it on your own, even if you had not found me."

"I have changed my mind," he said abruptly, before they had taken more than a few steps. "I will return to the drawing room with you. I have been wandering about this house long enough that I will most likely find my friend there as well."

He silently invited her to place her hand on his arm.

Ellen accepted his offer, appreciating the firm muscles concealed beneath the sleeve of his evening coat. "The drawing room, it is," she said, trying not to sound too excited by the prospect.

Derrick was acutely aware of the lady at his side as they ascended the staircase. She was not what he had expected. The tall, willowy female with the elegantly upswept dark brown tresses, the stubborn chin, and vulnerable blue-green eyes did not require the additional enticement of a sizeable dowry to lure a man into marriage. What was wrong with the bachelors in this town? Why hadn't some lucky gentleman slipped her from the watchful eyes of her governess and married her before her family deduced he was unworthy of her? Her slender waist should have thickened over the years because of the sons and daughters her husband had planted in her belly.

Instead, fate had given him a goddess who possessed too much wealth for her own safety.

"So how do you know my brother?"

"I confess, I have never spoken to him until this evening," he admitted, slowing his pace to prevent her from stumbling. "Since I am alone, Lord Ravens has taken me under his wing."

"In my opinion, it is a precarious position. It astounds me Lord Ravens would trouble himself since he is not known for his charitable deeds. According to my brother, Lord Ravens . . ." Biting her lip, she realized her frank opinion might be misconstrued. She offered him an apologetic smile. "I did not mean to insult your good friend. Perhaps like my brother and the other Lords of Vice, the gossips overlook the gentleman's good qualities and speak only of his misdeeds."

"So Lord Ravens is not one of your suitors?"

She appeared flustered by the question. Her blush revealed as much about Ravens as it did the young lady.

"The earl does not *court* any respectable lady."

Lady Ellen did not have to add that her brother would have quietly castrated Ravens for even considering it.

It shouldn't have pleased him that someone as dark and dangerous as the earl held little appeal to her. He had gleaned enough from Ravens to understand that the gentleman enjoyed a certain degree of depravity that no true lady would tolerate. Derrick deduced from her surprise at his friendship with Ravens that she did not cast him in the same light. It was a pity that he could not agree. His presence in London was not entirely noble, and before he was done, she might view him as a villain.

Before they entered the drawing room, he deliberately covered his left hand over hers, drawing her attention. "Good. I would not wish to face Lord Ravens at dawn."

Her blue-green eyes widened at his quiet admission. The implication that he had been willing to fight the earl for her affections startled her. He had hoped to flatter her.

Most ladies would have been thrilled to have two gentlemen coming to blows in their honor.

Lady Ellen's gaze nervously shifted from him to the elderly woman who was holding court across the room with several ladies seated around her. The visible relief on her face revealed that he had made a slight miscalculation in his attempt to impress her.

"Ah, I see my mother, Lady Netherley. She will likely scold me for tarrying too long with the flowers, when I promised to help with the children." To his dismay, her expression brightened at the prospect of abandoning him. "It was a pleasure to meet you, Lord Swainsbury. Will you be staying in town long?"

"As long as it takes."

Derrick's gaze narrowed as he noted that most of the gentlemen in the drawing room were observing them. Three of them were already making their way toward Lady Ellen in hopes of speaking to her before she reached her mother's side. He had the irrational desire to push her behind him and growl at the encroaching interlopers, but he had to earn her trust first.

"I do not understand," she said, puzzled by his enigmatic response.

He was spared from responding by the approach of a fetching blonde.

The two women embraced. "Where have you been hiding?" Her gaze assessed him from head to toe. There was admiration and speculation displayed on her countenance. "Or more importantly with whom?"

Lady Ellen blushed again. "Margery, allow me to present Lord Swainsbury. My lord, this is my good friend, Lady Oxlade. Lord Swainsbury is a good friend of Lord Ravens's."

The lady's enthusiasm diminished when the earl's name was mentioned. "How do you do, my lord?"

Derrick was not offended. It boded well that Lady

Ellen had sensible friends who would not approve of her associating with Lord Ravens.

To discourage any concern that he was cut from the same cloth, he said, "My estate and far-reaching business interests have made me a stranger in town. Lord Ravens was kind enough to take pity on me since I am without family during the holidays."

Sympathy replaced the hint of disapproval on Lady Oxlade's delicate features. "Oh, it is simply terrible to be alone, when one should be surrounded by loved ones."

He longed to rub the ache in his chest. "I concur, my lady," he said, unable to conceal the wistfulness in his voice.

Lady Ellen had noticed. "Where is your family, Lord Swainsbury?"

Derrick audibly exhaled. "I am all that remains of my family." He saw the pity on both women's faces and silently cursed. He had hoped to gain Lady Ellen's interest in another manner, but he would have been a fool not to take advantage of her sympathy.

Her eyes shined brightly with compassion. "I am sorry for your losses, my lord."

Lady Oxlade nodded. "With the Courtland family, no man is a stranger. Especially at Christmastide, the house is open to one and all."

It was precisely as he had feared. Before he could respond, a gentleman approached them.

"Lady Ellen, may I have a private word with you before I take my leave?"

Derrick glared at the newcomer, but the other man's gaze was wholly focused on the lady. His annoyance climbed when Lady Ellen seemed to be quite familiar with the gentleman.

"I hope you are not bored with our family gathering, Lord Pountney," she teased, causing Derrick to grind his back molars.

"Regrettably, I have another commitment that I must attend," the gentleman confessed, clasping Lady Ellen's hand between his own. He was a good-looking man with dark blond hair and a face that was fashioned to set a lady's heart fluttering.

Derrick had witnessed enough. The man was not to be trusted.

Recalling her companions, Lady Ellen's gaze shifted to him. She offered him a half-smile. "Lord Pountney, I am being rude. You have met Lady Oxlade, yes?"

The blue-eyed scoundrel acknowledged the lady by inclining his head. "Indeed. Pray, give your husband my regards."

"I will," Lady Oxlade replied. "He will be disappointed to have missed you."

Lady Ellen extended her hand toward Derrick. "And this is Lord Swainsbury. My lord, may I present Thomas Josland, Viscount Pountney."

Lord Pountney's expression was bland, but Derrick noticed his stance and bow were stiff with annoyance. It appeared they shared something in common, after all.

"Swainsbury." He frowned. "I thought you were elderly."

The dry statement had Lady Ellen gaping in shock at her friend. "Pountney, could you be any more obnoxious! Apologize at once."

The viscount's mouth tightened at her order. He was clearly reluctant to yield, but he did not want to lose the lady's affection. "Forgive me, sir. I must have been mistaken."

"Perhaps you have confused me with my uncle," Derrick said, his teeth flashing as he grinned. "I inherited the title from him six years ago."

The anger faded from Pountney's flawless face. "Ah, then that explains it." He turned, deliberately positioning his body so Lady Ellen could no longer see Derrick. "My darling lady, walk me to the door. I have a few things to tell you, and then I must dash off."

"Oh, very well." Lady Ellen surrendered too easily to Pountney's ploy to separate her from Derrick and Lady Oxlade. She peered over the viscount's shoulder. "Margery, will you tell Mama that I will return so she does not send Vane after me?"

"Leave the task to me." The blonde tilted her head at the viscount. "Lord Pountney, I trust you will behave yourself?"

"And risk Vanewright's ire?" He dismissed her question with a laugh.

"Lord Swainsbury," Lady Ellen glanced back, even while Pountney was leading her away. "I hope we get a chance to talk again."

The couple disappeared from view. Every muscle in his body urged him to follow them.

Lady Oxlade cleared her throat to gain his attention. "You needn't fret over Ellen."

The woman thought he was jealous. "Was that what I was doing?"

"My dear friend has been expertly managing gentlemen like Lord Pountney since her first ball."

Lady Ellen did not appear to be managing anyone. In fact, Derrick was certain she was a willing participant in her departure.

"She seems fond of him," he said, striving for neutral tones.

"And he has gone to great lengths to endear himself to her and the family."

Derrick was pleased to see Vanewright leave the drawing room with a dark-haired gentleman. At least Lady Ellen's departure had not gone unnoticed by her family.

"Of course, not everyone likes him." Lady Oxlade leaned closer. "Can you keep a secret?"

"Upon my honor."

"Lady Ellen will marry, but it will not be Lord Pountney," she whispered.

"How do you know?"

"I know my friend," the blonde said with resounding confidence. "However, the viscount is determined to claim that dowry, but he is not the only gentleman in this room who hopes to succeed."

Derrick had counted thirty guests this evening. More than half of them were male. "Who else is seeking Lady Ellen's hand?"

"New admirers present themselves each day. By Twelfth Night, who knows?" she said with a delicate shrug.

He was running out of time. Lord Netherley's intent to marry off his youngest daughter had brought a murderer into their midst, and not even Derrick could identify him. How could he subtly investigate dozens of suitors without drawing attention to himself or alerting the man he sought?

The dowry was the key.

Unfortunately, that placed the comely Lady Ellen in the unenviable position of being the bait.

Chapter Four

"Well, that was unpleasant," Ellen declared after her brother and the Earl of Chillingsworth—who went by the nickname Frost—had ensured that Lord Pountney had not lingered in the front hall with her as they had said their farewells.

Afterward Vane had taken her by the hand and practically dragged her into the library for a private chat.

"Brandy for your nerves, brat?" Frost held up the bottle in silent invitation.

She stomped over to the nearest chair and sat down. "No, thank you," Ellen said with false politeness. She glared at her brother. "You do realize that you owe Lord Pountney an apology."

"I disagree. Pountney is a fawning arse." Vane sneered over his glass of brandy. "The only reason why he didn't try to kiss you before our timely arrival is because he's too weary pressing his lips to our father's boney backside."

"Vane!" she exclaimed, appalled by her brother's accusation.

"Pountney isn't the only one puckering up," he ruthlessly continued, warming to the topic. "Even without Father in attendance this evening, I counted five greedy bastards . . ."

"No, there were at least seven," Frost countered.

"Seven!" Ellen wailed. She had been excusing herself from the drawing room since her arrival, and had not bothered counting them all. "Papa has gone too far."

"Greedy bastards, each and every one of them." Her brother seethed with indignation. "I want the names of every gent who dares to touch you without your permission. A few dawn appointments should cool their ardor."

"You will need someone to act as your second," Frost said, always relishing a fight. "I volunteer for the task."

Frost's new bride would never forgive her if something happened to her husband. "Emily will not approve," Ellen said tersely.

"No, she will not," the earl said, too agreeably for her liking. "However, I thoroughly enjoy working my way back into her good graces. When all is said and done, she will thank us both."

The notion was too disconcerting. "Why would she thank me?"

"It isn't for innocent ears, my sweet." He waggled his eyebrows. "I will explain everything in detail once you have bedded one of the desperate gents you have panting after you."

"You mean after her dowry," Vane corrected, sounding as bitter as she had been their father had revealed what he had done. "And there will be a wedding before there is any bedding. Is that clear?"

Ellen shook her head in disgust. "I cannot believe it."

"Believe what, sweet?" Frost asked.

"That I am actually listening to you two charming dissemblers." She raised her hands and implored to the heavens. "You are aware that I am acquainted with your wives, are you not? I *know* things."

Actually, Ellen was guilty of lying, too. Isabel and Emily were too polite and ladylike to mention anything so intimate. However, the Lords of Vice had earned their reputations, and she had heard rumors about their conquests. It was a safe bet that Vane and Frost had been impatient and claimed their ladies before their weddings.

In truth, she thought it was wonderfully romantic, though she was too vexed with their interference to admit it.

Vane paled as he considered the possibilities of what she had been discussing with the married women in their family. Frost, much to her dismay, appeared mildly curious.

"*Things* . . . too generalized a word and not very gratifying." The earl patted the armrest of his chair. "Come closer and we'll explore—"

"Frost."

The man sighed. "Naturally, you would deprive me of what would likely be a very entertaining exchange."

"If you are finished lecturing me about my unwanted suitors, I will return to the drawing room." Ellen stood and stifled a yawn. "There is no need for any concern. I doubt anyone will try to seduce me in front of Mama and the other ladies."

Her brother and Frost were too astute to miss the sarcasm in her tone. She pivoted and headed for the door.

"What about the other one?"

Perplexed, she glanced back. "Who?"

Frost spoke up. "Brown hair, gray eyes . . . wearing the dark blue waistcoat. He was very displeased when Pountney showed up. Thought we were going to have a brawl in the drawing room." He grinned at his friend. "Best of all, someone else would be to blame for a change."

Ellen thought of those final moments in the drawing room. "You are wrong. Lord Swainsbury was a perfect gentleman."

"Swainsbury . . . are you positive that is his name?" her brother asked as he turned to address his friend. "I remember an older gentleman sitting in the House of Lords."

"I heard he died. Thought the title had died with him." The earl finished his brandy and reached for the bottle.

"I assume both of you are correct," Ellen said, recalling what Lord Swainsbury had revealed. "The earl inherited the title six years ago from his uncle. He mentioned that he is the last of his line and travels often so he has few friends in London. Well, except for Lord Ravens."

"What of Ravens?" Vane sent his friend a sharp, meaningful look.

"Simply that your friend knows him. Lord Swainsbury is here as Lord Ravens's guest. I thought you were aware of this?"

Frost shrugged. He was not concerned by her news, because he considered the other man a good friend.

"Perhaps I should speak to this Swainsbury in private," her brother muttered just as she was about to walk away.

Instead, she pivoted and marched toward her older sibling. After observing her brother's humiliating behavior with Lord Pountney, she did not want the earl to suffer the same fate.

"I forbid you to approach Lord Swainsbury." Ellen poked a finger in Vane's face. "Lord Ravens has vouched for him—"

"Ravens possesses a very generous nature," Frost said to no one in particular. "I will speak to him about Swainsbury. Discreetly, of course."

"And he has suffered loss. Mayhap recently. Where is your charitable heart, dear brother?"

Vane closed his eyes as he struggled not to lose his temper. "Have you considered, dear sister, that your Lord Swainsbury is just another gentleman in pursuit of your dowry? Perhaps he is cleverer than the rest?"

"Nonsense! He is Lord Ravens's friend and nothing more," she said, deciding not to mention her reaction to the stranger. There was no point in provoking her brother. "Besides, I did not sense any flirtation or interest from Lord Swainsbury."

Ellen walked out of the library before her brother could argue.

"That is where you're wrong, little sister." Vane stared at the vacant threshold where his sister had stood. "Whatever his reasons . . . Swainsbury is most definitely interested in you."

Ellen had had overheard her brother's parting remark, but chose not to remain and debate him. Vane was just being overprotective because he was unhappy with their father's high-handedness with the dowry. Susan had accused her of sulking, and she supposed that she was to a certain extent. What overshadowed her sense of injustice was her increasing despair toward the man who had caused all of this mischief.

Lord Netherley.

They had made plans for him to attend this evening's rout at Vane's house. It was to be their father's first outing since his last debilitating attack. Even though he was no longer bedridden, Lord Netherley had politely declined joining his family at the last minute.

"Isn't it enough that Lady Netherley has invited half of London into my house this month!" he had thundered when it was suggested that Dr. Ramsey should be sum-

moned. *"I won't have a single minute of peace until Twelfth Night has passed. Leave me to my conservatory. My plants and trees need tending."*

Ellen had seen through her father's bluster. He had not wanted anyone to know he was too weak to endure an evening out of the house. *"I wish you were feigning illness in a futile attempt to avoid my displeasure, Papa,"* she sadly whispered. *"We have so little time left and you want to saddle me with a husband that I do not desire."*

Espying a bench just outside the drawing room, Ellen sat down to compose herself. It wasn't as if she was precisely against marriage. The seven notorious Lords of Vice had each fallen in love and married. Many considered it a miracle. The *ton* had yet to recover from the shock. Was it wrong for her to wait for someone so unexpected and wonderful to come into her life that it seemed equally astounding?

Yes, it is.

With a soft groan, she rose to her feet. No more hiding. Her admirers awaited just beyond the doors of the drawing room.

"Lady Ellen."

Fulton Tovey, Marquess of Hawksword stepped in front of her when she entered the room. He was not alone. Valentine, or rather, Troy Alexandra Valentine, Earl of Montridge had joined him.

"Gentlemen," she said genially. "How most unexpected to see you here." Surely, that cursed dowry had not prompted her friends to consider sacrificing their freedom and common sense at the marriage altar.

Her acquaintance with both gentlemen spanned an unflattering amount of years. She had been introduced to Hawksword when she was six years old. He had proven his devotion by pushing her down into the mud and ruining her favorite dress. She had returned the favor by blackening his left eye. When Vane had learned of the boy's cruelty, he had blackened Hawksword's other eye. After a few more childish incidents, they had gradually become friends.

Ellen had crossed paths with Valentine just before her eighteenth birthday. Admittedly, her romantic heart had swelled and pounded within her breast as he impressed her with his dark, sultry looks that suggested his lineage included a Roman conqueror. He had been the first gentleman to boldly kiss her. At the time, she had thought herself in love, but the earl's affection had not been constant. An hour later, she had caught him kissing one of her friends.

"Valentine and I were arguing who should escort you to supper," Hawksword explained in a cheerful manner that revealed that she did not have to worry about them coming to blows. "I told him that I deserved the honor because of our long-standing friendship."

"You pressed my face into the mud the first day I met you," she reminded him. Ellen noticed her mother's regard and waved. During her absence, Lord Ravens and Lord Swainsbury had joined her. Her mother gave her an encouraging smile. Perhaps she was hoping either Valentine or Hawksword were swearing their undying affection to her wayward daughter.

"I have different recollections of that day. I recall you planted your tiny fist into my eye and slipped spiders into my shoes when you challenged me to wade into a pond," the marquess replied without rancor. "You were always such a fierce little thing, determined to have your way."

Ellen laughed, her heart lightening as they reminisced. "If I had had my way as a six-year-old, you would have gotten more than your feet wet." Before Valentine could mention the kiss she preferred to forget, she said, "Hawksword may claim a longer association with me, my lord, but he is not the only one I thought deserved a good dunking so you will have to make your decision without me. I have neglected my mother and I seek to remedy my error."

How long had Lord Ravens and his companion been sitting with Lady Netherley? Two handsome gentlemen would give her mother all sorts of ideas that did not bode well for her.

"If you wish to settle the argument between you, the rules of precedence apply. Hawksword outranks you, Valentine." She fluttered her eyelashes flirtatiously. "Until later, gentlemen."

She ignored Valentine's soft appeal to stay. It was likely she had tarried too long, she mused. Mama was looking too pleased with herself. Lord Ravens and Lord Swainsbury immediately stood at her approach.

"I pray you are behaving yourself, Mama." To take the sting out of her gentle scolding, she leaned down and kissed the elderly woman's cheek. Ellen straightened. "Good evening, Lord Ravens." Her gaze switched to Lord Swainsbury. Unknowingly, her voice softened. "So we meet again, my lord."

"Please, join us." Lord Swainsbury stepped aside and offered his seat next to her mother. "You must be weary after Pountney's long farewell."

Lord Ravens snorted, but he swiftly bridled his amusement at his friend's not-so-subtle insult. He sat down, and the earl mirrored his actions by selecting the chair closest to Ellen.

"What's this about Lord Pountney?" Lady Netherley asked. "He's such a sweet and attentive young man."

Was the earl implying that she had slipped away in order to kiss Lord Pountney? "The viscount had no time for prolonged farewells," Ellen said, her explanation directed at Lord Swainsbury. "I was detained by my brother and Frost in the library."

His right brow lifted at the name. "Another suitor?"

"No, another annoying, overprotective brother," she said, her tone revealing her fondness for the gentleman. "You probably have met his wife, Lady Chillingsworth."

"Did something happen with Lord Pountney?" Lady Netherley inquired, sounding concerned. "And why on earth would Christopher and Frost escort you to the library when I distinctly told them to . . ."

"Told them what, Mama?" Ellen asked, when her mother did not finish her sentence. "Well, there is nothing to worry about. They wanted to ply me with brandy."

"They did *what*?" exclaimed her mother.

Lord Swainsbury's face darkened and his mouth narrowed with disapproval.

Lord Ravens was the only one with a sense of humor. He deduced almost immediately that Ellen was baiting her mother to repay her for sending her brother to watch over her.

"Naturally, I refused," she blithely added, which appeased her mother. Lord Swainsbury, on the other hand, was not persuaded. It was time to change the subject. "Lord Ravens, will you be joining in on our family celebrations? Mama predicts our Twelfth Night masquerade ball will be remembered for years to come."

Lord Ravens acknowledged her deliberate attempt to sway the conversation with a quick grin. "I was expressing my regrets to your lovely mother. I received word that my presence is required at my northern estate, and I will be leaving at dawn."

"How disappointing! Will you be gone long?" she inquired out of polite concern.

"Worried over losing one of your suitors?"

Ellen gasped in disbelief. Lord Swainsbury's bland

delivery had been so careless that she had not felt the sting for several seconds. "Not at all! Lord Ravens is not one of my so-called suitors." She sounded so appalled at the notion that she felt the need to apologize. "No offense."

Lord Ravens placed his hand over his heart. "None taken, my dear lady. I am, after all, an utter scoundrel. I have no redeeming value. Do you not agree, Lady Netherley?"

"Indeed," her mother heartily concurred. "You would be a terrible husband for our Ellen."

Lord Swainsbury sat rigidly in his chair. Ellen was tempted to demand an explanation for his outlandish behavior. It was not her fault that her father was determined to see her married. He had no right to judge her.

Lord Ravens seemed immune to the growing tension between her and the earl. "I do not leave London without a few regrets. Take Swainsbury, for example. Alone during Christmastide without friends or family."

"Think nothing of it," Lord Swainsbury muttered, his expression silently informing his friend to hold his tongue.

"Never fear, Ravens, I will not allow your friend to sit alone in a hotel when I can do something about it. Lord Swainsbury will stay with us at Netherley House."

Lord Ravens's eyes gleamed with approval. "An excellent and most generous offer, my lady."

Ellen's lips parted at her mother's announcement. "What? Mama, I do not think . . ." She cast a wary glance at the man seated next to her.

Lord Swainsbury was shaking his head. "I do not wish to intrude."

"Nonsense," her mother said, dismissing his protest. "The staff is already preparing for overnight guests. What's one more?"

"And Father?" Ellen pressed. "What do you think he will have to say about all of this?"

"Nothing at all. Lord Swainsbury will not be the sole bachelor residing under our roof, and Lord Netherley is an indulgent husband." Leaning forward, she confided to the gentlemen, "He spoils me dreadfully."

Ellen had little choice but to surrender gracefully.

Chapter Five

"I owe you," Derrick said solemnly, hours later when Ravens had proposed that they end the evening at Nox. His companion had managed the impossible. Not only had the earl introduced him to the Courtlands, but he had secured a coveted invitation from Lady Netherley, allowing him to watch over Lady Ellen.

"No words of thanks are necessary," Ravens had assured him. "One day, however, I would like to hear the real reason why you are so interested in that family." Derrick had been tempted to assuage Ravens's curiosity, since their association had proven advantageous. However, he was a man who had learned to keep his own counsel. "The dowry isn't enough," he countered, thinking of Lady Ellen's reaction. She had not been overjoyed by her mother's impulsive decision.

After a few minutes of contemplative silence, the earl slowly shook his head. "Not for you."

Lord Ravens's astute observation still echoed in Derrick's head the next day, when the Courtlands' butler escorted him to his bedchamber. Lady Netherley had not been exaggerating when she mentioned that he was not the only overnight guest. Many of the people he had met the previous evening would eventually show up at the Courtlands' town mansion in coaches laden with their bags and trunks. There were already indications that every room would be filled by the eve of Twelfth Night. He had recognized the Marquess of Hawksword as he strolled past the music room. No doubt his friend who had been flirting with Lady Ellen was in residence. Squires had also mentioned the recent arrival of a Mr. Giddings. He had no idea who the devil the man was, except that it was another name to scribble down in his journal.

Derrick was unaware of Lady Ellen's whereabouts. He was not arrogant enough to believe that she was deliberately avoiding him, but he was certain that she had been told of his arrival. He spent the afternoon casually exploring the interior of the large house and the vast collection of antiquities. It bespoke of what he assumed was generations of wealth and influence.

He marveled at its beauty, and wondered if Vanewright pondered the weighty mantle he would one day inherit from his father or if he simply accepted his birthright. Derrick had not been raised in impoverished circumstances, however, his father had been the second son of the Earl of Swainsbury. Everything his father owned, he had labored for it. When he had been five-and-twenty he had purchased his first top-sail schooner. It had been barely seaworthy, but his father had taken that single sailing vessel and turned it into a prosperous fleet. When he had something to offer a good woman, his father had married and sired a son and daughter. Even as a boy, Derrick had worked alongside his father. No task had been too menial because their hard work fed and sheltered his mother and sister. It had provided him with an education that rivaled any nobleman's son.

Derrick hesitated at the entrance of what he assumed was a connecting arched enclosure to the conservatory. The butler had revealed earlier that the flora within was Lord Netherley's passion. Curious, he walked down the short chilly passage and opened the door to peer inside.

Humid warmth blasted his face. He did not know much about hothouses; something more complicated than sunlight kept the room heated.

"Stay or go, but shut the damn door, if you please!"

The gruff order came from the left, beyond a row of potted citrus trees. Derrick stepped inside and closed the door. "Lord Netherley? Forgive me for intruding. I was exploring your marvelous house and—"

"I cannot hear a word you're saying. If you want to apologize, do it properly and give me a hand with this."

A man with a weaker disposition might have turned and fled. Derrick followed the narrow maze to meet the elderly Lord Netherley. The marquess's harsh tone was reminiscent of his own father. He discovered the man sitting on a stone bench. His breathing was labored and his complexion was pasty.

"Perhaps I should summon your physician."

"Leave me be." The man waved him off and pointed at the trough of rotting vegetation. "If you would be so kind to dispose of that for me. I cannot . . . I cannot . . ."

Derrick removed his frock coat and placed it on the bench. "Say no more. Just point me in the right direction."

"The wall . . . left of the entrance." Lord Netherley nodded and gasped for air. He gestured in the general direction Derrick had emerged from. "There is a worktable. You will understand when you see it."

"Just rest while I take care of this for you."

The scraping marks on the stones told their own story. The marquess had tried to lift the four-foot-by-two-foot wooden trough filled with dirt and decaying plant material. When he lacked the strength to raise it, he had attempted to drag it.

God save him, it was heavier than it appeared. Derrick gritted his teeth as he put his back into his task. He staggered a few times as he made his way to the workbench. His shirt was ruined, but he'd soil a dozen more to prevent the elderly gentleman from lifting another pot.

"There are three more," Lord Netherley said, his color improving with each passing minute. His hand shook as he pointed out their hidden locations. "Over there . . . and another set in the next section."

"Very well, my lord."

With a brisk nod, he was striding toward the next trough. By the time he was finished with his task, his thin linen shirt was clinging to his skin. His manservant, who he had left behind in Ferrystone would have mourned the condition of his waistcoat.

When he was finished, he sat down next to Lord Netherley on the stone bench.

Instead of thanking him, the man asked, "Which one are you?"

"Derrick Hunt, Earl of Swainsbury." He removed a handkerchief from the inner pocket of his frock coat and wiped his hands.

"Swainsbury?" He squinted as he inspected his companion's face. "I thought he died years ago. Are you his son?"

"His nephew. My uncle passed away six years ago."

The marquess digested the old news. "I knew your uncle. A very disagreeable gentleman, if you want to know the truth. I assume you must have lost your father before your uncle or else I would have had the pleasure of issuing orders to him?"

Derrick smiled, imagining the two gruff gentlemen bellowing orders at each other. "Yes. My mother, too, but I was still a boy when we buried her."

And my sister. God, Eloisa.

His heart clenched as if he had lost her yesterday.

Unaware of his companion's sad musings, Lord Netherley gave Derrick a measured look. "So you have come to claim my girl, have you?"

"I . . ." Derrick was uncertain how to respond to the blunt question. If he agreed, he might be giving the man false hope. If he lied and said that he had come because he was curious about the dowry and the lady who inspired it, then he would be no better than a common fortune hunter. In truth, he did not know what sort of reply the man was expecting. "I fear I have spent much of my time traveling. When Lady Netherley learned that I was in town alone, she generously invited me to join you and your family."

The marquess began to wheeze. Concerned, Derrick began to stand, but sat back down when he realized the man was laughing. "You are either richer than Croesus or a fool. What say you, daughter?"

"Lord Swainsbury is not participating in your little game, Papa. Leave the man alone."

Startled, he raised his gaze to meet hers. Derrick had not heard the doors open or her footfalls on the paved stone and gravel. He reached for his coat, slightly embarrassed he was not presentable for a lady. For Lady Ellen.

Standing, he slipped his arm into one of the sleeves, he shrugged into his frock coat. "My lady, if you wish some privacy with your father, I will take my leave."

She wrapped her arms around her body as if to ward off a chill. "Actually, I came looking for you. It's Christmas Eve, and Mama thought you could help me prepare the games for the children."

Derrick was delighted to assist her. He glanced down

at her father. "Of course, with your permission, my lord. Unless you have some other . . ."

"No, I can continue on my own. Run along." He gave Lady Ellen's hand a hesitant pat when she bent down to kiss him on the cheek. "There, there . . . none of that. Save your kisses for your admirers."

Her cheeks were a vivid pink that had nothing to do with the chill in the corridor as they walked back to the main house.

"How long had you been listening?" Derrick quietly asked, sensitive to the fact that Lord Netherley's comment had upset her.

Lady Ellen halted in front of the closed door. She placed her hand over his to prevent him from opening it. "Long enough to understand that you are a good man."

Derrick stared at their clasped hands. There was a rightness to it that worried him. "You are mistaken, I am not a good man. Do not fool yourself into believing a kind act toward an enfeebled—"

Lady Ellen tenderly caressed his jaw with her free hand. "Hush."

He froze, fearing he would break the magic of the moment. Unexpected hunger rose up within him. In spite of her height, she seemed so delicate. Her pale, flawless skin reminded him of the finest porcelain. She made him feel clumsy and unsure of himself.

"My father is dying, Lord Swainsbury," she said, the admission clearly painful to her. "He often refuses to acknowledge his limitations. Your kindness gave him dignity. Do not belittle yourself in my presence. I will only call you a liar."

Lady Ellen reached up with her other hand and cupped his face. She tilted her head as she studied his face.

His gray eyes narrowed until all he could see was her

face. "What are we doing?" His voice was flat and disinterested, but if the lady glanced down she would have had another excuse to insult him.

Lady Ellen moistened her lips with the tip of her tongue. Her blue-green eyes were alight with undisguised humor. "I believe we are about to kiss, my lord."

"What if we are caught? A scandal wouldn't be good for your reputation." He immediately regretted his words when the anticipation faded from her eyes.

"My dowry will polish away any tarnish." Her hands dropped away from his face.

Lady Ellen was in full retreat. She had been so brave, so daring up to this point and he had ruined it with a few careless words. With a muffled denial, he pulled her into his arms and covered her lips with his. She tasted like sunshine and innocence. Derrick longed to bask in her warmth. His arm curved around her waist as his mouth explored her tenderly. He did not want to frighten her.

A few minutes later, he lifted his face and was pleased to see that she appeared to be as dazed as he was by their kiss. The look she gave him had him reaching for her again. A few minutes later, she was gasping for air when she stepped away.

"You . . . are . . . a very dangerous . . . man, Lord Swainsbury," she declared as she pressed her hand to her heart. "And very distracting. I have games to plan."

She waited for him to open the door. He obliged, and followed her through the doorway.

"A lady who kisses me is permitted to use my first name. And I have games to plan, as well, since I am supposed to be helping you," he reminded her, amused that he had managed to scatter her orderly thoughts.

Lady Ellen clasped her hand over her mouth as she gasped and whirled to confront him. Her blue-green eyes were so expressive and so damn sweet that he wanted to pull her back into the chilly corridor again. He could probably keep her there for another fifteen minutes before someone began to search for her.

She placed her hand on his chest to keep him at a distance. "*You* will be returning to your bedchamber to change your clothes." At his confused expression, she elaborated, "Your shirt and trousers are filthy from carrying those old troughs for my father."

He had forgotten about his clothes. "You've muddled my good sense, my lady."

"Any man who kisses me should be allowed to call me by my first name," she said cheekily. Before he could respond, she rushed up to him and brushed a kiss against his mouth. "Join me in the small parlor when you are presentable."

She stepped back, but it was too late. Lord Pountney appeared around the corner with one of the servants. The high color in her cheeks and her slightly swollen lips and his rumpled clothing revealed he and the lady had been soundly caught in a bit of carnal mischief.

"Lord Pountney, you have arrived," she announced unnecessarily to everyone. "Good. You can assist me as well. Follow me. Lord Swainsbury, I expect to see you later."

"Yes, my lady."

Derrick smiled as the viscount glanced back over his shoulder to deliver a parting look of hatred toward the man he viewed as a rival.

The feeling is mutual, Pountney. Don't count on us ever being friends.

Chapter Six

Ellen never anticipated that she would enjoy Christmas-tide in London. This time of year was generally reserved for family and a few close friends, and she had always found solace in the rural winter landscape. When they were unmarried, Vane and his friends had spent time together hunting wild game on Netherley lands. The New Year was celebrated with good food, strong spirits, and presents were exchanged.

Her father's poor health and this dowry business had turned her world upside down. Instead of a quiet family holiday, they had a full house with more promising to pay their respects on Christmas and the days leading up to Twelfth Night. The servants had been busy, placing greenery across every door and window. The scent of roasted meats and spicy pies, cakes, and puddings filled every room in the house. Her stomach gurgled with anticipation.

In spite of his weakness, her father had joined them downstairs this evening. Overjoyed, her mother rarely strayed from his side. He sat in his favorite chair and watched over the children. Ellen had even caught him smiling and tapping his foot when a particular tune caught his fancy.

She could not even criticize the gentlemen who thought to court her despite her objections. Hawksword and Valentine entertained the children with mock sword battles. The son of one of her father's business partners, Mr. Giddings, played several instruments so he entertained them throughout the afternoon. Lord Pountney possessed some skill with the pen. He wrote several short plays that would be performed by their guests over the next few days. He even composed a poem that he had dedicated to her beauty. His gift had not gone unnoticed by the other gentlemen, and an awkward silence ensued for the next half hour. Susan and several of the female guests were sewing costumes for the various plays and the masquerade.

Lord Swainsbury, or Derrick, eventually joined her and the others in the informal parlor. The possessive glint in his gray eyes made her toes curl. Aware they had an audience, neither one of them mentioned what had transpired in the corridor. With their heads together they made a list of possible games that could be played, and cheerfully debated about which ones deserved to be placed at the top of their list.

Everything was perfect.

So much so that like all dreams and good things, it would fade and give way to something less satisfying.

"Is something wrong?" Susan shouted in her ear to be heard over the music and dancing.

Ellen shook her head. "Not at all." Since her reply would not appease her sister, she added, "I am worried about Papa. His health has been improving, but he is tiring easily. He refuses to listen to anyone, and I would never forgive myself if all of this excitement overtaxes him."

Instead of brushing aside her concern, Susan clasped her hand and squeezed. "Rejoice that he is happy, Ellen." The two sisters glanced over at their sire. Lord Netherley glanced up at his wife and smiled. "There is nothing you can do to stave off the inevitable."

Her father had once told her that he did not wish to die in his bed. Ellen briskly nodded and wiped away a stray tear. "Where is your husband?" Pypart had a way of disappearing, especially when there was work to be done. She had encountered the gentleman only once since he had arrived at the house.

"He took the five-year-old upstairs. The little one was falling asleep on her papa's shoulder," Susan said, content that her child was well cared for.

Ellen had rarely glimpsed this side of Pypart. Most days, he could not recall the names of his twelve children. He had always seemed content to leave the children in her sister's hands, while he spent his time gambling or dallying with a mistress. Over the years, she had never understood why Susan had bothered forgiving her husband for his many indiscretions. Ellen had always been so focused on her sister's pain that it overshadowed the apparent love between them.

"Have you seen Lord Swainsbury?"

Distracted, Susan absently nodded as she watched the dancers on the other side of the room. "Mama had the card tables set up in the library. Most likely, you will find him there with the other guests."

"He has the list and my notes," Ellen murmured.

Susan clapped along to the lively tune. "What did you say?"

"Oh, never mind. I have to find Swainsbury. Will you keep an eye on Papa?"

When her sister didn't reply immediately, Ellen touched her on the shoulder. "What? Yes, I will. We'll be fine."

Ellen went downstairs and peeked in the library to search for the earl. When she did not see him among the cardplayers, she climbed several flights of stairs to seek out the bedchamber Lord Swainsbury was occupying. Under normal circumstances, she would never consider knocking on a gentleman's door. However, there was nothing routine during the holidays.

She knocked on the door.

When Derrick did not open the door, she stood there and contemplated what to do next. Perhaps he had left the papers within the bedchamber when he had dressed for the evening. It was a reasonable explanation.

Ellen opened the door. "Lord Swainsbury?"

Satisfied there was no one in the bedchamber, she entered. One of the servants had already come and gone. Several lamps were lit so the occupant would not have to stumble into a dark room. She searched several tables, but saw nothing that resembled their notes.

For a man, Derrick was quite tidy. Nothing was out of place. Ellen took a step backward as she surveyed the room and bumped into the writing desk. A book fell to the floor with a distinct *thud*. As she bent down to retrieve the book and the leaf of paper that spilled out of it, she noticed that there was a gold chain tucked between the pages.

Grabbing everything, she straightened and frowned. She moved closer to one of the oil lamps. What she held was not a necklace, but a portrait miniature. Skillfully painted in watercolor was the image of a dark-haired young woman. She was quite lovely, and someone important to the earl.

Ellen opened the folded piece of paper and almost dropped the portrait miniature. Written in Lord Swainsbury's distinctive handwriting was a list of the names of every gentleman she had encountered in the past fortnight. At the top of the list was the amount of her dowry. The earl had circled the number.

She almost fainted on the spot when she noticed Lord Swainsbury in the doorway.

"So you have figured out all of my secrets," he said, sounding oddly flat and resigned.

Ellen fought down the panic bursting like fireworks inside her. "Not all, my lord."

The earl shut the door. "I suppose it was unavoidable. I do not have what it takes to be a spy."

"Is that what you are doing? Spying on us?" *On my family.*

He threaded his gloved hand through his hair. "You misunderstand me. I am not a spy, Ellen. I just thought a spy's unique skills would be useful."

Lord Swainsbury did not seem angry that she had uncovered his secrets. Emboldened, she extended her hand and revealed the small portrait miniature. "Is this lady your betrothed?" she asked, her voice cracking with emotion.

The earl reclaimed his property. In silence, he studied the lady's features for a minute before he slipped it into one of his inner pockets. "To answer your question, no, I am not engaged to the lady. Eloisa was my sister."

His sister. Relief flooded through her so quickly she felt light-headed. Belatedly, she recalled that he had told them that he was the last of his line. "And this paper . . . the names on this list. You have written down the exact amount of my dowry. When we first met, you insisted that you knew nothing about what my father had done—about the dowry."

"I lied."

Ellen flinched at his admission. He was succinct and brutally frank, and she could return the favor. She threw his journal at him.

Lord Swainsbury caught it before it struck him in the face and tossed it onto the bed. "No, wait!" he said, wrapping his arms around her and spinning her around so she could not reach for the doorknob.

"Let me go!" She seethed with fury. "I want you out of my house. You are nothing but a . . . a fortune hunter. For all I know, you are not even the real Lord Swainsbury."

"I am the real Swainsbury," he muttered as they struggled. "Why would I lie about that? Damn you, will you listen to me?"

"Never!" she spat out. For good measure, she kicked him to gain her freedom.

The earl retaliated by tossing her onto the bed. Before she could express her outrage, he joined her. He seized her wrists to keep her from slapping him, and used his body to pin her in place. "You bloodthirsty minx. I am not your enemy. I'm trying to protect you."

"How convenient," she said, straining against him. "Let's see if your story changes when you are dragged in front of the magistrate."

Ellen was tiring with each minute. She was no match for his strength. When she opened her mouth to scream, the blackguard kissed her. She silently howled at the injustice. It was unlike any kiss she had ever experienced. It was unyielding, relentless, and held an element of desperation and violence. She moaned against his mouth and he used his tongue to push past her defenses. He was demanding her surrender and she gave it to him.

The earl ended the kiss when he felt her relax beneath him. He raised his head and their gazes locked. "Are you ready to listen or do I have to kiss you again?"

A small part of her longed for him to kiss her again. It only proved that she was a madwoman. "Release me, and . . . and I will listen, my lord."

He hesitated, probably debating if he could trust her.

She was having the same problem so she could sympathize. Suddenly, he grinned down at her. "Derrick. A lady who has shared my bed has deservedly earned my trust and the right to call me by my given name."

He rolled off her and waited.

Ellen warily sat up and rubbed her wrists. He had tried not to hurt her as she had struggled fiercely against him. With her body rubbing against him, his body had reacted to her silent invitation. His unruly cock was still aching, but he ignored the need to finish what they had started. The lady sitting beside him had been through enough surprises for one day. Out of modesty, he shifted his position to conceal the hard length straining against the front of his trousers.

"I am not a fortune hunter." It annoyed him that she thought so little of him. "However, I will not lie—again," he amended at her smirk. "News of your dowry lured me to London, but it was not you or your fortune that enticed me."

"Such flattery will go to my head," she mocked.

Derrick gritted his teeth in frustration. "I did not know *you,* my lady. Nor your family. However, I did know something of the man who would travel to London to find you once he learned that he had a desperate father and a very rich heiress to seduce."

She stared at him as if he were daft. "What man?"

"The man who murdered my sister." He rubbed the grit from his eyes. "Perhaps I should start at the beginning. I was raised to be a merchant's son. It's been a good life, and I have traveled all over the world. Then my father died when I was twenty-two years old. I had Eloisa to look after and a business to run alone so I stayed in England. Four years later, word reached me that my uncle had died and the earldom had been passed to me." He made a vague gesture with his hands. "My uncle had no business sense. The estates were in disarray. What money he had was taken to settle gambling debts."

"It must have been difficult for you."

He laughed at her understatement. "My business suffered as I struggled through my uncle's affairs. I traveled often. I left Eloisa alone for months at a time."

"She wasn't a child."

Derrick thought of the portrait miniature in his pocket. "No. She was twenty-two when she was introduced to Brice Ayliff, Earl of Varndell. According to her letters, she was madly in love with him and they were impatient to marry. I immediately wrote her back and begged her to wait until my return, but it was too late. They were already married by the time I posted my letter. When I returned to Weymouth, I learned that my sister was dead. She had been strangled in her bed."

"Good grief! And you believe her husband was responsible?"

His gaze hardened. "Varndell murdered Eloisa. When I searched for him, he had already disappeared with her jewelry and all the money she had access to . . . And like you, she was an heiress. Vulnerable and too damn trusting."

"I resent that!"

"You still don't understand. Varndell never existed. He made up the name to gain my sister's trust."

"How many years have you been searching for him?"

"Almost five." His shoulders slumped in defeat. "I managed to trace some of my sister's jewelry, but no one could give me an accurate description of the gentleman. Whoever he is, he studies his quarry. He is familiar with your world. I suspect he had heard news of my inheritance and the problems that it had created."

"Our world," she softly corrected. "Why are you convinced this man would seek me out?"

Derrick shrugged. "A feeling. For months, I have heard

rumors of your father's illness. When he increased your dowry, I knew every miscreant would seize upon the opportunity of claiming that prize for himself, including Eloisa's murderer."

She grimaced at the notion of being any man's prize.

"You could have told us."

"Told you what? I had no proof, no description of the man, and I was a stranger. I didn't expect anyone to believe me so I decided to come to London to watch over you. If I was wrong, then I would have returned home."

She straightened as something occurred to her. "How did you convince Lord Ravens to vouch for you?"

"I didn't. He came to the decision that I was trustworthy on his own."

"We have to tell my father."

He swore under his breath. "No, we do not have to tell your father. And I would prefer that we not tell your brother. Vanewright glares at me as if he's measuring me for a shroud."

"He thinks you intend to seduce me."

Vanewright was more intelligent than he credited him. "Let's not give him a reason to shoot me on sight, shall we?"

"We have to tell someone," she said stubbornly.

"I disagree. If Eloisa's husband is planning to approach you, then the less people who know, the better. He is not to be underestimated."

Her eyes widened. "You're using me as bait to catch your sister's killer."

His brow furrowed in irritation. The denial stuck in his throat. "I prefer to view your dowry as the bait. And let us not forget that I could be wrong."

"So what are you planning to do?"

"Court you," he blurted, surprising himself. She appeared bemused by his statement, too. He rushed onward, not wanting her to debate the issue. "It is expected, and many of your friends and family assume those are my unspoken intentions. A courtship gives me an excuse to remain faithfully at your side. Ellen . . . I would never allow anyone to hurt you." He reached out and placed his hand over hers. "You can trust me."

She offered him a tentative smile. "I cannot explain it, but I think I already do."

Chapter Seven

The days passed without incident.

As Twelfth Night approached, Ellen's confidence increased. Although she kept her opinion to herself, she thought the chivalrous quest that had brought Derrick to London and his heightened fears about her safety had been induced by heartbreak. A tragic tale of a gentleman who had been unable to save his beloved sister from an unscrupulous, faceless stranger that he could not vanquish. Now she understood what was driving him to take extraordinary lengths to spare another family his sorrow.

A lady could fall in love with a man who was eager to slay dragons on her behalf.

"You like him."

Ellen glanced up from her book. She batted her lashes at him. "I like many people, Papa."

Tucked between the pages of romantic prose was a copy of the list she had helped Derrick create. After an evening at the theater, they had added another four names.

Before he was finished, he would have placed most of London's bachelors on the list.

Not far from where she sat, her father was near his worktable. He looked like a man of science as he mixed the proper ratio of compounds to increase the fertility of the soil he was using. It was not common knowledge, but her father had written several papers on the subject.

"Do not be coy with me, young lady." He huffed. The sound of pottery clinked against glass. "I was told by a reliable source that you were kissing that young viscount."

"Oh, you are speaking of Lord Pountney," she said, her good humor dimming at the memory. "It was on Christmas Day, Papa. Someone had nailed a sprig of mistletoe above one of the thresholds to trick unwary ladies. When we were taking Christmas boxes to the kitchen, I was soundly ambushed and I had to forfeit a kiss."

Derrick had not been amused when he had learned of the incident. Several of their male guests had taken advantage of the trick. Sprigs of mistletoe kept appearing above random doorways all day.

"Do not presume to think one kiss will help you select a husband for me. I kissed several gentlemen that day and I cannot marry them all," she teased, giving the list a final glance. She closed the book with a snap. "Furthermore, I—"

The almost musical collision of glass and pottery brought Ellen to her feet. She saw her father crumple to the ground. "Papa!" she screamed, dropping the book and running to his side.

When she turned him over, she noticed that his breath was labored and his lips were bluish in tint. "Not again," she muttered, lightly tapping him on the cheeks. "Papa, can you hear me? Do you know who I am?"

"S-Stub-born and im-mmm . . . impertinent," he said faintly, his words slurring as he struggled to breathe.

"That's me. And I will not let you die. Do you hear me?" She hugged him and pressed a kiss to his temple. "I love you. Hold on. I'm getting help."

Ellen ran as fast as her skirts and legs could carry her. She opened doors and did not worry about the cold air seeping in. Her heart was pounding and she could barely breathe when she stumbled into one of the main halls.

She did not even know the words she was screaming until Derrick and her brother emerged from the library. Derrick reached her first and caught her before she could fall to her knees.

"Papa"—she gulped more air—"Conservatory."

"I will summon Dr. Ramsey," Squires said from behind her.

"Go!" she ordered her brother. "I'll follow."

Vane took off with the lethal speed of a large muscled beast. Derrick helped her stand. Curious about the commotion in the hall, guests began to wander into the front hall. Someone offered to get her a brandy. She waved them off and staggered toward the side passage her brother had taken.

"He was teasing me about the mistletoe kiss," she said, her lungs burning with grief. "And then he collapsed. I called out, but no one heard me."

"I heard you." His arm tightened around her waist. She had not even realized that she was not standing on her own. "You kept screaming my name. I thought someone had attacked you."

Vane's complexion was ashen when he reappeared in the outer corridor with Lord Netherley in his arms.

Is he . . . ?

"He's alive," her brother announced and she sagged

against Derrick. He marched past the couple. "I'm taking Father to his bedchamber. Send Dr. Ramsey upstairs immediately."

He did not glance back to see if she was following them. "Someone has to tell Mama."

A high-pitched shriek announced that Lady Netherley had learned of her husband's failing health. Ellen glanced up at the man holding her so tenderly. She was startled by the fierce expression on his face. Straightening, she drew on his strength.

"Come, Mama needs our help."

Six hours later, Derrick found Ellen sitting on the floor just outside her father's bedchamber. It had been a close call, but Lord Netherley was resting peacefully with a liberal dose of laudanum.

"I have been searching for you," he said, crouching down beside her.

Her tearstained face and the utter anguish broke his heart. "Mama is sitting with him." She sniffed into her damp handkerchief. "Dr. Ramsey does not want anyone upsetting him. A room filled with sobbing people will assuredly convince Papa that he is not long for this earth." Her features twisted in misery at the terrible thought. "And he is correct. Papa would not like it."

"Your sister said that you refused to eat."

Ellen shook her head. "I am not hungry."

God, she was stubborn. "It is too cold for you to be curled up on the floor."

"I am fine," she said dully.

No, she was not. The lady was in pain and she was struggling to be brave for the sake of her family. "Come with me. Let me take care of you."

Without asking her permission, he pulled her into his arms and stood up. Derrick carried her down the hallway.

Most of the guests had retired for the evening so the house was silent. He did not know where he was taking her until he had reached the closed door to his bedchamber. Ellen rested her cheek against his shoulder as he shifted her in his arms so he could open the door. He swept her into the room with a romantic flourish and placed her on the bed.

She solemnly watched him lock the door so no one could intrude on their privacy.

He turned his back on the door and returned to her. He knelt down and removed her shoes. "I have never acted as a lady's maid," he said, his voice sounding hoarse to his own ears. His hands caressed the curve of her calves as his hand traveled higher to untie her stockings. "If you tell anyone, I will be forced to deny it."

Ellen had lovely, graceful bare legs. She also had a body he longed to worship. He gave into temptation and kissed her right knee and then her left.

"Derrick," she whispered, the longing in that single word slipping beneath his skin. It resonated with his soul. He understood her need.

"I'm cold," she admitted.

His hands moved upward until his fingers found her hips. "Let me warm you." He tugged her closer and leaned up to kiss her.

Their lips touched. Derrick felt her hands on his shoulders. Without breaking contact, he helped her remove his frock coat. With each layer of clothing that fell away, the more desperately he needed to feel her bared flesh against his.

Derrick had taken the occasional lover over the years to ease the loneliness of his travels. Although no one would ever accuse him of being as notorious as Ravens, or even the Lords of Vice, he had the skills to pleasure her. To make her crave the feel of him moving inside of her.

He unfastened her dress. She tugged and pulled his shirt over his head. They added to the pile of discarded clothing, kissing and touching new unexplored areas of exposed skin until they were naked.

His cock was primed and rigid with lust as he gently pushed her onto her back. His fingers slipped to the scented flesh between her legs and he stroked her, savoring the wetness that coated his fingers. Ellen instinctively arched against him. He wondered if she would like it if he buried his face into the curly thatch of hair and tasted her desire for him. Would he shock her if he suckled her tender flesh, pleasuring her with his tongue until she begged him for more?

He satisfied himself by nuzzling her nipples. Her breasts were small and perfect. Ellen gasped in surprise when his mouth covered one. He drew deeply as if she could nourish him.

Her hands threaded his hair. "Too much . . . I cannot bear it."

"Take more. Belong to me," he murmured between kisses. Blindly, his hand enclosed around his heavy cock. He rubbed the thick head against the opening of her sheath.

"Yes." She moaned again, her hips undulating in invitation. Her thighs widened to accommodate him and his cock slipped deeper.

Derrick felt her stiffen as her body took more of him, but it was too late for either one of them to turn back. He gazed into her eyes. Both of them were hurting, and the pain had coalesced into a need that he knew how to assuage. His hand cupped her buttock, pulling her closer and her body stretched and yielded to his demands. Her innocence faded with his claiming stroke.

He set the pace, a slow, delicious rhythm that made him break out into a sweat. Ellen rose up to meet his decisive thrusts. Her nipples grazed his chest as her fingernails dug into his back. The slow grind quickened as their bodies raced for completion.

When she cried out in pleasure, his body responded. Derrick pressed his face into her neck and whispered her name as he spilled his seed into her. He had never experienced anything so satisfyingly perfect.

Greedy for more, he wondered how long he would have to wait before he could fill her again.

"What is it?" Ellen murmured when he laughed.

"You have ruined me good and proper, my lady," he said, kissing her before she could reply. They were both breathless when he ended the kiss. "You might want to consider giving up your independent ways and marrying me."

Derrick was too intelligent to demand an answer from her. He reached over and pulled the bedding over them. Ellen snuggled against him, her cheek pressed against his heart. Too happy to question the wisdom of their lovemaking, they fell asleep.

Chapter Eight

Twelfth Night.

It astounded Ellen how quickly the days had flown by. The Yule season was almost over. Tomorrow, the servants would take down the greenery and burn it in the fireplace. All of the guests would return to their homes. Many would journey to their country houses, and she would not see her friends until warmer weather enticed the *ton* back to London.

Her father was recovering from his latest collapse. Dr. Ramsey had forbidden Lord Netherley to return to the conservatory. His health was too fragile. To soften the order, Derrick and others had volunteered to look after her father's prized plants until someone could be hired to care for them. Lady Netherley was touched by everyone's kindness. Most of her day was passed at her husband's side.

Susan had suggested that they cancel the grand masquerade, but Lord Netherley stubbornly refused to ruin the event everyone had been looking forward to. Despite her concern about her father's health, Ellen was relieved that her sister did not get her way. Perhaps it was selfish, but she was not ready for the magic to fade.

She was not ready to let Derrick go.

The night they had become lovers, he had mentioned marriage. His words had been more of an observation rather than a proposal, leaving Ellen mildly perplexed. She half-expected him to say something, but he never broached the subject again—not even during the late hours when he slipped into her bedchamber and made love to her until she fell asleep sated and exhausted.

Perhaps he had regretted his hasty words. Her brother had seduced countless women before he had met Isabel. It hurt her pride to consider it, but she was practical enough not to bind herself to a man who did not love her. No amount of threats could change her opinion, and the gentlemen who had joined the Courtlands in hopes of claiming her dowry would leave disappointed. In time, she would persuade her father to accept her decision.

Her scandalous nights with Derrick had revealed something about herself. She had been unaware that she could not give away her body without her heart. Derrick Martin Hunt, Earl of Swainsbury owned both, and there was a chance he would leave her, never realizing the truth.

Eloisa's murderer never revealed himself. She and Derrick had gone over his list. No one seemed to fit the description of a violent fortune hunter set on seducing her for her money. Most of the gentlemen present had connections to families that her parents had been acquainted with since their youth. In truth, Derrick was a more likely suspect, even though he was loath to admit that his instincts had failed him.

Ellen studied her reflection in the mirror. She was attired as a fortune-teller. Valentine had encouraged her to choose the costume, since she alone could reveal the name of the gentleman who had a chance of winning her.

The fortune-teller was one of the many roles Lord Pountney had created for the play. Earlier, she and several ladies had cut paper into small slips. Traditionally, the names of each guest would have been written down and placed into a hat. Later, a king and queen would be selected and they would reign for the rest of the night. This year, everyone had agreed to fill the hat with only two names—Lord and Lady Netherley. They were everyone's king and queen, and she wanted to give her parents a night to remember.

A brisk knock had her turning away from the mirror and heading for the door. Had Derrick decided he wanted to escort her to the ballroom? It was a bold declaration for a man who had arrived at their door with the intention of using her as bait to catch his sister's murderer.

Ellen opened the door. "Lord Hawksword. This is unexpected," she said, hiding her disappointment that her visitor wasn't Derrick. "Is something amiss?" The marquess had not donned his costume.

"Forgive me, my lady. If this was not about Lord Netherley, I would have sent a servant," he explained, his handsome visage etched with concern. "Your presence is needed. Someone saw your father enter the conservatory. He has gotten it into his head that a few more orange trees are needed around the thrones."

It sounded precisely like something her father would do. "Good heavens! The man is determined to give me heart failure." She nudged Hawksword aside as she exited her bedchamber and shut the door. "Do you know how many assurances I had to make to Dr. Ramsey to convince the good doctor that the most strenuous task my father would engage in this evening was *sitting*?"

"Do you want me to join you?" the marquess offered as they made their way downstairs.

"Thank you, but it's unnecessary," she said. "I would appreciate it if you looked after Lady Netherley. Assure her that I won't permit Papa to touch a single potted tree."

"Have your father handpick the ones he desires," he called out as they parted ways. "Valentine and I will see to it that they are in the ballroom at the appropriate time."

"You are a good man, Hawksword."

"Just not the right man for you, eh?" He winked knowingly at her before he sauntered off.

Unable to form a proper response, she watched the marquess disappear around the corner. "Perhaps I should have pushed him in the pond when we were children," she muttered.

Ellen was breathless when she entered the conservatory. Most of the interior was cast in shadows. The servants would be lighting the lamps later so guests could tour her father's private sanctuary.

"Papa?" She stepped deeper into the maze of flora. "Come out of hiding. I know all about the orange trees. Why didn't you take one of the servants with you? Dr. Ramsey will personally throttle me if you lift a single pot."

To her right, a gentleman stepped out of the shadows. "I agree, Lady Ellen, you deserve to be punished, but you needn't worry about Dr. Ramsey." It wasn't his presence that startled her, but rather the large pistol he had aimed at her heart. "I am completely capable of seeing to the task."

In the library, Derrick was seated and surrounded by seven very stern gentlemen. When he had answered Vanewright's summons, he had been introduced to the man's friends, the other founding members of Nox: Saint, Sin, Dare, Reign, Hunter, and Frost.

He believed every man deserved to know the names of his executioners.

"I do not recall the part of the Twelfth Night tradition that called for a human sacrifice."

"Sounds very pagan," the dark-haired gentleman with the odd blue-turquoise eyes murmured.

"An inappropriate time for humor, Frost," the man who had introduced himself as Sin replied. He glanced at Vanewright. "He doesn't look as dim-witted as you had described. Perhaps we can finish this without bloodshed."

"Gents, I have a very pregnant and restless wife sitting in Lady Netherley's drawing room while she awaits my return," Saint said, uncrossing his arms. "Unless you want my son born in this house, I recommend we handle this in a manner that will not upset our wives."

Derrick allowed his gaze to drift from face to face. He could think of only one thing that would provoke a brother into a killing rage, so much so, that he invited his friends to commit murder. The man knew Derrick had bedded Ellen.

Without warning, Vanewright delivered a sharp, brutal punch to Derrick's diaphragm. He doubled over and groaned. The man hit like he pounded stone walls each morning with his damn fists.

"Frost and I had a chat with your *good* friend, Ravens."

So Lord Ravens had confessed all. Protecting his stomach with his hand, Derrick shook his head. "It isn't what you think."

Vanewright crouched down to meet Derrick's gaze. "And what do I think, Swainsbury? That you talked Ravens into vouching for you to gain access to my family. My sister. You heard news of the dowry and thought to seduce my sister to claim it."

He tried to stand, but hands gripped his shoulders and slammed him into a chair. "No . . . you're wrong. I never cared about the dowry. *Ever*. Keep it, for all I care." The next part was going to hurt, but this man was going to be his brother-in-law if he had his way. He grinned at how fate had kicked him in the arse. "Now, your sister. She's the one I want."

"You can't have her!" Vanewright snarled.

Derrick shrugged. "Already have."

"Oh Christ, you shouldn't have said that," the blond-haired gentleman muttered.

Whatever else he said was muted by the earl's outraged bellow as he lunged for Derrick. His friends moved out of the way as the chair was knocked over. He tried to roll away but Vanewright sat on top of him. Grabbing him by the cravat, the man punched Derrick in the jaw.

Sparks danced like fireflies in his vision.

"We can't let him murder this lovesick fool in Netherley's library," someone argued.

Lovesick? Who accused him of being in love with this madman's sister? He struggled to avoid the next punch.

"Only a man in love would beg his lover's family to kill him," was another man's dry retort.

Vanewright drew his fist back and froze. "You are marrying my sister."

It wasn't a question.

"No bloody dowry," Derrick said, bracing for another punch. He did not want Ellen or her family to think he'd approached her to feather his pockets.

"Now that's the first sensible thing I've heard this gent utter," the one called Dare said. He clasped his friend on the shoulder. "You can't kill him."

Vanewright snorted, his fisted hand dropped to his side. He shook his head, and surprised Derrick by offering his hand. "Welcome to the family, Swainsbury."

Before he could accept, the door burst open and Lord Hawksword rushed into the room. His eyes widened as he realized he had walked into a potentially violent situation. "Has everyone lost their minds this evening?"

"What is it, Hawksword?" Vanewright snapped, his temper on edge.

"I came to warn you—something is amiss. I sent Lady Ellen to the conservatory to stop Lord Netherley from exerting himself."

"Let me up, Vanewright, and I will go help her," Derrick offered.

Hawksword wasn't finished with his news. "But that's not the oddest part. When I returned to the ballroom, your father was sitting on the throne beside his lady. I cannot fathom why he lied to me."

"Who?" Derrick said, his stomach aching with dread.

"Lord Pountney."

"Damn, I knew there was a reason why I hated him on sight." He shoved his future brother-in-law aside.

Frost scowled. "Besides the obvious, what's wrong with Pountney?"

"You are in luck, Vanewright," Derrick said, allowing him to assist him to his feet. "You might get to murder a man who actually deserves it."

Ignoring his companions, he ran out the door to catch up with Ellen. Perhaps he could reach her before she stumbled into Pountney's trap.

"Lord Pountney, I looked upon you as a friend."

The viscount studied her face and sighed. "My dear, Lady Ellen. I had thought—I was wrong. Until I had Hawksword lure you here, you had not figured out the truth about me." Another weary sigh. "It was quite careless of me. You see, nothing has gone right since Swainsbury's arrival at Netherley House. I panicked, fearing he might see through my disguise."

Staring at the pistol, she silently debated whether lying to a murderer was prudent. In hopes of calming him, she edged away from the door and moved toward her father's worktable where he concocted his various fertilizer mixtures for the plants and trees in the conservatory. "Your secret is safe. I won't lie to you and tell you that I haven't heard the tragic tale of Eloisa Hunt's death. The loss has tormented Lord Swainsbury. He believes his sister's murderer is a man named Lord Varndell. A man he has never met . . . a man who doesn't exist." She smiled at him and appeared to clasp her hands behind her back. "I have always liked you, my lord. Mistakes can be forgiven. Allowances made. I see no reason why we cannot let the earl continue to chase Varndell's elusive specter across England. I will keep your secret."

The viscount's grip tightened on the pistol. "Is that what you promised Swainsbury when you parted your thighs and welcomed him into your bed?"

Her blush confirmed his suspicions.

"Foolish little heiress," Lord Pountney mocked. "I had already spoken to your father before your lover's arrival. Netherley was merely giving you a few days to accept your fate before he announced our betrothal." His face twisted into something dark and ugly. "The dowry is mine!"

"Wrong!" Ellen tossed the contents of the jar she had retrieved from the table into the viscount's face. Deducing his response to her attack, she lunged to the left as he discharged his pistol.

"Ellen!"

She heard Derrick's anguished cry and the thunder of footsteps. He had come with reinforcements. Staying just beyond Lord Pountney's reach, Ellen picked up one of her father's large pots.

"You are wrong about my father. Dowry or no dowry, the decision is still mine to make."

She raised the pot high, and smashed it against Lord Pountney's thick skull. The viscount ceased scrubbing his eyes and collapsed without a sound.

Derrick found her standing over Lord Pountney's unconscious body. Vane, Hawksword, and the other Lords of Vice surrounded them.

"It looks as if your sister beat you to it," Frost cheerfully announced.

"My lord, I believe I have found your sister's murderer." Ellen swayed, feeling a bit unsteady. "Drat, I am going to faint."

Derrick rushed to her side and she collapsed into his arms. "Don't worry, love. I've got you."

She nodded and surrendered to the swallowing darkness.

Epilogue

"I cannot believe I fainted," Ellen complained hours later after the constables had carried off a barely conscious Lord Pountney and had interviewed everyone who was involved. Some of them had lingered to enjoy the Twelfth Night cake.

"You were not the only one feeling dizzy." Derrick pressed a kiss to her temple. "Did you see your brother's face? Dare had to wave your mother's smelling salts under Vanewright's nose when you retold your harrowing tale to the constable."

"I missed that part." Her fingers drew tiny circles on his palm. "It is Catherine who has my sympathies. Mama said that the poor woman went into labor when Pountney fired the pistol. Before the night has ended, you and the others might need to use those smelling salts on Saint."

Derrick wondered if he would ever recover from finding Ellen standing over his sister's killer.

"He was planning to shoot me. All that mattered to

him was my cursed dowry," she fumed. "It has brought me nothing but trouble, I tell you."

Derrick stilled. "I disagree. If not for your father's high-handedness about finding you a husband, I would have never come to London."

"Or caught Eloisa's murderer."

She tried to stand, but he dragged her back onto his lap.

He tilted her chin up with his finger. "You caught Pountney. I only viewed him as a rival for your affections and was too blinded by my jealousy to consider he was pursuing you for less noble reasons. After all, he was a friend of the family."

Ellen wrinkled her nose at the reminder that Pountney had fooled all of them.

"Do you think we'll ever learn his real name?"

Derrick was no longer interested in talking about the viscount. "I doubt it. His name won't do him any good when they hang him for murder." Eloisa would have justice thanks to the woman in his arms. "There are more important questions that need to be addressed."

Ellen gazed up at him with her vulnerable blue-green eyes. "Such as?"

Just because Vanewright was resigned to having him for a brother-in-law, it didn't mean he had won his lady's heart. "You never gave me your answer."

"About what?"

He had the urge to shake her when he caught on that she was teasing him. "Marry me, Lady Ellen Courtland. I've already told your father that I don't want your dowry. I want . . ."

He floundered at the objection darkening her face.

"What do you want, my lord?" she asked tenderly.

"I want to marry you," he said without hesitation. "I want to share my home by the sea with you . . . show you the world if you'll let me."

"And children?"

His eyes gleamed with unshed tears. "If you have no objection, I would like to name our first daughter Eloisa, to honor my sister."

"I have only one question."

"What is it, my love . . . the only true keeper of my heart?"

Ellen wrapped her arms around his neck and tried her best to throttle him. "Oh, never mind, you have already given me my answer. I love you, too," she whispered into his ear. She pulled back. "However, I disagree about the dowry. You should keep it."

Derrick glanced over her shoulder and sighed. "Let's argue about this when we have less of an audience."

From their gilded throne that was surrounded by her father's orange trees, the newly crowned king and queen of Twelfth Night surveyed their subjects, who were observing their exchange with undisguised interest.

Not far from the couple, Lord Netherley wiped his eyes with the handkerchief his beloved wife handed him.

The Scandal

Before

Christmas

❄

Elizabeth Essex

Prologue

It was only fitting that a ramshackle fellow like Ian Worth should arrange to take a girl to wife in the dim, drafty taproom of the Ball and Anchor, a tumbledown public house on the road to nowhere. Nowhere—in Ian's case—being Portsmouth Harbor, where his ship rode restively at anchor in the dripping, swollen Solent.

Time and tide were running out.

"We're agreed to it, then?" His companion struck out his hand, and took one last, narrow look at Ian through the tavern's thin blue smoke, as if he were belatedly trying to gauge the level of Ian's sobriety.

But Ian wasn't drunk. He *was* hungover. And desperate. "Agreed."

This was what he had come to—ordering up a wife with the same casual trepidation he normally reserved for stowing volatile powder aboard his cutter. Gingerly taking on dangerous, combustible cargo.

The likelihood of a hasty, patched-up marriage *not* blowing up in his face like so much black powder was practically nil, but no less than he deserved for trying to become engaged in a taproom.

But damn his eyes if such hazardous odds weren't exactly his favorite sort of gamble.

Chapter One

The event that precipitated such a dire state of wagering, and the casting of Ian's anchor deep into the still waters of matrimony, had been the arrival of his father, the esteemed Viscount Rainesford. The old man barged into Ian's until-that-moment-peaceful breakfast room within the cozy confines of Gull Cottage, and barked, "I need you to marry."

His father the viscount, despite the advantages of wealth and breeding—or perhaps because of them—was forever barging in. And forever barking. Forever insisting upon having his way.

But even at such an early hour, Ian was not about to let the old man gain sea room. "Certainly not before breakfast, sir." Ian made his voice as bland as bathwater. "Do you care for coffee?"

"Don't you try to give me the dry end of your wit." The old man ground the words out of his mouth like grist for his unreasoning anger. "Your brother has broken his damned fool back. Fell from that bloody-minded hunter of mine three days ago. They tell me he'll never walk again, much less sire children, damn it all to hell. So I need *you* to have a wife by Christmas."

"Good God." Not Ross. Dutiful, obedient, golden Ross. Ian tried not to react to his father's latest blatant manipulation, but fear for Ross exploded like grapeshot in Ian's chest, propelling him up and out of his chair, even as his father flung himself down into one. "What has been done for him?"

His father pounded his fist on the table by way of an answer. "Nothing can be done. He's a damned cripple. If he lives. Useless to me. You will need to take over his duties immediately."

Devil take the poor bastard. How could this have happened to Ross? Ross—the brother who had spent his entire life trying to please their unpleasable father, willingly living as the old man directed, serving the family name honestly and dutifully, without a murmur of complaint. Unlike Ian, who had gone to his duty—the career his father had chosen for him in the Royal Navy—grudgingly at best, and cursing his father every queasy step of the way.

And all Ian could think was that it should have been he who was crippled—*he* was the expendable one. Their father had always said so, and no doubt the old man had always expected his recalcitrant younger son to be put to bed with a cannonball. More than twelve years in the service of His Royal Majesty's Navy had put Ian in harm's way enough times to make his early death both possible and entirely probable.

But Ian had always had the devil's own luck, and despite those twelve years spent staring down the business end of a cannon, he had emerged relatively unscathed—still the irascible, standby second son.

But now his father wanted him to do more than stand by. He wanted Ian to take his broken brother's place.

"Sell out of your navy business immediately, and return home. We must see to the business of making your brother's betrothal over to you instead."

The thought was not to be borne. Ian could only be appalled at the idea of so cold-bloodedly transferring his brother's betrothal—his brother's very life—to himself. In the face of his father's angry bluster, he strove for calm. "What has been done for Ross?"

"Nothing. I've had them all, the doctors—locals from Gloucester, consultants from London, and specialists from the continent alike. They all say the same thing. Nothing further can be done. Nothing. I wouldn't have bothered to fetch you if I thought anything more could be done."

"Jesus God."

"Best accommodate yourself to being my heir. Sir Joseph Lewis's daughter Honoria is his only child and his heir, and I expect . . ."

Ian had shut his mind to his father's expectations and machinations. It mattered little what else his father had to say. His initial instruction had been all that mattered— the same as all the previous directives that had come with regularity throughout all the years of Ian's life. The Viscount Rainesford spoke, and expected the world to jump to do his bidding.

But Ian was no longer a boy to be intimidated by his father's perpetual scowl. He was an officer of His Majesty's Royal Navy. Devil take him, he'd learned to eat colder stares for breakfast.

No. He had accommodated his father enough. He had done his duty, against his will and against his inclinations, and learned to do it brilliantly. And he'd not have it said that Ian Worth had robbed his brother of his rightful inheritance before he'd even breathed his last. All it needed to make a miserable scandal was for the Viscount Rainesford to settle everything on his vagabond younger son, only to have Ross recover.

No. While his brother lived, Ian would do all he could to protect them both from his father's selfish thoughtlessness.

And if he could do only that for Ross, Ian would also do this one thing for himself. "I can't possibly accommodate you, sir," he lied. "You see, I'm already married."

Chapter Two

Which was how Ian found himself staring down the empty end of a tankard in the Ball and Anchor. He'd given his word.

He'd also seen Ross—dosed into a stupor of laudanum—and after accepting that there really was nothing to be done but give Ross time to try and recover, Ian had retreated to the public house full of morose desperation.

Ian knocked the empty tankard against the table, and motioned to the stout publican. "Another bitters." Marriage, he felt sure, should not be contemplated on an empty stomach, or with an empty glass.

Marriage. A wife. A woman to have, to hold, and to keep until death did them part. God help him and the devil take him, she'd have to be a lady, especially if the dire prognostication about Ross's eminent demise proved to be true—which Ian did not believe—and not just another one of his father's tricks to get him to do his bidding. Because God knew the old man didn't want Ian to be the next viscount.

Yet Ian had given his word, and therefore needed to find himself a wife. But damn his eyes, he hadn't the faintest idea of how to go about the business. Ian didn't actually know any young *ladies*. Females—barmaids, widows, and women of all sorts of earthy, working denominations—yes. Ladies of the gently bred and gently spoken type—not at all.

Unlike his obedient older brother, Ian had never gone to London and done the pretty with the society ingénues and their ilk—because he was reasonably sure that you couldn't have a romping good fuck with an ingénue the way he had with Betty, the charmingly sympathetic, milky-thighed barmaid last night.

How on earth was he going to abide some gently bred young lady—the same woman day in and day out—for the rest of his life? God's balls. Here today and gone tomorrow had been the way of his life. And it was the only way he wanted to continue.

And while many men—navy men in particular—would have been perfectly content to breeze through marriage taking their pleasure where they may, the idea held little appeal to Ian. Blame it on his father's hypocritical example—Ian may have been a bit of a libertine, or at the very least a thoroughgoing sensualist, but it seemed downright dishonest to require fidelity from one's spouse if one were not prepared to be faithful in return. And he knew, despite thoroughly enjoying sowing his wild oats, that in his own marriage he would require absolute faithfulness. He just hadn't counted on requiring it quite so soon.

So therein lay the rub. And the trap. And there wasn't enough ale in all of England to get him out of it.

"I say . . . Worth, is that you?" A hearty voice boomed across the low-ceilinged taproom. A tall, ruddy-faced man in his forties strode toward Ian with his hand extended.

"Colonel Lesley." Ian pushed back his chair to rise and greet the marine. "God's balls. I haven't seen you since the old *Audacious*. What brings you to the Ball and Anchor?"

"This filthy weather," Colonel Oliver Lesley answered jovially, slapping Ian on the back. "I'm selling out, Worth, my boy, selling out. You poor navy fellows can't sell your commissions to turn any profit like those of us with the foresight to go into His Majesty's Marine Forces. Ho, Barkeep!" He sat. "Selling out before I'm put on half pay for the peace, like at least half the fleet. And the wife wanted me back. Need to see to the business of my own family the way I've seen to England's, she said. And what about you? I'd heard you'd landed a plum little commission commanding a dispatch cutter."

"I *have*," Ian agreed. The perfect commission for a navy man who did not like the sea. A commission he did *not* mean to give up. Channel service put him home—his own home where everything was cheerful and easy, with no one to please and no one to disappoint—once a fortnight. "But come have a drink with me, and keep me from being morose."

"Happy to oblige. Ale and kidneys if you have 'em." The colonel ordered his breakfast, and eyed Ian with some amusement. "But what on earth would a young man like you have to be morose about?"

Ian was too desperate for secrecy—his misery wanted company. "My father requires that I be married by Christmas."

Lesley let out a low whistle. "Six days? But marriage is a young man's lot—once he has a career and a fortune, he must marry. Still, all in all, I'd rather have your job than mine. You only have to marry—I have daughters I've got to marry *off*."

Desperation made Ian prick up his ears. "Daughters? Any you'd like to part with by Christmas?"

"Come, come. Young man like you—a handsome man with all his hair and teeth, not to mention limbs, as well as a fortune—shouldn't have to go a-begging."

"And yet I must." Ian rubbed his hand through his hair, as if he could chafe some sense into his brain.

Perhaps he should go to town, to enlist his mother's aid? But if he were honest with himself—something he had very little experience with—he wouldn't be able to abide the kind of girls his mother or her cronies would see that he met: bright, chatty young misses with plenty of conversation and a love of society, as an antidote to what she called "your dark tendencies."

Dark tendencies, indeed. He liked the uncomplicated company of his navy friends, he liked to drink, he liked to gamble, and he liked to fuck uncomplicated barmaids. Hardly the sort of things mothers approved of, naturally, but all in all, there was nothing particularly dark about them. It wasn't as if he were married. Yet.

"But I've not the faintest idea how to go about it."

"Perhaps you ought to figure out what sort of girl you want first, and then it might be easier to find her." At his age, the colonel was nothing if not practical.

A barmaid was the first answer that came readily to Ian's mind, but the Viscount Rainesford would turn out an inappropriate daughter-in-law faster than a ship's carpenter could sniff out wood rot. Just the thought of his father's cold, manipulative rage made Ian's gut turn as sour as a barrel of brine. And his hangover wasn't helping.

"A quiet girl," he mused out loud. "Young enough to comfortably adapt to my ways, but not so young that she can't manage anything by herself. Because she'll be by herself when I'm at sea. A quiet, country girl," he continued as the idea gained merit, "who isn't forever craving society, and wanting to go to London, and give insufferably tedious balls and dinners."

A fairly short list of requirements, but that was the gist of it. "Appearance doesn't matter. Not really. I don't care if she is blond or brunette, long or short, so long as she can manage herself, and leave me in peace." Most of the time anyway—he supposed she ought to be pleasant enough to look at, to make it easy to do his duty by the family, and get a brat on her. Poor girl.

At that less than cheering thought, Ian buried his face in his bitters, draining the tankard to the last. He surfaced to find the colonel regarding him as if he had sprouted two heads. "I know, I know. You think me mad."

"I don't know what to think," the older man answered with a wary sort of wonder. "Are you quite serious?"

"I am entirely serious," Ian said with a young man's laughing bravado. "A quiet, easygoing girl is all I require. Even a bit of a cipher. But they're damned thin on the ground this morning."

"Not so thin as all that," the colonel said carefully. "I may have exactly what you require."

Ian felt his breath bottle up in his chest. "Are *you* entirely serious?"

"Quite. I do have a daughter who might do. My eldest, in fact. A girl who has just turned two and twenty, and a quieter, more unassuming girl you'll never find. Born and bred in the country, without a thought for London. A quiet, sensible girl. Very happy to be left on her own. Prefers it, actually."

Ian's tankard fell to the table with a thump. "Does she have a portion?"

The colonel's answer was swift and sure. "A thousand. And she's not one for the fripperies. Never exceeded her allowance, very economical."

It was enough to consider. And really, what choice did he have? It was not as if he had any other options or ideas to hand. "When might I meet her?"

"By Christmas, you said? I suppose you'd best come with me now, to Somersetshire, to meet her."

Such a trip would take too much precious time, and Somerset was too close to the whole sphere of his father's influence in Gloucestershire for comfort.

"Perhaps it might be better to have her see where I live presently, which is where she'll be for the foreseeable future? Gull Cottage, out on the Isle of Wight, across the bay." Ian made a vague motion out across the gray Solent, but he subdued his hands, and changed tacks at the sight of Lesley's frown. "It's lovely, really. And much larger than it sounds. A very handsome property and . . . it would be her dower property in the event of my death."

Yes. The plan was forming in his brain, a plan that would serve both his father and himself. If he married the girl and got her with child quickly, his father would get what he wanted—a secure heir whom he might raise to the title instead of Ian, who knew nothing about estates and land management. And once Ian had safely gotten the girl with child, he would be free to return to his command.

Ian firmed his voice. "I had rather you brought her to see the property, as well as me. So she can see if living there will suit her."

The colonel chewed on his bottom lip for a long moment of shrewd contemplation before he spoke. "I suppose I don't see why not. A visit of a few days' time, to see if you'll get on together?"

"Yes." Ian swallowed over the hot mixture of trepidation and excitement climbing up his throat. It would work. It had to work.

"We're agreed to it, then?"

Ian extended his hand. "Agreed, sir."

And so it had been arranged, right there in the taproom of the Ball and Anchor. Just as he deserved.

Chapter Three

Six days wasn't much time in which to change one's life. Still, more drastic changes had happened in fewer—his father had taken him from home, and deposited him at the Portsmouth Naval Yard all those years ago in less than three days. And the three-day interval waiting for the colonel to retrieve his daughter from Somerset had also given Ian enough time to travel to Doctors' Commons in London to pay through the teeth to procure a special license.

He was, legally and ecclesiastically speaking, as ready as he could be.

Yet, now, as he stood on the steps of his rambling cottage, his gut knotted up tighter than a bosun's fist at the sight of the hired chaise that drew down his long, meandering drive. He had faced French cannon with less trepidation.

But damn his eyes and his rising pulse, he would see it through. He would make it work.

Ian temporarily pushed all thoughts and concerns about Ross from his mind, and forced himself to concentrate on the task at hand. He gave his coat a firm, surreptitious tug—his long-suffering mother would have been near giddy at the change in his attire. Normally, he didn't give two farthings for his appearance, but today he had taken care to tog himself in his best dress uniform bedizened with the gold braid. And his man Pinkerton had polished his Hessian boots to a blindingly glossy shine. All ridiculous vanity to look his best for Miss Lesley.

Ian let the winter wind chill the heat in his face, and took a deep, calming breath. Then he plastered his inscrutably professional naval officer's smile upon his face, and prepared to meet his fate.

Colonel Lesley was the first to alight from the hired coach. He greeted Ian warmly, much as he had at Portsmouth—"Worth, my boy"—and then turned to assist his wife from the carriage.

Mrs. Lesley proved to be an exceptionally short woman of indeterminate middle years, who was clearly enamored of the sound of her own voice. She greeted Ian so effusively, he was nearly blown aback by the ceaseless chatter. "Oh, Lieutenant Worth. How very nice to meet you at last. I'm sure I've heard ever so much about you from the dear colonel. I'm sure I don't know how to thank you for the invitation to spend a few days here by the sea. So thoughtful! I'm sure the sea air will do me no end of good. I said to my dear colonel, I said . . ."

If the daughter proved herself to be anything in the same pattern as the mother, he would have to learn to like staying out to sea.

". . . how much nicer it is to visit a private home than to stay at an inn. Oh, what a lovely house you have here. Very pretty property. No, no," she said, directing her servant girl. "We'll leave the bags for the footmen. I'm sure the lieutenant has footmen enough, him being a viscount's son."

Actually, despite being a viscount's son—or perhaps because of it—Ian hadn't footmen at all. Old Angus Pinkerton normally acted as butler, valet, and cook all in one, but Pinky had wisely convinced Ian to bring on a local woman, Mrs. Totham, as a cook, along with her two stout daughters for the scullery, laundry, and cleaning for the duration of the Lesleys' visit. He had assumed the Lesley ladies would bring a servant, or servants of their own, but there appeared to be only the one maid, hovering at the side of the carriage, whom he hoped could be impressed into serving at table for dinner—neither Pinky, with his odd assortment of sailorly clothes, nor the Totts, as he had come to call Mrs. Totham and her daughters, were fit to be seen in a drawing or dining room. As a habit, Ian had never kept comely, or even presentable, young girls on staff at Gull Cottage. Not with his ramshackle friends.

"Well now." Mrs. Lesley recalled Ian from his contemplation of servant problems by taking up the arm he had yet to proffer. "I thank you for your assistance, lieutenant. It is so nice that you are such a tall, strong, young man. A young man ought to be tall if he can help it, I always say. Well," she repeated breathlessly as she puffed up the three short steps to the front door. "It is so fatiguing, all this travel. A body can get no rest with all the swaying and bumping and jostling. All the way from Somerset . . ."

She towed him along in her wake, swaying and bumping and jostling him so forcefully that he hadn't even had a moment to catch a glimpse of her daughter. And there had to be a daughter. She was the whole reason for the visit. The tholepin of his future. "And Miss Lesley, ma'am?"

"Oh, she'll get my satchel. You needn't carry it for me."

Well, damn his inattentive eyes. He had assumed the girl by the carriage was a servant from Mrs. Lesley's tone of voice. But Mrs. Lesley had pointed the considerable prow of her bosom down the corridor, toward his private study, and was sailing him onward, still laying down covering fire with her constant stream of chatter. "A lovely house, with a very pretty aspect, to be sure, as I was saying to the dear colonel as we drove up. And this would be the drawing room . . ."

"No, ma'am. The drawing room would be over here." He steered her helm back toward the front of the house, where Pinky held open the drawing room door, looking like a hopeful, aged cherub.

"Oh, yes. Very nice," Mrs. Lesley exclaimed as she took in the sunny, warm room. "I expect she'll do very well here. I'm sure she'll like this room with all its sun and cozy seats. Very comfortable, to be sure, and not too grand."

Mrs. Lesley was overawed by his ancestry. But Ian had rather meet the girl—who still had not appeared within his vision—than assure the Lesleys that he was nothing like his too-grand family. Such a misapprehension was exactly why he had wanted them to bring the girl here, to his cottage, instead of anywhere else.

But where was she?

A quiet, unassuming girl, Lesley had said. Perhaps she was shy. Yes, shy was better than the alternatives playing the devil in his mind, turning her into an ogre, or worse, a nothing. Damn his eyes. He didn't know what he'd do if she were a nothing. He taunted himself with the idea that ugly would at least be better than plain. Ugly was at the very least interesting.

Ian's gut hitched itself into a tighter knot. But still he was the host. "May I offer you some refreshment before you are shown up to your rooms?" Ian turned to speak to Pinky about bringing in the coffee and tea when suddenly Ian felt, rather than saw, a small brown shadow behind the colonel.

Ian could have sworn that he had not heard or seen her enter, yet there she was, a sudden silhouette in the sunlight, creating a small presence behind her father.

The knot in his gut strangled itself in disappointment. Ian was entirely underwhelmed. The girl was as plain and unappealing as a pikestaff.

A pikestaff he had no alternative but to marry.

So plain and unassuming and quiet, even the colonel and his wife seemed unaware of her—the lady carried on without any acknowledgement of her offspring, while her father only noticed her belatedly when he stepped back from his inspection of some aspect of the room's decoration—a model frigate Ian had constructed years ago when he had been a midshipman—and trod all over the hem of the girl's gown.

Not that the gown would have been any great loss—it wasn't much as fashion went. Certainly it was as plain and unadorned and dun-colored a traveling dress as he had ever seen, and it did very little to enhance the very plain appearance of its wearer.

Who was herself as plain and brown as a marsh wren. Brown bonnet, brown hair, brown gown, and quite possibly brown eyes. Ian wasn't sure, because she kept her face turned resolutely down even as he came forward to greet her. "How do you do? I'm Ian Worth. Welcome to Gull Cottage."

The girl curtseyed well enough, but would not look at him, and said not a peep. Ian was quite sure Miss Lesley—whose name no one had thought to offer him yet—was as unassuming and uninteresting as a dishcloth.

Just as he had so carefully specified, damn his eyes to hell.

He retreated behind the defensive barricade of civility and politeness, when Pinky bustled in with hot coffee and tea to revive the road-chilled travelers. "Would you take some tea, Miss Lesley?"

"Oh, yes, I thank you." Mrs. Lesley took command of the entirety of the conversation like a jealous admiral. "I'll arrange it."

At that moment, Ian wanted nothing so much as a large glass of brandy or whisky. A very large glass. Large enough to drown himself in.

"What a lovely prospect down the lawn to the sea. And such furnishings," Mrs. Lesley enthused. "Very tasteful. Not at all what I had envisioned for a bachelor's establishment. But I wonder if your mother, the Viscountess Rainesford, might have taken a hand in assisting you with the decoration of the house? I had no idea you might be used to having everything so fine."

With that remark, Mrs. Lesley turned an assessing eye on her daughter, as if she feared the girl were not fine enough for her potential surroundings. And though the daughter did not raise her eyes, she had clearly understood her mother's uneasy perusal, for a sweep of high color blazed up her pale cheeks. Yet still, she did not speak.

But with the mother still carrying on—"This chimney appears to draw well. So important to have a fire that draws cleanly, don't you think? I always say . . ."—no one could get a word in edgewise. It was no wonder the girl was as silent as the tomb.

God's balls. Maybe she was a mute, who never spoke. Or couldn't. Maybe—

"I'll take tea, of course, and the colonel will take coffee." Mrs. Lesley set herself directly next to the tray, but motioned meaningfully for the brown wren to do the actual work of pouring the cups of coffee and tea.

The girl did so, silently fulfilling her mother's wishes,

until she needed to address Ian's choice. He waited hopefully for her to speak, but she merely glanced up at him, and with the barest lift of her brown eyebrows, asked for his preference by holding up an empty cup in question.

Yet Ian was intrigued by the spark or flash of something—something less docile than her outward behavior suggested—he fancied he saw in the depths of her otherwise ordinary brown eyes.

"Coffee," he answered firmly over Mrs. Lesley's observations on the salubrious effect of the local climate.

". . . the sea air is bound to do a body good. Oh, how I envy you the sea air, Lieutenant Worth."

She wouldn't envy him when a freezing gale came howling down the Channel out of the North Sea and rattled the windows with lashings of sleet, but Ian let the comment pass. And kept his gaze on the quiet girl while she poured, giving him only a floating glimpse of her darkly intelligent eyes when she raised them in silent inquiry over the cream and sugar.

He shook his head in answer, and tried to give her an encouraging smile.

She didn't smile back.

Well, damn his eyes. Perhaps she really was a mute. Perhaps that was why the colonel was so willing to be rid of her. On the other hand, perhaps a wife who was unable to nag would prove a boon to domestic harmony. He had to hope.

Had he imagined that flash of something more? Had he invented a glimpse of keen intelligence to ease his disappointment? Her head was back down now, hidden behind her straw bonnet, merely a muddy brown marsh wren.

He had to find out. He turned to the colonel. "Is there something wrong with her? Is there a reason she isn't able to speak?"

"No." The girl's gaze came swiftly to his, sharp and

incisive. As was her voice, though it was so small, it was beyond quiet. "There is nothing wrong with *me*."

But for the first time, she looked at him fully, her gaze level and direct, and Ian could see without any doubt that the expression he thought he had seen dancing in the dark depths of Anne Lesley's golden brown eyes was in actuality, a subtle, refined rage.

Chapter Four

It was everything Anne Lesley could do to sit still, and not throw the entire pot of coffee at Lieutenant Worth's big, thick, absolutely perfect head.

Not that she had ever thrown a coffeepot in her life, but the moment seemed ripe to start. And it made a nice change from wanting to throw pots and pans and anything else to hand at her mother, who chattered and nattered on and on, just as she always did, until Anne thought she would drown in the rising sea of endless, useless, suffocating noise.

And from the slightly seasick look on the impossibly handsome lieutenant's face, he now felt the same way. About her.

"If you will excuse me, ma'am." The lieutenant broke in the moment Mama paused for breath. "I have some business I need to attend to. Pinkerton"—he gestured to the cherubic-looking old salt who had brought in the tray—"will show you to your rooms as soon as you may like."

Anne liked that very moment, if it would take her away from the drawing room. Away from her parents, who took her obedient compliance for granted because she let them. Away from the wretchedly perfect young man, who was exiting the room as if she stank like day-old fish. Away from her foolish, girlish hopes.

Clearly the perfect young man was already regretting his impulse to offer for her. But he had offered—through her father, of course—and she had accepted, and she meant to keep to the devil's bargain now. For what else was she to do? How else was she to escape the suffocating, endless noise of her mother's house? This was her chance, and she meant to take it. At the advanced age of two and twenty, she was so firmly upon the shelf that another offer was not likely to be forthcoming—her father was more than unlikely to have another acquaintance who would bargain for a bride sight unseen.

No. As imperfectly perfect as Lieutenant Worth appeared, she meant to keep him, and Gull Cottage, to boot. The charmingly eccentric cottage was poised by the edge of the sea, and was situated in an equally charming garden—beautifully disarrayed, even in winter. The whole place looked as if a good stiff wind might catch it up, and sail the antique amalgamation of rooftops and chimney pots straight across the marvelously brooding bay.

It was enchanting. And absolutely perfect.

Her father said she was to be left on her own here. She could not imagine a happier fate. Anne wanted nothing more than to be out-of-doors, exploring the frost-covered garden, and finding a way down to the beach that beckoned to her from outside the window, where the howling wind could drown out every other sound so she wouldn't even have to hear herself think.

Since her parents took no more note of her than they would the furniture—until they had need of her—it took no more than a moment for her to don her heavy cloak, and make her quiet way down the stone corridor toward the back of the house, where she had glimpsed a path leading away to the sea.

But the way out of the house was blocked—the cherubic old sailor was poised over the threshold of what looked like a book room.

"I've put the young maidy up above." He bobbed his white head, and Anne could see his apple cheeks had been polished a glowing red by his exertions in bringing in their baggage. "In the big airy room with the windows over the bay. Best view in the house."

"Put her wherever you like, Pinky," came the unseen answer. "Just keep her well away from me."

Anne knew she should move on. She knew no good could ever come of eavesdropping. But the sharp words were like a blade, carving up her determination. Her confidence had already fallen through the bottom of her belly to land somewhere around her knees, leaving her too unsteady to go any further.

And it was best she knew how Lieutenant Worth really felt about her, without her father's blustery, inept kindnesses to blunt the blow.

"Now, young sir." The man Pinkerton shook his head like a sad-faced hound. "Things seem to be going so well. She looks the sort to like it here."

"Devil take me if she does. We'd best get in considerably more whisky, Pinky, if she's to look the sort that *I'd* like to have here."

"Now, now. Perhaps a little more time, young sir, to get to know the little maidy." The old tar sounded full of sympathetic caution. "Afore ye go about consigning yerself to the whisky."

"All time in the world couldn't turn that girl into something more attractive. And I don't think there is anything on this earth that will convince her to like *me*. I saw the look on her face. She'll never have me. Not in a hundred years." The still unseen lieutenant heaved out a frustrated sigh. "And it's just as well. Save us both a world of hurt. I can't abide plain, Pinky, you know that. I like to be entertained, and to all appearances Miss Anne Lesley is as dull and unentertaining as a house wren, and it's clear that she already hates me."

It was not news to her, this unflattering assessment of her looks, for it was nothing more than she had known from staring into her own mirror. But hearing it stated so bluntly by another hurt all the same. The words had torn some unseen part of her, deep inside, and all she could feel was the numbing heat of leaking blood inside her chest.

"But I haven't got any choice." His voice ground inexorably on. "So whisky, I think, Pinky, applied with liberal vigor, as the only effective recourse."

Damn him. Damn him for an arrogant, unthinking bastard. Damn them both, because there was no alternative for her either. She could not abide the thought of going back. Of returning home a failure.

Anne turned blindly to go, to escape into the frigid air, but she ran straight into a little table set beside the door, bashing her shin, and giving herself away.

The old tar reeled around, his chalky blue eyes taking in everything in an instant. "Oh, miss! I didn't see you there."

Behind Pinkerton, a blue oath streamed from beyond the book room door.

So before she had to face her humiliation in person, Anne fled though the doorway, and pitched herself down the nearest path. She followed the salt scent of the wind blindly, until she burst out upon a gray beach where the sand gave way to slate gray water stretching almost as far as her eyes could see. And she could see a long way. Years and years stretching in front of her as flat and overcast as the winter sky.

Years filled with the stink of stale whisky.

Anne picked up a pebble and dashed it into the choppy water with every ounce of mortified frustration she possessed. The stone disappeared without a splash, swallowed whole by the sea. If only she could disappear as easily.

She should have known. She should have anticipated that her father's scheme would be as harebrained and half-thought-out as all the rest of his interactions with his family had been for the past twenty years—minimal and fleeting.

"Worth." Her father—a man who had only recently come home from the Royal Marines for good—had given her the name like a souvenir prize captured in battle. "Knew him when we both served on *Audacious*. Good lad. Sure you'll rub along quite well. There's a good girl."

And that was all the explanation of her marriage and potential mate she had been given. And all she had wanted. The news that she was being offered a chance to marry had been like a lung full of fresh air to a drowning woman—an awakening, as if, after years of merely existing, of putting up with her circumstances, her life had finally, finally begun. She had listened to her father's kind assessment of the lieutenant and his wish to marry, and had been filled with hope. Enough hope to keep her opinions, and the questions that had swirled around in her head, to herself.

But now she had the answers to her unasked questions anyway—Lieutenant Ian Worth didn't want her for a wife at all.

How incredibly lowering. In fact, Lieutenant Worth's reaction had been more than lowering—it was only just short of appalling. Because she would rather face the humiliation of being wed to a man who thought her so plain he could barely abide her, than go home again. What other option did she have but to swallow her pride the way that pebble had been swallowed by the sea? How many other chances for escape was she likely to get?

At the age of two and twenty, the answer was obvious—none.

Oh, why could Lieutenant Worth not have been what she had hoped—a good lad. A young man as unpretentious and unassuming as herself. A man who had been a colleague of her father, unaccustomed to company after so many years in the navy, who needed an old acquaintance to arrange his marriage? Why could *he* not have been as dull as dishwater? Why could *he* not have been a quiet, weather-beaten sailor man who did not expect to be entertained?

Instead he had been a handsome, polished—such a profusion of gold braid and gleaming boots—worldly young man. She had nothing to entertain—no accomplishments, no wit, no sparkling conversation, and certainly no smile dazzling enough for the Lieutenant Worths of this world. As it was, she could barely speak, let alone entertain. She simply had no words.

No, that was not entirely true. She had plenty of words, masses of them, swirling around in her brain, dammed up behind the barrier of her mouth. But there they stayed. Because words were too powerful to play with so carelessly, like the lieutenant, or her mother. Words could so easily and lastingly cause division and hurt—her mother's words flowed out in an unabated rush, careless and unthinking, streaming over everything in her path, and so often wounding those around her. Especially Anne, whose ways and demeanor always managed to put Mama in an ill humor.

"A body likes to be doing!" her mother was always exclaiming. "A lady is never idle. How you can be so still, so quiet, saying nothing and doing nothing, is beyond me. A good woman is industrious, not idle and still. I cannot abide you when you are so awfully still and quiet."

Anne was not industrious or busy. She could never be. She could never concentrate on the things her mother cared about, and constantly pressed upon her—tatting, embroidering, mending, or some such. All Anne wanted to do was think, and read, and walk. All she could do was shut her ears, and bide her time until her mother's miniscule attention was invariably turned, and she could escape to her attic window seat, or slip away to the quiet windswept hills she loved in silence. A silence she had hoped to find here, with Lieutenant Ian Worth.

But he was as careless with his words as her mother had ever been. And his words had cut her more deeply, for she had invested herself with the one thing that made her vulnerable—hope.

"Miss Lesley." The smooth voice came from behind her on the sand.

Lieutenant Worth. Of course. She turned toward him because she knew she must, allowing herself only a peek at him before she turned her flaming face resolutely to the sand. But it was enough to see his handsome face creased with something very much like remorse. "Miss Lesley, you needn't look at me so."

She hardly knew where to look. The wide expanse of the Solent seemed the safest alternative. "I'm sorry," she forced herself to say, because she felt she must say something.

A bark of a laugh escaped him. "Don't be. It's only right that you should give me a look that makes my cods shrink up into my body for protection. I've been in the navy long enough to get used to such looks, and to know when I deserve them."

Had she really given him such a look? "I didn't mean—"

"You, Miss Anne Lesley"—he had learned her name—"are a dreadful liar." He advanced to stand next to her, but thankfully kept his gaze focused out at the sea. "While I am simply dreadful."

The candid admission startled a reply out of her. "Yes."

"I should like to apologize. Most profoundly. I know I'm a ramshackle, shallow fellow, Miss Lesley, but I've never been thoughtless. Or cruel. But I can see that I was both."

"Yes." She could think of nothing else to say. But neither could she say any more. And though she could not bring herself to look at him—at all his noble, handsome misery—she thought she could hear sincerity in his voice.

"Do you think, Miss Lesley, you might be kind enough for both of us, and forgive me?"

What a strange, unsettling, lovely feeling to have such a man ask her for her forgiveness. It almost made her feel merciful. Almost.

"Do you think it would help if I begged? If I got down on my knees, and begged your forgiveness? Like a supplicant in front of a queen."

The thought of such a man prostrating himself in front of her was such a fanciful, ridiculous image that Anne forgot her anger and humiliation enough to actually look at his face. But it was as if he had been waiting for that moment, because he lavished her with a smile so sweet and so rueful, that Anne was almost ready to forgive him for being so handsome. Almost.

"Please. I beg you." And here he *did* drop to one knee before her in the sand. "Dear, gracious Miss Lesley. Please forgive me. Please give me another chance to earn your trust. Only say the word and we can start again."

Say the word.

But that was the problem. She never could *say* the right

word. She could think it. She could think of scads of them. But she could never get them beyond the heat that bottled up in her throat.

So she gave him the only word she had. "Yes."

"Wonderful," he said. "I am honored to make your acquaintance, Miss Lesley." He rose as he spoke, and made her a bow—a lovely, deeply respectful bow—to which she found herself making a graceful-enough curtsy in return. "How do you do? I'm Ian Worth. And you're Anne. And, I think, you're very shy."

It was not news, this assessment of her timidity, but no one had ever forced her to acknowledge this truth. Within the busy confines of her mind, she had merely thought of herself as private. Deeply, persistently private. And perhaps secretive.

But she could no longer be secretive—not if she were to be married. Here was her chance standing before her— the only chance that fate had ever been kind enough to drop into the sand in front of her—to become a new version of herself.

"No." She forced the words over the hammering of her heart. "I sometimes have difficulty in speaking. But I will overcome it."

"I don't mind if you're shy. I'm not." The lieutenant observed pleasantly. "As I said, I'm . . . Well, whatever I am, I'm not shy."

"No." Another whispered, astonished agreement. But it was impossible for her not to agree with such self-deprecating openness.

He turned from the sea, moving a step away, and then back, looking about in a rather restless fashion, as if he found it as much of a trial to keep still as she did to keep busy. He gestured back the way they had come down from the house. "So this is my home, Gull Cottage. It is, of course, much prettier in the spring. The wood above is full of daffodils and such."

"Yes. But I like it as it is now." She tried to speak normally, as other people did, but her voice was still barely a whisper, because he had to bend his head down to hear her before he straightened back up.

"Do you? I'm very glad to hear that. Because if you like it now, at its worst—well, let's say 'less than best'— you're sure to love it the rest of the year." He gifted her with another dazzling smile, all shining white teeth and charming, crinkled blue eyes. "And I'm sure the house would look all the more charming if you wanted to take your hand to it. Spruce it up for Christmas or some such."

As if he thought she would be staying all the way until the feast of Christmas. And beyond. As if he thought they should be married.

Oh, Lord help her, but he was handsome. As handsome as they came. Too handsome for his own good. Far too handsome for *her* good.

He was all shining, bright blue eyes and gleaming mahogany hair that curled across his forehead just so, as if he had only a moment ago risen from his valet's chair. But he hadn't. The wind was buffeting them both, but it only made him appear more tousled, and effortlessly handsome. And only served to make her feel even more like that small, insignificant brown wren he had named her.

Anne felt the return of all her insecurity and insignificance. Heat gathered at the back of her throat, and prickled behind her eyes. She turned to walk on, away from him, completely flustered by his appearance and flummoxed by his attention.

But he fell into step beside her. "I hope you don't mind if I join you?" He carried on pleasantly, as though she had answered. As if he were actually interested in their one-sided conversation. As if he didn't think her dull as dingy dishwater.

He forestalled her descent into helpless, frustrated rage with more of his strangely cheerful honesty. "I am sorry if my thoughtlessness drove you from the house."

"No," she lied before she made herself stop, and pause to gulp down another dose of newfound courage. "Yes. I needed the air. After the carriage and . . ." Her voice strangled away into nothingness.

"Can't abide closed carriage rides myself," he rambled on, easy and breezy—her complete opposite in every manner and way. "I'd much rather be out-of-doors, sailing, riding, or driving. But I didn't suppose ladies felt that way." He smiled again with the air of someone comfortably sure of his charm.

"No!" she breathed, determined to resist his charm, and determined to assert herself. "I much prefer the air. I rode up top with the coachman when I could."

Let him make of that what he would. But when she peeked up at him to gauge the effect of such an opposition to his ideas, she was astonished to find him still smiling down at her with that amused, charming smile.

"Did you?" he asked, with the same easy grin. "Well, we've plenty of air here at Gull Cottage. Have you visited the seaside before?"

Anne shook her head. "No."

But she couldn't go on giving only the briefest of answers. She knew that she needed to exert herself, and actually add to the conversation—entertain him. And because he was so tall and gleaming and worldly and sophisticated, despite her self-admonitions, she could not bear to have him think she was a graceless simpleton as well as provincial. So she ignored the hammering in her chest and admitted, "I have never been from home, from Somerset, before."

"And I have been to the ends of the earth, and I can assure you that this stretch of beach is one of the prettiest places on all the globe." He smiled again as he said it, and gestured around. "And I like to think that Gull Cottage is rather pretty itself. What do you think of it so far?" He turned the invitation of his easy grin and twinkling eyes toward her.

She ducked her head away from his almost over-whelming glamour. "I find it very pretty, sir," she said, and then, unaccountably she blurted, "I like to walk."

"Do you?" he asked in that strange, amused manner that didn't seem to need any response. "Well, I daresay there are any number of picturesque walks hereabouts. I haven't walked much myself. Do you ride?"

"Yes, sir." She was a country girl, and every country girl with some pretension to gentility could ride. Did he still think her simple? Or too awkward and ungainly for such sport?

She could find no answer in his response. "Mmm," he mused. "But you didn't bring a horse?"

"No, sir. My sisters and I shared."

"Ah. Yes, of course. And what about sailing? I have a small ketch—very small, mind you—that I use to sail to Portsmouth and back."

"I've never been in a boat, sir. Except a rowboat once. On the River Parrett. Near home. In Bridgwater." But Anne didn't think a drifty little rowboat would count with a seagoing navy man like the lieutenant.

"Do you think you should like to learn?"

She glanced up at him, and noted that although he smiled, he appeared to be serious enough. Though why he should ask, she had no idea, except that perhaps, just perhaps, he was trying to hold out a sort of olive branch. An olive branch she could ill afford to refuse. "Yes, I should like to try it sometime, sir."

"Look." He stopped, and stepped directly in front of her. His blue eyes were a stunning, exact amalgamation of sea and sky.

He reached out, and laid his hand to her elbow. The press of his bare fingers through the stout wool of her cloak was a jolt of something new and entirely different that made her breath seize up in her chest.

"I know it's not the done thing," he was saying, "but do you think, given the circumstances, that you could stop calling me 'sir'? You make me feel quite ancient, like my father."

"No." There wasn't an ancient thing about him, a foot away from her and towering over her like a tall yew tree.

"No? Do I overstep the proprieties? But see here, Miss Lesley, I'm not one for flummery. You do know why you've come, don't you? To see if we can get on. To see if, despite everything I've said, we can be married. And made to become as one."

Chapter Five

As one.

The words echoed down from her ears, through her chest and deep into her bones, until Anne felt her resolve begin to give way beneath the relentless sunniness of his smile.

"We are contemplating marriage, you know, Miss Lesley, not just a couple of country dances at an assembly. Some . . . informality is called for." He smiled at her in a way that was probably meant to knock her knees out from under her—very slowly, with the corners of his mouth slowly curving upward until his eyes warmed. And just as slowly, his eyes dropped to stare at her bottom lip.

And despite herself, despite her determination *not* to be charmed, his smile made her insides turn little cartwheels of unbridled delight.

Informality is what he said, but *intimacy* was what he had meant. Anne knew it as plainly as if he had said it out loud, because she felt a shiver of something prickly and not altogether uncomfortable skitter down the length of her spine. Despite all his easy, almost boyish charm, he was clearly a man. A man who lived alone, said what he wished, did as he pleased, and arranged for a wife as casually as if he were buying a horse from the market-place on a three-day trial.

"Forgive me." The all-too-familiar admixture of indignation and embarrassment made her tone pert. "I will address you however you wish, sir."

"Will you?" His smile spread wider, making his eyes crinkle in mischievous delight. "Good. But as you're clearly loath to give up 'sir,' I'm going to make a bid *against* lieutenant, and *for* just plain Worth, if you can manage it. I can see that it will be quite some time before I can convince you to attempt 'Ian.' "

This, then, must be his version of teasing. But was he laughing at her as well? It was hard to tell from his steady smile. She had been acquainted with him for less than an hour, but it seemed to her that he smiled rather easily—as though his mouth were completely at home relaxing into a ready grin. As if he were quite *used* to being happy. As if he *expected* to be.

Anne didn't know when she had last felt like that—happy. Or when she next expected to be. The anticipation of the journey there had only made her feel hopeful, however fleetingly. "Pray tell me, lieut—Pray tell me if what my father says is true . . . that you mean to return to the sea?"

"Yes. In three days' time." This time he looked much less sure of himself, those smiling blue eyes sobered with apprehension. "It is my intention to return to the sea, to my career in His Majesty's Navy, if we marry—indeed, even if we do not. That is the life of every sailor. And every sailor's wife. The colonel said he thought you would not mind. Would you? Do you think, even alone, you could be happy here?"

The admission was exactly what she wanted to hear—and everything that she had been too afraid to hope for. "Yes." She *was* determined to be happy in her own way. She did not need to smile easily, or laugh out loud to be happy.

Yet it was seductive, his laughter—his breezy way of seeing the world.

But his breezy laughter and charm would wound her as easily as his careless words, were she not careful. So she would be careful. She would keep reminding herself that a man like him—a young man, handsome and carefree, and in possession of his own fortune—was only seeking her for a wife because he had no other choice. He was ready to marry her to suit his own ends, just as surely as she would marry him to suit hers.

The thought gave her something to use as a shield while he accompanied her in blessed silence on the rest of her walk down the cold, windswept beach; the only sound accompanying the wind was the simple rhythmic crunch of their boots in the ever shifting sand.

Miss Anne Lesley spoke only eight words at dinner. Ian counted.

God's balls. If they continued to have this little to say to each other when their every topic of conversation was fresh and new, what on earth would they have to say years from now, when his store of suitable topics had already been canvassed? She had spoken with him this afternoon, although not quite easily, then at least clearly, but at dinner, she seemed to fade before his eyes. Whatever her declaration about overcoming her shyness on the beach, she had reverted to type in the presence of her parents.

Of course, it could have been the mother. The confounded woman nattered on endlessly, asking all sorts of inquisitive questions about the house and the income from the property. "And do you entertain often, Lieutenant Worth? Such lovely porcelain plates," Mrs. Lesley praised in between bites. "I see that this dining room is large enough to accommodate a larger party. How many have you been able to seat here for an evening dinner?"

Ian was sorely tempted to shock the dear old biddy right out of her overstrained stays with an account of the long-ago night his friend Marcus Beecham, and half a dozen other assorted rogues and rascals, had turned this very dining room table into a live buffet of young, nubile opera dancers. The entire *corps de ballet* had been served up as hot, fresh, and steaming as any Christmas pudding.

Having fortified himself with ample whisky before dinner, and sufficient claret throughout, Ian had nearly persuaded himself to recount the whole of it, with special attention paid to the stout construction of the mahogany table. But that was also the very moment when the little brown wren chirped up.

"I understand you have traveled quite extensively, sir."

Eight elegantly breathless words, all at once.

He rewarded her with an encouraging smile, and redoubled his effort to be charming. "Hard not to in the navy. Isn't that true, colonel? Well, let's see. All over the coast of France and Spain—Brest, Saint-Nazaire, La Rochelle. Beautiful and treacherous, the coast of France is, especially the Finistère, in Brittany. Then Lisbon, Cádiz, Cape Trafalgar, and Gibraltar—and into the Mediterranean in old *Audacious,* under Captain McAlden. But it was nothing compared to the lush green islands of the West Indies and the Bahamas, where I went on several cruises under Captain Colyear. Marvelous days, those. Do you remember, colonel, the night Will Jellicoe nearly set the old *Audacious* ablaze with his illicit fireworks? And when *she* caught fire as well, and Captain Col grabbed her up and went right over the side? Famous night."

"Oh, my. I'm sure we ladies don't want to hear such colorful tales," Mrs. Lesley cautioned.

Ian thought differently. Ian thought the look on Miss Anne Lesley's face—a narrowing frown above her wide, dark eyes, and the open "o" of her mouth when her mother interrupted his narrative—was surely disappointment. For a moment there, when he had leaned back in his chair and relaxed into telling her his tales, she had appeared almost animated—her dark eyes had sparked with keen curiosity as he had described the wonders of the wide, unseen world beyond her experience.

She had been entirely, lividly still, her eyes pinned to his as he spoke. She had seemed almost . . . interesting.

Or perhaps she was merely interested. Or just being polite.

Whichever it was, it was gone now, the spark, snubbed out just as quickly as it had this afternoon, when he had inadvertently—no, he had done it quite deliberately, though he had not done it on purpose—insulted her beyond all bounds of propriety. But propriety and following of rules had never been his strong suit. Not while growing up under the exacting and dictatorial hand of his father, and not during his formative years in His Majesty's Royal Navy, learning the hard way to acquit himself in the honorable and proficient execution of his duty.

But in the navy he had had friends—friends who had looked after him and showed him the way to get things done, even if it occasionally meant bending the rules. Friends who stood by him. Friends who had shared his good luck.

And what he needed to do was make Miss Anne Lesley his friend, and get her alone again so she might talk to him as she had on the beach—as if she did not hate him.

Ian refilled his glass with claret from the dusty bottle at his elbow—purloined from his father's expensively overstocked cellars—and let Mrs. Lesley have her noisy way with the rest of the conversation. "How often do your parents, the Viscount and Viscountess Rainesford, come to visit you here? Or are you quite at home in Ciren Castle? I understand it's a very large estate . . ."

Ian shut his ears to her ceaseless drone, and concentrated on that glimpse of whatever it was—intelligence, defiance, curiosity—he had seen in Anne Lesley. His intended bride—and despite their monstrously bad start, he reckoned he still had a chance with her—was smart. He had not imagined her quick-wittedness when she had exerted herself on his behalf.

Of course, it wouldn't do to have her so enthralled with him she wanted to wander the world with him. Bugger up his career quite badly, a wife aboard would. On the other hand, if she were content to wait at home, and listen with breathless attention to his *colorful* stories, that would be another thing entirely.

And she really wasn't as ordinary as he had originally thought. There was something about her—he was not yet quite sure what—that was intriguing. Her eyes *were* too brown, her nose too long, and her mouth too wide to conform to any accustomed standards of beauty. But there was something else, some glint of something wise and warm in the golden depths of those eyes. And there was something elegant in the length of her nose, which made her something of a silent, dark swan among the more conventionally plumed beauties. And what was more, there was something desperately solemn in her countenance, that made him want to exert himself to ease the grim line of her mouth, and make her smile.

And really, what choice did he have but to make the best of it? Even if he did bolt off to London, there was no guarantee he could find something—someone—better.

Pinky was right—a wren in the hand was worth more than the possibility of an empty bush.

He made himself consider her afresh. Her skin, though it seemed pale, appeared smooth and even enough. And for another thing, now that he looked closely, he found her figure—at least the small portion of it he could discern across the top of the table—quite unobjectionable. She was tallish, but fine-boned. Though her clothing was rather nondescript—plain brown wool, buttoned up to the collar, and entirely unadorned—the high-waisted garment fit well through her shoulders. And, oh, yes, there at the top of her bodice resided the lovely evidence that she was in fact a young woman. The sweetly rounded swells of her breasts might just about fill his palms, if he—

God's balls.

Dining room. Claret. Smile and nod politely, and keep eyes well away from bodices, and all thoughts of the corset that must be pushing her small but perfectly formed breasts up, presenting them for his perusal and enjoyment.

Devil take him. So much for indifference.

Ian shifted restlessly in his chair. He was sure he could find more mitigating faults, if he but looked for them again.

Her dark hair was parted severely down the center, as was the current fashion, but instead of dangling ringlets, it was pulled back and severely knotted at her nape, each and every strand kept scrupulously in place. The severity of the hairstyle, and the dark, unappealing color of her hair did little to set off her high cheekbones and firm chin, making her appear a bit grim and angular.

That was it, concentrate on grim and angular, and forget about the appeal of her lovely breasts. She was rather slight, and perhaps too tall—side by side at the table, she was a full head taller than her mother. Yet, out on the beach, the girl's head hadn't reached any higher than his collar. Of course her unassuming, fadeaway air probably made her seem smaller. But perhaps once he got her alone, and got her angry, he would see that spark. Perhaps, if he took matters literally in hand, and simply backed her up against a wall, and filled—

No. He would not think about walls, or bending over chairs, or spreading upon dining room tables, though it was nearly impossible not to think of such things when all he was meant to be doing was deciding if he liked the girl enough to get her with child. But judging from the growing state of his own arousal, he liked her bloody well enough, indeed.

"Cap'n?" Pinky—tricked up in an old blue bosun's coat that he evidently thought suitable to the grandness of the occasion—was at his elbow, bending to speak in close confidence, as he presented Ian with a plate of fruit.

Ian snagged a tangerine orange. "What is it?" Devil take him if they'd run out of claret.

"I was thinking as maybe how it might be a lovely time to show the maidy round the house? While I bring the colonel and his missus some port and chocolate. The music room, cap'n? Per'aps the maidy plays? We could sore use some music round here."

For all of Pinky's lack of subtlety, it was an excellent suggestion, just as the old tar's prompting to follow the wren down to the beach had been. One that would give him time alone with her.

"Miss Lesley," Ian said as amiably as possible once he had finished both his callow ogling and his fruit. "Would you care to take a tour of the house?" An informal tour would be an unobjectionable activity that would occupy them away from her parents for a decent interval, and give him another chance to charm her into agreeing to the marriage.

"Oh, goodness, no," Mrs. Lesley objected. "It's far too late for that. Anne will need her rest, and want to retire, I'm quite sure."

To Ian's eyes, Anne did not look ready to retire. Anne looked ready to advance. Anne looked, in fact, as if other people making decisions for her might be kindling the fire of that magnificent, contained rage he was so curious about.

"Nonsense." Ian skated a glance at the clock on the mantelpiece—it was not yet nine o'clock. "It's early yet." He rose, and simply reached out and took his would-be bride's hand, and he walked her toward the door. "We'll leave you to your sherry."

"See if you can get more than two words out of her," the colonel mouthed as they passed.

Ian saw Anne color deeply—a hot flush streaked up the side of her neck, and she turned her face to the floor in mortification. Or perhaps in that subtle, restrained anger that so intrigued him. Ian found himself eager to find out.

"Well, you have your marching orders, Miss Lesley," he said for her ears alone as he ushered her out the door of the dining room. "You are hereby required to contribute more than two words as you inspect the premises. Or perhaps you might defer them until some later time. Perhaps in the morning, on another walk, when we march resolutely toward the village of St. Helens."

His teasing had goaded her into looking at him then, giving him a glimpse of heat firing in the depths of her eye. "As you wish, lieutenant."

The words were quiet, but hot.

"Four already. But I shan't let you off that lightly. And you did promise not to call me lieutenant."

"I never did."

She was so resolutely battened down, he could feel his own sail shaking loose to run before the wind. "Ian," he insisted, just as determined as she. But he was determined to find out what made the quiet, serious Miss Lesley tick. So far, her pleasure was limited to walking.

"Sir—"

"Ian. Give it a try." He gave her his best, most winning smile—the one that made barmaids forget to charge him for his beer, and offer up other delights instead.

And it was working. She was having trouble keeping her determined look in order—she had to keep pursing her lips. "I—"

"Almost. Almost. But you didn't say 'sir,' so I shan't object any more this evening. This way." He walked her all the way up the central corridor to the other side of the house, to begin the tour in the small front parlor that Ian had come to think of as the music room. There was a pianoforte and a harp that had come with the house, but they were never used. Well, just that once by the corps de ballet—a lovely "performance" involving a picturesque shedding of clothing that had preceded the memorable dinner the night he had moved into the house. Ian was half afraid there might still be a silken shift left carelessly about, draped over the harp perhaps, but thanks to the able Totts, there were no echoes of evenings past.

"Do you play, Miss Lesley?"

"Yes." Her voice was hushed, and almost reverent. "I had no idea you would have—May I play on it sometimes? When you're not here?" The words came in a quiet rush, as if she didn't know quite what to do with them in her mouth.

He did—use them to charm and ease her along. "Excellent. Of course you may play it. Anytime you like."

She was trailing her fingers along the keys in a lingering, loving caress—the first hint of physicality or sensuality he had seen.

"Why not now? I'd love to hear you play." He flung

himself into one of the large armchairs in the corner and prepared himself to be surprised.

But she didn't oblige him. She snatched her fingers back as if they had been burned. "Oh, no. I couldn't."

"Why not? You must do as you please."

She looked at him as if the idea were as foreign and far-fetched as a South Seas island.

"Truly, Anne. If we marry it will be *your* pianoforte—I don't play. It will be your house, to do with as you please."

But even this piece of generosity—and he thought it enormously generous of himself to give his marvelously comfortable house, that he had paid for with his own prize monies and made into such a comfortable haven, over to her without a sigh—could not produce a smile. Her solemn gravity lightened not a whit. In fact, she looked dangerously close to tears.

"Is this how you always get your way?" Her eyes were wide and luminous, and her voice, quiet and ravaged. "By charming everyone into doing your bidding by giving them their heart's desire?"

Ian had forgotten what it was to feel pity. He couldn't afford such a costly emotion in his professional life. But his heart ached for her, this girl whose expectations of life were so low that he could have so easily and unthinkingly provided her with her heart's desire.

But he had no idea how to stem the tears. He could only tease.

"Yes." He rose, and went to her, and took the hand she had raised to cover her mouth. And provided her with his most cajoling smile. "Exactly. I should very much like to give you your heart's desire. And I have already got you to do my bidding. That's fifty-odd words already, by my count."

It worked.

"Fifty-two." She tried to make her whisper tart, to pull

away and hide behind the shield of her solemnity, but she could not hide the luminous sweetness of her first watery smile.

He felt his lips stretch into an answering grin. "Oh, Miss Lesley. I really ought to warn you, I'm desperately fond of impertinence. And pert intelligence most especially. If you get any more pert, I think I might just have to kiss you."

Chapter Six

Anne felt a slow spreading panic—like the strange, suspended lethargy of a dream, where she tried and tried to run but could not manage to move—creep upon her. Even her breath felt heavy and mired in indecision. It was not like her, this indecision, this not knowing what to think. Inaction she was accustomed to—bottling up her reactions and wants—but indecision, never.

"Why would you want to do that?" It was an idiot's question—a nonsensical placeholder until she could adequately order her wits, and use that pert intelligence he was teasing her about.

And he *was* teasing. He must be with his strong hands, and his slow smiles, and his soft, crinkled blue eyes as inviting as a warm bath.

"Because you are letting me." His answer was low and languorous, and he watched her steadily, his eyes open and his attention settled singly upon her. By slow increments, he lowered his head toward hers. So, so slowly, as if it were some sort of test of patience she did not know how to pass.

So she held herself still and watched him approach, until she could no longer meet his eyes. Because she had to look at his mouth—his laughing, teasing, open mouth—as his lips continued to descend toward hers. And then, because she did not know what to do, other than try to hold herself entirely still, she turned awkwardly with him when he ducked, and then angled his head so his lips might finally reach hers.

But they did. He was kissing her.

His lips were softer than she expected, and harder all at the same time. Firmer, she supposed, not knowing how one was supposed to describe a man's lips. But she thought his were like raspberries—pliant velvet with the barest hint of prickle.

He brushed his lips across hers, once, twice, back and forth, testing her out before he settled more properly upon her. The whiskers just lurking beneath his clean-shaven chin roughed gently against her skin, and she felt everything—every part of her body and every inch of her skin—come to startled, prickling awareness,

His lips plucked at her gently, imploringly, begging for her attention as he had done on the beach. But he had all of her attention, all of her alertness, all of her astonished hope. But her astonishment soon faded, leaving in its empty path awakened curiosity.

She wanted to catalog and remember each and every strange and interesting new thing about him—he tasted of claret and the sweet winter orange he had eaten at dessert. He smelled aromatic and exotic—of sunny, sandy places beyond the sea. He was warm and tall and patient, lacing his fingers through her hands. He played his lips across hers until she was doing the same, and kissing him back.

Little sips of kisses, tentative and polite—not wanting to do it wrong, or embarrass herself by presuming too much.

And then the ordinary, orderly wheel of her brain simply stopped turning, and she could not think. Because his tongue was in her mouth, invading her, filling her with nothing but the taste and feel of him within her.

She turned her head abruptly and shut her mouth, and shut her eyes. But that only made her more aware of the height and weight of him. He rested his forehead against her temple, his breath hot and unruly against her cheek. "Too much too soon?"

She hardly knew. She had no idea of the correct progression of the passage of time *vis-a-vis* the allowable amount of kissing. And for the first time her determination wavered, and she had no idea if she really could submit herself to this marriage. And to this man.

For he was young and handsome and a man of the world, who teased and kissed as easily and naturally as he breathed. He made her tremble with a feverish mixture of uncertain hesitation and certain want. For already she wanted to kiss him again—to taste again the astonishing raspberry of his lips.

"Too much, I think. But not too soon." He eased away, but kept his fingers enlaced with hers, holding their hands between them. "Not too soon to discover that you kiss very sweetly, Miss Anne Lesley."

She felt all the pleasure and heat of the compliment blossom across her cheeks. She found herself ducking her head instinctively, trying to hide.

He would not let her. "Are you sure I cannot convince you to play?"

"No. I cannot. Not in front of other people." Certainly not in front of her mother—who was not there in person, obviously, but who was no doubt straining to listen from the other room. And most certainly not in front of handsome Lieutenant Worth, who she barely knew except for his charm and his kissing and his height.

"Then I must tempt you with something else to try and find your heart's desire."

Her heart's desire was turning out to be a fickle changeable thing. For at the moment Lieutenant Worth's lips were featuring prominently. As was his charm—*you kiss sweetly,* he had said.

The lieutenant steered her out of the music room, and down the unlit corridor to another room. "This is my book room," he said as he opened the door. "And if you like, and marry me, it can be your book room as well."

The room was a small jewel box of dark, lacquered wood and bright, colorful bindings. The man Pinky had heaped up the fire so the room was warm and toasty and glowing with mellow, yellow light.

She stepped into the room the way a novitiate must walk into a church—full of awe and wonder. "Are these all your books?"

"All." He was smiling again, that incorrigibly pleased smile that curved up one side of his mouth, and made a dimple slide deep into his cheek.

And she wanted to kiss him again. She wanted to fling herself at his chest in wonder and joy and thanks. Of all the things she had come to think and expect since her arrival, she had never thought that he—so breezy and athletic and careless and tall—would be a reading man.

But he had turned, gesturing to the shelves. "They are all mine, and if you are very kind, and forgiving to me, and marry me," he said again, "then they will all be yours as well. But only if you are sweet, and very, very kind."

"I don't know," she said honestly, "if I can."

"Be sweet, or kind?"

"Either."

"Of course you can. Just say yes. Or come here and kiss me. Or both."

Lieutenant Worth sprawled himself back in a chair, his long, long booted legs stretching out to nearly touch hers. He was all manly, animal ease, like a great unthreatening dog lying in the sun, who would be pleased to have his belly scratched. And he was still smiling that roguish, sideways smile.

Anne had very little experience of humor, and even less experience of men—the combination of the two was proving maddeningly perplexing. "Are you laughing at me, sir?"

"No. At myself, perhaps. A little. Why don't you come sit, so we can talk and get to know each other better without the distraction and anxiety of kissing?"

Goodness, but he had an easy way of stating the obvious—something most other people tried to avoid like the blackest plague. Even when such forthrightness mortified her, she could not but approve. "Thank you."

She stepped around his feet, and sat in the armchair facing his. The fire was warm and cheering, and she hoped, a cover for the flush still heating her cheeks.

He finally turned the amused focus of his devastatingly clear blue eyes elsewhere, to the dark walls hovering just beyond the circle of the fire's bright light. "I take it from your expression that you approve of the room. Do you like to read?"

Did he not think her capable, or educated enough? "I love to read. It is my greatest pleasure." Doubtless because it was solitary—a pleasure she could only take in the absence of her mother, who took no pleasure of any kind from books.

"Ah. So noted. I think I will have something more to say to that point later, but for now, I should like to gift you with this room. You can read here, anytime, anyway, anything you like. The collection"—here he looked around, and gestured at the shelves with an expression of great fondness—"is extensive, gathered in my travels. What do you like to read?"

"Everything." She would show him—and herself— that she had something of refinement to go along with her *pert intelligence,* even if she did look as plain and dull as dishwater. "Poetry and history. Novels."

Let him make of that what he would. Let him try not to show his contempt.

He astonished her by looking surprised. He turned his mouth down at the corners, and his eyebrows rose, all at the same time. The effect was comically charming. "Excellent. I have a great number of novels. I already have all three volumes of *Emma,* the new novel from the author of *Pride and Prejudice.* I defy even you to resist such a lure."

"*Even me?*" What on earth could he mean? "Lieutenant Worth, I—"

"Just Worth, if you can't manage Ian. Or Worthless, if you should like to join the opinion of many of my intimates."

"—don't think you know *me* well enough to make such a judgment."

"Perhaps not." His smile showed he took no objection to her hot tone. "But I'm getting to. Getting to know you better and better with each and every word above the recommended *more than two.*"

He was teasing again. And possibly even flirting. She had so little practice, she did not know. "Are you amusing yourself at my expense? Mocking what you no doubt see as my naïve provincialism?"

"No. I am *intrigued* by what I see as your naïve provincialism." The lieutenant let his flyaway eyebrows resume their lazy position shading his too-bright, too-sharp eyes. "Deeply intrigued."

The pulse at the base of her throat began to pound at a seriously indecorous pace. He *was* flirting. In his book room. How very . . . strange. And interesting. And nice. "And what do you read?"

"Everything," he admitted. "I have no discrimination. They're all my books—I've read them all, novels, histories and trigonometric instruction alike." Here he had another sweeping gesture toward the dark shelves. "Why don't you look for yourself, and see what you can find to your taste."

Anne was glad of the chance to stand and move away, down the rows of bright, calfskin-bound titles that glowed like jewels upon the shelves. She trailed a finger along the spines of some large folios with particularly beautifully gilded lettering, astonished at the wealth—both literal and figurative—that the titles must represent. She had no access to such expensive books at home. "You must spend a great deal of time reading."

"When I'm here, at home. When I'm not kissing." He remained sprawled in his chair, with his head tipped back against the back, following her progress along the room.

There was nothing that she could think to say to that particular piece of provocation. The words that usually whirled around her brain like a flight of sparrows had deserted her.

"I must say, that for someone who has never been kissed before, you did exceptionally well."

Her pulse continued to hammer as if she had run up a mountainside, instead of only walking down a room. Good Lord. She really was a naïve provincial. But he had said he liked that—said he was *intrigued* by it.

She took a deep breath, and made a foray into the frigid water of flirtation. "I—How do you know I've never been kissed before?"

His smile spread full across his mouth, like marmalade smeared profligately across warm bread. "My dear Anne—"

"I don't believe I've yet given you leave to use my Christian name." Anne was trying desperately for pert, but her voice only sounded breathless and small.

"Yet." He laughed and closed his eyes, and rolled his head back against the chair, and he looked warm and edible and delicious. "Oh, my darling Miss Lesley. You may have little experience of men—I can tell—but you're learning fast."

"And is that a good thing?"

"I think it is a very good thing. It gives a wonderful place to start. I shall remember it always—the night when my wife Anne learned to flirt."

"I have not yet consented to be your wife."

"But you give me hope with your 'not yet.'"

She turned away, and resumed looking at the shelves, but her mind was only half attendant—the other half was still quite firmly engaged in Lieutenant Ian Worth's large, comfortable, relaxed physical presence.

"So tell me, *Anne*—was I right? Have you never been kissed before?"

There was nothing she could tell him but the truth. "No."

He nodded and smiled, and then frowned—concern pinched up between his brows. "Anne, what do you really know about men, and married couples, and what goes on between men and women?"

Despite her distance to the fire, Anne felt her face flame a scalding red. She was a country girl, and while there were some truths that must be universal, she rather thought he was talking of kissing and flirtation and pert intelligence rather than rude coupling. Still, she could not say so. "Only what my mother has told me."

"What *has* your mother told you?"

Her face grew so hot, she was going to boil freckles into her skin. "She told me that once we were married, you would rend me asunder," she whispered, her eyes fixed squarely on the toes of her boots peeping out beneath the hem of her gown. "And that I was to permit it, and bear it without complaint."

He laughed out loud at the idea. "How preposterous. I'm not going to *rend you asunder*, Anne. I'm going to make love to you."

Love? In her astonishment, Anne said the only thing that occurred to her. "But you couldn't possibly love me."

Anne Lesley's voice was quiet and threadbare. And absolutely, devastatingly honest.

With any other woman he would have lied. With *many* other women, he *had* lied readily enough. But he could not, he would not lie to this solemn girl. Besides being a very wrong way of starting a marriage, he reckoned that she, with her pert intelligence and steely self-control, would be able to tell.

So he spoke as kindly and as truthfully as he could. "No. You are right, Anne. I do not love you," he admitted. "We have hardly known each other long enough for love. But I have faith that I will—I will come to love you, just as you will come to love me."

"How can you say what may happen? You don't know that any better than I do."

She was a cynic, this intelligent, self-controlled girl. The thought of anyone, especially a young woman, being so disappointed by life as to not believe in even the possibility of love made him unbearably sad. He rose and crossed to take her hands again, and lace her fingers through his. "But I do desire you, Anne. Very much. And I do think that is a very good place for us to start. And I also think, despite the fact that you say so little, and show even less, that you desire me, too."

She tried to pull her hands away, to turn and evade him, and hide behind the fortress of her self-possession. "That is lust, sir, not love."

He held on, insistent but gentle. "Perhaps. Yes, you are right—some of what I felt, and what I feel now, *is* lust. I feel lust because every time I look at you now, I want to see what lies beneath your clever, conventional camouflage. I want to kiss you intimately. I want—" He wanted to spread *her* out on the hard, flat expanse of the dining room table, and bury himself in her subtle, controlled rage. But he wouldn't. "I want to kiss you for my pleasure. And I admit, that is lust."

The hot color had drained from her face, leaving her as pale as the dark, cloud-washed sky.

Ian stepped closer still, so that his chest was just barely brushing hers. "But I want to *give* you pleasure, as well. To teach you the pleasure and joy of your own body. To show you the joy of our bodies together. And that, my Anne, is all the difference."

Chapter Seven

She turned her face up to him, in censure or astonishment—he was not sure. Nor did he care. He only wanted to kiss her again, and explore the extraordinary sweetness and sensuality—the passion—he was sure floated just beneath the surface of her skin.

"I want to kiss you." He wanted more than that, but he was a gentleman, and if there seemed to be nothing else he could control in his life, he would at least control his baser urges.

So he tucked his head to kiss the soft skin beneath her ear instead, and was rewarded by the sound of a sigh winging its breathless way out of her. But she said, "It's not right."

"It's not wrong," he countered. "We are nearly engaged, Anne. More than engaged. Say the word, and we shall be married upon the spot."

That surprised a tiny huff of laughter—cynical perhaps, but still laughter—out of her. "I defy *even you*, lieutenant, to produce a parson who would marry anyone this late at night."

"In the morning then. Say the word. Say at least that you shall think on it."

"Of course I shall think on it." Her whisper was only slightly defensive. "I've thought of almost nothing else. It is the only reason I'm here."

Her candid reply surprised a laugh out of him. He ran a hand through his hair, in the hope that he could rub some better sense into his kiss-obsessed brain. "Fair enough." But she had been so sweet and so fresh and so eager, in those few seconds, that he wanted nothing else but the taste of her lips, the way an opium eater wants his pipe.

Yet he controlled himself enough so that she quieted, and stopped resisting him quite so stiffly. But her voice was just as solemn. "Do you really think we can learn to love?"

"Certainly. I had to learn how to lust—learn how to kiss and—" Ian broke off the thought. Again, too much, too soon. "Let me just say I have faith we will learn."

"And how did you learn?"

Since he had already admitted that he had not yet learned to love her, she must be talking about—"How to lust? And kiss?"

"Yes."

Ian was vastly encouraged. So encouraged, the blood in his brain made a hasty descent to more interested parts of his anatomy. Practical application, he wanted to say, and a very great deal of practice.

But one didn't say such things to one's hopeful wife. "From books."

It was a somewhat facetious answer, but there was enough truth in it to pass muster. His time as a lonely, lowly midshipman had been immeasurably lightened by his shipmate Marcus Beecham's small but instructive collection of erotic *facetiae*.

She scrunched up her nose to suppress her amused disbelief. "What sort of books teach you to kiss?"

Ian hesitated for a very long moment, unsure of how exactly to sail across this particular shoal. His moral compass didn't reliably point true north, but even he knew that showing a shy, gently bred, quiet girl like Anne Lesley his rather stunning collection of erotic books would not be the act of a gentleman.

But he was who he was. And he did own a rather marvelously stunning collection of erotic books. And the house would indeed be hers to explore without censure or governance once he was gone back to sea. Best she not come upon it by chance. Best for him to begin as he meant to go on. And best for her to know exactly who the man offering for her was, before she married him. For truly, once they were married, his true nature, like his books, could not be hidden.

"Novels," he said, to pave the way. "Full of the tempestuous emotions that come with things like kissing."

" 'Things like'? Really? I've never read such novels."

"Well, now you may." He looked meaningfully at the shelves, hoping to tempt her into matrimony with the thought of such freedom. "And there are other books as well of instruction as well. Books . . . from other cultures, where the whys and wherefores of what goes on between a man and his wife are not so hidden, and frowned upon."

She did not take his meaning. She looked around at the shelves with perfectly innocent curiosity. "May I see them?"

"I think not. I'm sure even a ramshackle, rapscallion fellow like me ought not let a sheltered, young Englishwoman read a translation of an Indian marriage manual."

"A *marriage* manual?"

"Yes." He hitched his hip on the edge of the desk so he was not so much taller than she, and could see eye to eye. "It is meant to instruct young Indian men and women on how best to please their spouses." He brought their enlaced fingers up to rest against his chest. "In the marriage bed."

"How sensible that sounds," she managed after a long moment. The fragile pulse at the base of her throat became thready.

"Eminently so." He strove for an even, instructional tone, as if he were teaching a young untutored midshipman his maths. But she was only young and untutored, and not at all like a midshipman. She was not noisy and rollicking and brash and male. She was soft and quiet and female, and growing compliant under his hand, still enlaced with hers. "If I show them to you, I must warn you that they might be . . . shocking as well as instructional."

She said nothing, and made no protest when he let go of her hand to choose his book—a large folio, but one of the tamest of his volumes—and returned to lay it before her. And then he moved away, and went back to stand next to the fire so she might have some semblance of privacy while she contemplated the shocking sight of erotica for the first time.

But she neither screamed nor fainted, and when he chanced a glance her way, he found her tipping her head and frowning, and turning the book for a better vantage. So he ventured closer.

"Do all married people," she finally asked, "do . . . that?"

He glanced over at the book, and cleared his throat, and said in as normal a voice as he could possibly muster, "No, not all. I should think portly men would find *that* especially difficult."

* * *

Lieutenant Ian Worth wasn't portly at all. He was as long and lean as a wolfhound, and his relaxed, comfortable attitude did little to hide his whipcord strength.

"And if we marry"—she heard the question whisper past her lips—"will we do that? What the pictures . . ." Suitable vocabulary evaded her.

"Yes," he said softly and kindly, but truthfully. He reached over, and pointed to the picture with his long, lean index finger. "Yes, Anne. You and I would do *that*."

It felt as if his words vibrated through her, deep into her very bones.

"And"—he flipped a page over—"that. Especially that. And many other things as well."

Her breath began to heat in a way that had nothing to do with her embarrassment, and everything to do with his nearness. Silence stretched between them until the air became as hot and smoldering as a Christmas fire. She could not keep herself from glancing down at the new image spread out in front of her. The picture showed a couple locked in an intimate, nude embrace, and each part of their private anatomy was showing. But the picture also depicted the man and the woman with pleasant, secret smiles upon their faces—much like the lieutenant's smile a minute ago—which seemed extraordinarily far removed from her mama's ridiculous instructions about honor and duty.

That book didn't look like anyone was thinking of honor or duty.

"And could you make out any of the writing?" he asked in the same low voice that rumbled through her. "I don't want to assume, with all your *pert intelligence,* you can't read Hindi. No?" She shook her head, and he continued. "The words are more like poetry than instruction."

"Oh," she said for lack of a better thing to say. "I like poetry."

"Hmm, good. This is erotic poetry."

"Erotic?" The word was the shiver of a whisper.

"Erotic." He repeated the word slowly, so that it tumbled around inside her, wearing itself down into something she could manage and understand. "Meant to soothe and enflame all at the same time. So that your breath comes short in your lungs, and you begin to feel warm and strange all over."

It was exactly how she felt. Especially since he was looking at her quite intently, actually staring at her with those sail-away blue eyes across the top of the book. "And do you feel that way?"

His brows rose very slowly, but he did not smile that purposefully charming, amused smile. He merely nodded. "I daresay I do," he murmured. "Now."

Heat swept like a wind across Anne's skin. Not just on her cheeks, but all over, amazing her with its strange intensity.

And then he reached out very slowly and took her hand, reeling her gently back toward the table. Anne didn't resist. There was nothing to resist. He didn't do anything else, merely touched her hand, holding her there.

His hands were quite nice. Long and lean, and beautifully articulated—her smaller hand seemed swallowed in his. And strong—though he held her hand very lightly, she could feel the strength in his muscles and bone.

He covered her hands completely with his, letting the warmth and strength flow into her skin. "Do you like that? The way it feels when our hands—our flesh—touches? The way I am making you feel?"

Anne held her tongue, almost literally—she found she was unconsciously biting down on her lower lip. She also found that her breath was coming fast and shallow in her chest, and that her breasts were rising and falling in rather rapid succession. And she felt all warm and quivery inside, as if her bones were turning to unbaked pudding.

The quivering intensified when his thumb slipped down, and began to graze along the sensitive skin on the inside of her wrists. Anne tried to hold herself very, very still, but she could not stop the surprising feeling of her breasts tightening inside her shift in reaction. And she could not stop from trying to pull away.

He held on. "Are you afraid?" he asked in a low, quiet voice.

His eyes were sober and intent upon her—no trace of the laughing, ready smile now—and she *was* afraid. Afraid of everything she did not know. Afraid that he still thought her as uninteresting and unappealing as a dishcloth.

But for some reason, or no reason at all, she didn't want him to stop.

"Don't be afraid of this, Anne. Of these feelings. Or of me."

She shook her head slowly, and just as slowly, he raised her hand up in his own between them, and brought it very carefully to his lips, while he looked down at her from under the fall of chestnut hair across his forehead. And then he pressed a slow kiss across her knuckles before he turned her hand, exposing her wrist to kiss that same sensitive spot on the inside of her wrist that he had been stroking.

Everything inside her furled and unfurled all at once. "Lieutenant Worth?" Her question was a mere whisper, and she was unsure of what she asked, or if she even asked anything.

He shook his head. "Ian." His voice was low with gentle insistence. And he had very nice, soft-looking lips.

While she contemplated them, he was busy, slowly undoing each and every one of the small buttons on the cuff of her sleeve. As he freed each one in turn, he peeled back a little bit more of the woolen fabric, exposing more and more of her pale forearm to his gaze. When he had loosened the last one, he pulled her arm out straight before her, and bent his head to kiss it. But he didn't just kiss. He nipped, just a little. Just enough to make her hunch her shoulders involuntarily, and squirm within the confines of the wool dress. And then with his free hand, he ran the backs of his fingers over the spot, soothing the hurt with a gentle caress. But his hand kept moving onward and upward, stroking up her arm, onto her shoulder and up the side of her neck, until he was stroking her cheek with the backs of his fingers.

His touch was feather light and exquisite. Exquisite because she could feel it travel everywhere under her skin, skittering down and around below the surface of her flesh. Her mouth opened instinctively, to assure the passage of the air she had forgotten to breathe into her strangled lungs, and she had to close her eyes, to concentrate on the exquisite feeling. She held herself completely still, nearly oblivious to everything else but the tumultuous, slippery feelings leaping around inside her.

She opened her eyes again when he slid nearer along the edge of the desk, until she felt the greater warmth of his body pressed tight to hers. His breath fanned gently across her cheeks. He smelled of spice and claret and fresh winter wind.

The lieutenant continued to hold her right hand with his left, while his other hand continued to roam. Up over her forehead to her hairline, and then down and around, over the sensitive whorl of her ear, and down again over the flushed skin on the side of her neck. She felt her head lean into his touch, tilting into the breath-stealing sensations.

He curled his hand inward, and let the backs of his

fingers slide along the line of her collarbone, and then down very, very slowly across the top of her bodice. Beneath the layers of cotton and wool, her breasts tightened so suddenly, she let out an involuntary, but very audible, gasp.

But he did not stop, nor did she ask him to. Nor did she move away from his touch.

His fingers traveled farther down, along the underside of her breast, and down to her waist before sliding behind to her back. He traced the line of her spine up through the soft wool of the dress until he reached her nape, all the while saying nothing, but watching her face, which she tried desperately to keep shuttered.

But she could not. Especially when he slid his hand up her side until his hand rested just below the curve of her aching breast. And whispered, "Well, damn me for a fool, Anne Lesley. There is nothing, absolutely nothing, plain or uninteresting about you now."

Chapter Eight

Ian stopped with one hand just below the tempting curve of her breast, and the other resting momentarily on the wispy hair at the back of her neck while his mind luxuriated in the nearly perfect way she fit against him. Extraordinary. He was as hard as a carronade, and feeling dangerously intoxicated by her willingness to submit to his touch.

He brought his hand forward under the line of her jaw until his thumb was under her chin, lifting it so she was compelled to look directly into his eyes. "This is more than just lust, Anne. This is attraction—deep and abiding. This is the two of us and no one else."

Anne was mere inches away—his breath was making the soft tendrils of hair along her temple flutter—and she held herself utterly, precisely still. No coy batting of lashes or dramatic sighs from her. No, nothing so overt or easy. With this one, he had to pay attention to the details.

To the delicate flush that warmed her skin, smooth as

winter cream. To the leaping pulse that shuddered in the hollow at the base of her throat. To the shining golden eyes that went dark and dreamy as her lids slowly slid closed.

He moved the hand at her breast to her waist, and let his fingers fan along her rib cage, to join his other hand curving around the slim circumference of her bodice. "You are exquisite."

"Do you really think so?" she asked in her solemn way.

"Yes." And he had to kiss her again to prove it.

He kissed her slowly, carefully, barely brushing his lips along hers in invitation, exploring the plush softness of her lips—such a surprising contradiction to the tense angularity of the rest of her—waiting until she accepted him, and then did more than accept him, until her lips began to move tentatively beneath his.

"My God, Anne. You taste so sweet." He slid his hands up her sides to her neck to cradle her face, and fan his thumbs along the taut line of her jaw. To hold her while he began to explore her open mouth with his tongue, tasting first her lips, and then the pearly softness inside.

The honeyed warmth of her mouth suffused him as she began to kiss him back in earnest.

He tipped her head to the side, increasing the angle more to his liking, encouraging her with his hands and his mouth and his response, to deepen the kiss. Her response was slow but steady and in another moment, she was timidly tasting his lips, opening her own to let him explore the tart sweetness of her mouth as he wished. And soon she was kissing him as if she were born to it, her tongue twining with his in heat and abandon.

Her hands crept up to his lapel, fisting up his coat, pulling him closer so the wool of her bodice pressed against his chest.

His hands swept down the graceful column of her neck to find the soft sliver of bared skin so he could—

In the distance, a loud slam penetrated the warm cloud of his brain—someone was at the door. He turned his head to listen. "Pinky?"

Anne pulled away and stood for a moment with the back of her sleeve pressed against her mouth as she tried to recover herself. And then she began to hastily button up her sleeves. "Oh, Lord. Pray it was he, and not my mother listening at your door."

"Shite." He swore before he could think better of it. But there was no time for apology.

Pinky's voice was raised to carry down the corridor. "No, sir. If you'll just but wait a spell, I'll fetch the captain for ye."

Shite, shite, shite. Ian knew exactly what that sort of noise meant. He cursed his luck and set Anne away from him, and found he had to draw a deep breath into his lungs, and clear his throat before he could speak. "Anne?" he asked as he quickly set to rebuttoning her clothing. "We have to get you all to rights."

She nodded and put her hand up to make sure her pins were still in place in her hair. And then she said, "Wait. Your cravat." She tugged it into place and smiled—a small, shy, disheveled smile that made her seem young and pretty, and he had to kiss her again.

But he could press only the quickest of busses to her swollen lips before the sound of the door opening made them spring apart, and his father, the Viscount Rainesford, barged his way into the room.

The viscount doused them with one cold, assessing glance. And then he said in his usual, sneering way, "When you're done with your doxy, I'd be pleased to see you in the drawing room. Although why you cannot act like a gentleman, and keep yourself from toying with the servants in your own house, is beyond me."

Ian felt, rather than heard, Anne's silent gasp. And

there was nothing else he could do to protect her, but brazen it out, and once more lie for all he was worth. "For pity's sake, Father! She's not my servant, she's my wife!"

The moment Ian said the words he wished them back. "Wife? Her?"

For now he had exposed her to an even greater scrutiny. His father took another step or two into the room, his narrow gaze focused on Anne, his displeasure and condescension written all over his face.

Ian stepped in front of him, belatedly blocking his way. "I will meet you in a moment, sir. In the drawing room. You intrude upon our privacy, and are not welcome here."

"Interrupted a little *tête-à-tête,* as the damn French would have it? Well, at least I know you've been doing your duty on her. Have you gotten her with child?"

"Not here." Ian's voice was as commanding and cutting as he could make it, and his father, thank God, for once responded as a normal human being should.

He stepped back. And though he did not apologize, as a gentleman ought, he at least said nothing else inflammatory.

"Pinkerton, show my father to the drawing room, if you would."

"Aye, aye, captain." Pinky came to attention—or as close to attention as a superannuated old tar dressed in his hodgepodge of checkered waistcoat and calico scarf could do. "This way, sir."

Pinky held the door open for Ian's father, who stalked through and down the corridor, and then turned to speak in a whispered aside to Ian. "Right sorry I am, cap'n. I tried to stop him a-comin' on through, but . . . And things seemed to be going so well between you and the maidy."

Anne colored crimson, and turned sharply away, back to the warmth of the fire. But as she stood there with her head down, recovering her breath, the light of the fire silhouetted her figure in the high-waisted brown wool dress. And Ian's eyes were drawn to the outline of her surprisingly lithe frame—the perfect indentation at the bottom of her spine, and the lovely upward sweep of her breasts where they thrust out against the now tightly buttoned material.

Ian felt himself grow hard again—right there, standing in his book room, in advance of a severe dressing-down from his father.

Who would have thought that the sight of a high-necked, dark wool gown that covered her as effectively as a nun's habit would have him straining at his breeches, and wondering how on earth he was going to navigate himself out of his present crisis so he could marry her, and get her locked into a private room where he could finally remove her drab clothes, and see what lay beneath the little wren's camouflaging plumage?

"Thank you, Pinky. Just see to him, devil take him. Get him a drink." Another thought intruded. "Oh, devil take *me*. Where are the colonel and Mrs. Lesley? Keep him away from them. Bring my father back in here—we'll remove ourselves in a moment—just keep the three of them apart until I can think of . . ."

But he couldn't think. Not while the blood that ought to have been in his head was still taking its pleasure in other, more attentive parts of his anatomy.

"I'll go." Anne whispered so low Ian was sure only he could hear her—retreating into her shy, silent shell. "I'll see to my mother."

And before he could say anything else, or apologize, or say he would speak to her just as soon as he had dealt with both her parents and his father, she walked silently out of the room, and was gone.

Their lovely interlude together was over. But, Ian reflected with a vast deal of satisfaction, she had said considerably more than two words.

Her mother was comfortably situated in a very pretty, well-upholstered bedchamber. Anne expected to be given an enthusiastic catalog of the fineness and cost of the furnishings, but her mother, it seemed, for once had other ideas.

"What on earth were you doing with the lieutenant, Anne, all that time? I should not have let you alone with him. It's not seemly. I worry that he'll think—"

"He thinks we are contemplating marriage, Mama, not just a couple of country dances at an assembly. A greater degree of informality is called for."

But a greater degree of intimacy is what had occurred.

Lovely, marvelous intimacy. Much better than she had ever imagined. And she had imagined quite a bit in her narrow bed at home, and on the long trip from Somerset on the Post.

But all was not as it should be. And clearly, in the wake of the arrival of his father, the handsome lieutenant had a good deal of explaining to do. And so did she.

"Mama, did you hear the Viscount Rainesford's arrival? We didn't hear anything as we were at the back of the house." And engaged in an altogether much more *engaging* activity.

No question could have pleased her mother more—she was wild to talk about it. "Well." She sat up on the very edge of her lovely slipcovered chair. "We were in the drawing room. That funny old servant had brought me a pot of *very* good chocolate, and your father his port, there, while you were wandering the house with the lieutenant. What could you have to talk about all that time, I should like to know?" Her mother paused only to draw breath before chattering on. "But we heard the carriage draw up—a traveling carriage it was, a beautiful chaise and four with a crest on the door. So smart and elegant. And we heard his footman clatter up the steps and knock, but the man—the *viscount* himself—simply burst through the front door. *Burst* through it, without waiting for it to be opened. We heard it slam open. Did you ever?"

Anne shook her head in response to keep her mother moving along.

"And then he *shouted*. Shouted out, 'Worth, where are you?' And then to the servant, 'I knew I'd run him to ground. Where is he, man?' And then he threw open the door to the drawing room, where we were, and said, "Who the hell are you?" And then he walked off down the corridor, and then that butler, Pinkerton, came into the doorway and bowed to us, and shut the door. And that was that for a bit, until the butler came back and said he would show us to our rooms."

At this point her mother sat back— at least as far as her stays would allow her—and clasped her hand to her bosom dramatically. "Such a to-do. Such manners, and him, a *viscount*. Makes me wonder if all is right between the viscount and his son. There seems to be something very strange there."

"Yes." Anne judged it best to give her mother the bare facts. "The lieutenant has told his father that we are already married."

For the longest moment her mother said nothing—it was for the first time in Anne's life that her mother was at a loss for words.

Goodness, there must be quite a storm coming if more than Gull Cottage was freezing over.

"Why on earth would he say that?" her mother sputtered. "I can't imagine—"

"He will have his reasons," Anne interrupted. "The same reasons that made him seek out Papa to arrange this marriage."

"But—Well, I never—"

"You *always*." Anne firmed her resolve. "But for once you won't. You won't say anything. Not to the lieutenant. And not to his father."

"Anne!" Her mother's voice was laced with disbelief and outrage.

"No." She made herself speak before she could wish it back. "Our marriage is our private business, not the viscount's."

"It is certainly the viscount's business," her mother chided severely. "The lieutenant is his son, and stands to inherit—well, certainly not the estate, but something. Something that will concern you as well. And it is only right that the viscount should want to approve of his son's marriage."

"I should think, Mama, that that is exactly the reason why the lieutenant should like to make his father think the marriage has already happened."

Her mother could not follow. "What on earth do you mean?"

Anne swallowed the bitter tonic of her pride, and let loose the words that had been flying about in her brain like a wheeling flock of sparrows. "I mean, that the lieutenant thinks his father will not approve of me as a wife. I mean, that if you wish to see this marriage happen, you will keep quiet, and keep to yourself, and not be speaking to the viscount. I mean, that if you should like to see *me* married, you will for once hold your tongue."

Again her mother was dumbstruck for a full minute. "Why Anne, I-I think that is the longest speech I have heard from you in years."

It was. It was the longest speech Anne had *made* in nearly her whole life. And it felt good. It felt right to say what she thought, and not try to keep it within for fear of displeasing.

A knock came at the door, and at her mother's call, a stout young woman entered, bobbed a graceless curtsy, and said simply, "I'm to do for you, ma'am."

Anne rose to take her leave before her mother could argue, or detain her, or say anything revealing in front of the servant. "I beg you would think about it, Mama." She sketched a quick but respectful curtsy. "I must go."

"But Anne—"

"I beg you. Good night." She left before her mother could say any more, and headed down the stairs to find Ian, when the servant Pinkerton—Pinky, Ian had called him—came bustling up the wide, twisting stairwell, half humming, half singing an old Christmas carol.

"We three kings of Orient hmmm," he was lilting in a well-worn tenor until he saw her. "Mistress," He bobbed his head as he addressed her. "I've got a hot posset here for your mam. I'll just give it to the girl, then, shall I?" He gestured up the stairs. "But is there anything I can get for you, mistress?"

"Miss will do, if you please." She felt her face heat with all the usual trouble of speaking to strangers. "I'm not your mistress yet."

"Ah, but I've great hope you will be." He lowered his voice to a whisper, and slanted his eyes meaningfully down the stairs. "Grand hopes. But I'll say no more. No more. Is there nothing I can get you? It's coming on for a raw night."

"No, I thank you, Pinkerton—"

"Oh, now call me Pinky, if it please you, mistress. We're to be friends and all."

Anne had no idea on earth what "and all" might include, but she was nonetheless happy for the offer of friendship, even from a servant. Especially from this cherubic old sailor, who looked to be kindness personified. "I'm honored. I just thought I'd go down, and . . . perhaps get some air." It was so much easier to think in the fresh, open air. "I'm very fond of the out-of-doors."

"Oh, well, we've plenty of out-of-doors here at Gull Cottage. But mistress, it's coming on for a nasty raw night. I can feel it in my bones, I can. But if you'll allow me . . ." He bustled up the rest of the stairway and disappeared for a moment, until she heard him knock upon her mother's chamber door. And then he was hustling himself back to her.

"If I may suggest instead the glasshouse, mistress? A bit of air without going out into the night? I'll get your cloak for you, shall I, and show you the way?"

The long glasshouse stood just off the far northwest corner of the house, and was reached by a small and frigid covered passageway. Pinky shambled ahead with a lantern.

"Holds the heat of the day for some time after the sunset, the glasshouse does, even on such a raw night. We'll be having snow, you mark me, mistress. Be out of the wind here, you will. I'll be done my business in a moment, and you can enjoy yourself in peace."

He left the lantern, and swayed off to a corner, but the full silver moon cast enough light for her to take in her surroundings. The tables were covered with wooden flats full of a variety of different growing things, and in the middle of the space was an old stone well, as well as a modern hand pump. The slate-paved glasshouse must have been built around them. What a marvelous convenience to provide water for the plants and keep the well itself from freezing.

"Brilliant."

"Oh, aye. That was the cap'n's idea, mistress, to keep the old well here, and add the pump, when we built the place. 'Build it around the water, we will, Pinky,' he said."

He was draping some sort of heavy holland cover very carefully over some bushes in a deep boxed planter.

At her inquisitive look, he explained. "Raspberries, mistress. So's we'll have fruit. Important for the cap'n's health with him still at sea. But tetchy they are, with the cold, the raspberries, so's I like to wrap them up, and wrap them down with a tarpaulin or two. But my old bones tell me we're in for a cold spell, so needs must cover them all. At least for the night." He gestured to a neatly folded stack of the tarpaulins under one of the tables. "But you make yourself at home. I'll be done in a moment or two here, and leave you in peace to yourself."

"You needn't hurry on my account." She heard the words—so antithetical to her former feelings—come out of her mouth with something of astonishment. But Pinky seemed to be a font of interesting information about his master. "How long have you known the captain—rather, Lieutenant Worth? I take it you sailed together?"

"Aye, mistress. Back in oh-six, that were, and him just a wee young gentleman. I took care 'o him, all those years ago, seeing that he got spice and eggs and fish, and he's been good enough to see to me, all these years now, and give me honest work."

"That's very good of him."

"The best. They all were, him and the other young gentlemen. But he's the best."

Anne could hear the gratitude and esteem in the old sailor's voice, and it brought a warm feeling welling in her chest. Lieutenant Worth, it seemed, was a man worth trusting—a man of steadfast loyalty and honor, as well as a handsome rogue. And a particularly marvelous kisser.

His task done, Pinky touched his forelock and shambled away, and Anne made a lovely slow promenade of the place, looking indoors and out. She wiped the film of condensation off the panes and peered out through the darkness. Beyond, across the lawn a line of arthritic apple trees made up a small orchard, reaching beseeching arms up into the night sky. There were brown, frost-covered borders with their shrubs hunched down against the weather.

But she could see more. She could see into next spring, when the ground thawed and the borders greened and bloomed, and the wood below would be full of bluebells. It would be peaceful. And she would be blissfully alone.

But would she be happy?

The better question was, would she *let* herself be happy?

Chapter Nine

Pinky, God bless him, still seemed able to scent the wind. "I've got the colonel and his lady above. And I let *himself*"—Pinky's disapproving emphasis reinforced exactly what he thought of Ian's father—"back into the drawing room until you're ready to see him."

"Right." Ian took a deep, deep breath into his lungs. Pity he couldn't inhale patience. "Time to beard the lion."

"Aye, sir. But if you'd just—" Pinky had somehow retrieved Ian's dress uniform coat, and was easing away his evening coat over his shoulders. "For the authority of the senior service, sir."

"Well put, Pinky. Just the thing." Ian squared his shoulders. "Show the bastard in."

A more imperious, colder man than his father had yet to be born. His usual manner was enough to quench the warmth of the fire. And so it did this day. The viscount stalked in and seated himself behind Ian's desk as if he owned the place.

Which he did not.

"Well." His father gave him a full helping of his scorn. "At least I know you've done your damned duty on her. Have you gotten the chit with child?"

"Father, Anne is my wife, and—"

The Viscount Rainesford was interested in but one thing. "I will need to see the evidence that you are actually married, and she's not some—"

"Sir." Ian used the nonchalant, disobliging tone that so infuriated his father. "I will thank you to keep a civil tongue in your unmannerly head, or I shall be obliged to rip your throat out."

"You wouldn't dare—" His father's laugh was nearly a sneer.

"Try me." Ian called upon every ounce of *sangfroid* he'd acquired over the years, and calmly stared his father down. "I've been twelve years at sea, sir. Twelve. Death and destruction day in and day out. I've killed better men than you before breakfast." Ian flicked at an imaginary speck on his chuff. "State your business, and then I'll thank you to get out of my house."

"Don't you speak to me in that tone of voice. I'll cut you off without so much as a farth—"

"Do it. For the love of God, do it." Ian used his height to his advantage and looked down the length of his nose at his father. "But we both know you won't."

They both knew he couldn't. Not while Ross was in such a state. For the first time in Ian's life, he knew his father was both unable and unwilling to carry out his threats. And for a moment, the old man was actually taken aback. And then he tried to bluster his way out of his embarrassment—or at least what ought to have been embarrassment. The viscount had gotten his way for too long to have enough sense to know when to be mortified.

"Registry, settlements, and such. I'll want to approve

or amend them, as I see fit," he insisted. "And you'll have to give up this fool cottage, and come to Ciren Castle, of course, until we know it's a boy."

"Impossible." Ian swallowed the hollow feeling in his stomach and asked the question sitting heavy in his gut. "How is my brother? How does he fare? Mother wrote that she had returned to Ciren to nurse him, but did not give any other news."

The viscount dismissed his long-suffering wife's care for their eldest son with an impatient gesture. "You will quit this navy business. It has served its usefulness to me, but now I need you at my side."

"No, sir. I cannot."

"Will not, is what you mean. But I'll have obedience out of you yet."

"Will not, indeed. Unless you bring me news that Ross is dead—which I pray every day and with every breath of my body is not true—I am pledged to return to my ship and my duty."

"Your damn duty is to *me,* by God, not to the king or the Admiralty."

Ian ignored his father's sulky wrath, and asked again, though fear and dread were like acid in his throat. "Is Ross dead?"

"No."

Devil take his father for the surly bitterness in his answer.

"Then you already have my answer. I return to my commission directly."

"Then you'll leave the girl with me, to take to Ciren." His father narrowed his eyes, as if contemplating her. "And you'd best to get a brat on her, if you know what's good for you. But knowing you, you're hot enough for a piece of ars—"

"Enough." Ian's voice was as stealthy and sharp as a

saber. "You are beyond insulting. You are disgusting. See yourself out." The habit of respect alone kept him from bodily tossing the old man out.

His father ignored Ian's order, and retreated into silence for as long as it was possible for him—a half a minute, no more. "Tell me about her. Where did you find her?"

As if she were breeding stock at a fair.

Ian felt the smoldering, slow-burning fuse of his temper ignite. "I will *not* discuss my wife with you."

His father was too stubborn to realize his danger. "Damn you. Who is she? Who are her people? Surely you don't expect me to change my will for some fortune-hunting bit of muslin without knowing—"

"Shut. Your. Mouth," Ian roared. "She is the daughter of a former colleague—a King's man—and is the future mother of your heir, as you would have it. And if you want a lick of influence over any future child, you'll learn to mind your manners with the mother, and keep a goddamned civil tongue in your head."

"So there is a child?"

Ian forced himself to cool the hot end of his temper by taking savage delight in his lies. He would not dignify his father's insolence with a reply. "The fact remains that I shall not be going to Ciren Castle, nor shall my wife. This is her house, her home—deeded to her in the settlements— and we shall both stay here. The answer to any and all of your questions is no."

"What do you mean, 'no'?" the Viscount Rainesford barked, and pounded the flat of his palm against the table, turning the full brunt of his wrathful insistence upon his recalcitrant son.

"No," Ian repeated simply. "Again, no. So now you may go." He crossed to the bellpull and tugged, hoping to God that the damn thing actually worked, and Pinky, not one of the Totts, was going to toddle in.

"Be damned to you. I'm not leaving until I—"

Pinky, bless his bright pink cheeks, appeared in no time, throwing open the door sharpish, though he looked out of breath with exertion. His face was practically glowing.

"Pinky, his lordship is leaving. Please be so good as to see him out," Ian instructed.

His father remained seated, red-faced with ire. "Are you mad, or just insolent?" he bawled. "I'm not going anywhere in this weather. The horses are winded from the run down. Think of the cattle and the coachmen, out in this weather, if you can think of no one and nothing else."

Ian had known that it had grown colder since the afternoon—he could feel the weather in his bones—but his father's scathing setdown forced him to take a keener look out the windows. The barest beginnings of snow flurries were whirling through the damp, frigid air, and the December night was turning nasty.

In the corridor Pinky was now engaged in consultation with the coachman and two postilions, who were shaking their heads and frowning deeply in a manner not suited to put Ian's mind at ease.

"Don't like to risk my animals, sir." The coachman appealed directly to Ian. "They've not even rested from the journey here. I can't see them even making it so far as Ryde without any rest, and I don't like the looks of this weather. Best stay put until the storm breaks."

"No," Ian insisted. "Send someone on to Ryde, to see if there's a fresh team to be had there. Or—"

"Begging your pardon, sir, but we come through Ryde on our way here, and the ostler there was closing up. Only taking horses in, he said, as long as the inn could hold 'em, in this weather."

Devil take him all the way to bloody hell.

Devil take him quickly. Gull Cottage was a large cottage, as cottages went, with six principal bedrooms, but it wasn't so big that both his father and the Lesleys could pass each other unseen, and especially not unheard.

Ian looked at Pinky, who ruefully agreed. "Afraid he's right, sir. Fearful blow it is out. Coming on hard to storm. Shouldn't like to send any of these *landspeople*"—Pinky sniffed his compassionate opinion of the inferior species—"out in weather like that."

"So be it. Show the viscount to a room for the night—he will leave on the morrow. Put him at as much a distance as possible from our other guests," Ian said in a quiet aside to his man. "At all costs, keep them well away from one another."

Ian left his father to Pinky's capable ministrations, and retreated to his desk to write a long, imploring letter to his mother to please, for the love of God, keep him apprised of Ross's condition. It was torture knowing that he could do nothing for his brother but stall their father, and keep the old bastard from acting before it was time, and pray that his brother would recover enough to resume his duties at some level. Ross was too young to suffer such a heartless fate.

Ian was still crouched around his scrawl of a letter, his fingers smeared with ink, when Pinky returned.

"Settled the viscount at the end of your wing," he advised. "Opposite end of the house from the colonel and his missus."

"Good man. Thank you, Pinky." Ian signed off the letter and sanded it, and pushed back from the table. "God knows what I'm supposed to do next."

"A bit of air, cap'n. Clear the head, it will. The glasshouse will do the trick, in this weather. It's coming on to snow, you mark my words. You seal that up—wouldn't want your father to be finding it, I'm sure—and go across, and I'll have a cup of something hot and bracing along to you in a minute."

"Something alcoholic, I hope you mean."

"Aye, it's thirsty work, sir. Thirsty work. You get along now."

Ian did. He sealed the letter and, taking the advice to clear his head after such a day, headed toward the glasshouse through the bitterly cold passageway. The wind nearly pushed him across the slick slate floor, and he was about to curse Pinky for a fool and turn back, when the old tar bustled along humming a familiar Christmassy air—and come to think of it, Pinky'd been doing a powerful lot of bustling and humming that day—with two steaming mugs in his hand. Two.

"Pinky? What are you up to?"

"Sailing while the breeze is up, sir. Breezing up." His words frosted in the air above his head as he shoved the mugs into Ian's witless hands. "A Christmas nog, cap'n. For you to share." He put his back to the glasshouse door. "In you go, sir. While the breeze is up."

"It's more than a breeze, Pinky," Ian said, laughing into the teeth of the wind, which was picking up to a gale, because Pinky's sailorly expression had nothing to do with the weather, and everything to do with the girl he hoped was within the glasshouse. But it was damn cold. "We're likely to have more than just snow this night."

Devil take them if the weather stranded his father. God only knew what he would do if he were trapped in a house with the viscount. Patricide seemed the likeliest result.

"Then best get on with it, and then be off to bed. But take a moment for a bit of the yuletide cheer." Pinky nodded at the steaming mugs. "Nothing like a bit of yuletide cheer."

"Thank you, Pinky." Ian slipped into the glasshouse,

and waited for the peaceful hush of the shelter to clear his ears after the harsh whistle of the wind. But what he heard instead was a song. A carol.

A beautifully fine, clear voice was softly singing an old country carol.

> " 'Arise and go,' the angels said,
> 'To Bethlehem, be not afraid.
> And there you'll find this blessed morn
> A princely babe, sweet Jesus born.' "

She was musical. She played the pianoforte and she also sang like a reverent angel, her voice a glorious combination of clear and bright and intimate that made him feel as if she were singing for him alone. But of course she wasn't—she was singing for *herself* alone.

Her song faded into silence the moment his boot sounded on the slate floor.

"Anne? Is that you?"

It was of course she, standing at the end of a row, her cloak turned silver in the moonlight.

"I heard you singing."

She did not answer, but disappeared a bit, back into the voluminous folds of the cloak. Only the long, elegant slide of her nose peeked out of the hood.

"It was very pretty," he assured her. "But you must be cold. Here—I've brought some Christmas cheer. Although you sounded rather wonderfully Christmassy." He handed her the mug, and stopped himself from telling her Pinky had sent it. He didn't want to give all the credit to Pinky. The old tar had told him to make sail while the breeze was up, hadn't he?

"Thank you." She took the hot drink gratefully, wrapping her hands around the mug to warm her fingers.

"Mmmm. That's divine. That's"—she blew out a rum-flavored breath—"potent. Goodness, what is that? I feel like I have turned into a fire-breathing dragon."

He smiled at the image. "Rum, my girl. Dark, Barbados rum. A stiff drink for a stiff breeze. Christmas cheer as Pinky would have it."

"Did that old cherub make this? Goodness," she said again on a laugh. "Christmas cheer, indeed. Who knew he had it in him?"

Ian knew exactly what the old lad had in him, and at the moment he was more than glad. Pinky's penchant for finding the best in people had proved to be more than a boon to Ian this long day and evening. And speaking of evening. . . . "It must be getting on for midnight."

Anne turned her face to look at the sky, steely white with heavy clouds. "Makes me think of 'Oh Holy Night.'"

"Sing it for me."

She shook her head—a swift negative. "No. I couldn't."

"You were singing before. As I said, it sounded very pretty."

She could not be convinced. "It's the acoustics. The glass makes the sound sharper, clearer."

He tried a smile upon her. "Then it must have been you who made it sound so sweet."

Again she did not answer, so Ian bided his time, and let the rum do its work for him, softening her up.

He came to stand beside her, as if he, too, were contemplating the sky overhead. She seemed more comfortable when he wasn't looking directly at her, though he himself wanted nothing more than to look at her again, and figure how she had gone from someone plain to someone rather astonishing in his eyes within the space of one day.

But standing so still, the cold began to seep through his boots—the price of his vanity in wearing the stylish

Hessians. "Devil take us, but it's cold. Raw and damp with a rising wind out of the northeast. I can smell it coming on to snow."

"I should think the snow were the least of your worries." Her voice was as quiet as always, but had something more of that pert intelligence he liked so much. "That was quite a lie you told your father."

Ian winched up his face in a show of ruefulness. "You're not going to let me sail on by this particular shoal, are you?"

"No." The hood of her cloak tipped up to look at him. "You seem to have put yourself—put us all—in a considerable quandary."

He laughed, the sound turning cold and bleak as it bounded off the glass walls. "That would be an understatement."

"Would you care to explain?"

"No. I wouldn't care to, but I know I must. I may be a ramshackle fellow, Anne, but I do know right from wrong, however, and I did lie to my father." His breath was frosting in front of his face as he looked up. She must be frozen. "Do you care to sit? There ought to be a bench here somewhere, where you can rest." And he could snug her up beside him, wrapped up tight.

He led her to the end of the row, past covered plant boxes full of tender seedlings. No lush, tropical setting for seduction, this. It was a working glasshouse, where every spare inch of table space was covered with wooden flats of seedlings—evidence of Pinky's penchant for the husbandry of herbs.

Ian wanted to take Anne to his bedchamber, and cuddle her against him and warm her there, and forget everything else and damn the consequences. But he was an officer and a gentleman. And there were her parents, not to mention Pinky—who had clearly appointed himself as her guardian angel—standing ready to make sure he did not.

There it was, a bench, plain and unadorned, sitting in an unused corner. "Let me warm your feet." He turned and sat, holding out his hands.

She stood before him for a long moment, and with a whisper of a glance down at her feet, said, "You are avoiding making an answer."

"So I am," he agreed reasonably. "But I can warm your feet while I answer."

There was another long, still pause before she agreed. "All right. They *are* cold." She was nothing if not practical, this terrifyingly straightforward, logical girl.

"If I'm to keep my ancestors from rolling over in their graves at my ungentlemanly manner, and warm your feet, it would help if you would sit."

She collected her skirts, and carefully sat at the far end of the bench. The pale oval of her face peeking from her hood was all that was visible of her in the darkness.

"I should light a lamp."

"No, if you please. Pinky left a lantern, but I prefer the darkness. And I'd prefer that you explain your lie."

Ian took up one of her feet, and set himself to unlacing her boot. "I lied to him before. Seven days ago. I told him then that I was already married."

Ian could almost feel the wave of astonishment evolve off her, before she ever spoke. "Why?"

Ian busied himself pulling her half boot off, and plying his thumbs into the arch of her foot, to chafe some warmth back into her chilly extremities. He needed some action to occupy him while he sorted out what to say. Finally he said, "Because I wanted to choose for myself. I wanted to choose a young woman who was her own person, and wouldn't be swayed, or fall prey to my father's machinations about the title and the succession."

"Oh." She drew her foot away, and pushed it back into her boot. "I see," she said in a whisper so bare he had to lean toward her to hear it. "But—I don't see. Why should the title and succession matter at all to you?"

Ian turned his face back to the barren, frozen sky. "Because my brother is dying."

Chapter Ten

"Oh, Ian!"

Even as the seeping heat of worry savaged his chest, Ian had to smile at her use of his Christian name. Finally. "See? That wasn't so hard."

She was not to be so easily distracted. "I'm so sorry. What happened?"

He might as well tell her all—there was no one else to whom he could speak, or even try to articulate the seething roil of anger and fear within. "He took a fall. From a bloody hunter that my father had scorned him for not being able to ride. A bloody, fractious, monster of a beast that should have been put to bed with a bullet years ago. There was no reason my father should have kept him on, except to taunt Ross. Poor Ross, whom my father knew would do anything to please him. *Every*thing he had ever asked." Ian flung himself off the bench, and began to pace back and forth in the welcome dark, glad that the night would not truly reveal him in this agitated state.

Anne's question was full of pity. "What has been done for him?"

"Everything possible, I am assured by my mother, who has gone to care for him. But on the advice of some of the doctors, my father despaired of his ever being whole—of ever walking again. He is especially fraught at the judgment that Ross will no longer be able to sire children."

Though she said nothing, Ian could hear Anne's sharp breath of distress.

"Yes." He could only agree. "Hence his sudden interest in me. And my entry into the state of holy matrimony. And thus you. And the potential fruit, as it were"—he gestured hopelessly to the swathed fertile greenery about them—"of your loins. No. I've got it all wrong." He let out a mirthless laugh. "Your womb. My loins."

She exhaled the breath she had just taken in. "Oh heavens. I think I'm going to need more rum if I'm to contemplate my womb being fruitful." She took a deep draught from Pinky's mug.

"I don't know." Ian was happy to feel his face stretch into a smile. "If you have come to making jokes, I should think you've already had too much rum."

"I don't think too much rum is possible, given this news." She patted her chest to dispel the effects of the strong spirits. "But I am sorry. You were talking seriously, when I interrupted."

"Not an unwelcome interruption." Not at all unwelcome. Very welcome in fact. *She* was welcome. Very welcome.

"Is it a sure thing, that he will not recover?"

"I don't know." He ran his hand through his hair. "I don't think anyone knows for sure. I can only hope. And pray. And worry."

"Yes. Of course." She shook her head, even though she was agreeing with him.

"God, Anne. I used to envy him, you know? I used to be jealous of all the things I thought Ross had that I had not. The inheritance . . . the privilege of someday being the viscount. The attention that I thought he received from our parents. The trappings of the heirdom—the hunters and the dogs and the assemblies and the girls. The holidays at home—Christmas full of fire-breathing nogs and family and fun. Damn my eyes, Anne. I was twelve when my father took me from all that. Twelve years old, and forced to give it all up to go to sea."

This time, her distress could not be hidden. "Oh, Ian. I can't imagine."

He tried to dispel both her pity, and his own, with a laugh—gallows humor. "Neither could I. I could not believe it. I thought it was all a bloody awful mistake. A cruel hoax. I thought for sure they would take me back, and let me come home. I was wrong."

"Twelve years old. That's monstrous."

"That is life, and life in the navy. I wasn't the only one, by any means. Just the only one who didn't want to go. But I was wrong, about Ross. And I learned. I learned better. And I have long since outgrown such foolishness. I have long since realized that he has had the far harder road—the expectations and the ludicrous pressure to perform, and to perform perfectly. He has had day after day of our father baiting and berating him, always telling him that he is not good enough. Always. Devil take me. All I had to do was not get myself killed."

She made another sound—of pity or distress, he could not tell. "Anne?"

She shook her head, but when she finally turned her face up to his, he could see the liquid path of tears streaking down her cheeks. "I'm so glad that you didn't die."

Ian stopped thinking, and simply pulled her into his arms. "Don't cry, Anne. Please, don't cry. I'm here in one piece." Ian concentrated on giving her some comfort, so he could not have to feel the enormous relief and gratitude at the evidence that she cared for him.

It was incredible really, to feel that anyone could care for him, the scapegrace, ramshackle man that he was.

He drew her closer. She felt good in his arms. She felt right.

"I will pretend that we are married."

Her words were spoken against the wool of his coat, and he was not sure he heard her right. "Anne—"

She raised her voice higher. "I'll send my parents off, so they can't give the ruse away. I'll tell your father—"

"Anne. They'll never go without knowing you are legally married. I wouldn't expect them to."

She let out a watery sigh, so he went on. "But I thank you for the offer." He took her cold fingers in his. "You cannot know how much it means to me that you should offer." He clasped her closer, until she was snugged tight against his chest. "I'm a man of the navy, Anne. A man defined by my friendships. Friendships with the men—and women—who have helped to make me the man I am today. Loyalty means everything to me. Everything." He swallowed over the scaling heat in his throat.

Her voice came back, low and solemn, and full of the woman she was. "I may be a dishcloth with only pert intelligence to recommend me, and nothing much else by way of entertainment, but I will say I am loyal."

The heat in his throat ripped down through his chest. And he knew it for what it was—shame. "My God, Anne. My God." His voice was cracking open like a split timber. "Devil take me. How am I ever going to deserve you?"

Her heart felt so full, she could only smile. And tease him. "You could dance with me."

"Dance?" His tone was both amused and incredulous all at the same time.

"Well, we neither of us got to go to any assemblies," she explained. "I just thought it might be . . ." Romantic. The sort of thing she dreamed about but never allowed herself to believe. The sort of thing that happened to other girls—dancing in the moonlight with a dashing, handsome man.

Ian turned his kind blue gaze upon her. "No? Have you not even been to village dances?"

"No." Such events were an agony to her, standing under the eyes of strangers. "We live very far from the village. Too far."

"Ah." He took another deep breath, and smiled his rueful, I'm-a-shallow-fellow smile. "Why not? Although, I do feel I ought to point out that in the normal course of things—in the normal course of a courtship—dancing would typically come before kissing and midnight talks in glasshouses. But I suppose that we'll just have to accept that this"—he pointed his finger back and forth between them—"is not the normal course of things."

Anne could feel her mouth stretch into a smile. He really was irresistibly charming. "Does that mean that this is a courtship?"

"A rather backward one, it would seem. But as I was saying, before you butted in with all your pert intelligence—in the normal course of things we would have met at a village dance in . . . Somerset, was it? And gotten to know each other as friends before we might have progressed to . . . other things. Like kissing. And . . ." He hesitated over the top of his wickedly teasing smile. ". . . like feeling the sweet flair of your waist, and the delicious curve"—he lowered his head to whisper in her ear—"of your breast. Which I should very much like to do again. But we must do it all in the proper order, as my lady bids. So let us pretend. Let us pretend we are at a village dance."

She gave into the smiling charm in his warm voice. She could not help it—the mental image of him, so tall and powerful, so full of leashed energy, doing the pretty in one of Bridgwater's tiny, tired-looking assembly rooms was ridiculous. "I cannot picture you at a village dance."

"Well, no." His broad smile gleamed in the moonlight. "Neither can I. Which is, I suppose why we find ourselves in this predicament, talking rather improperly of kissing and breasts—very lovely breasts I might add—in a dark, frozen glasshouse, instead of dancing in a low-roofed assembly hall."

It *was* rather silly. And fun. And wonderful and breathtaking. Because the offhanded compliment heated her skin afresh, and made her breasts feel full and aching. Beneath the enveloping layers of cloak and clothing, her nipples contracted and rasped against the practical starchy white muslin of her shift.

She ducked her head to retie her boot, thankful for the darkness that made it easier to hide her reaction to him.

"Now then—our imaginary village dance."

"Do you actually know how to dance? I don't." She had learned—her mother had insisted—but she had never danced with anyone other than her much younger sisters. "Not really."

"I do." His reassuring smile was a bright slice of moonlight. "I did learn—all of the exalted Viscount Rainesford's offspring must learn the art of the dance."

Another small flash of pain tore across his face, and she knew he must be thinking of his brother—his poor brother who could no longer dance. But he recovered his smile, and stood directly in front of her, and bowed very formally and properly, and said, "Good evening, Miss Lesley. How nice to see you this evening."

Anne had never practiced formalities with her sisters, or made conversation, so she had no idea how to go on.

But Ian didn't mind playing the dancing master. "You're supposed to say something back, like, 'Good evening, Lieutenant Worth.' Or, 'Lieutenant Worth, how delightful to see you.'"

"Delighted, Lieutenant Worth." She made him a passably graceful curtsy.

He clapped a fist to his chest in mock pain. "And there's that pert intelligence I like so much. Well played, Miss Lesley—a hit direct. But now it is my turn to fire, and I say, 'Would you care to dance, Miss Lesley?' No, no, that won't do—a mere shot across your bow. Something better aimed, like, 'May I have the honor of this dance, Miss Lesley?'" He bowed to her again, as smooth and fine and polished as if he stood in some castle's drafty ballroom.

He was so handsome and sad and gay all at the same time. Anne felt her heart turn over in her chest—a gentle, happy pain. To have such a man flattering and teasing and dancing with her. She had never thought such a thing possible. "You may."

He held out his hand, and slowly, because she rather thought that it was going to be a momentous thing, she placed her hand gingerly upon his. And she was right. Somehow the power within him—within his flesh and bones and sinew—translated itself from the palm of his hand to hers. She felt light and suspended as he led her out upon their imaginary dance floor, as if she could float along, buoyed up by a cloud of make-believe.

"And we go like this." He began to hum an easy air, and then promenaded forward two steps and then back, until she caught the movement, and was comfortable enough to stop looking at his feet. He turned her around with the pressure of his hand at her back—sure and warm and solid—and repeated the movement on the other side.

"How delightfully you dance, Miss Lesley. And now you lie, and compliment me."

"But you are the one who is lying, Lieutenant Worth. You do dance very well."

"I thank you, but that is only because I have had the benefit of a dreadfully expensive and exacting dancing master, who quite despaired of me in my youth. And I have it from a reliable source that now that I am grown so tall and gangly, I am too big, and simply loom over my partners."

How strange that he should see himself that way—he who was nigh unto perfection. Easy, breezy, laughing, handsome, sad perfection.

"So now we circle around each other, like this." He twined their fingers over her head as they slowly rotated around each other. "And as we dance in our little imaginary village assembly, since you very politely decline to disparage my dancing, I will take the opportunity to compliment you. Because I cannot help but notice"—here he appeared to look at the glass ceiling and think something up—"the delicate warmth of your hands. Actually, I notice that your hands are ice cold, and I am moved to warm them up. I hold them a fraction of a second too long as we pass through the figures, drawing my fingers along the length of yours for as long as possible."

He slid his palm slowly out from under hers as he stepped apart, turning away in a small circle.

It was riveting—all this focused attention. She lost the way of the step, and stopped, and he was compelled to touch her again, to put her right. He stepped up close next to her—so close his shirtsleeve brushed against the length of her arm, and her skin tingled within her clothing just as if her arm had been bare to him.

"I take advantage of when we come together, side by side like this, to place my hand in the small of your back."

He suited words to action, and sent his hand exploring under the loose covering of her cloak, pressing the wide span of his hand into the curve of her spine. "And I find I like the feel of the smooth, tiny line of your waist."

He took up one of her hands, and drew her closer before he moved her in a slow circular rotation around him with the warm pressure of his hand. "I catch a hint of your scent as I lean in close. You smell delicate and delicious— like citrus." He dipped his head down close to the curve of her neck, and his breath fanned across the sensitive shell of her ear.

Anne shivered despite the relative warmth of her cloak—a delicate skittering of sensation across the surface of her skin.

"I come close to feel the heat from your body, dip my head to smell your perfume, and then I'm here, so close. I can span your waist with my hands. But all I can think about is how sweet your lips taste."

Her lips were already parted in unconscious readiness, and she stopped thinking and let herself fall into the heady pleasure of his kiss.

This was nothing like their careful, teasing dance. Nothing like the gentle exploration of the book room. Nothing like she had ever imagined.

His kiss was hot and tight and close and needy and fierce.

He kissed her as if this moment, this meeting of flesh and desire was everything. As if he actually wanted her. Wanted her lips upon his, her tongue twisting and twining with his, licking and sucking and tasting her. As if he needed the nourishment of her love. Needed the press of her body to his.

Her hood fell back, and his hands were along her face, holding her to him, angling her head so he could get close, and closer still. As if he could not get close enough.

And she was kissing him back, pressing her lips and

her body to his. Kissing him as if this moment of passion between them *were* all that existed. As if she did not need air or water or heat. As if she needed only the cold burning torch of his touch.

He tasted of rum and spice, and winter and need and loneliness—and she ached for him. For all the years he had not been able to dance or kiss. For all the years she had not had the chance to dance, or be kissed.

For all the time that they would never have together.

She would make up for it now. She threw her arms around his neck, anchoring him to her, pulling him down upon her so she could feel the heavy thrill of his weight. He was bending her back, pushing her over his arms with the press of his mouth and nose and cheeks.

"Anne," he said, and he did not need to say more. She knew. She understood. She wanted everything that he wanted. She wanted more.

More of the fiercely tender way her held her face within his strong hands. More of the weight and strength of his body as he pulled her to him.

More of the hot greedy pleasure blossoming out of her. More.

As if he could hear the unspoken thoughts within her head, he speared his hands into her hair, upsetting the pins. "I want to see your hair down. I want to see you undone. As undone as I am."

"No." But her hair was already coming loose, springing free from the severe constraints of her hairstyle. A riotous profusion of unruly curls tumbled over her face and down over her shoulders. "No. Please."

Ian drew away from her, staring down at her, with something stronger than confusion writ across his face.

"Damn my eyes, Anne Lesley," he breathed. "What in God's name have you been hiding from me?"

Chapter Eleven

Her composure, the fine-tuned, steely composure that had lasted through the long day, shattered.

"Don't do that. You mustn't," she stammered, and abruptly tore away to gather her hair up in her hands. She twisted it viciously to subdue the wild corkscrew of sable curls that sprang from her head in wild abandon, and stab it back under the hood of her cloak.

"No. No, no. no. My God. What have you been hiding?" he asked again. His fingers nearly itched to get at her, to fist in the untamed abundance before him.

"I'm sorry," she repeated, and scrabbled up the pins scattered across the dark, uneven slate floor.

"No, stop. Stop it." Ian went down on his knees beside her to cover her hands.

She snatched back her hand, and went instantly still, like a wary wild animal—even her erratic breathing seemed to strangle to a stop.

He was breathing too hard and too fast, as well, but for

an entirely different reason. His breath was sawing in and out of his chest because he wanted to . . .

He wanted to rip off the shapeless cloak clothing her frame and see what else she was hiding behind her careful little wren's defensive plumage. He wanted to see the glorious riot of her hair unrestrained. He wanted to see the color of the peaks of her small high breasts—apricot— they would be the same apricot hue smeared like jam across her flaming cheeks. He wanted to see all of her. He wanted to light every lamp he could find, and assuage his ravenous curiosity by—

Ian closed his eyes to try and blot out the image. The devil must have already taken him, because he was clearly in hell—a hell of his own making. Because he was a gentleman, and an officer of His Majesty's Royal Navy, and she was a naïve, shy, untried young woman, his not-quite-betrothed, under his bloody glass roof. A guest in his house.

He opened his eyes to find hers wide and dark with something beyond fright. She looked, for the first time in their short acquaintance, entirely vulnerable—stripped of defenses in a way that was nearly too intimate, too personal, to take advantage of so callously.

Ian willed his body and his mind into self-discipline. He gathered up a few of the hairpins, and placed them carefully in her hand. "Please, Anne. Please. Do not think that I am displeased, or in any way disappointed. In fact, quite the opposite. I am . . ." Words failed him—polite words, that wouldn't have her running back to Somerset as fast as her legs could carry her. "Please understand, I like your hair. I am enthralled by it."

Her hair was the exact opposite of her disciplined restraint—exuberant, unfettered, and abandoned.

"I find it inordinately beautiful." He reached out to finger an errant strand curling below her ear.

She turned her face away and closed her eyes. "You mustn't."

"Whyever not?"

She kept her face turned resolutely away, withdrawing from him in every way, though she did not move. "It's not ladylike. It's not seemly."

"Anne. I don't give a damn for ladylike—I've never given a care to seemly." What he wanted was her—this glorious unbound creature lurking behind her tightly controlled facade, unrestrained by shyness and convention. He wanted *her* for his wife.

"Do you mean it?" she asked, her voice full of doubt and a pain he could not fathom. "Do you mean any of it? Truly? Or is this just another one of your convenient lies, like the one you told your father?"

Damn, damn, damn his eyes.

The truth was a stunningly sharp blade between his ribs. Hoisted on his own insidious petard.

He took her hand again very slowly and carefully, and held it very lightly, very reassuringly. "Anne, I admit I am a ramshackle sort of fellow. I *have* lied a great deal in my life. I have lied to my father almost from the day I was born. And I lied to him again today. But I will pledge here and now, I will never, ever lie to you."

She did not speak. She did not move. She was barely breathing. Finally, she whispered, "How can I trust you?"

"I will show you. I will show you in my action and my deeds how much I like *you*. Very, very much. I *like* the way you try to contain your thoughts and words by crushing the soft cushion of your lips between your teeth. I like the way your breath throttles up in your throat, and you sound a little scared, but also curious, all at the same time. I like talking to you. I like kissing you. I want to kiss you again, to prove to you how much I want you."

He could not tell if she believed him or not, so he went

on. "I will tell you that you taste like melted snow and wintergreen mint. I will tell you that I like the hint of chapping on your bottom lip where you bite it in your shyness, or to keep from speaking. And I will tell you I want to kiss those lips, to taste you, and feel you in my arms."

He had to kiss her then—he was helpless not to. Because she needed to be kissed. She needed to be reassured. And he needed to reassure her.

And tease her. "Your lips are cold."

"I'm sorry," she said in that strange solemn way that made him smile, and made him want to make her smile.

"Don't be. Because if they weren't"—he angled his head to take her bottom lip between his lips, and worry at it gently—"I wouldn't have the pleasure of warming them."

He teased the kiss out of her, gently nipping and sucking until she opened her mouth and let him into her rum-laced warmth. He moved along the line of her jaw, pressing his lips to her chilled cheeks, nosing his way to the sweet hollow beneath her ear, where he could take her lobe between his teeth.

"I need you, Anne," he whispered. "I could not lie about that."

She made a soft sigh of capitulation, before her hands stole around his neck, and she was kissing him back. Kissing him as if she, too, wanted and needed this—this closeness, this sharing of warmth and affection.

His head tipped into the cup of her hand, and he knew he was grinning like a boy, enjoying the fresh delight of the back of her hand grazing along the curve of his ear.

Ian was rewarded for his encouragement when she laid waste to his cravat, and, unshackled the buttons marching from his collar halfway down the front of his shirt. The air felt cool against the exposed vee of heated skin, and he was floating in the warm, swirling waters of anticipation, buoyed up by confidence and lust.

Confidence and lust and rum.

She plied her lips to the hollow of his throat, and then moved on, kissing along the line of his collarbone, nipping and worrying the sensitive, straining tendons there. He was dying by tiny degrees, shot through with painful pleasure. "My God. Let me touch you. Let me—"

In answer, her nimble fingers stole down over the buttons on his waistcoat, and in another moment her clever hands were inside, stroking over the linen of his shirt, kneading into the muscles of his chest. His flat male nipples tightened against the press of linen, and when her hands found the rumpled tips, she thumbed him through the thin fabric of his shirt.

"Devil take me. Anne."

She kissed him, and Ian felt as if he were coming out of his skin, and he could only wonder at how she, with her untutored, tentative touch, could bring him to such a state of bloody, glorious arousal. He could feel himself slipping under her spell. Under the control of her fragile curiosity. Under the power of her delicate, clever hands, and soft lips, and cleverer teeth. Dragged under gladly, happy to drown in the ineffable pleasure.

It was all the permission he wanted to do the same to her. He parted the concealing curtain of her cloak to slide the dress off her shoulders. Her skin was a living pearl, smooth and luminous white in the silvered light from above.

Ian knew he had never seen anything so beautiful. But he had no time for spoken reverence. He could only worship her with his body—with his hands and mouth. He turned his attention to her exquisite breasts. Pale and pink and perfectly formed, they fit exactly into the curve of his palm. He drew his thumbs across the tightly furled peaks, and she gasped—a startled sound of keening delight. Thus encouraged, he tweaked the sweet tip, rolling it between

his thumb and forefinger, until she cried out with pleasure.

"Ian."

He had never wanted to hear his name more. This was
what he wanted—this unbridled response, this revelation
of her hidden passion. He lowered his mouth to join his
hand, taking her between his lips, sucking and lavishing
her with every ounce of his skill and care.

She clutched at his head in response, and drew him
nearer, fisting her hands in his hair, tugging and straining
to find the pleasure. Learning the way of her own delight.

He arched her back over his hands, nipping and tongu-
ing her until she closed her eyes, and threw back her head
in submission and triumph—submission to the pleasure,
triumph in her delight.

He returned his lips to her mouth, ravenous for more of
the taste of her. Hungry for more of the untutored pleasure she was giving him. He held her close, and she all
but wrapped herself around him, pressing her breasts into
his chest in painful bliss.

It wasn't until he thought of lowering her to the cold
slate floor, or backing her into the icy glass walls that Ian
realized he had to stop. She had never so much as kissed
a boy until this day, and here he was thinking of taking her
in the uncomfortable, freezing glasshouse. She needed a
bed and care and soft words, not an animalistic coupling
in the cold.

But Anne had other ideas. She took his lip between her
teeth and bit him. "Now."

There was no mistaking the urgency in that message.
Or in his body's ferociously hungry response.

Ian swallowed his moan of frustrated arousal. "Anne.
Please. We can't. I can't—"

"Please," she whispered low into his ear. "Pretend. Just
pretend I'm not plain. Pretend you aren't marrying me out

of need, or some misguided notion of honor, or duty. Pretend you've never even seen me."

She never should have said it. She never should have opened her mouth. Once words were said, there was no recalling them back. Never.

He froze. And then very carefully set her away from him.

She had revealed too much.

Anne pulled the arms of her dress back over her shoulders, gathered the edges of her cloak together, and tried to fasten the clasp. But her hands were shaking, from grief and anger and unaccustomed, unstoppable lust. No wonder he liked it so much. But unlike him, she had no experience in stopping the heedless surge of feelings and emotions sliding through her veins. Once loosed, she could not seem to recall herself.

He set his hand over hers to still them. "Why would I do that, Anne? There's no need."

"Oh, there is every need." Her voice was less emphatic, but no less revealing. She had nowhere left to hide. She turned away from him, trying to protect herself with distance.

He would not let her go. "You're wrong." His voice followed her with calm insistence. "I want you for my wife, Anne, not just a groping tumble in a cold glasshouse. When I have you—when we have each other—I want you warm and comfortable and happy and mine, before God and all men. I want you. You. Quiet and composed. Solemn and pert. Lemons and snow."

His words were both a balm and a rasp upon her soul. They were everything she wanted to hear. And everything she was afraid to believe. "You are only trying to be kind."

He shoved his fingers through his hair in a gesture of

rumpled, end-of-his-tether frustration. "I should hope I'm trying to be kind. I should hope you would expect me to be so. I want to marry you, Anne. To have and to hold from someday soon—someday very soon. As bloody damn well soon as I can manage it—forward, 'til death us do part. You should expect that I should care for you and take care of you, just as I can only hope that you will care for me. And I can also only hope you want to marry me."

She did. She wanted it with all her body, and with all her soul. She wanted to believe him. She wanted everything he promised—warmth, and comfort, and companionship. And happiness.

Above all, the damn elusive happiness.

Chapter Twelve

Ian slept late, and woke the following morning to the steady hush of falling snow. Which meant the storm had not abated. Outside the window the flat press of iron gray sky revealed a thick cover of snow blanketing the ground.

Which also meant his father could not have left, damn his probing eyes. And damn Ian's own, because the snow that would prevent his father from leaving, would also prevent Ian from being able to fetch a parson. His wedding day would have to be put off at the same time he would have to pretend it had already happened.

He would have to ask Anne to pretend to be his wife after all.

If, in the light of day, and in the absence of potent "Christmas cheer" to influence her thinking, she agreed, there really was no way he was ever going to be able to deserve her.

Ian flung himself out of his warm bed and put himself to work. His next stop was the kitchens, to find Pinky and the Totts, and to inquire after both his invited and uninvited guests. But when he went looking, he found only Pinky and the Rainesford coachmen. The Totts, it seemed, had decamped.

"Left last night just before the storm. Gone down the footpath to the village like badgers gone to ground. With the snow coming on, they didn't like being away from their own farm any longer," Pinky explained. "Didn't rightly know how I could stop 'em, them being women and all."

Ian could only sympathize. "Indeed, Pinky, I understand entirely. Nothing could be done. As long as they left the larder stocked—it is well stocked, isn't it? As long as both the larder and the coal scuttle are full, we should be able to survive even my father's presence."

Pinky shook his head, and shot a sideways glance at the coachmen. "Too deep, they say, for the horses. Don't like to risk their animals, or their own necks overturning in a ditch. But, no need to worry about the coal, sir. If it comes to it, I've got a grand yule log all picked out near the edge of the wood. Should be able to fetch it up to the house, even in all the snow. And Christmas day is tomorrow. We ought to burn it then, regardless. Keeps the spirits bright, the yule log does."

"Then burn it we shall, Pinky."

If Ian did not first burn the house down around his ears with his lies.

Because their survival—his and Anne's, and their marriage—would hinge largely upon his skill with subterfuge. With the Totts gone, and only Pinky to shift for all of them, there was absolutely no way for his uninvited guests to stay out of the way of each other. It was going to be absolute hell to keep them apart—especially his probing father and garrulous Mrs. Lesley. Gull Cottage was only so big, and no larger—his father's outsized sense of entitlement could barely be contained by the vastness of Ciren Castle.

Devil take them all. But clearly, not even the devil would take them in weather like this.

"Make them comfortable," he told Pinky. "But country hours, and country food. And"—he had a marvelous moment of insight—"lock up all of the good liquor. Don't give my father any reason to linger."

"That'll be all the good French brandy?" Pinky followed Ian across the kitchen with a sad, hangdog countenance. "I was going to make her a Christmas pudding. Can't light it afire without the brandy."

No need to ask which "her" Pinky was trying to turn up sweet. But if Pinky could manage it where Ian could not, so much the better. He needed all the help he could get. "Just keep the brandy hidden in the kitchens, Pinky—I doubt my father has ever set foot in one in his life."

It occurred to Ian to simply avail himself of that bottle of brandy, and drink his breakfast, sliding off into a happy stupor in the comfort of his own room, but that was hardly kind—it was in fact rather cowardly. Best to start as he meant to go on.

He found Anne at the top of the drafty kitchen stairs, coming down the corridor in a flattering claret-colored gown. She looked so different from his first impression of her that the change knocked him hard in the chest. She looked nothing like a drab little wren. In the claret, she looked like the perfect warm wine punch on a cold winter's day. "Anne."

She colored deeply at just his mention of her name—a vivid swath of apricot pink streaked up her cheeks, and disappeared down the front of the admirable claret-colored gown. But she smiled as if she were very much pleased to see him.

His body set up an interesting hum of anticipation that vibrated down into his bones. "Good morning. You've dimples, you know. Right there, in both cheeks. I never noticed them before."

He knew the compliment warmed her, because her smile widened full across her mouth, though she only asked, "Is he gone?"

"No, damn me," he answered. "I must apologize. Again. We are stuck with him. The weather is too severe for him to think of leaving." He shoved his hand through his hair, as if he might pull a better idea out of his head. "I can control neither the weather—though in ten years at sea, I have often wished to God I could—nor my father. I shall endeavor to keep him well away from you. And from your parents as well."

"You may certainly count on my assistance. I'll go to my mother just as soon as she wakes, but that should not be for several hours yet."

It seemed the whole house had kept late hours last night. "And your father?"

"I'm afraid I do not know his habits well enough to venture a guess."

"From what I know of your father, I should think as a military man he'll be afoot long before mine. Service to the King is a long habit to break, while the Viscount Rainesford serves no master but God—and God, only when it's convenient to him. With luck, he'll stay abed, or at least stay out of our way, for the rest of the day."

"Then let us hope that we shall be lucky."

We. Ian liked the sound of that. It sounded hopeful. It sounded promising. "Oh, I'm counting upon it." He gathered his supple, almost-bride into his arms. "I've always had the devil's own luck." He kissed her sweet lips. "It's brought me you."

"Well, isn't this cozy." His father's cold sneer took all the warmth out of the air. "At least you'll have no trouble getting a brat on her. You're too much my son to fail me on that score."

The viscount's tone was knowing and snide in a way that made Anne feel embarrassed and dirty. Twice now he had come upon her tangled in his son's arms.

"Aren't you going to introduce me?" he asked.

Ian's quick rueful glance was an apology, but Anne was ready for the coming lie. There was no way around it. "My wife, Anne Worth. Anne, my father, the Viscount Rainesford."

The viscount looked at her down the length of his imposing nose, as if she were a particularly pestilential insect. He did not speak, though his nostrils flared in disdain. But if he thought his silence was a punishment, he was wrong. Anne welcomed his not speaking to her, if it would save her the trouble of having to talk to such a man.

She took satisfaction in vexing him by smiling serenely.

The viscount immediately grew tired of trying to intimidate her, and turned back to vex his son. "Am I going to be kept in the corridor all day, or has that doddering old fool of a servant prepared a proper breakfast?"

Ian stepped aside, and swept out his arm in a mocking imitation of a courtly gesture. "Don't let us keep you from breaking your fast. I'm sure there are kippers and eggs aplenty for you to complain about."

The two were barely civil to one another.

"You'll starve if you hope to dine on your wit, boy." The viscount gave as good as he got, before he stalked down the hall.

Ian turned back to her, his eyes full of that self-deprecating, bittersweet regret. "Forgive me. I hate to inflict such a man upon you."

"It cannot be helped."

"No, it can't. Have you eaten? Are you hungry? You hardly ate much last night. I fear Pinky would be insulted if he did not see you eat a good breakfast. He will take it as a mark of your disfavor."

"Oh, no. There is no disfavor on either side. He brought me a pot of chocolate earlier. It was divine."

"I'll make sure he knows so. Unfortunately, I am ravenous this morning—or rather this afternoon, so I shall have to brave the breakfast room."

"I won't make you face it alone."

"Thank you, Anne."

But when they got to the breakfast room, they found it occupied with not one, but two fathers. Her father had already taken a seat, but now stood greeting the viscount.

"Colonel Oliver Lesley." Her father brought himself to attention, his back ramrod straight and his gaze level before he made a bow. Though he wore no uniform his bearing declared him every inch a military man. "At your service."

"I take it you're the father?"

If her father was aware of the slight in Rainesford's voice, he hid it well. "I am, sir. I take it you are Worth's good sire?"

Whatever the viscount might have made in reply was forestalled by Ian, who reached across the table to shake her father's hand in greeting, in an attempt to draw him away. "Good morning, sir. I trust you slept well? Can I get you some coffee? Come. Let me refresh your cup."

"No, no. I thank you." Her father waved Ian's assistance away. "I am quite fine. Anne."

Her father held out her chair, so Anne took the opportunity to brush close to him, and whisper, "Say nothing of the marriage, please. I beg you."

"Anne? I beg your pardon? I could not hear."

"So you approved of this marriage, did you?" The viscount turned his probing stare on her father. "Of course you did, thinking to ally yourself with a viscount's son."

This time, her father did take note of the barely veiled insult, but he maintained an admirable calm. "I thought to ally myself with a shipmate. A colleague and a man whose worth and character, in times of peril and times of peace, were well known to me."

The viscount snorted. "Ian, do you mean?"

"Of course." Her father shot a glance at Ian, standing by the sideboard, to see what he thought of such a remarkably derisive attitude from the young man's own father.

"Who knew? You were on one of his ships then, were you? I didn't know if you were just some colonel of the local militia."

"I was until quite recently a colonel of His Majesty's Royal Marines."

"And how long ago did you two cook up this marriage between these two? Did he have to come a-begging you for your daughter?"

"No, sir." The denial was out of Anne's mouth before she even had time to gather her courage. "I am the one he begged."

The wide sash of Ian's smile was all the reward she needed for being so bold.

Her father looked back and forth between her and Ian, and then between Ian and his father, before he answered. "I met young Worth on his first cruise as a young gentleman of the navy—as we call midshipmen—and took a liking to him then."

"So how much did she bring him?" The viscount turned the full cutting power of his disdain on Anne. "I can only assume you dowered her well, as she's not much to look at. I told *him* I'll want to see the settlements." He shot an equally derisive look at Ian. "Not that anything can be changed. It's too late now that the deed is done."

Again, her father looked from father to Ian and back. "What do you mean, too late?"

"Father . . ." Anne began at the same time that Ian spoke.

"Speaking of settlement, colonel, sir, I have that . . . If you'd come along then, sir, I'll have the . . ."

Viscount Rainesford slowly sat up from his slouch, like a canny fox scenting up the wind. "What goes on here? How much did she bring?"

Anne knew enough to answer swiftly, "A thousand pounds."

The viscount subsided into his usual, curling sneer. "Is that all you could afford?"

"He did not ask for more, sir." Her father returned his own canine smile—the cagey dog guarding the henhouse, who knew the fox will always come to him.

The viscount smiled back, though it was clear he did not think it amusing. "No, he wouldn't have. I would."

"Ah." Her father leaned back into his own chair, and steepled his fingers across his wide chest. "I begin to see why you are here. You think to make the bargaining tougher. Well, do your worst."

Viscount Rainesford's answer was deceptively casual. "Are the settlements not done?"

Her father answered before either she or Ian could keep him from responding. "Not even begun."

"Sir—" Ian tried.

The viscount was as quick as he was tenacious. "Then how is it that you allowed the chit to marry?"

Her father looked first to Ian in his confusion, and Anne leapt to try and avert the coming disaster. "It was a love match, sir. My father wants me to be happy."

"Yes, of course," her father added in loyal support. But

he was frowning at her, and looking back and forth between her and Ian.

And Anne could not stop herself from looking to the viscount. Who saw it all. And understood.

"I knew it. They're *not* married. I knew it." He slapped his palm against the table and pushed to his feet, staring at her, his fierce dark eyes—so unlike his son—boring into her. "This is all some sort of elaborate, godforsaken sham."

She could not keep the sweep of mortifying heat from blazing across her face, and he saw and understood. Her face proclaimed her guilt as clearly as if she had spoken.

"Jesus God." The viscount spat the curse at his son. "You fool. You stupid impetuous fool. Thank God I came when I did. There's time enough to stop this unless—" He narrowed his gaze upon her. "Christ Almighty. You were practically buttering her parsnips in the corridor—"

Another scorching swath of humiliation burned across her face and neck.

"Enough," Ian snarled in a voice gone low and quiet with anger. "I've already asked you to keep a civil tongue in your head, but I should have known that even that is beyond you."

His father paid no mind to his lethal tone. "But have you had her, boy? That's the question."

"It is none of your business."

"It is my business to find out if you are married or not!" Viscount Rainesford shot back.

Ian looked at her then, and she saw the same bittersweet apology in his eyes, almost as if he were asking her permission.

It would have been easiest to continue the lie. It would have been better for them both if he did. But it would have been wrong. "We are not," he said.

"Jesus God," the viscount swore again. "You're nothing but a walking scandal."

"There will be no scandal unless *you* make it one. The only people who know are in this house, and are trapped here by the snow. If word gets out, if a scandal is created, then it will have been you who created it. Is that what you want?"

His father had his answer at the ready. "What I want, is for once in your miserable life, you will do as you are told, and come back to Ciren Castle immediately, and marry the wife I have chosen for you. And mark my words, I will use whatever means I have to, including turning you into a scandal, if that is what it takes to make you obey."

Ian advanced on the table. His eyes blazed with the commanding authority he must have used on his ships. "I am not a chess piece for you to move about your board at whim. I am an officer of His Majesty's Royal Navy. I have a duty and a career—the career you picked out for me—to fulfill. And I will do so, no matter what you threaten. My duty and honor compel it."

"Duty. Honor." The viscount hammered out the words as if he were pounding them on an anvil. "You trot your duty and honor out whenever you don't want to do as you are told, like guard dogs for your will."

Ian leaned forward onto the table, and smiled like a pirate, armed to the teeth with elegant menace. "Mark *my* words. I will do whatever it will take to convince you that I am not your puppet. Nor is Ross."

"Ross? He is not *anything* anymore."

"He is alive, and he is your son, and my brother." Ian spoke as if his grief and anger were burning his mouth. "And if you cannot have some pity and compassion for him, then you are no father to me either." And with that final salvo, Ian threw himself from the room.

Anne immediately went to go to Ian, but her father followed her into the corridor so they might speak privately. "Anne? What goes on here?"

There was nothing to say but the truth. "The lieutenant told his father we were already married. I think he feared the viscount's interference."

"With good reason it seems." Her father rubbed his hand along his jaw. "They go at each other hammer and claw—two sides of the same tool."

"Yes," she admitted. "And I fear they will injure us all."

"Never you fear. Worth will see this out. He's a good lad, Anne. A good lad. That's more than I can say for most. I'll put my faith in Worth."

Chapter Thirteen

She found Ian, gone to cover in the kitchens, where Pinky—dressed in an outlandish getup—was handing him a mug of steaming coffee.

He raked his free hand through his hair in a now-familiar gesture of rumpled frustration. "I'm sorry that you had to witness that, Anne. I'm used to my father's vile demeanor, but I dread inflicting him upon others."

"It cannot be helped. As you said, you cannot order the weather."

"More's the pity." He took several scalding gulps, and turned his keen blue eyes on Pinky. The old cherub was wearing layer upon layer of clothing—a woolen coat over a knitted jumper, with several scarves swathed around his neck, and topped off by a bright crocheted scarf that he had knotted on top of his head. Anne had never seen the like of it in her life.

But Ian did not bat an eye. "Now where do you go in

such a sartorially resplendent, top-man's getup, Pinky? Is the well frozen over?"

"No, cap'n, sir. Not a'tall. The well is in fine shape, it is. I'm bound for the wood, to fetch in a yule log. I've my eye on a good one, I have. I just hope I've the strength for it. I'm not so young as I once was, you know," he said in a confidential aside, as if it were fresh news. "But I suppose I can rouse those lazy coachmen from their naps if the snow proves to be too deep."

A low chuckle rumbled out of Ian. "You needn't try to cozen me with your mock innocent looks, Pinky. I'm onto you. I know when I'm being bamboozled into doing something. And God knows I could use some air after being in the same room as my father. Just let me get my seaboots and coat, and I'll be ready presently."

"Oh, aye, sir! I could certainly do with your good strong help. That I could," Pinky said with great satisfaction, before he turned his hopeful cherubic charm upon her. "And you, mistress? I could do with your eye as well. Perhaps gathering some holly and ivy to put along the mantelpieces? It would make the old place powerful pretty for the yule."

Ian's smile was an even more powerful charm. "What say you, Anne? Would you like to bundle yourself up for an afternoon in the snow? We've nothing else to do but avoid my father."

Relief and pleasure made her nearly giddy. "Yes, please." She would have begged him to include her, had he not asked. Because another plan—an alternative set of words—was wheeling and swooping about her brain. "I should very much like that."

It was no more than a few hundred yards to the wood. Ian led the way, trudging a path through the deep snow for Anne to follow, but it felt good to be out and moving, doing. He could think better when he was out in the bracing air.

And he could look at the revelation that was Anne. Out-of-doors she was an entirely different creature than even the shyly happy girl of the corridor in her wine-punch gown. Though she was dressed for the cold with her thick country cloak over a nondescript wool redingote that could only be considered the last stage of fashion, she glowed.

The cold painted her skin a luminous milky white, and her cheeks a delicious rosy pink. The light reflected from the snow illuminated her hair beneath the hood, gilding the brown with warm shades of cinnamon and amber spice. But it was her voice that brought him to a standstill in the snow.

Once in the wood, they had wandered slightly apart—Ian to hewing Pinky's chosen log down to a size to fit into the hearth, and Anne and Pinky to strip ivy from the trunks and trailing branches of trees. And Pinky, being Pinky and some sort of aged guardian angel, had started singing. At first it was only a throaty version of "God rest ye merry gentlemen," that Ian was sure could only end in a chorus of nautical yo-ho's.

But once they set to their assigned tasks, the sentimental old tar slipped into a quiet little rendition of "The Holly and the Ivy."

And in another moment or two, Anne's voice joined his. And Ian was nearly struck dumb. He had heard her in the glasshouse, but she had stopped so quickly, muting herself within his hearing. But today she did not hold back.

Pinky encouraged her, pitching his warm tenor to harmonize, and let her carry the melody. And as he raised his volume, so too did she.

"Oh, the holly and the ivy,
When they are both full grown,
Of all the trees that are in the wood,
The holly bears the crown."

The song rose, soaring slowly through the empty trees. Her voice was clear and bright, and so soft and intimate and powerful, it was angelic. When she sang, everything about her was clear and bright.

How had he ever thought her plain? He must be even more of a shallow, ramshackle bastard than even he had thought. Too shallow and ramshackle a fellow to deserve her.

But he had somehow earned her, and keep her he would. By hook or by Pinky's crook, which the old cherub leaned on heavily to make his way through the deep, wet snow with an armful of ivy.

"I'll just take these in for the mistress." Pinky toddled vaguely off in the direction of the house. Leaving them alone.

Alone with the idea Ian had been drawing up in his brain. His father had been crudely specific in his quest for Ian to get him another heir. But if he did beget that heir on Anne, then not even the Viscount Rainesford could gainsay the wedding.

And with both his invited and uninvited guests, including the coachmen, all at the house with Pinky—and most likely to be kept there by the canny old tar—the small carriage house was empty. The hayloft there would provide just enough comfort and warmth for the endeavor.

It wouldn't take much to get either of them so inclined—they had both been on fire for it last night. And in the bright, flat light reflecting off the snow, he would be able to see her, and look his fill, even in the dimness of the hayloft.

Ian paused with the axe resting in his hand. He would

peel back her cloak, and open her coat buttons, and untie her laces and fill his hands with her—

"Ian?" She was so close it startled him out of his daydream. "Are you all right?"

Apart from a rousing cockstand, thankfully hidden by both the long hem of his sea coat, and the fall of his breeches, he was. And to prove it he simply gathered her into his arms.

"I found some mistletoe, to bring the spirit of the spring into the house." Between their almost-touching bodies, she held up a tiny sprig of green. "It's an ancient country tradition. It would be powerful bad luck not to honor the spirit of the season."

He took the sprig from her hands, and threaded it through her hair. "And how do you think we ought best honor that spirit?"

"By kissing beneath it." She held tight to his coat sleeves, drawing herself nearer.

Ian nuzzled at her ear. "We ought not dishonor the spirit."

"No." Her words were nothing but breath and anticipation. Nothing but nascent want. "We'd best not."

"So." He kissed his way across her throat to the other ear. "I suppose that means that you'd like me to kiss you? On your lips?"

"I would be much obliged"—there was nothing left of her voice but a thin, taut string of breath—"if you would make it a good one."

"Oh, Miss Lesley, you *are* a clever, naughty girl to taunt me so. You have no idea how very, very much I like pert intelligence."

"I was hoping you would show me. And Ian?"

"Yes, my love?"

"I've been thinking." She tilted her head to the side, and gave him a small, rather shy smile that struck him as clear as a ship's bell. It was a winsome smile. In fact, it was *his* winsome smile, the smile he had tried to give her that first afternoon on the beach, to win her over.

Ian's gut tightened from something beyond hunger. "What of?"

"I might have chanced upon a solution. Your father seemed concerned with . . ." She took a steadying breath. "Making sure we had not fully . . ."

Hunger flooded his veins. But still he could think. And speak. "Consummated our bond?" he supplied.

"Yes. Consummated." She nodded, gingerly trying out the dangerous word. "What if we did? What if we did . . . do that and if I were to . . ."

"Get with child?"

She looked up, and finally met his gaze with eyes glowing with topaz hope. With desire. "Yes."

The word was like a rumble of thunder rolling through him—every part of his body vibrated with anticipatory heat. The rush of blood from his brain nearly made him stumble.

But he did not. He was sure-footed. And sure-handed. He was sure.

Ian picked her up in his arms and forged his way through the snow to the stable. He set her down on the threshold and followed her in, rubbing his hands together and clapping the snow off his boots to ward off the cold, damning himself for his impatience.

Ian felt his own body quicken and heat another ten degrees at just the sight of her, standing and looking at him with her innocent lust shining in her eyes. He would make it good for her.

He gifted her with his most disarming smile, furrowing his brow and tilting his head to starboard to tease her. "Are you sure, Anne Lesley? Are you quite sure you're ready for me to rend you asunder?"

Her voice held the whisper of a smile. "You said you would make love to me."

"And so I did. And so I shall." He stepped closer, and kissed her.

And fell under the spell of her wide, pliant lips and honeyed taste. He kissed her until he began to think of backing her against convenient stall walls and having his way with her there without bothering with the hayloft.

His lips were on her mouth, and his hands were in her hair. And he was finally, finally going to do exactly as he wanted. She was already kissing him back, already returning his heated, openmouthed kisses with a fervor all her own, and he felt himself falling into her softness and sweet, intense solemnity.

Ian saw it then—her beautifully refined passion he had mistaken for rage. It wasn't anger that had burned in her luminous brown eyes, it was passion—all the passion she must have denied herself for years. All the passionate thoughts and passionate feelings that had lived behind the wall of her tongue-tied shyness. Not just physical passion, but a passion for life, a passion for living, and living right. He saw all the life in her.

She wasn't a wren at all. He had been fooled by her camouflaging plumage. She was a small, nimble sparrow hawk—a small, swift, elegant falcon.

His kiss was everything he was—confident and brash and exuberant and strong. So strong and sure and powerful, she felt as if the strength of his hands along the line of her jaw was the only thing holding her up.

Because she couldn't feel her knees. She could only feel the rough, taut texture of his lips, and taste the tang of rum-laced coffee on his tongue. She could only hear the rush of his breathing, and smell the sharp, heated spice of his body. She could only understand that this, more than the hand-holding, or foot-rubbing, was at last *pleasure*.

So much pleasure it left her shaking—quaking like an aspen in the winter wind.

He wasn't shaken at all. He looked solid and sure, and in his right senses, as if he were well used to the powers of such pleasure—well used to the ride. But his voice had none of that surety. It was softer, blunted around the edges, as if he had taken a blow to the head and could not see straight. "My God, Anne."

She drew the pins from her hair slowly, one by one, for the first time not caring if she loosed a riot of curls springing from her hands, unladylike and untamed.

His sigh of satisfaction was very nearly a groan. "I like your hair down—I love it. I want to tangle my hands in it." He matched action to words, and set his hands drawing through her hair, tugging on her scalp sending streaks of warm, tingling sensation sliding deep into her belly and back out to surface just below her skin.

He was on her, around her, picking her up in his arms, slinging her legs around his waist while he walked into the harness room and set her upon an empty worktable there.

He leaned his forehead against hers, and looked at her with those fathomless blue eyes, as if he could see all the way through her. As if he could see who she really was inside—the passionate person she was in the privacy of her own head. The person she felt herself to be when she played the pianoforte. Clever and intelligent.

Not shy. Never again shy.

His fingers emboldened her to do the same, to spear her fingers through the short waves of his hair. To find the sensual delight for herself in the feel of the thick, glossy strands slipping through her hands, as well as to give him pleasure.

He kissed her again, pressing his height and his weight and his being upon her, giving her everything of him. His mouth was on hers, and his hands were around her back, and at the back of her neck, holding her to him, supporting her as kissed and kissed and kissed her.

Under his tutelage, her skin—the plain, ordinary covering of the body she had lived in for two and twenty years without noticing—now felt extraordinary. It felt sensitive, alive to every change within and without. Something fierce and finer than heat blossomed under the surface of her skin. "It feels like I'm new."

"You are new. We are new together."

His voice was low and heartfelt and sincere, and set off an answering, indecorous thudding of her heart within her chest.

He let go of her, leaning his hands onto the table on either side of her, hemming her in, tipping her back farther and farther. "Anne? Will you say my name?" he whispered against her lips.

She smiled, and breathed it out on an exhalation. "Lieutenant Worth."

"Anne."

She laid her lips alongside his ear. "Ian."

He put his hands on her shoulders, and slid them down her arms and around her waist, drawing her lightly against his chest. He pressed a kiss to the side of her neck. Heat and something more, something that must be longing, slid under her skin. "Say it again, Anne."

"Ian."

He kissed his way down the sensitive tendon below her ear, and her skin caught fire. He kissed her, hard and purposeful, holding nothing back. He kissed her with heat and passion, with tongue and teeth, and a hunger she was beginning to recognize in her own wants.

He was everything and everywhere, his hands at her

face and in her hair, holding her tight against him. He was everything she felt, the smooth probe of his tongue, the firm possession of his lips, the sharp edge of his teeth as he took her lower lip and worried it between his own. She felt the rough rasp of his morning beard against the sensitive skin of her neck and chest. He was everything heat and passion, and he was showing her how to be so.

He levered himself back so he could look at her, and turned his attention to her small breasts. "You are exquisite—perfectly rounded, made for my hand." He dragged his thumbs across the tightly furled peaks, until bliss was blossoming within, and she was arching her chest into his hands, letting her head fall back, and her eyes fall shut so she could not see, and could only feel. Blindly seeking pleasure and release.

He followed his hands with his mouth, and closed his lips around her sensitive nipple, licking and sucking her, sending shards of want and need and omnivorous hunger prowling deep into her belly. The sound of shocked surprise came from so deep inside her that it was barely audible by the time it winged its way out of her mouth.

Anne kept her eyes closed, and let her mind concentrate on the feeling of her body. Let herself feel the cool air as it made her nipples contract, and made the flesh along her belly pebble up with gooseflesh. She felt the pleasurable tension begin to snake through her body, and she wanted to move, to appease the strange need to feel more.

"Shh," he said as if sensing her need, stilling her with his words, making her quiver with anticipation when he stepped between her legs, and gently pried her knees apart as he kissed her again, diverting her attention with his clever tongue from the hand that reached down the side of her leg to drag up the hem of her skirts. And then his hands were back at her breasts, fondling her until heat and something else, something bright and shining budded to life within, teasing and swirling into her belly. Between her thighs, her body clenched into a pleasurable ache.

Which Ian seemed to understand. "Hold your skirts up for me, Anne. Please." His voice had gone to pieces, each word a shard of sharp urgency.

She hauled the material back tight against her waist, baring herself to him. She closed her eyes, and turned away.

"Open your eyes, Anne. Open your legs for me, please. Wider. Please, Anne. Yes."

She did open her eyes and followed his focused gaze to the tangle of dark curls at the apex of her thighs. Her body seemed to shift deep inside her, loosening a shaft of pleasure within.

She watched his hands come to rest upon the pale white skin of her thighs. "Anne." His voice brought her back to meet his gaze. "Tell me what you like. Tell me how you want to be touched."

"Yes." She wanted to—she wanted to meet him measure for measure in this dance of passion. She closed her eyes, and concentrated on the sensual tug of his hands against the sensitive flesh of her upper thighs.

"Yes." He gathered her to him, cradling her against his chest with his forehead resting against hers, as he watched his hand part her folds.

She felt open and vulnerable and wanting and waiting, and when he touched her she felt her muscles clench with delight. Pleasure, heavy addicting pleasure lapped up through her torso until she was arching toward him, trying to get closer to him, and closer still.

"Anne. Your sex is so soft and wet and warm and tight."

Anne had never heard the word used in such a way before, but she knew from the tone of his voice, from the heat and gravel of his words, what he meant.

He slid one long, articulate finger inside her, and a little ripple of delight radiated from her core, growing stronger, becoming a wave of sensation and heat that surged within her, making her gasp and pant with delight and want.

"Yes," he encouraged her. "I want to hear you. Do it again. Always so. quiet, so composed," he whispered, as he worked his hands under her skirts to cup her bottom and pull her closer to the edge of the table. And then he bent her backward to take the tight, needy peak of her breast between his lips.

She made a loud, inarticulate, animal sound at the shock and almost overwhelming pleasure that shot through her, streaking deep into her belly and radiating out to the very tips of her fingers.

"Oh, yes. That's it, Anne," he whispered, his breath harsh and strained at her ear. "I want to make you lose that calm, collected composure. I want to make you scream."

And the fierce feeling, the need that was so deep it was a rage, rose up in her. "Please, make me. Make me scream."

His head swooped down and captured the ruched peak of her straining breast roughly, abrading it with his teeth and sucking fiercely, just as he positioned himself at the opening of her body.

She could hear his breath now, coming in audible pants, as if breathing had begun to pain him. She planted the soles of her boots flat against the front of the table and pushed herself toward him, her hips bucking gently into the pressure of his hand.

Now it was he who made an inarticulate, harsh sound as he grappled the close of his breeches, working to free himself. "Easy, love," he gritted. "I need to—"

She needed, too. She needed him as bare and exposed as she. So she ripped away the confining screen of his waistcoat, and laid waste to the buttons of his linen shirt, in her haste to bare what she could of his chest. Her hands burned to touch him, to rove over the tight muscles of his chest and around to his back, and lower, to his sleek flanks, pushing down his breeches, using her feet and toes to shuck his buckskin breeches and small clothes from his tensed buttocks.

And still she needed more. She needed the blunt velvet probe of his body pushing its way into hers. She needed the strength of his hands, pulling her into him, holding her as he bore down into her body. And then he was inside her and around her, and filling the emptiness inside with his hungry, ravenous need.

She felt tight, and full, and unsatisfied, sure there was something more, more of the pleasure that built and built inside her like snow piling high upon a treetop—one small movement would send her crashing to the forest floor.

And then he touched her, there, where their bodies were joined, and it was too much effort to talk. It was far too much effort to think. She abandoned herself to his rhythm, driving her higher along with himself.

She could hear the gasps he wrenched from her with each nearly mindless stroke. "Please," she heard herself beg him. "Please."

He answered her by grasping her bottom and pulling her toward him, and she wrapped her legs around his waist, changing the angle of their bodies. The sound he made in response was nothing more than a growling howl. Above her, his face was shadowed, his hair falling forward over his brow, his lips parted even as his jaw was clamped closed. He looked so young and full of anguish, even as he gave her such pleasure.

She reached out to stroke his face, and he turned into her caress, and kissed and nipped her fingers, until she rubbed the sweet wetness of her finger over his tight, dark nipple. He cried out at the same moment, his head thrown back, his eyes closed, and she turned inward, letting the hot wave push through her. Her climax broke over her and she let go of the sound building in her throat, the high keening call of a falcon diving for its prey.

Chapter Fourteen

Christmas day dawned quietly. The slight chill in the quiet air, the hush of the slumbering house, and the harsh blue-bright edges of light seeping around the curtains told Ian it was full morning.

Beside him, Anne slept on, her hair spread across the pillows, messy and undone. She looked like some sort of angelic urchin. They had snuck back into the house late, in the early evening, when the slate twilight had already fallen on the cover of still-falling snow. And once they were above stairs, they had not wanted to part. They had slept still-clothed upon the counterpane, with Ian's sea coat for a blanket.

Something sharp and pleasurable, and not altogether peaceful, filled him at the sight of her—the guilt and re-membrance of what they had done in the quiet hours of the night, and what they had yet to do.

They had yet to marry.

They had yet to find a way around the inconvenient

weather, or the even-more-inconvenient Viscount Rainesford.

Ian drew in a deep breath, and was contented when Anne snuggled closer. He would be happy if they could simply pass the day in peace, avoiding the old man and his directives, without doing anything more interesting than making a quiet toast around the burning yule log Pinky was sure to have hoisted inside. And giving Anne a lovely, long kiss underneath her sprig of mistletoe.

And then Ian's ears picked up a new sound. Outside the window the chatter of winter birds—cardinals and sparrows—and the quiet drip of snow melting from eaves and the branches of trees, meant the storm had passed and the snow had stopped falling. The roads would be clearing.

No sooner had he formed the thought, than the bells of the village church began to toll in the distance.

"Anne. Wake up." Ian surged out of bed, his feet bare and cold, not giving a damn. They had to be up.

"Wake up." He came back to the bed, and began to kiss and shake her awake. "Do you hear that? Church bells. The church bells in the village calling us to worship. So that's what we're going to do. We're going to get married. Right now. Before anyone else arises. Even if it takes us all day to wade through the snow."

That brought her bolt upright on the bed. And then she smiled. A slow, spreading smile that lit her face like a rosy dawn. He was all but slain by her sweetness. "I'll get my boots."

They snuck down the creaking service stairs at the back of the house like thieves, only to find Pinky up and bustling about the kitchen.

"Mornin', cap'n." The old cherub bobbed his head. "Mistress."

"You haven't seen us, Pinky," Ian instructed. "If my

father is so rude as to inquire after my whereabouts, you may tell him I've gone to the devil."

"Ha ha! Not to the devil today, though, sir? Somewheres else entirely today?"

"No, Pinky, not today. Wish us luck."

"I wish you more than luck, sir—I wish you happy. But mistress, wait." Pinky shambled away, but less than a minute later he was back with a tiny bundle of cloth that he handed to Anne. "That's for you now, mistress, so everything's proper for the luck."

"Thank you, Pinky."

Ian pulled Anne through the door. "No time to tarry, Pinky. Mum's the word."

"Aye, aye, cap'n. But mind you see here—I've got you out a sledge just big enough for the two of you. Right here outside the door. If you take the right turning at the end of the hedge, the path'll put you up at the top of Farmer Boscowan's hayfield. You ought to be able to slide down the hill, and come out on the other side of the churchyard."

"You're a wonder, Pinky. A bloody wonder."

They did exactly as the old tar instructed and in less than ten minutes, breathless and nearly giddy with delight, they were inside the church and knocking at the vestry door.

"Are you ready?" he asked as they stamped the cold from their feet.

She hesitated. "Will your father be very upset with you?"

"Yes. Serves him right. This is for us to choose, Anne. We can do whatever we want. We will do whatever you want. But I want you to stay with me always. Will you?"

"I will."

The poor, round-eyed young curate had probably never before seen anything so reeking of aristocracy as the special license Ian pulled out of the pocket of his blue uniform coat. But they must have looked presentable enough for the august document, for the curate did not, as Ian half expected, look back and forth between the two of them in a manner that might suggest disbelief or censure, but opened his prayer book, and set them to it.

In no time at all it was done, and Anne was Mrs. Lieutenant Worth. Or probably just Mrs. Worth. Not that it mattered. Nothing mattered, as long as she was with him. As long as she was his.

She looked like a bride—glowing and radiant. And happy, despite the lack of flowers or adornments. So happy she looked like she might come apart at her seams and melt into a warm wine-colored puddle in the snow.

"I am sorry it was not a grander affaire, with flowers and toasts—"

"But it was. Did you not see? Pinky made me a little nosegay of flowers. Ivy for endurance, rosemary for remembrance, and snowdrops for eternal hope. And all tied with a blue calico ribbon. So thoughtful. He must have known."

"I rather think he must have *hoped*. And he was not the only one with hopes." He kissed her then, right there on her lips, in front of God and all men.

Because she was *his* bride.

And it was a new day—Christmas day.

Last Christmas he had been pounding his way across the freezing North Sea with dispatches for the Admiralty. And maybe next year, or even tomorrow, he'd be doing the same thing. But this Christmas, he was happy, and happily married. All within three days.

It had been only three days since he had met his peregrine, his swift little falcon. It already seemed a lifetime. And with a sharp jolt of awareness that lanced through him, and shook him to his boots, Ian realized that he did not want to leave her.

There was still too much for them to learn, too much for them to talk about and share and decide. Too many hours he wanted to spend learning the hidden secrets of her body.

But the Admiralty could not wait. The business of duty could no longer be put off.

He laced his fingers with hers. "Anne, I've been thinking—About you. About leaving you here alone when I go back to sea."

"I'll be fine. And a two-month isn't that much time, is it? Not compared to other captains who have voyages of years."

"No. A two-month isn't too much time, but as it isn't that long, I wondered if you would consider coming with me?"

"To Portsmouth?"

"To Portsmouth, and beyond, aboard my ship. Come with me. Come live with me on my ship and sail with me."

She smiled her astonishment. "Do you really mean it?"

"Yes. I've decided I shan't go, unless you decide to come with me."

"You would give it up—your ship and your career? You would let your father have his way?"

"It would seem so. But as you seem so very good at opposing him, I wondered if you might take pity on me, and thwart him, if only for my sake."

"I should like only one thing better."

"And what is that?"

"To always be with you. To follow you to the ends of the earth if you will let me."

"I shall do more than let you—I shall insist. Come with me, Mrs. Worth. Let us go home. To our home, and wherever else we might choose to go. Where we shall have each other, always."

He pulled her close to walk slowly down the bright-shining, snow-covered lane. Anne tipped her head toward him, and laid her head against his chest, and began to sing.

The sweet clarity of her voice rang out across the fields like a bell, shining and bright.

"Good people all this Christmastide,
Consider well, and bear in mind
What our good God for us has done,
In sending His beloved Son.
With Mary holy we should pray
To God with love this Christmas day
In Bethlehem upon this morn
There was a blessed Messiah born."

He did indeed take the moment to consider the blessings of the day. And in that moment Ian Worth found something he never could have anticipated. True friendship. True understanding. True compatibility.

And something else a ramshackle fellow like himself had never thought to find. True love.

Epilogue

The letter came by express—galloped across the snowy fields and roads to reach them late that afternoon. The muffled clatter of horses' hooves on the hardpacked drive, and the pounding on the door pulled all of them—even his father, who had until then chosen to remain in chilly high dudgeon in his assigned chamber—away from the warmth of the yule log burning steadily in the drawing room grate.

Ian's hands began to shake the moment he recognized his mother's swirling hand. It could be nothing but bad news. There was no other explanation for the speed and expense of the express on Christmas day.

Pinky, God rest him, was there with a steadier hand, to pay out the coins into the cold gripped hands of the rider, and to steer him toward the stable with the promise of a warm meal and a hot fire in the kitchen once he had seen to his animal.

"What is it? What does it say?" His father would have

snatched the letter from Ian's paralyzed hands had not Anne taken charge.

"It is addressed to Ian, sir. To Lieutenant Ian Worth."

The direction steadied him. Surely there would have been some other indication in the address if what he feared were true. If Ross had passed away.

The thought—the very real possibility—was a pain so large Ian could not fathom how to breathe, or think, or open the letter as he knew he must.

"Let us go inside, out of the cold." Anne's voice, calm and sensible, directing their parents away from him. Giving him privacy.

Giving him time to do what he must.

Ian broke the seal and opened the missive.

The words, the looping hasty scrawl of his mother's news was nearly unintelligible. And then he saw it.

He has moved his toes.

Ian frantically went back to the beginning, and found them, the words he had longed for. The words he had almost despaired of ever seeing.

Inflammation of his spine has receded. Brought to consciousness. Reducing the reliance upon the laudanum. Believe he will recover.

"Ian?" Anne was at his elbow, her heart, her concern wide in her eyes.

"He lives." Cool air poured into his lungs. "He lives and recovers. My mother writes that he gets better, little by little every day."

"Thank God."

Ian would thank his mother before God, but he had no quarrel with the Almighty if his brother's recovery was the result. His lungs filled with blessed, clear air, and he felt almost light-headed, as if he would float away—the result, he reckoned, of the enormous weight of dread being lifted from his shoulders. And he had Anne to help him carry the burden. Loyal, steadfast Anne. "I should not be too happy just yet, my love."

She frowned at him, even as she smiled with her own relief. "Whyever not?"

"Because she bids us keep my father here, so he may not impede Ross's recovery with his malicious, managing ways."

She laughed. "He can stay here all winter, and into the spring, if it will make you happy."

"Then he shall. Because it will not matter if he is here, because you are going to come with me. Come with me upon the seas and be spared."

They had all, every last one of them, been spared.

It was—as he never could have believed—their very own Christmas miracle.

The miracle of life and love.

It Happened Under the Mistletoe

❄

Valerie Bowman

To Cerian Halford who introduced me
to a beautiful name I just had to use and to Candice
and Becky who love cake and cats,
perhaps in equal measure.

Chapter One

Hunted. That's what he was. Hunted like a fox. And just like a fox, he'd been forced to . . . run.

Oliver Townsende skidded across the perfectly polished marble floor in the foyer of Lord Medford's country house. He rounded the imposing column at the edge of the space and took off down the nearest corridor. Behind him, the slapping of slippers against the parquet floor indicated that his flight was not in vain. He was, indeed, still being chased.

He glanced to his right. By Jove, was that a cat hurrying alongside him? He resisted the urge to rub his eyes. He looked again. Yes. There was indeed a furry feline romping to his right. Medford owned a cat? And more importantly, who was the cat hoping to avoid? Surely not the same young lady?

Oliver smiled to himself as he continued his flight.

Why exactly had he agreed to attend Medford's Christmastide house party? Yes, he'd become friendly with Lord Perfect and his wife Kate in the last year since Kate had been acquitted of his cousin's murder. Oliver had inherited the dukedom, but he knew better than anyone how hunted he was in Society. He was an eligible young duke, for heaven's sake. Of course Medford's house party would be filled with young, eligible ladies with their hearts set upon becoming a duchess. Hence, the running.

Oliver and the cat rounded the bend in the hall, the slap of Lady Selina Kinsey's slippers still echoing somewhere behind them. She was gaining on him. He could hear it in the steady increase of the slaps. If he didn't know any better, he'd think the earl's daughter had picked up her skirts to run after him full tilt. This particular young woman had somehow caught him under a bough of mistletoe. She'd not so subtly demanded a kiss just before Oliver had unceremoniously ripped the offending plant from the door frame upon which it hung. Mumbling something about how he was quite certain Lady Medford had been looking for this particular bough, he'd taken off as quickly as his legs would carry him. Only to realize soon after that Lady Selina was not one to give up easily.

There was nothing left for it. He must find a way to gracefully leave this party. Lady Selina was only one of several young women who refused to take no for an answer. And their mamas? Those formidable matrons were even worse.

Oliver nearly slid past the next corner before he noticed the cat had stopped running and was sitting next to a small door inlaid in the wall, licking its paw as if it hadn't a care in the world. The glint of a brass door handle caught Oliver's eye. He examined the door. The silver closet! An excellent place to escape. Lady Selina would never think a duke would hide inside a silver closet. *Please don't let it be locked.*

He wrenched open the door with his unoccupied hand. Ah. Unlocked. Such luck. No doubt Medford's servants were too perfect to even consider stealing from the butler. Oliver skated inside the closet. The cat promptly followed him, twitching its tail proudly. Oliver shut the portal behind him, leaned against the solid wood with his empty palm (the other still clutching the mistletoe bough), and willed his breathing back to rights.

It was dark in the closet and a bit stuffy. It smelled like silver polish and the tang of metal. Not a bit of dust, however. Of course Lord Perfect wouldn't stand for a dusty silver closet.

"You'd best not meow and give me away, cat," he warned in a whisper. The cat, wherever he was, remained silent.

Oliver waited, holding his breath. The slap of slippers drew near, paused for a bit in the corridor outside, and then continued their slap-slap-slap, completely passing him by.

He expelled his breath. Excellent. He'd done it. Evaded Lady Selina. For now.

But it was only wise to wait a few more moments. Lady S was not one to be underestimated. She might swing back around and surprise him. No. He'd linger in the silver closet until he was absolutely certain he was entirely out of danger.

A small feminine cough behind him made Oliver's spine snap to attention. That was no cat. He spun on his heel. Was it possible that Lady Selina had somehow tricked him? Made her way into the silver closet through some other entrance? Or was this another potential future duchess? One who was perhaps a bit more clever than the Kinsey chit?

In the next moment, a candle burst to light not two

paces away. It illuminated a lovely female face. Dark hair and bright green eyes that blinked at him. A lady too, from what he could see of her clothing. He hadn't just stumbled upon the work of a maid assigned to the silver closet. He peered at her, studying her features. No. He hadn't met this particular young lady since he'd arrived at the party this morning. He was certain of it. He would have remembered *her*.

But he didn't have long to contemplate the matter.

"Let me guess," the beauty said, one dark eyebrow arched in the shadows. "Lady Selina?"

Oliver eyed the unknown woman carefully and then slowly nodded. He wasn't certain yet if she was friend or foe. For all he knew, this young woman was Lady Selina's cohort, there to flush him out so Lady S could find her prey once again.

"How did you know?" he asked.

The lovely brunette placed the candle on the sideboard next to her and slid easily off the cabinet upon which she'd been perched. She straightened her light green skirts with both hands and gave him a saucy smile. "I could tell by the whiff of desperation in the air."

Now *that* made Oliver laugh. When was the last time that had happened? Especially with a female anywhere near marriageable age. Young, beautiful women never made him laugh. They made him run.

"That pungent was it?" he asked, returning her infectious smile.

"I'm afraid so. I'm quite familiar with it unfortunately." She had the barest hint of an accent he couldn't quite place.

Oliver cocked a brow. What did that mean? "Familiar how?" He couldn't help himself. He had to ask.

She laughed, and the sound ran over his skin like a

brisk spring breeze. He felt it in his chest. Oliver shook his head. When had he ever been affected by a lady's laugh?

"Why do you think *I'm* hiding in this silver closet?" She winked at him.

He furrowed his brow. First of all, she was adorable when she winked and secondly, now that she mentioned it, it did seem odd, her hiding in the silver closet too. He wasn't about to be an arrogant boor and accuse her of waiting in here in hopes of running into *him* eventually. What *was* this pretty young lady doing in the silver closet?

"Why are you hiding?" he asked, curiosity riding him hard.

"For the same reason you are, I suspect," she answered, stepping past him to press her ear to the door. Her movement afforded Oliver a whiff of her perfume. Just a hint of the sweet scent of lilacs. Normally, he found women's perfume cloying, but this teased his senses.

He arched a brow. "You're hiding from Lady Selina as well?"

She turned back to face him, a smile on her lips. "No, not Lady Selina."

The cat, who had heretofore remained still, chose that particular moment to leap up to the cabinet and present his overly fluffy tail to Oliver.

"Is this your cat?" the young woman asked, rubbing the cat on his head.

"No. I'm not particularly fond of cats to be honest. I have no idea where this one came from. He must belong to Medford."

The young lady picked up the cat and examined him. "Er, *she* must belong to Medford," she corrected. "And it's funny. Kate never mentioned a cat to me."

"This cat and I found ourselves running together and when it came time to hide, I wasn't about to shut her out."

He grinned at the young lady. "But you never answered my question. Whom were you hiding from?" Perhaps her mother was overly solicitous. God knew most mothers were.

She deposited the cat back upon the cabinet and rubbed her head again. The feline shamelessly purred. "Lord Esterbrooke," the young lady replied simply, counting off on her fingers. "Lord Dashford. Lord Meriwether. Oh, and Sir Gilliam."

Oliver blinked. Esterbrooke, Dashford, Meriwether, and Gilliam? All decent blokes, to the one, well, except for Gilliam; he was a bore. But they were all also exceedingly eligible and exceedingly titled. Did this young lady mean to imply that she was being courted by these men and meant to avoid them? Whatever for?

He narrowed his eyes on her. He didn't recognize her, and he'd been introduced to every single eligible young woman in London. Was it possible this young lady had been hiding in Oxfordshire this entire time? He needed to come out to the country more often.

The beauty sighed and crossed her arms over her chest, offering, "You see, my cousin Lady Medford invited me to this party. She told my mama there would be eligible young men here. And she's correct. The problem is that I am uninterested in them."

Well, that was a first. He'd never met a young woman who was uninterested in securing a good match. In fact, he *only* met young women who were interested in securing a good match. Oliver blinked at her. "You don't wish to marry, Miss . . . ?"

"Blake, Cerian Blake."

Cerian. What an intriguing name. He'd never heard anything like it.

"Not particularly, Mr. . . . ?"

"Townsende, Oliver Townsende." Oliver couldn't help

himself. He couldn't bear to introduce himself to this young lady as the Duke of Markingham. She proclaimed to be uninterested in titles but what if she was bluffing? He couldn't stand to see her eyes light up at the mention of the title. Everyone in town knew he was a newly minted duke and an eligible one to boot. Yes, she might recognize the name but he wasn't about to piece it together for her.

"What about you, Mr. Townsende?" she asked, the hint of a smile playing around her soft pink lips. "Do you have an objection to all young ladies or is it just Lady Selina you seek to avoid?"

He smiled at that. She was funny, this Miss Blake.

"I'm a bit . . . popular at the moment," he allowed. "Sounds as if you are, as well."

The edge of her mouth quirked up. "If you're so popular, why are you carrying around your own mistletoe bough? Doesn't seem prudent for someone who proclaims to want to be left alone."

Oliver looked at her twice. He nearly opened his mouth to respond when he realized she was teasing him. Good thing, that. He couldn't very well tell her the tale of how he'd snatched the bough from the ceiling and ran. Too idiotic.

"It's a long story." He cleared his throat, suddenly wishing he could use the bough of mistletoe with her.

"The best stories always are," she said with another beautiful sigh. She scooped up the cat and set her on the floor before pressing an ear against the door again. Oliver had to concentrate on not looking at the lady's enticing backside poking toward him. He shifted uncomfortably on his feet and glanced away. The cat twined herself around his ankles, purring contentedly. That's all he needed, this cat to trip him. Leave him in a prone position for Lady Selina to pounce.

"It sounds as though we're safe," the lady offered. "I think we may be able to leave now."

An unexpected surge of disappointment rose in Oliver's chest. "You think?"

"Yes. Yes, I'm certain of it."

Oliver rocked back and forth on his heels, rolling the bough of mistletoe between his fingers. What exactly did one say to a gorgeous young woman to whom one had not been formally introduced yet with whom one had spent several minutes conversing while mutually hiding in a silver closet? Good day? Nice to have (sort of) met you? See you next time we're hiding from people?

Miss Blake didn't give him long to contemplate the matter. She whisked open the door, blowing out the candle as a result, and stuck her head into the corridor. She looked both ways. "All clear," she announced before turning back to him momentarily. The cat made her way toward the open door as well.

"Excellent," he said, not understanding the tug of disappointment in his middle at the prospect of the young lady leaving.

"Let's agree to pretend we've not met before, Mr. Townsende." She gave him a conspiratorial smile. "And then when Kate introduces us later, we shall play completely ignorant. That way, we won't have to explain our penchant for milling about in the silver closet."

Oliver pressed his lips together to keep from laughing. He liked Miss Blake's style. He liked it a great deal. This young lady was game enough to hide in a closet and flaunt propriety. Quite game was Miss Cerian Blake. Quite game, indeed.

"Agreed," he replied with a bow. "In the meantime, I wish you the best of luck avoiding eligible gentlemen."

"Oh, if only it were that simple." She gave him one last look over her shoulder. "Kate has already informed me that she intends to introduce me to yet another potential suitor this evening."

An unexpected bit of envy rankled in Oliver's middle. "Who's the unworthy chap?" he asked, wondering just how long the list of Miss Blake's suitors would be.

She rolled her eyes. "The Duke of Markingham. Can you imagine? A duke? Sounds like a dreadful bore to me."

And with that, she and the cat were gone.

Chapter Two

Cerian had to remind herself for the thousandth time to stop tapping her foot. It wasn't her fault her mama had forced her to stand here all done up in her pink ball gown, with diamonds twined through her hair, feeling like a deuced prize horse on parade, while Mama exchanged witty banter with their host. Lord Medford's country house was an imposing structure to begin with, but with its scores of rooms decorated for the holiday season, it was even more grand. Every room was draped with evergreen boughs, holly, ivy, hawthorn, and Christmas rose. The smell of cider floated through the air and the burning of logs in the many fireplaces gave the house a warm, cozy feel.

They were waiting in the drawing room before dinner. Many of the guests were mingling and laughing. Lord Medford was entertaining her and Mama with stories of his friends in London.

"I'm sorry you won't be able to meet Lord and Lady Colton and Lord and Lady Ashbourne," he said. "Both of

those ladies are well into their confinements with a new
marquis and a new earl on the way. They are expected to
deliver at any moment."

Cerian smiled at that. Kate had written to Cerian and
told her about her friends Lady Lily and Lady Annie. The
two women were sisters. They sounded quite nice and
had been good friends to Kate.

Kate? Where was Kate? Cerian glanced around the
drawing room. She wished her cousin would appear and
get the introductions over with so Cerian could smile
politely at the Duke of Markingham and then settle down
to the business of eating dinner. She was much more interested in the menu for tonight's meal than meeting her
first duke.

And hadn't Mama been all aflutter when Kate had announced that she would introduce Cerian to the man?
Mama's dream. To make the most advantageous match
for her daughter. It didn't matter that Cerian's dream was
oh, I don't know, to actually fall in love with the man who
she married. And one never fell in love with a duke. She
doubted it was possible. She had even imagined more
than once winging back through history and trying to
find a duchess who actually loved her duke. Oh, she supposed it may have happened, but it had to be extremely
rare. But she couldn't convince Mama that love was important. "You've been reading too many romantic novels,"
Mama would say. "And poetry."

The fact was that Cerian didn't belong here. She came
from a small village in Wales. Papa had worked hard and
made a fortune in the copper trade but even with their
riches, nothing could make up for their poor connections.
Well, they'd been poor until cousin Kate had written to
them. Seemed after a bad marriage—to a duke, no less—
that she didn't speak much about, Kate had wedded a viscount, and Mama, seizing the opportunity to receive entrée

into London Society at last, had written back posthaste fishing for an invitation.

Cerian remembered Kate as a beautiful, friendly spirit from her childhood. Their fathers were brothers, and now, Mama would do anything she could to use her cousin's connections to make an advantageous match for Cerian, even if she had to sweeten the pot with a large dowry.

So they had traveled to Oxfordshire for Kate's Christmastide house party. Mama had tested Cerian on etiquette and proper decorum for hours in the coach. It was clear that her mama intended her to come home with a betrothal well secured, and the duke, of course, was the biggest prize of them all. The devil may care about the man's disposition, humor, or looks. Why, the Duke of Markingham probably resembled a toad. Or perhaps he was angry and hateful like Kate's husband had reputedly been. Cerian wanted someone handsome, dashing, funny. Someone a bit like . . . Mr. Townsende from the silver closet this afternoon.

Now *that* man had been swoon-worthy. All tall, dark, and handsome. From what she'd been able to see of him at least. His broad shoulders filled out his jacket, his smile forced her to steady herself against the wall, and his cerulean blue eyes caused her to shake herself. Combine that with short, dark hair, a bold brow and chin, and a compelling sense of humor, and she was downright taken.

Of course, Mr. Townsende was probably someone's pauper cousin. He was a mere mister, after all. Not someone whom Mama would want her looking at twice. Oh, what did it matter? Mr. Townsende was already in high demand, it seemed, if Lady Selina Kinsey was after him. She'd only just met Lady Selina that morning but she could tell the young woman was entirely intent upon marriage. Or at least intent upon chasing handsome young men down the corridor, possibly with a cat in tow.

Cerian had her own troubles. Since Mama had apparently let it leak that she was the cousin of a viscountess with a large dowry, the gentlemen suitors had begun nipping at her heels like dogs on a hunt. It was ludicrous, actually, when one stopped to contemplate it. She'd only just been in London for the Christmastide Season and already Mama had a steady group of admirers at her door. Money, it seemed, attracted a certain group of men. Kate had promised that the house party would be full of eligibles, and so far that proved to be true. But Cerian had managed to live her twenty-two years in Wales, rejecting all advances that seemed monetarily motivated. She'd hoped to come to England to meet a man who cared about . . . her. The longer she was here, however, the more hopeless that particular goal seemed. The *ton*, as they called themselves, valued money and titles above all. Love wasn't high on the list if it was there at all.

Kate came floating into the room just then wearing a gorgeous ruby-red gown. She gave her husband a peck on the cheek and greeted Cerian's mama warmly. Then the viscountess turned to Cerian, her beautiful red-gold hair shining.

"Cerian, there you are." She hugged her cousin. "You're an absolute vision. I cannot wait to introduce you to the duke tonight." She leaned in with a conspiratorial whisper. "But just between the two of us, I fear Lady Selina has already set her cap for him. I doubt he's interested though. But she's already informed me that she's conceived a handful of house party games in order to facilitate the mingling of the eligibles. One can only imagine what she has planned."

Cerian widened her eyes. Good heavens, Lady Selina certainly was a bit man-crazy, wasn't she? She'd been chasing poor Mr. Townsende through the house earlier, and now she'd set her cap for the unwitting Duke of Markingham.

No matter. Lady Selina could have the stuffy old duke, and Cerian would take the dashing Mr. Townsende.

Cerian shook her head at that saucy notion and concentrated on listening to what her cousin was saying.

". . . unfortunately, we had to invite her because she's distantly related to James," Kate said. "And I've heard she's making a complete fool of herself in London over the duke. She did everything short of demand an invitation to the house party."

Cerian wrinkled her brow. "Are we still speaking of Lady Selina?"

Kate rolled her eyes. "Yes. A bit of stuff if you ask me. And her mother?" Kate shuddered. "A dreadful woman. I pray the duke has the sense to stay away from her. At any rate, once he sees you . . ."

Cerian winced. She hoped Kate didn't expect her to make a match with the duke. Her cousin clearly liked him a great deal, despite her own previous association with a duke, but as far as Cerian was concerned, a duke was hardly someone in whom she was interested.

"I met your cat this morning," Cerian offered in a bid to change the subject.

Kate blinked at her. "My what?"

"Your cat."

"I don't own a cat."

"Whose cat is she then?"

Kate shook her head. "To my knowledge there is no cat in this house. Perhaps one of the guests brought him."

"Not a him. She's a female and she's fluffy and gray and has pretty green eyes. She's exceedingly friendly and seems to like people a great deal. Acts something like a dog, this cat. I found her in the silver closet."

Kate's eyes widened. "I won't even ask what you were doing in the silver closet," her cousin said with a laugh.

The door to the drawing room swung open just then,

and Mr. Townsende stepped inside. Cerian sucked in her breath. If the man had been handsome in the dim light of the silver closet earlier, he was an absolute Adonis when illuminated by the drawing room's candle-filled chandelier. Wasn't there some way to convince Kate to introduce her to him instead of the Duke of Whoever?

"Ah, Oliver, there you are!" Kate's melodic voice drifted across the room.

Mr. Townsende looked over at them, a wide smile on his indecently handsome face. He made his way toward them, and Cerian's foot tapping increased exponentially. A nervous habit Mama detested. Oh, good grief. She couldn't stop it. She sounded like a woodpecker. Whatever would the dashing Mr. Townsende think of her? She gulped. *Ninny. Ninny. Ha' a penny.*

Mr. Townsende came to a stop in front of them and bowed decorously to Kate while taking her hand. He smelled like a combination of spice and soap. And he was even taller and more broad-shouldered than Cerian remembered.

"Oliver, may I present, my cousin, Miss Cerian Blake."

Cerian curtsied. Oh, good. She got to meet Mr. Townsende after all.

"And Miss Blake, may I present my friend, Oliver Townsende, the Duke of Markingham."

Chapter Three

If the dinner, which consisted of ten courses of some of the most beautiful food anyone had ever laid out in front of her, was delicious, Cerian would never know it. There was boar's head and turkey, marchpane, plum pudding, and gingerbread. Rows and rows of sweetmeats, roast and goose, and potatoes and squash. There were Brussels sprouts and carrots, eggs and pies, and raisins and lemons and apples and brandy. And it had all tasted like nothing to her mostly because she couldn't manage to swallow more than a bite or two.

Instead she sat far down the long dining table from Oliver Townsende, Duke of Markingham, and remembered every idiotic moment of their formal introduction, specifically just what sort of a fool she'd made of herself.

First of all, she must have looked as if she'd been about to swoon, because Kate had taken one look at her, eyes widened, and grabbed her arm to steady her. "Are you all right, Cerian?"

Cerian had nodded, vigorously. What else was she to do? Something inane like, "How do you do, your grace?" had somehow made it past the embarrassingly large lump in her throat, and then Mama had turned around. She and Lord Medford had joined the conversation. And if her own introduction to the duke had been mortifying, Mama's had been excruciating. Her mother made such a show of hanging on the man's every word, laughing too loudly, standing too close, and generally making a giant cake of herself. Oh, what the man must think of her and her mother.

Not that it mattered. A ridiculously handsome duke wasn't about to look twice at her at any rate. She was sought after for her dowry, something a duke certainly didn't need, and she was a mere Miss when all manner of ladies, including Lady Selina, were throwing themselves at him.

No. There was absolutely no chance of Cerian catching this particular nobleman's interest. Why, oh why, did she have to find him so . . . attractive? And why did he have to be a duke? Unfair that. Most unfair.

And there was another question. Why hadn't he told her who he was when they'd met in the silver closet? *Oh, Cerian, you ninny, no doubt it's because he knew you'd have jumped into his arms and kissed him.* She smiled at the thought. The man had been carrying mistletoe, hadn't he? Dangerous for a gentleman that handsome to have a bough of such a potent plant in his hands. No wonder he had ladies chasing him down the corridor. The cat had probably been chasing him too. Wise cat. Cerian pressed two fingers against her lips to keep from laughing.

Her dinner companion, Sir Gilliam, turned to her. "I say, Miss Blake. How're you finding the weather in Oxfordshire compared to that in Wales this time of year?"

"It's quite agreeable," she replied, halfheartedly pushing a cold bit of potato around her plate.

"I don't like it," the knight replied. "My gout is acting up quite a bit, not to mention the dryness of my skin. I hate to think how poor Aunt Margaret is doing in the North. She's up near Manchester, you know."

Cerian nodded sympathetically, but try as she might to focus on Sir Gilliam's lament about his aunt's aversion to inclement weather and his grandmama's latest attempt at a poultice for her skin ailments, Cerian's thoughts kept wandering back to Mr. Townsende.

Just how was it that Mr. Townsende was a duke and as handsome as he was? Weren't dukes supposed to be old and decrepit and gouty? Or completely arrogant louts? Yes. Gouty or louty. That was the way of it. It was completely unfair of him to be so good-looking. The man needed to wear a warning sign.

She glanced over to where Lady Selina Kinsey sat, batting her eyelashes at the duke. Oh, wasn't Lady Selina subtle?

For a moment, the duke's bright blue gaze caught Cerian's. She blushed and looked away. Why was she behaving like such a ninny? He hadn't been looking at her. It was random chance. No need for it to make her insides flip like a Christmas flapjack.

She turned back to the lovely plum pudding a footman had just placed in front of her. Oh, what a delight. She grabbed up her dessert spoon—she *hoped* it was the right spoon, there were far too many of them—and plunged it into the concoction. Yes. Sweets. Now this was a course she could readily enjoy. Much better to concentrate on her meal than her unsettling thoughts about the Duke of Markingham.

Oliver scoured the ballroom. After dinner, the dancing had commenced at the ball that was held to commemorate the beginning of the house party. Where was Miss

Blake? He didn't have long to find her. A handful of marriage-minded misses were already skirting around the sidelines clearly intent upon hunting him down. At the front of the room, Medford's butler intoned the names of guests arriving to the ballroom.

Oliver turned. There she was, standing in a group of admirers, her pretty pink gown hugging her curves in ways he shouldn't think about at the moment. Her bright green eyes shining and her dark hair piled atop her head.

Cerian. Miss Blake.

She'd given him a funny look when Kate had introduced them in the drawing room earlier and seemed as if she might actually swoon for a moment. Had he shocked her so thoroughly then? How would he explain exactly why he hadn't told her his title when he'd first met her? He didn't know, but he had to try.

Oliver stalked up to the group where she was standing. "Gentlemen, if you'll excuse me, I was hoping I might steal Miss Blake for a dance."

It was obvious that none of the men liked that idea one bit, but Oliver didn't wait for permission. He merely offered his arm to Cerian and said, "Miss Blake?"

To his everlasting relief, she put her gloved hand on his arm and allowed him to escort her to the middle of the floor. He whirled her into his arms as a waltz began to play.

She tipped her head back and looked up at him, an inscrutable expression on her breathtaking face.

"Thank you for agreeing to the dance." He smiled at her.

"Thank you for saving me from them." She motioned with her chin toward the group of gentlemen from which he'd just extracted her. The gentlemen in question shifted on their feet and gave Oliver narrowed-eyed glares. Sir Gilliam looked positively foiled. No, Oliver hadn't made any friends in that group stealing Miss Blake away, but he didn't give a bloody damn.

He cleared his throat. "I owe you an apology. I should have introduced myself properly in the silver closet."

That earned a laugh from her. Oliver beamed with pride. He'd made her laugh.

"Yes," she agreed. "You should have. But I suppose you can be forgiven. It was a bit of an unconventional situation. I mean it's not every day that I find myself hiding in a silver closet with a handsome duke carrying a bough of mistletoe and accompanied by a cat."

He grinned at her. "Did you just call me handsome?"

"Wh . . . ? What? No!" Her face turned the most adorable shade of pink, nearly matching her gown. She glanced away.

"Yes you did." His grin widened.

She bit her lip, still averting her eyes.

He pulled her closer. "It's not every day I find myself hiding in a silver closet with a lovely young lady."

"That I don't believe," she replied, giving him a saucy grin.

"Why not?" Was she trembling a bit? He was glad it was a waltz.

"I can imagine you're chased around quite a bit. That can't have been the first time you sought refuge in the silver closet."

He laughed out loud at that. "Oh, the silver closet is a favorite refuge of mine, Miss Blake. However, I am not usually accompanied by a lovely young woman and a bough of mistletoe."

"What about the cat?"

"Also a first for me."

Miss Blake wrinkled her nose. "That reminds me, Kate tells me that cat doesn't belong to her. She says there is no cat in this house."

He inclined his head. "There's a cat in here, all right. Whether it belongs to Lord and Lady Medford is a different issue."

"I've yet to see that cat again," Miss Blake replied. "I'd hoped to learn her name."

Oliver shrugged. "You'll have to ask around, I suppose."

"Oh, I do hope the cat doesn't belong to Lady Selina," Miss Blake said. "She's such a pretty cat. So well-mannered and friendly."

"And you don't believe such a cat would belong to Lady Selina?" he asked, a hint of a laugh in his voice.

Miss Blake gave him a look that could only be described as skeptical. "What do you think?"

He spun her around in the dance. "I have my doubts that the cat belongs to Lady Selina too."

"Speaking of Lady Selina, I don't see her here tonight. You may just have a bit of room to breathe. Though if those ladies giggling on the sidelines have anything to say about it, it looks as if you'll be quite busy this evening."

Oliver glanced over at the ladies eyeing him like a side of beef. "And what about your suitors?" he replied, arching a brow. "I could barely find you in that sea of evening coats."

Miss Blake's cheeks tinged pink again. "You were looking for me?"

Oliver spun her around again. "Merely making the point that this morning's episode couldn't have been your first time hiding in a silver closet either. You seem to be quite popular, Miss Blake."

The side of her mouth quirked up in a way that Oliver was coming to realize was uniquely her own; he still couldn't quite place her accent.

"Tell me, why are you so bent on avoiding young

women, your grace? Do you not intend to marry one day and beget an heir?"

She was straightforward, this young woman. He liked that about her.

"Ah, but I might ask you the same question, Miss Blake. Why are you so intent on avoiding *your* many suitors?"

She laughed at that and gave him a smile that he'd looked forward to. She lowered her voice to a whisper and glanced about. "I'll tell you why I avoid my suitors if you tell me why you avoid yours."

He nodded. "Agreed. You go first."

The butler continued to intone the names of the arriving guests and Oliver spun Miss Blake around and around in the dance. It seemed the young lady was an accomplished dancer indeed.

"Very well. But you must promise not to laugh," she said.

"I would never be so ungentlemanly."

She quirked a brow at him.

He smiled and blinked innocently. "What? You don't believe me?"

"I shall have your word," she insisted.

He shook his head lightly. "Very well. On my honor, I will not laugh. No matter how outlandish your answer."

She appeared satisfied with that and nodded. "It's because I refuse to settle."

Oliver raised both brows. "Hope Princess Caroline takes a nasty spill from a carriage and the Prince Regent becomes available, do you?"

She wrinkled her nose again and for the first time in his adult life, Oliver had to concentrate on the steps to a dance.

"No, no. I mean the opposite actually."

"The opposite?"

"Yes, you see, I am a romantic and I believe in falling in love. My mother is more concerned with a title but I"—she cleared her throat—"I'm more concerned with ensuring that I make a love match."

He narrowed his eyes on her. A woman unconcerned with titles? Such a woman existed? "And you don't think you'll find a love match with a gentleman of the *ton*?"

She smiled. "I suppose you could say I find it highly unlikely. The *ton* is filled with political ambition and the desire for wealth and power. I'm not interested in all of that. Besides, I'm from Wales. My father is a copper tradesman. There's nothing remarkable about me. I fear Mama is quite out of her element attempting to marry me off to the Quality."

Oliver begged to differ that there wasn't anything remarkable about her. She was remarkably pretty and remarkably funny to name two things. But her story interested him. And it explained her accent. "Wales? What brings you here then?"

She blew out a deep breath. "Mama. Well, Mama's letter to Kate. You see, Kate's my cousin, and she graciously invited us here for Christmastide. Mama saw her opportunity to trot me out in front of Society and here we are. I made my debut during the little Season just a few weeks ago in London. Kate was kind enough to sponsor me."

Ah, so that explained it. He'd been away on business at the coast the last few weeks. Miss Blake had only just arrived in England. "So, that's it? You refuse to consider a gentleman with a title?"

She smiled. "Refuse is a bit harsh. Let's just say I hold no expectations of such a thing happening. Now. I've told you my secret. It's your turn. And I promise not to laugh."

He quirked a brow at her. "Very well. My issue is quite the opposite of yours. I've realized that I should have married before I inherited my title."

"Why?" she asked, blinking rapidly at him.

Oliver sighed. "Because now I'll never know if my wife wants me for me or for my title. And between you and me, I think it's quite the latter with these young women I've been running from."

Cerian laughed then. She nearly had to stop dancing. "I'm so sorry. I don't mean to be rude, but it's just so . . . funny."

He couldn't help his smile. "It is a bit, isn't it?"

The dance ended then. Oliver reluctantly let go of her and bowed.

The butler's loud voice intoned the arrival of another guest. "Lady Selina Kinsey."

They both winced.

Chapter Four

The house party began the next morning with a late, lei-surely breakfast followed by a variety of equally leisurely activities enjoyed by the guests. Some sang songs along with the pianoforte in the music room, others engaged in painting watercolors in the conservatory, and Oliver found himself reading in the library.

He'd made an early night of it after Lady Selina had ar-rived at the ball. That determined young woman had made her way directly to his side and practically pounced on him. Miss Blake had deftly offered her excuses and left, while he'd been forced to claim a headache of all idiotic things in an effort to disentangle himself from the earl's daughter.

As a result, he'd gotten quite a good night's sleep, had woken up early this morning, and made his way to the library hours ago. He'd been caught up in re-reading *Much Ado About Nothing* when he glanced up to see Miss Blake curled up on a settee in the far corner of the room. Had she been there the whole time? No. Surely he would have noticed. He closed his book with a soft thud, stretched his legs in front of him, and stood. He'd just go over and say good morning.

Miss Blake gave him an enchanting smile when she looked up to see him approaching. She moved her legs off the settee and pushed a wayward dark curl behind her ear. Fetching, that.

"May I?" he motioned to the open space beside her.

"By all means," she answered, closing the book she'd been reading.

He sat beside her and gestured to the book. "What is it?"

She self-consciously turned it over in her lap. "Oh, it's . . . nothing."

"May I?" he asked again, reaching over and pulling the tome from her hands.

She glanced away.

He read the spine of the book. Shakespeare's *As You Like It.*

"I know; it's silly but I've always enjoyed his comedies," she began.

Oliver slipped the book he'd been carrying into her lap. She looked down at it and flipped it over. A smile lit her pretty face.

"You too?"

He nodded. "Guilty. I've never been one to enjoy a tragedy."

She laughed. The other occupants of the library looked up from their books and gave her a series of disapproving stares. She clapped her hand over her mouth and lowered her voice to a whisper. "I quite agree. It's so much more pleasant to read about Rosalind and Beatrice's antics then the melancholy Hamlet or the tragic Othello."

"I couldn't agree more. Tell me, Miss Blake, are you enjoying the house party?"

She smiled at him again, and Oliver felt a bit light-headed. Odd, that.

"I am," she said. "So far. At least I haven't been forced to hide in the silver closet again."

"I've managed to avoid that fate as well," he agreed with a grin.

"Of course," her voice remained low. "I haven't seen Sir Gilliam yet this morning. So I haven't completely ruled out a trip to the silver closet."

Oliver's smile widened. "You're most likely safe in here. Something tells me Sir Gilliam isn't much of a reader."

Cerian nodded in agreement. "What about Lady Selina? Have you been forced to dodge her this morning yet?"

"I have my doubts that Lady Selina rises before two in the afternoon. Makes one want to hop out of bed and start the day early, doesn't it?"

Cerian fluttered a hand lightly over his sleeve, play slapping at him. A few glances around the room told Oliver others had noticed. Miss Blake was innocent. And she obviously wasn't accustomed to the ways of the *ton*. In the *ton*, a lady touching a gentleman, even for a moment was the makings of a scandal or at least the start of a good gossip. He wondered if she did that a lot at home, touch young men she was flirting with. It made him a bit uncomfortable to think of her laughing and talking like this with another man.

"The irony is I'm on my way back to bed myself," she said.

He cleared his throat. "What's that?"

"Mama insists I take a nap every afternoon. She claims it's good for the complexion. I have my doubts." She stood and clutched her book against her chest.

She was wrong. Her complexion was flawless. "And do you? Take a nap, I mean?"

"Oh no. I read novels under the covers." She winked at him and his stomach flipped.

"Novels? No more Shakespeare?" he asked.

"Not at all." She gave him a conspiratorial grin. She glanced toward the door. "I'd better go or Mama will come looking for me. I live in fear of her causing a scene."

"Surely she wouldn't do that if she hopes to make a good match for you."

Miss Blake laughed. "You don't know Mama very well. She cannot help herself. She's a bit loud and . . . unconventional."

Oliver nodded toward the door. "Go, then, and if your Mama comes looking for you, I'll inform her that the last time I saw you, you were headed to bed intent on your beauty rest."

Was that a blush that lit her cheeks? The slight pink tint was captivating.

"Thank you, very kindly, your grace," she said with a laugh.

"Will I see you at dinner?"

"You will indeed," she replied. Then she turned in a swirl of bright yellow skirts and jauntily made her way from the library.

After Miss Blake left, Oliver stood and made his way back to the shelves where he replaced the copy of *Much Ado* and began half-interestedly looking about for something else to read. Perhaps he should try a novel. He smiled to himself and shook his head. He made his way around the large mahogany bookcases and found himself in the back of the room, obscured by an entire set of shelves. He'd been quietly perusing the selection there when a pair of voices drifted across the room to him.

"Did you see Markingham and that Blake girl?" said a woman's voice he didn't recognize.

"I did. Seemed to be quite friendly if you ask me," answered another woman's voice.

"Who'd have thought for a moment that those two would have an affinity for one another? Why it defies convention. I cannot believe it," the first voice replied.

"She may be a nobody from Wales but she's a pretty chit, you must allow that," the second voice answered.

Oliver had to nod.

"No doubt why the duke is interested," the first voice answered. "They appear to be courting."

Oliver nearly choked. Courting? Based on one conversation? Wasn't that just like two gossiping matrons of the *ton*, starting rumors out of thin air?

The second voice added, "If those two keep up their acquaintance for the duration of the house party, I fear there will be many a thwarted young woman and her mama here."

"You're absolutely right about that," the first voice replied.

The two matrons' conversation drifted away as they left the room, and Oliver rested a hand against the bookshelf next to him. He smiled and drummed his fingers along the wood. Hmmm. They didn't know it, but those two ladies had just given him a brilliant idea.

Chapter Five

Whist. Whist was the after-dinner amusement the ladies were participating in when the gentleman joined them after drinks.

Oliver's gaze scanned the room for Miss Blake. He was eager to tell her his plan. Well, eager for her reaction to it, that was. He'd found himself looking forward to their conversation all afternoon actually.

Luckily, Miss Blake was just tossing in her hand of cards on a table toward the back of the room when he spotted her. She was wearing a bright, pretty violet-colored gown, and her dark hair was piled atop her head, a few tendrils left to stroke her porcelain cheeks. He made his way over to her.

"Miss Blake?"

She glanced up and swallowed. Had he frightened her?

"Your grace?" she replied, glancing nervously around at the other ladies who were all watching him with adoring eyes. Bloody uncomfortable, that.

"May I have a word, Miss Blake?" he asked. Of course, such a display would do nothing to quell the rumors that they had an affinity for one another, but that was exactly what Oliver wanted.

Miss Blake stood and made her excuses.

He nearly dragged her into the corner he was so eager. He turned to face her. "I have a proposal for you."

She glanced over her shoulder as if she wondered if he were speaking to someone else. "A proposal? So soon? Why, your grace, you flatter me." She laughed and he gave her a sarcastic eyebrow raise.

"Not funny?" she asked.

He shook his head.

"Very well, then," she said. "What is this proposal of yours?"

He leaned a shoulder against the wall next to her, effectively blocking off the view to the rest of the drawing room. "I heard a rumor today. One that's going 'round the house party."

Her teeth tugged at her bottom lip. "Enjoy gossip, do you?"

She was relentless. He gave her another sarcastic eyebrow quirk. "Endlessly."

"Go on," she offered.

"The rumor is that you and I are courting."

Her mouth fell wide. "Pardon?"

"You and I are supposedly courting," he repeated.

She looked almost horrified. "And I suppose us being seen together over here in the corner talking quietly is not helping matters." She made a move to step around him, but he placed a hand on her arm. A sharp spark passed between them. She stepped back.

"Wait," he said. "Listen."

She looked a bit like a hare trapped by a fox but she stayed. "Yes?" Her breathing had increased and her chest rose and fell. It was distracting and he had to force himself to keep from looking at her enticing décolletage.

"I have an idea. One I hope you'll agree to."

She eyed him cautiously but she appeared intrigued. She crossed her arms over her chest. More distracting. "I'm listening."

"I was thinking about it. You're being pursued by unwanted gentlemen, correct?"

She nodded. "Correct."

"And I'm being pursued by unwanted ladies." He glanced back to the room at large where Lady Selina stood eagerly watching him. He turned back to face Miss Blake.

She nodded, a slight smile on her lips. She also eyed the lady who stood behind them. "Seems so," she agreed.

"What if we didn't want to stop the rumors?"

Her eyes narrowed on him. "I'm not entirely sure I follow."

"Perhaps we want to *encourage* them."

"Encourage them? What exactly are you saying, your grace?"

He kept a smile on his face. "I'm proposing that we pretend to be courting in an effort to keep our suitors at bay. For the remainder of the house party, that is. We'll be left alone, at least more so than we are at present."

Miss Blake's lovely green eyes momentarily clouded, but she appeared to be contemplating the matter. She bit the end of a fingernail. What she was thinking? The plan had merit, did it not? The more he considered it, the more merit he saw in it actually. The arrangement seemed perfect. He enjoyed her company and he believed she felt the same way. Not to mention, he was intrigued by her. More intrigued than he'd been with a young lady the entire time he'd been looking for a wife. She appeared to be the only woman he'd ever met who didn't give a toss that he was a duke. A rare quality to be certain.

But he couldn't tell what she was thinking. Couldn't tell, that was, until she smiled brightly and said, "Why, I think that is a perfect idea."

Cerian's stomach dropped. *A perfect idea?* Had she truly just told the handsome Duke of Markingham that their *pretending* to be courting was a perfect idea? It sounded awfully like she'd said such a thing but Cerian couldn't quite believe it. She pressed a hand to her throat. Perhaps she'd only imagined it.

"Excellent," he replied, letting out his breath. He couldn't possibly have been nervous, could he?

He glanced back over his shoulder most likely to see if they were being watched. When he returned his gaze to Cerian, she hoped she'd settled a calm look upon her face. A look that was the complete opposite of how she felt. It was true that if she agreed to the duke's proposal, she might have a bit of peace from Sir Gilliam and Lord Esterbrooke, but Mama would be devastated if she thought the Duke of Markingham had been in her grasp and she'd lost him. Which is exactly what Mama would think if they were to embark upon this farce.

She eyed the duke. He remained leaning against the wall, his booted feet crossed at the ankles. Cerian forgot to breathe. Instead she made a noise that was something between a wheeze and a cough. Most unladylike. She pressed a hand against her cheek. "I . . . um . . . that is to say . . . I'm not quite sure . . ."

"Don't tell me you don't think it will work," he continued, glancing over his shoulder once more. "It appears to be doing the trick already." He turned back to her and flashed a smile that made her brace her opposite hand against the wall to steady herself. She peeked around his shoulder. It appeared he was correct. In one corner, a few of Cerian's admirers were assembled, watching the two of them with ill-concealed irritation, while Lady Selina and a handful of other young ladies openly glared at them from the opposite side of the room.

Cerian ducked her head back and looked up into the duke's captivating blue eyes. "It appears you're correct. It does seem to be working."

He flashed a bright grin at her. "Does that mean you'll agree to it?"

Chapter Six

They'd all been playing draughts, innocently playing draughts, when Lady Selina suggested they change the game. Cerian should have known at the first indication of that young lady's pink cheeks and tittering laughter that something else was afoot. Of course it took her all of half a minute to realize what Lady Selina was up to.

"It's time for our first Christmastide game. Miss Cosgrove and I have hidden special boughs of mistletoe throughout the manor house. We shall each go on a hunt for them. When a lady finds a bough, she must kiss the first gentleman who happens along."

Cerian let out a breath. Draughts had been so much less dramatic. Why couldn't they simply continue to play nice, safe draughts? And kissing a gentleman who found you with a bough of mistletoe seemed a bit scandalous even for the fast Lady Selina. Where was that girl's mother? Hmm. Standing back while her daughter roped in a duke, no doubt.

Lady Selina's giggles were quite getting the best of her. Cerian briefly wondered if she would choke. But even that would interrupt her draughts game. There was no help for it. Either way she wasn't playing draughts anymore this afternoon.

"The gentlemen shall begin at the west end of the house and the ladies, the east," Lady Selina explained.

Cerian glanced over at the duke. He arched a dark brow and gave her a comical look that made her guess he was thinking exactly what she was, that Lady S didn't know her right from her left. Let alone the east from the west. This game was clearly set up.

Lady Selina was busily ushering everyone into two lines, one for gentlemen, the other for ladies. Cerian dutifully stepped into line behind the Davis twins. The poor young women looked horrified at the prospect of finding a bit of mistletoe and being forced to kiss a gentleman. Cerian leaned forward and whispered, "Remember ladies, just because you find it, needn't mean you must admit it." She smiled at them both and the two sisters exchanged relieved looks.

Cerian nodded. The gentlemen's queue was quickly forming to her right, and she glanced up to see Oliver step into line beside her. His grin was unrepentant. "Are you thinking what I'm thinking?" he asked, shoving both hands inside his pockets.

Cerian gave him a sideways smile. "That Lady Selina knows exactly where every sprig of mistletoe lies and intends to trap you with it like a hare?"

He coughed lightly into his hand, hiding a laugh. "Something like that."

"Yes, well, one can only wonder how she has worked out how to catch you first. I expect a catfight in the dining room within minutes."

Oliver shuddered. "I intend to stay far away from the dining room."

"So do I," Cerian agreed.

The queues moved then, as the ladies shuffled out the door to the left and the men, the right. Cerian swallowed a horrified giggle. "What'll I do if I find a bough?"

Oliver wore a frown on his face. He nodded toward Lord Esterbrooke and Sir Gilliam who were craning their necks to see Cerian. "I expect you'll have quite a bit of company," he warned.

Cerian wrinkled her nose. "Ugh."

She and Oliver were the next to part. They stepped toward the door and Oliver leaned over and whispered, "We might as well begin to put our plan into action. Meet me in the library. It's directly in the middle."

Plan? Into action? Oh, that's right. She had agreed to the duke's tempting offer, hadn't she?

Before Cerian had a chance to answer, Lady Selina quickly stepped between them and pointed in their respective directions while giving Oliver a bright smile. She completely ignored Cerian.

Cerian halfheartedly followed the Davis twins down the corridor until those two decided to take off into one of the drawing rooms. Cerian briefly considered sneaking up to her room to retrieve her book. Surely reading was a more noble pursuit than this outlandish game, but every time she remembered Oliver whispering 'meet me in the library', gooseflesh popped out along her arm. She quickly walked down the corridor in pursuit of that large room, taking the time to pause along the way in an attempt to pretend to be searching for the elusive sprigs of mistletoe.

The closer she got to the library, the more quickly she walked. She'd probably gone too fast. There were no young ladies behind her any longer and no gentlemen appeared to be approaching from the opposite direction. She was lost. That's what she was. She spun in a circle, completely unsure of the location of the library. She turned back in the direction in which she'd come.

Sitting in the middle of the corridor, staring at Cerian as if she hadn't just appeared out of nowhere, was the cat.

That same gray cat she'd met in the silver closet. Only this time, the cat had a sprig of holly tied loosely around her neck. Quite a jaunty Christmastide cat, Cerian had to admit.

She bent down and held out a hand. The cat walked directly toward her, passed her by, ignoring her hand, and kept walking, swishing her bushy tail as if to say, "Follow me." Cerian plunked her hands on her hips and watched the cat go. She'd never met such a bold cat. Cats, in her experience, were mostly concerned with staying out of the way and avoiding people they didn't know, this cat seemed to relish attention. She marched down the corridor. When the cat stopped about twenty paces away and turned back to give her a doleful look, Cerian realized the animal did indeed intend for her to follow.

Her brow furrowed and shaking her head, Cerian rapidly fell in line behind the cat. The feline plodded along, making three turns, bypassing several rooms, and finally coming to stop in front of two large ornately carved wooden doors. Cerian followed the entire way, though not without questioning her sanity for being led about by a household pet. Finally, she glanced up at the doors and blinked. The library. Why, that ever-so-helpful cat had led her directly to the library.

Cerian slipped through the doors holding her breath. The cat happily trotted in behind her. That cat was unique, no doubt about it. Cerian watched the animal prance past Oliver who was standing next to a large desk, his legs crossed at the ankles. The cat bobbed past him, the sprig of holly hugging her neck like a jolly little Christmas decoration.

Cerian looked up at Oliver. A brace of candles sat on the desk behind him and he appeared to be staring at something on the ceiling.

Cerian glanced up.

"Behold the errant mistletoe," he said with a laugh.

And there it was, fastened over the settee, hanging from the chandelier.

Cerian made her way over to where Oliver stood. "How did you know there would be mistletoe in here?"

"Merely an educated guess. Stood to reason since this is one of the first rooms both the ladies and the gentlemen will stumble upon together."

"Ah, so I expect we'll have company soon, then."

"No doubt," he replied.

Cerian twisted her fingers together and concentrated on keeping her foot from tapping. "'Twill be interesting to see who it is, actually."

He laughed at that.

"My money is on Lady Selina," Cerian added.

"I think that would be a safe bet, my dear Miss Blake."

Cerian swallowed. Ooh, the way he said, 'My dear Miss Blake' made her tingle inside.

She crossed her arms over her chest to quell her nerves and took a few steps over to the settee to stare up at the mistletoe. "Seems a bit of a letdown, really." She sighed. "The mistletoe wasn't the least bit difficult to find."

"I have a feeling the ladies in charge of this particular charade intended ease of locating the mistletoe to be of the utmost importance."

Cerian nodded. "No doubt."

"What should we do with it?" he asked, his question hanging in the air like the spicy scent of mulled wine. "Now that we've found it?"

For a moment Cerian wondered if he meant . . . If he meant . . . No, he couldn't mean *that*. Cerian gulped this time. Then she snapped her fingers. "We should hide it," she announced, a mischievous smile on her face.

"Hide it?" The duke blinked twice.

"Yes. Won't that be the most fun? Then when Lady Selina comes rushing in, we can pretend we know nothing about it."

He regarded her with something akin to admiration alight in his eyes. "Miss Blake, I like the way you think."

Cerian couldn't tamp down her answering smile. "Thank you, your grace." She executed a perfect sweeping curtsy. "Now if you'll just . . ." She righted herself and stepped upon the settee. "Help me up."

The duke offered her his hand, and she stepped up and reached for the bough of mistletoe. She pulled it down, tripped over her skirts, and fell into his arms, just as the door to the library opened and Lady Selina, Lord Esterbrooke, and Sir Gilliam came rushing inside.

Chapter Seven

Cerian's feet barely touched the ground, before the duke cleared his throat, straightened his shoulders, and announced to the room at large, "Miss Blake, I believe you owe me a kiss."

Her eyes wide, all she could do was stare at him, her heart thumping like an insane rabbit's foot in her chest. Her breathing hitched; the room spun. Did he really expect her to—?

The moment the duke's lips met hers, her head tipped back and she stumbled a bit. His arms went around her to hold her, steady her, and her hands went up to grasp at the lapels of his coat. His mouth continued to move over hers, so warm, so strong, so intoxicating. And then . . . .

Her lips parted. Had she done that on purpose? She groaned a bit in her throat. Had that been on purpose too? Then the duke's tongue slid in between her lips and she forgot to think. It was the most amazing feeling. She shuddered and grasped at him. She stood there, bent slightly backward over his strong, warm arm, lost in a sea of emotions she didn't even understand until someone—it had to have been Lady Selina—cleared her throat, loudly.

The duke pulled away, his mouth leaving Cerian's. He straightened her and steadied her and kept an arm at the small of her back while the two of them turned to face the small group of onlookers. Cerian glanced up. Her cheeks must be bright red. A few more of the gentlemen and ladies, including the Davis twins, entered the room. Oh no. Had they seen too? Was the entire house party a witness to her scandal?

"Yes, well, seems the two of you were overly enthusiastic about the game," Lady Selina said in a voice ripe with pique.

"Those were the rules, were they not?" the duke said with a charming smile. How could he be so nonchalant after . . . after   that kiss? Cerian felt as if she couldn't even stand up straight, let alone deliver witty repartee to their audience. Thank goodness for the duke and his quick wit. He'd made it out to be nothing more than part of the game. And yes, of course, that's what it had been, hadn't it? But Cerian couldn't stop thinking about the way his hot tongue had played inside her mouth. That hadn't been part of the game. It couldn't have been.

To their credit, Lord Esterbrooke and Sir Gilliam had glanced away and were busily examining paintings on the wall as if they hadn't seen anything, and the Davis twins, with all four cheeks a lovely shade of pale pink were doing their best to seem intently engaged in their own conversation. Something about cake.

"Have you seen the cat?" Cerian offered, but a quick scan of the room yielded no cat. The twins, who'd seemed interested at the mention of a cat, both quickly became disinterested once no feline was produced.

Meanwhile Lady Selina swept her bright blue skirts

into her hand. She arched a brow. "It seems the mistletoe has been found in this room, ladies," she said, ostensibly to the twins. "We might as well look elsewhere." And then they were off, all of the other occupants of the room including the two other men. The twins hurried after them as if they were unwilling to stay in the same room with Cerian and the duke.

Cerian couldn't look at him. She could only stare at the tips of her slippers barely visible beneath the hem of her gown. "I should . . . It's time for . . . Mama will be waiting." She curtsied quickly, excused herself, and hurriedly made her way through the door.

Cerian rushed upstairs to her room as fast as her legs would carry her. She'd never been so glad of Mama's afternoon nap rule. She couldn't breathe. Her mind kept replaying the moment in the library when the Duke of Markingham—no, Oliver—had kissed her. The firm pressure of his mouth. The nervous anticipation in her belly. And then, the feel of his tongue sliding across her closed lips and the moment her lips had parted just barely, barely and then . . .

Ooh, she just couldn't think about it. She pressed a hand against her roiling middle and took several deep breaths. Her maid came running up to her. "Let me help you out of your morning dress, Miss."

"Yes, thank you," she breathed.

Several minutes later, once Cerian was settled into bed in her shift, she still couldn't relax. She snuggled under the covers and closed her eyes, intent on actually falling asleep for once. She counted ten. Nothing. Twenty more. Unsuccessful. Fifty. No results. She squeezed her eyes shut and wrinkled her nose. *Sleep. Sleep. Sleep.*

But instead of fat little sheep jumping over a fence, all she could conjure was Oliver Townsende's strong hands on her arms, pulling her closer, and his mouth lowering to hers.

Lady Selina had been shocked no doubt. As were the other occupants of the drawing room. And the looks on their faces when he'd said she owed him a kiss. Why, it was without a price.

Mama bustled into the room just then. And Cerian squeezed her eyes shut more tightly, hoping Mama would leave her alone if she believed her to be asleep. Of course, that was too much to ask.

"Cerian. Cerian, my dear. Wake up."

Reluctantly, Cerian pulled the coverlet away from her head. "Yes, Mama?"

But she knew exactly what her mama would say even before she said it. Mama came hurrying over and sat on the edge of the bed, jostling her. "My dear, you are the talk of the party, and I could not be more proud."

"Proud?" Of course she was proud. For once her daughter had chosen the most eligible, titled man in the room.

"The Duke of Markingham appears to be quite taken with you, dear. You've done so well. Oh, just imagine . . . a duchess in the family. Mrs. Halifax will be so jealous and I cannot wait to—"

A twinge of guilt tugged at Cerian. "Mama. Please don't get your heart set upon—"

"Perhaps we'll have a spring wedding. Yes. Yes. Early spring." Did Mama just wink at her?

Cerian shook her head. "Truly, Mama, it was only a Yuletide frivolity. I do not think—"

But Mama wasn't listening. She already had that far-off look in her eye. She stood and made her way back to the door. "Yes. Yes. Spring. You rest now, dear. Must get your beauty sleep for the dancing tonight."

Her mother left the room humming to herself. Cerian

winced. She should have thought the entire thing through a bit better. She hadn't exactly considering getting Mama's hopes up quite so high when she'd agreed to Oliver's proposal. And now, oh, Mama would never recover from the disappointment once she learned that the duke had absolutely no intention of proposing. Why exactly had she believed this was a good idea, again?

Cerian rubbed her temples. When had this all become so complicated? She didn't want to hurt her mama. Truly, she didn't. She and Mama just didn't quite see eye to eye on the issue of marriage. Mama had wed a copper tradesman, not expecting to rise to any greater heights socially, and then when Papa's business had done so well, that combined with Cerian's first cousin turning into a duchess and then a viscountess . . . well, it had all been too much for Mama to ignore. She truly thought she was doing right by her daughter by attempting to make an advantageous Society match. It wasn't Mama's fault that Cerian was horribly frightened and intimidated by the idea of having a title in front of her name. The scrutiny, the responsibility. It was all too much for her. Cerian didn't know how to behave in front of these beautiful perfect people. She was much more comfortable hiding in a silver closet with the Christmas cat.

For some reason, Mama had allowed her to remain unmarried in Wales. Perhaps she'd always hoped Cerian would make it to London Society. Oh, Cerian didn't know. All she knew was that Mama was now hell-bent on securing the best match possible and Cerian had gone and got her hopes up to ridiculous heights by agreeing to the Duke of Markingham's little game. Oh, she wouldn't blame Mama if she disowned her when this was all over. And where was Papa? Safely back in Wales happily working while his wife and daughter pretended to be a part of the London winter Season, that's where he was. She envied Papa at the moment.

Groaning, Cerian slunk back under the covers and squeezed her eyes shut again. The image of his grace's captivating blue eyes haunted her until she fell into a fitful slumber.

Oliver went outside. Straight outside. Out onto the balcony. He needed a blast of cold air. Freezing cold air to cool the ardor his supposedly innocent kiss with Miss Blake had caused.

He counted ten. He counted twenty.

Still not working.

He hadn't brought a coat. The icy wind blew across his exposed skin. He braced his hands along the frosty balustrade in front of him and stared off across the barren winter landscape. What the deuce had that been about?

He'd kissed Miss Blake. Kissed her a bit too long and far too enthusiastically. And now he was suffering for it. It was true that they'd planned this, this supposed courtship, and it had come as no surprise to him when they'd been discovered under the mistletoe. No, that had all gone quite according to plan. What had *not* gone according to plan, however, was his reaction to her simple kiss. And the fact that he was beginning to actually like Miss Blake. Like her quite a bit. Even more disconcerting?

He thought about her a bit too often.

Chapter Eight

He was waiting for her when she came out of the retiring room. Cerian glanced over both shoulders, convinced that the oh-so-handsome Duke of Markingham was *not* standing in the corridor in his formal black evening attire waiting to speak with *her.*

"Miss Blake," he said, confirming what she'd already suspected when she'd realized no one was behind her. The oh-so-handsome Duke of Markingham *was* standing in the corridor in his formal black evening attire waiting for her.

"Your grace." Did she look a fright in her golden evening gown that Mama had insisted brought out the flecks of color in her eyes? Oh, she knew she wasn't hideous. Enough gentlemen had made unwanted overtures for her to be somewhat assured of the fact that she possessed a modicum of good looks. But she was still far from a beauty. She was no Lady Selina and the duke had been actively *hiding* from that lady. There was very little hope he was actually attracted to Cerian. Why, the man was in search of a duchess for goodness sake, a gorgeous incomparable, not a nobody from Wales who merely had a bit of coin jingling in her pockets.

"I had hoped you'd allow me to escort you to the drawing room so I might have a word with you," he added.

Cerian pasted a smile on her face, but her insides fell. After their kiss that afternoon, she hadn't quite known how to treat him or how he would treat her, but a talk wasn't exactly what she'd expected. If he wanted to talk, however, so be it.

"I'd like that very much," she replied, wondering if that were true. It depended upon what he said.

He offered his arm and she slipped her hand around it, marveling at the strong warmth emanating from beneath his dinner jacket.

Cerian concentrated on watching her golden slippers move along the parquet as they made their way to the dining room.

"Seems the entire house party is talking about us," he began.

She pursed her lips. "No doubt they're agog at our antics."

He nodded.

"It is what we wanted, after all," she pointed out.

"Indeed."

He opened his mouth to speak, then closed it again. Then he repeated both actions. Twice.

"Your grace?" she prompted.

"Forgive me, Miss Blake, but I seem to find myself in a singularly unique position this evening."

She cleared her throat slightly, and they began walking again. "How so, your grace?"

He cracked a smile. "Because I feel as if I ought to

apologize to you and beg your forgiveness for my behavior earlier today in the library."

Cerian's face went hot. She pressed her free hand to her cheek. "Oh, there's no need to—"

"But, the problem is I don't feel sorry for it. The truth is, I rather enjoyed it."

Now her face was on fire. Of all the things he might have said to her on the way to the dining room, this had certainly not been one Cerian had imagined. Not at all. "You . . . you enjoyed it, your grace?" She concentrated twice as intently on not tripping.

"I did indeed." He had a look on his face that could only be described as devilish. "So, I'll ask you, Miss Blake. Do you *want* an apology from me? I'll certainly offer you one if you'd like."

Cerian took a deep breath. Asking her if she wanted an apology was tantamount to asking her if . . .

"I find myself wondering, Miss Blake, if you enjoyed our kiss as much as I did."

Cerian had no earthly idea how she made it into the dining room and back to her seat without breaking into a fit of hysterical laughter or crying or both. She was mad, that's what she was. She had to be mad or she wouldn't have stopped the Duke of Markingham in the corridor a moment ago, turned to him, looked him in the eye and said, "Actually, your grace, I quite enjoyed it."

What manner of saucy hoyden had she become? Why, Mama would wash her mouth with soap. Well, perhaps not, given that an eligible duke was involved, but Mama should. And Cerian hadn't felt a bit repentant of her words either. Instead, she'd given Oliver a sultry look over her shoulder and preceded him into the dining room.

What form of madness had overtaken her? Perhaps it

was some sort of Yuletide fever. Such a thing was possible, was it not? Perhaps that cat was infected with it, like the fleas carrying the bubonic plague. Oh, Cerian didn't know. All she knew for certain was . . . she *would* not, *could* not, fall in love with a duke!

Chapter Nine

Oliver sprawled across the divan in Medford's study.

"How are you holding up, old chap?" Medford asked, crossing over to the sideboard and pouring a drink. His big yellow dog, Themis, leaped up from the rug beside the fireplace and followed him. "Brandy?"

"It's barely noon."

"It's Christmastide."

"And it's not like you to drink," Oliver added, an eyebrow arched.

"Ah, I've been doing many things that aren't like me since I married Kate."

Oliver had to smile at that. It was true and the entire *ton* knew it. Lord Perfect had let down his infamous guard and strict set of rules since marrying the most scandalous widow of the season last year. Medford crossed back over the thick carpet and handed Oliver a drink, which he took with a nod of his head.

"I suppose there's no sense allowing perfectly good

brandy to go to waste," Oliver said. "By the by, when did you get a cat?"

Medford gave him a look that clearly indicated he wondered if Oliver had gone temporarily mad. "I don't own a cat."

The door to the study opened just then and Kate flew in, a mass of red-gold hair and emerald green skirts. "There you two are."

Kate dashed over to her husband's side and kissed the cheek he lowered for her. "Darling, I've just approved the final menus and Lady Selina insists upon another game after dinner." Kate rolled her eyes.

Medford lovingly trailed his fingers down his wife's arm. "I was just asking Townsende here how he's holding up."

Oliver raised both brows. "Here now. What's Lady Selina's game got to do with me?"

"Oh, give over, Oliver," Kate said. "You know Lady Selina is doing all this in an effort to catch your attention."

Oliver wrinkled his nose. Cerian had taught him that.

"And?" Kate asked, a sideways smile on her lips. "Has she succeeded?"

"Lady Selina?" Oliver snorted. "Hardly."

Kate plunked her hands on her hips and gave him a matter-of-fact look. "She seems to be quite smitten with you."

Oliver groaned. "I was forced to take refuge from that chit in the silver closet my first day here."

Kate's eyes went wide. "You did not!"

"Upon my honor, I did. Was in there nearly a quarter hour," Oliver added. *And met the most lovely young lady as a result.*

Medford let out a bark of laughter. "Now *that's* a first. A duke hiding in the silver closet."

"Next time, I'll most likely be hiding under the carpet in the foyer."

"Oh, come now, Oliver, she's not that bad, is she?" Kate asked.

"Let's just say, I'm not interested in any more of her games," Oliver replied.

Kate lowered herself into the rosewood chair that sat at odd angles across from Oliver. "Very well, if Lady Selina hasn't caught your fancy, tell me, has anyone here done so? There is a score of lovely young ladies here. I was quite hoping you'd meet someone you got on with."

A vision of dark hair and flashing green eyes danced in Oliver's mind. "I . . . I hadn't exactly . . . I don't know," he finished lamely.

Kate gave him a sideways smile. "What about . . . my cousin, Cerian?"

Oliver nearly choked on the brandy he'd just swallowed.

"The rumor is that you two are enamored of one another. Any truth to that?" Kate pushed, fluttering her eyelashes at him.

Oliver scrubbed his fingers through his hair with his free hand. "Miss Blake is lovely and accomplished. She's also quite intent upon marrying for love."

Kate's eyebrows shot up. "Is she now? She said that?"

"We—ahem—have a few things in common. It seems Miss Blake is being as ruthlessly hunted as I."

Medford nodded. "So you decided to team up, did you, and distract the suitors on both sides?"

Oliver nodded. "Precisely."

This time Kate's jaw dropped open. "You did not!"

Oliver stared at his glass and winced. "Guilty, I'm afraid."

"And whose idea was that?" she asked.

"Mine," he admitted, downing a hefty swallow of brandy this time.

Medford slapped his knee. "By God, I wish I'd have thought of that back when I was eligible."

Kate shot her husband a disbelieving look. "James, you cannot be serious."

Medford patted his dog on the head. "Why not? It's brilliant if you ask me."

Oliver hid his smile behind his glass when Kate turned back to face him.

"Is that why you and Miss Blake were in the library with the mistletoe? It was all an act?" Kate asked.

Oliver hesitated. No, he wouldn't call it an act. Especially his body's instant reaction to Cerian's kiss. There had been nothing false about that. But he wasn't about to admit that to Kate. "Sorry to disappoint you, but Miss Blake and I have formed a partnership of sorts."

Kate shook her head. "And here I thought you'd find someone to marry at this house party. You're only the new hope of the Markingham name. God knows George and I weren't going to have children."

"And don't I feel every bit of my obligation?" Oliver replied with a sigh. "Starting with restoring the family name."

Kate winced. "I'm sorry, Oliver. I know how trapped you must feel. Still, I did so hope you'd find someone here at the party. It's part of the reason I planned it. I'm trying to help."

Oliver lifted his glass to her. "I appreciate it, Kate, I truly do, but I'm not certain you can help."

"Very well. But, please have a care for Cerian's reputation, Oliver. She is my cousin, after all."

"I know. The incident with the mistletoe earlier was unfortunate, I'm afraid, but Lady Selina's antics left us little choice." That was his story and he refused to change it.

"Don't despair, my darling," Medford said, crossing over to where she sat and kissing his wife on the forehead. "There are still two more days of the house party remaining. Who knows what these young people will get up to?"

Oliver gave him a skeptical glance. "Young people? I'm merely two years your junior, Medford."

"Not the point, Townsende. Besides." Medford turned back to face his wife. "What's this I hear about Lady Selina coming up with more games?"

Oliver groaned.

Chapter Ten

Oliver nearly ran into her. He'd followed that blasted Christmas cat into the conservatory and practically fallen into Cerian's lap. She sat on a stone bench at the back of the room, alone. The same stone bench he'd been heading toward to seek his own solitude. It was one of his favorite places in Medford's house, and Oliver had wanted to come here to clear his head, be alone, breathe in the soft scent of orchids that grew nearby, and think about everything for a moment. He'd never expected the bench to be occupied. It was never occupied. And where had that blasted cat got to?

Cerian glanced up a bit frightful, perhaps because a six-foot man had come barreling toward her. Her features relaxed when she recognized Oliver, and she smiled.

"I beg your pardon," he said, ready to turn on his heel and afford her the privacy she no doubt wanted. But he couldn't quite bring himself to turn away. Why was he so reluctant?

Cerian moved over and patted the bench. "There's room enough for both of us."

Oliver eyed the bench. There was room, wasn't there? That's what drinking brandy in the early afternoon did to you. It made you believe very, very bad ideas were very, very good ones. Had Miss Blake been drinking brandy too?

He took two steps forward and slid onto the cold stone next to her, bracing his palms against the bench. "You enjoy the conservatory?"

"Very much. This spot especially. The orchids are my particular favorite." She reached out and plucked one of the exotic purple flowers from the nearby vine. She twirled it between her thumb and forefinger.

"I like it here too." Good Lord, had his voice just caught? When was the last time that had happened? He must have been a lad of fourteen. He was sitting close enough to her now to smell her light perfume, even more captivating than the orchids.

"Are you hiding again?" she asked, gesturing back toward the main part of the house with her chin. "From the others?"

He cracked a smile. "No. This time I was purely in pursuit of a bit of solitude. I reserve my hiding posts for the silver closet." He looked at her from the corners of his eyes.

She laughed at that. "Well, I'm hiding," she admitted. "Though I'm happy to go elsewhere to allow you your privacy if you'd prefer." She moved to stand and Oliver's hand shot out to stop her. He clutched her wrist and pulled her back down next to him.

"Don't go," he murmured.

She settled back onto the bench and nodded. "Very well, but if we're to remain here, make no mistake that I *am* hiding." She grinned at him.

"As long as you're not hiding from me." He winked at her. "Because I hate to be indelicate but if so, you're not doing a very good job of it."

She pushed a curl away from her forehead. "No, not from you."

"Excellent. Then your secret is safe with me. Who are you hiding from this time?"

"Sir Gilliam again," she replied with a sigh, bracing one of her gloved hands on the bench beside her thigh.

"Gilliam?" Oliver whistled. "Quite a determined chap, is he not?"

"Yes. He asked me to go for a ride with him."

"You dislike riding?"

"On the contrary, I adore riding. I dislike Sir Gilliam."

"Why's that?" he asked, arching a brow.

She brought the orchid up to her nose and inhaled deeply. "Oh, he's a nice enough chap. A bit overly concerned with the health problems of his elderly relatives perhaps. He's taken to reciting all of his family's inherited diseases to me. Most recently he treated me to a list of his own ailments."

Oliver winced. "It doesn't sound very encouraging."

"Oh, it's not. He begged me wait while he hurried to the library so that he might look up the correct pronunciation of his cousin's toe fungus."

Oliver pressed his lips together to keep from laughing. "No, he did not."

"I'm afraid he did."

"And that's when you left?"

"Made my way to the nearest door and have been hiding in here ever since."

Oliver couldn't control his bark of laughter this time. "Miss Blake, do you know that you never fail to make me laugh?"

She shrugged. "I must admit, Mama always says I have a bit of a jester in me. But I'm not jesting. If Sir Gilliam offers to show you the funny patch of skin on the back of his hand, do not under any circumstances assent to it."

"I'll keep that in mind," Oliver replied, valiantly attempting to keep from snorting. "And I'd hardly say you're a jester. You simply have a unique way of looking at the world."

She hung her head at bit, studying the flower that dangled from her fingers. "I suppose it's quite different from the way a duke looks at the world."

He shrugged. "I wouldn't know."

Her head snapped up. "Whatever could you mean?"

He blew a breath from his lips and it rippled the dark hair along his forehead. "Did you know that I only just acquired my title last year?"

She nodded readily. "Yes, Mama mentioned it, but I just assumed that your father—"

"My father was the second son of a duke who had an older brother and a strong healthy nephew."

Cerian looked hopelessly confused. "I don't understand."

"The fact is that Kate was married to my cousin, the former duke."

Still clutching the orchid, Cerian's palms flew to her cheeks. "Kate's husband was your cousin?"

Oliver nodded. "Yes. George. He was murdered, I'm afraid. It was quite a scandal, actually. I'm surprised your mother didn't tell you."

Her fingers were still pressed against her cheeks and the shocked look remained in her pretty eyes. "I feel like a complete idiot. Of course I should have known it. But I don't pay much attention to titles and all of that. I knew Kate's husband was a duke but I didn't put together the family connection until now."

"Did you know George was murdered by his valet and our dear Kate was blamed for a time?"

Cerian's hands fell away from her face. She stared glumly at the mulched floor of the conservatory. "Yes. An awful business. I so wanted to come visit Kate when she was imprisoned in the Tower but Mama forbade it. I know how horrible Kate's husband was to her. She was . . ." Cerian audibly gulped. "A duchess."

Oliver laughed softly. "You say that word as if it's an anathema."

"Oh, it is, to me. I cannot imagine the responsibility such a title must bring. Or the scrutiny."

"Believe me, I didn't know it either. And I'm under added scrutiny actually."

She twirled the orchid between her fingers. "More scrutiny than being a duke?"

Oliver braced his hands against his knees. "Yes, because I'm a duke who is living down a scandal associated with my family name. Everything I do is watched. I cannot go anywhere, do anything, have a moment's peace. There are bets at the gentlemen's clubs in London about who I'm expected to marry."

"It must be awful," Cerian added, shaking her head again. "More awful than I could even imagine."

"It is. And I must make a decision quickly," he said. "The sooner the better. The less scrutiny I'll be under and the less conjecture. But it's been nice, this week. You've helped me take the pressure off with our game. Thank you for that."

Still seated, Cerian made a mock bow at the waist. "My pleasure, your grace. And . . . and I'm quite sorry that your cousin died."

"Thank you. Though the truth is, while I certainly didn't wish death on him, George and I weren't exactly close, and you're right, he was absolutely abominable to Kate."

Cerian weaved her fingers together in her lap and looked at them. "So, you're not a duke? That is to say . . . you were not raised to be a duke?"

"Not any more than you were." He cracked a smile. "I had a comfortable life and a modest town house in London and now I'm not only heir to one of the oldest and most prestigious titles in England, I'm expected to marry posthaste and produce the next heir."

"Did you . . . did you not intend to marry? Before you inherited the dukedom, that is?

He let out his breath. "I suppose I did. I've always been fond of children." He glanced at her and Cerian blushed. "But I intended to marry a nice young lady who wanted me for me, not a power hungry young woman with visions of a duchy in her eyes."

Cerian wrinkled her nose. "Like Lady Selina?"

"Exactly like Lady Selina." He nodded.

Cerian sighed. "I know just what you mean. I've always wanted to marry too but all anyone sees is my dowry. And all Mama cares about is a title."

"You don't sound as if you relish Society one bit."

"Oh, I don't. It makes me so nervous. The minute I get around anyone with a title I feel completely awkward and awful and out of my element."

He grinned. "I must say you seem to be doing fine here with me."

She blushed. "That's . . . you're different."

"How so?" He watched her intently.

"I don't know." She seemed to contemplate the matter for a moment. "I certainly hope you don't take this as an insult, your grace, but you don't seem a bit as if you have a title. Not to me, at least."

He laughed so loudly he had to clap his hand over his mouth and hope no one undesirable heard him and came running. "Miss Blake, I actually take that as one of the greatest compliments I've ever received. And please, call me Oliver."

"Now you're making fun of me," she said with a small smile. "And you may call me Cerian."

"Not at all. I'm entirely serious. Society has always been a part of my life but the title, well, the title is quite new."

"You must think I'm the biggest ninny you ever met, but Society frightens me horribly. It's just so rigid and unforgiving, and Mama puts so much stake in it. If I'm not accepted, she'll be devastated and I will be too. I hate myself for feeling that way, especially with people like Lady Selina skulking about, but I do."

Oliver placed a hand over hers and squeezed. "You're just being honest. And believe me you wouldn't be the first person to feel that way. It's not an easy group to join. And you should feel doubly sorry for me, I'm the one who will be forced to marry someone like Lady Selina. Imagine my horror."

Cerian was able to crack a smile at that and Oliver felt as if he'd won a great victory. Making her smile and laugh the same way she made him do so was important to him for some reason.

"I just wish it weren't so imperative to Mama for me to marry someone with a title."

"Ah, Miss Blake, it's imperative to all mamas, I'm afraid. Mine included."

Her smile turned wistful. "I just cannot imagine myself marrying someone like Sir Gilliam. I'd rather return to Wales and marry a farmer, or a tradesman, someone who actually loves me."

Oliver moved his hand over hers and squeezed it. She turned her head slightly, looked up at him with those wide green eyes.

His head moved toward hers, an inch, two. He didn't

know why. His mouth met hers slowly, tentatively. Her chin tilted up to make room. The kiss was soft, exploratory. She sighed a little and his arms wrapped around her, pulling her close. At first, he wondered if she'd push him away but she didn't. Instead she wrapped her arms around his neck and kissed him back. Then his lips moved with more urgency. She tasted like apple-spiced cider and the soft sounds she made in the back of her throat made Oliver shudder. His lips moved to her cheek, her neck, her ear. Her eyes closed and her head was thrown back. Her body bucked when his tongue touched the sensitive spot in her ear. And then his lips were back on hers, his tongue moved inside this time. She grabbed the lapels of his coat, holding onto him, braced against him. He kissed her again and again and again.

Chapter Eleven

Cerian pulled away sharply and wiped a shaky hand across her lips. Oliver concentrated on restoring his breathing to rights and willing his overheated body back to normalcy.

"What was . . . that?" she asked, slowly pulling her fingertips away from her mouth.

"It was . . ." He couldn't answer it either.

It was a rhetorical question and they both knew it, but Oliver couldn't help but ask himself the same thing. What was that? This time there was no mistletoe, no excuse, no pretending in front of other people. They were alone, just the two of them now, and that had been the kind of kiss that made his cock throb. He blew out deeply through his nose and shook order back into his mind.

"It was nothing," Cerian said, answering the question for both of them. "It's Christmastide. It's romantic. That's all. Yes. Yes."

"Christmastide?" Did his voice sound less sure than hers?

"Yes. That's all. We mustn't let our little game confuse us."

"Our little game?" Christ. Now he definitely didn't sound sure of himself.

"Yes. You know, pretending to be courting?" She cleared her throat and glanced away. "For the sake of the others."

Oliver blinked. He sure as hell hadn't just kissed her for the sake of the others or because he was playing a game. He'd kissed her because he wanted to, damn it. Wanted to badly. But Cerian seemed intent on relegating whatever had just happened between them to a mistake and Oliver wasn't about to declare himself to a woman who thought kissing him was a blunder.

"Quite right," he responded, steeling his resolve. "I forgot myself, forgive me."

Cerian nodded. "I . . . we . . . It's quite all right. We should simply be more careful henceforth."

He glanced at her. She smoothed a hand over her hair and straightened her shoulders. She looked as prim and proper as someone's fussy maiden aunt, nothing like the woman who'd just responded passionately in his arms. And she'd just used the word 'henceforth'; no good could come of that. But it was another word she'd used that worried him.

"Careful?" he asked. What the hell was she talking about?

"You know? We should, well, perhaps we should stay away from each other."

Oliver fought his groan. Cerian suggested they stay away from each other just when he relished her company the most.

"Dear, come for a walk with me in the conservatory."

Cerian gulped. She couldn't very well say no to Kate, but the conservatory was the last place she wanted to go.

She'd spent the last hour trying to banish the memory of the kiss she'd shared with Oliver there earlier.

She smiled weakly at Kate. "Why don't we walk down the corridor, instead?"

Kate gave her a broad smile. "Whatever you'd prefer."

Cerian entwined her arm through Kate's and the two women began a leisurely stroll.

Cerian took a deep breath. "Kate . . . I . . ."

Kate glanced at her. "Yes, dear?"

"I wanted to thank you for inviting me here."

Kate squeezed her hand. "I'm so happy you came."

"And for . . . sponsoring me and introducing me to everyone."

Kate patted her hand. "You're quite welcome, dear. I hope you've enjoyed yourself."

"Oh, I have, very much and I just . . ." She squeezed her hand into a fist and bit her knuckle

Kate's brow furrowed. "Go on. What is it, Cerian?"

"I just . . . Oh, Kate, I'm so sorry . . . about your husband." She clapped a hand over her mouth, suddenly afraid she'd said the awful word too loudly as it echoed off the marble surfaces in the corridor.

Kate stopped and turned to face her, smoothing her hands over Cerian's shoulders. "Oh, Cerian, dear, you've no reason to be sorry. That was all a long time ago."

"It must have been a nightmare for you. And Mama wouldn't let me come, and oh, Kate, you must have felt as if your family had abandoned you. I'm so sorry."

Kate nodded. "Your mother would hardly be doing her duty as an apt chaperone if she'd allowed you to visit an accused murderess in prison. I should have written you myself, but I was just so embarrassed and ashamed."

"I cannot imagine how difficult it must have been," Cerian sobbed.

Kate tipped up Cerian's chin and looked her in the eye.

"I admit there were nights I went to bed praying that I wouldn't wake up."

Cerian gasped. "No! Kate."

Kate smiled wanly. "But then I met James and George's valet confessed to the murder and well, the truth is that my life is much happier now than it ever was when I was married to George. I spent many months feeling guilty for thinking that way, but it's true."

Cerian squeezed her cousin's hand again. "I'm just glad you're so happy now. Truly I am. I just didn't know about you and His Grace . . . Oliver."

Kate's brow furrowed. "What do you mean? What about Oliver?"

"I didn't know that he wasn't raised to be a duke. It just surprised me, that's all."

They resumed their stroll down the corridor. "I noticed you called Oliver by his Christian name," Kate said.

Cerian blushed profusely. "Oh, I—"

Kate shook her head. "No need to explain. Oliver tells me you two are pretending to be courting."

Cerian sucked in her breath. "He told you that?"

"James guessed actually and Oliver admitted it."

Cerian glanced away, examining the faces of the Medford ancestors in the portraits that lined the walls of the hallway. "It's true."

"And how do you feel . . . about Oliver, I mean?"

"Feel about him? I barely know him."

Kate gave her a skeptical look. "I heard about that kiss in the library. By all accounts it didn't seem as if you two were pretending."

Cerian hung her head. "Oh, Kate. Mama's fondest dream would come true if I married a gentleman with a title. But you know as well as I that I'm not cut out to be in Society. I didn't grow up in this world. I'd always be a horrible outsider."

Kate tucked a curl behind Cerian's ear. "May I give you some advice, dear?"

"Of course you may."

"First, stay away from Sir Gilliam. We invited him because he's one of James's business associates but I've heard rumors that he's in terrible debt."

Cerian nodded. "No trouble on that score. I wondered if he was only sniffing after me because of my dowry. It certainly isn't because we have much to talk about. Aside from his cousin's foot ailments."

"Ick." Kate shook her head. Then she continued, "As for Oliver, remember that I wasn't raised to be in Society either. I didn't fit in for many years. But now, I couldn't imagine my life without James."

Cerian nodded and Kate continued, "You don't want to marry just to suit your mother and I understand that perfectly. But be sure not to discard someone you may care deeply for just to spite your mother either."

Chapter Twelve

By the time Lady Selina's mother, Lady Kinsey, sidled up to Oliver in the breakfast room, he'd already mentally planned his escape. He'd been reading the paper, clearly indicating he didn't relish company and he'd just swallowed the last bit of his poached egg when the lady slid into the seat across from him.

"Good morning, your grace," she said in a gratingly pleasant voice.

How did that woman manage to make his honorific sound dirty? He fought the urge to grind his teeth and eyed her warily. Lady Kinsey had been good-looking in her day, no question. But now she wore a bit too much rouge and, if rumors were true, she was a bit too free with her favors with men who were not her husband. "Good morning, Lady Kinsey. I was just about to—"

Lady Kinsey leaned over the table, affording him a more than ample view of her aging breasts. She lowered her voice to a hiss-like whisper. "Please tell me you're not serious about that Blake chit."

The paper nearly dropped from his fingers. He clenched his jaw. "Pardon?"

"Why, she's no more qualified to be a duchess than the parlor maid."

Oliver savagely twisted the sides of the paper in his fists. "I fail to see how that's any of *your* concern, my lady." He nearly spat the words.

Lady Kinsey lowered her voice and glanced around. "She's Welsh for God's sake."

Oliver took a deep breath. "Again, none of your concern."

She leaned ever closer, her eyes narrowed to slits. "I don't have to tell you how tarnished the Markingham title became after Lady Medford's little escapade last year. I fear your family name cannot withstand another smear upon it."

Oliver stared at her with unblinking eyes. "Do you have a point?"

She raised her chin. "Must you force me to spell it out, your grace?"

"Seems so," he drawled.

She leaned back and crossed her arms over her chest. "Very well then," she said, her voice still low. "I am close, personal friends with Lady Jersey, Lady Castlereagh, and Lady Cowper, the patronesses of Almack's. As you well know, one cross word from them and your family name would be quite sullied beyond all hope of redemption. Not to mention if they don't approve of your new wife, she'll be given the cut direct by everyone in the *ton*."

Blood pounded through Oliver's temples. "Might I remind you that my wife shall be a duchess?"

"Indeed, but a Welsh nobody wouldn't survive as a

duchess, Markingham. Not without the backing of those ladies. Do I make myself clear?"

Oliver stood and tossed the crumpled paper to the tabletop. "What exactly is it that you want from me, Lady Kinsey?"

She grinned at that. An evil-looking grin. "Selina is the perfect choice for a duchess, Markingham. You know that. She's been raised to the title since she was a babe."

"I've no doubt she would fit the role to perfection but what about the fact that we don't suit? I'm looking for a wife who's more interested in me than my title."

Lady Kinsey smirked. "You're a fool, Markingham. Who cares about interest? This is about money and combining two great houses. And keeping your family name intact."

Oliver's knuckles cracked. "And you intend to ensure that my wife and I are given the cut direct by all of Society if I don't choose Lady Selina?"

"Precisely. Selina and I have invented a final game to play before the house party is over. Let's just say you'd do well to pick her when the time comes. Do I make myself clear?"

Oliver pushed back his chair with a loud scrape. "You've made yourself entirely clear," he spat. He stood up, turned on his heel, and stalked away.

Cerian turned away from the back entrance to the breakfast room. Whatever Oliver and Lady Kinsey had been discussing, it seemed intense. And intimate. She shuddered. Lady Kinsey had leaned over and touched Oliver's hand. That was the type of woman who populated Oliver's world, not Cerian. Not a silly little Welsh mouse who didn't belong in London Society, let alone on the arm of a duke. Lady Kinsey and her daughter were beautiful and worldly and self-possessed. No doubt they never said awkward, silly things like Cerian seemed to blurt at every turn.

Cerian thought back to her conversation with Kate and cringed. Kate had spoken about Oliver as if she actually had a chance at winning him. And Cerian had been so bold as to actually discuss it with her cousin. What an idiot Cerian was. It didn't matter that Oliver hadn't been raised as the heir to a dukedom. He'd still been raised as the grandson of a duke. He still inhabited the world of the *ton*, a world Cerian had no place in. Oh, she could travel to Oxfordshire for a Christmastide house party and put diamonds in her hair and dress up and pretend. She might even meet a real duke and—gulp—kiss him. But that was as long as that fairy tale would last, no matter what she or her Mama wished for.

And the most miserable thing was that she'd realized something watching Oliver and Lady Kinsey. Cerian was jealous. Desperately so. And one didn't get jealous unless one had feelings for someone.

She'd been having schoolgirl fantasies about Oliver and somehow managed to forget that he was the most-sought-after man in London. And she was seven kinds a fool for forgetting it.

Cerian shook her head. No. No. No. This was all wrong, not how it was supposed to go at all. The playacting must stop. She must end it all now before she truly got hurt.

Oliver slammed his fist into the bag of hay. He'd come to the stables to borrow a mount to ride but instead he found himself in an empty stall, driving his fist into the first in-animate object he found.

Damn Lady Kinsey and her smug innuendo. How dare that woman threaten him and his family name? And damn George and his treatment of Kate and his fight with his valet that got him killed and smeared the Markingham name to begin with. His grandfather's legacy was something Oliver had been proud of his entire life, and now it was somehow miraculously entrusted to him and he carried the burden of restoring the name to its former glory. By God, the Markingham name had been esteemed for centuries and it would continue to be, with or without the approval of the bloody patronesses of Almack's.

But even as he thought the words, he knew they weren't true. The patronesses could and did control the gossip and approval of the majority of Society. If they chose to cut him or his family, there would be little he could do to restore the good name. One miracle had already happened when Kate had been allowed to reenter the *ton*'s good graces. But that had been largely due to the reputation and connections of her husband, Medford. The Markingham name was no longer hers.

But the worst part was that even if Oliver didn't give a bloody damn about himself, he did care about Cerian. She'd told him how vulnerable she was when it came to fitting into Society. How she dreaded it, wanted no part of it. It made her nervous, made her want to rush back to Wales and marry a nobody who truly loved her and lead a simple life. When he thought about the viciousness of members of Society like Lady Kinsey, he couldn't blame Cerian for her wish.

Damn her to perdition, but Lady Kinsey had got one thing right, and that was that if those smug, awful women decided to give Cerian the cut direct, she would be an outcast. And she was already trying desperately to fit in. They could completely destroy her. Even if he did give her the protection of his name. And regardless of how he was rapidly coming to care for her, Oliver would not allow his new inconvenient title to ruin a young woman as sweet and loving and funny as Cerian. He slammed his fist into the bag again. No. He would stay away from her. He had to. For her sake. By God, he'd stay out here in the stables hitting hay bags for the rest of the bloody house party if that's what it took.

Chapter Thirteen

The moment Oliver strolled into the drawing room after dinner, Cerian made her way over to him, steeling her resolve. "Your grace, a moment of your time?"

He nodded, an inscrutable look on his face. "Of course."

He allowed her to precede him to the corner and followed her there. Thank heavens they were partially obscured by a large potted palm. But not before Cerian noted Lady Kinsey's dark watchful eyes upon them.

The words tumbled out of Cerian's mouth in a rush. She'd been practicing them all morning and now that the moment was here, the words seemed to have become hopelessly jumbled. *Typical.*

"Your grace, I want to . . . that is . . . I wish to . . . That is to say, I . . ."

"Perhaps you should take a deep breath," he offered.

Had that been the duke talking or the voice in her head? Regardless, it was a fine idea and no matter its origin, she would take that bit of advice. She breathed in deeply, sucking air into her lungs and then blowing it out evenly, briefly closing her eyes.

"Feel better?" he asked.

Ah, so it had been his idea.

"Immensely," she replied. *Courage, Cerian. Say what you've resolved to say.* She could only hope that the duke would be able to hear her next words over the insane tapping of her nervous little foot. "Your grace, I wanted to tell you that I think it's time we agreed to, I mean, that we decided upon ending our agreement."

He narrowed his eyes on her. "Our agreement?"

She lowered her voice and glanced over her shoulder glaring at the potted palm as if that sneaky plant might be listening. "Yes. The one in which we were pretending to have affection for one another."

She held her breath, waiting for his response. Would he be angry? Would he be sad? Would he be . . . ? No doubt about it. The look on his face was pure . . . relief. She wrinkled her nose. Deflating, to be sure.

"I do think that's best, Miss Blake." He nodded.

She blinked. "You do?"

"Yes. Most prudent."

Unexpected tears stung the backs of her eyes. Wait a moment. Why was *she* upset? She'd begun this conversation. It had been her idea. "Oh, I'm so . . ." She searched her mind for the correct word. Devastated? Shocked? Unhappy? "Glad you agree, your grace," she finished, trying her best not to choke on the words. "Because here I'd been thinking I'd be letting you down easily and you've clearly been wanting to do the same."

She bit the inside of her cheek. How humiliating. Her only comfort was that she'd been able to say the actual words first. Ugh and she'd got the "most prudent" reply. *Doubly humiliating.*

He nodded perhaps a bit too emphatically. "There is only one more day of the house party after all."

"Exactly my reasoning," she replied, the smile she posted on her face overly bright.

"I see no reason why we cannot fend off our respective suitors for that short amount of time."

Cerian refused to allow the smile to falter. "I quite agree. One day is most manageable," she replied. "Not that I haven't appreciated your help over the past few days."

"And I yours," he said with a bow.

Cerian swallowed the unwelcome and untimely lump in her throat. "So, we are in agreement?"

"Quite."

"Quite," she echoed, wishing she could somehow disappear into the potted palm.

She was saved from an awkward good-bye, however, when Lady Selina clapped her hands and announced to the group at large, "Gather round, everyone. It's time for the next game of the house party."

Chapter Fourteen

Hide-and-seek. Why did it have to be hide-and-seek?

Cerian knew exactly where she wanted to hide. In the coach on the way home from this dreadful house party. But instead, she decided the more prudent route would be to sneak up the staircase when no one was looking and go to bed.

She couldn't stand the thought of Lady Selina chasing after Oliver. And finding him. And God only knew what she'd do if she caught him. No, no, no. Not after Cerian had just declared an end to her mutual alliance with him. It was all too much.

"The ladies shall hide and the gentlemen shall seek," Lady Selina announced with a bit too much premeditated glee in her voice.

Cerian crossed her arms over her chest. "No doubt she'll hide in Oliver's bedchamber," she mumbled to Kate who stood near her.

Kate leaned closer. "What was that, dear?"

"Nothing." Cerian smiled sweetly.

"The gentlemen shall count one hundred," Lady Selina said. "Whilst the ladies hide on the ground floor."

Cerian fought her eye roll. The only place she'd be hiding was under the covers of her own bed.

The gentlemen, led by an overly enthusiastic Sir Gilliam, began the count while the mostly giggling ladies dispersed into the corridor. Cerian dutifully followed them out and then waited just outside the door until all of the ladies were gone before she tentatively made her way toward the staircase in the foyer. She made it up the first ten steps before her mother's voice stopped her.

"Just where do you think you're going?"

Cerian froze, closing her eyes. She had been so close to freedom. So close. She slowly turned on her heel to face her mother. "I have a ghastly headache?"

But even she knew she didn't sound convincing.

Her mother crossed her arms over her chest and slowly tapped her foot on the marble floor, giving Cerian the stern stare for which she was famous.

Cerian slowly plodded back down the stairs. Her mother pointed down the corridor. "Go! Hide. We've only one more evening here and you've yet to receive any offers."

"But Mama I don't think—"

Her mother pointed again. "Go!"

Cerian began walking. There was no arguing with Mama when she was like this, and even worse, the woman would remain camped out in front of the stairs. Cerian had no hope of slipping away. Unless of course she could manage to find the servants' staircase. With that bit of hope in her heart, Cerian made her way through the corridor, pausing every now and again to look back and see her mother's disapproving stare fading into the distance.

Sighing, Cerian rounded a bend just as a loud male voice boomed through the house, "One hundred!"

Oh, jolly, the men were finished with the count. She could just picture Sir Gilliam and Lord Esterbrooke barreling through the doors no doubt with mistletoe in hand ready to demand a kiss from the unwitting female foolish enough to be standing in the middle of the corridor during a game of hide-and-seek.

Cerian glanced around a bit frantic. There had to be somewhere to hide temporarily, just while the gentleman passed through. Then she could resume her quest for the back staircase. She glanced to the left. Nothing. She glanced to the right. Nothing. Wait a tick. Nothing but the door to the silver closet.

The silver closet it was. She scurried across the polished floor, flung open the door, and hurled herself inside the empty closet just in time to hear the raucous laughter as the large group of men passed by. She tried to still her breathing, pressing her ear to the door to listen. They seemed to all be gone, but just to be certain, she would count five and twenty before she ventured out. She moved back from the door, pressing her hand to her chest.

"One, two, three," she whispered.

She took two steps into the darkness, pressing her back against the far wall. No need to light a candle. She wouldn't be here long.

"Four, five, six."

She braced her hand against the cabinet behind her. Hmm. What was the most likely location of the servants' staircase and how might she get there the most expediently?

"Seven, eight, nine."

What was that noise?

"Ten."

The door cracked open and just before the room was plunged into total darkness again, Oliver Townsende's face came into focus.

Chapter Fifteen

Had he seen her?

Cerian's heart pounded in her chest so loudly she was certain Oliver would hear.

She'd been back in the shadows. She'd seen him from the light in the hallway, but had he seen her? He moved then, coming toward her; she could tell by the shuffling of his feet on the floor and the intoxicating scent of him moving closer. He bumped into something and cursed lightly under his breath.

Cerian pressed her lips together tightly. He was searching for the candle, she realized with a sinking feeling in her middle. *The candle that was perched in a stick directly behind her in the cramped space.* Oliver grunted as he knocked into something else and Cerian covered her smile with her hand a moment before realizing how entirely unnecessary that action had been. She held her breath, not daring to breathe, lest he hear her.

Could she somehow move the candle out from behind

her? Hand it to him perhaps? Oh, yes, because a candle floating in the middle of thin air would raise no questions. She bit her lip to keep from laughing hysterically. Her foot was shaking with the desperate need to tap. She had to do something. She could hear his movements not two paces in front of her. He seemed to be touching everything along the shelf. He'd get to her and the candlestick soon. There was no help for it. She must either declare her presence or put her back against the wall opposite the shelf, suck in her belly, and hope against hope that he didn't bump into her.

Clearly the former of those two choices was the intelligent, mature thing to do.

So she did the latter.

She knew the moment his hand touched the candlestick. "Ah, there you are," he said and Cerian's heart nearly stopped. She curled her toes in her slipper. *No tapping. No tapping.* The flint was sitting next to the candle. Her presence was about to be discovered when the candle illuminated the space, so she did what any reasonable person would do in such circumstances and squeezed shut her eyes. What she didn't count on, however, was that the man would accidentally drop the flint.

"Blast," he mumbled just before Cerian heard a clatter on the floor next to her foot. She briefly considered attempting to kick the flint into obscurity but she might hit him with it and reveal herself.

Instead, she kept her eyes closed even though it was dark. He turned and his coat brushed her arm. She nearly whimpered. Why did he have to smell so very good? Oh God. Could he smell her? All right, now she was being ludicrous. Ludicrous, it seemed, was the order of the day.

He bent down, she could tell by the sound of his voice when he said, "Where are you?" He was searching, searching along and the floor and—

His hand brushed her ankle and Cerian jumped. Jumped, and if truth be told, squealed the tiniest bit before quickly clamping her hand over her mouth, mortified.

Oliver took a deep breath and let his hand play over the shapely ankle in front of him.

Cerian was here: He'd know the sound of that voice anywhere. Not to mention he'd previously encountered her in this precise location. He hadn't noticed before, or perhaps he thought he'd dreamed it, but the scent of her perfume wafted in the air along with the scent of the silver polish. He brushed his hand against her ankle again, once, twice. A sharp intake of breath. He braced himself. Would she slap him? Or kick him? He had to smile to himself at that thought.

He took a deep breath. Yes. This situation called for delicacy to be certain. Delicacy and self-control. Another smile.

He drew one finger up her ankle, higher, higher. Another sharp intake of her breath. Her silken stockings beneath his fingers made his hands tremble. He clenched his jaw. He ran his hands up the backs of her calves to her knees. This time her breathing was ragged.

Then he stood. He remembered the space and he'd best have a damn good memory for what he was about to do. He hovered over her, their deep breaths mingling in the small cramped dark space. He reached down, picked her up, and set her on the shelf behind him. She made a small gasp.

"Cerian," he breathed, just before his lips found hers in the darkness. She was sitting at waist height and he pulled up her skirts and spread her knees wide with his hands. She gasped against his mouth. His arm went around her lower back and he pulled her against him, hard.

This time he gasped. "Jesus," he groaned. He might as well have entered her then, the feeling was that evocative. Her head fell back and she groaned.

"Oliver," she whispered just before his mouth found hers again.

His fingers found the buttons on the back of her gown and made short work of them. Her gown gaped away from her chest and Oliver pushed the fabric down, down until his hands found her full round breasts. He bent his head. He had to taste her.

Cerian whimpered when Oliver's scorching hot mouth found her nipple. Here, in the dark, it was as if all things were possible. As if they weren't really doing this. It was all pretend. But nothing pretend had ever felt this good before. Her neck rolled on her shoulders and she shivered as one of his strong, warm hands found her nipple while his mouth continued to play, hot and wet over the other one.

His mouth bit, sucked, lapped at her. Cerian's eyes rolled back in her head. She'd never felt anything like it; she didn't want it to end. Whatever had passed between them earlier, their agreement to stop pretending, was all a blur of words to her now. She couldn't even remember what they'd said . . . exactly. All she knew was that Oliver's hands were on her body, playing her like a fine-tuned instrument, and she didn't want him to let go. His tongue flicked against the sensitive peak again, once, twice, and she pushed her fingers through his short, cropped hair, hugging his head to her breast, never wanting to let go.

His second hand moved down, down to her exposed knee and he dragged it along the outside of her thigh up to her hip. Then he traced her skin in a feverish pattern with his fingers. He drew his hand back down to her knee, slowly, so slowly, and inched it up again, this time on the inside of her thigh. Cerian shuddered. She should stop this. Say no. Hop off the shelf, perhaps slap him, and leave. But all she could think about was what he would do next. She desperately wanted to find out.

She held her breath. He drew little patterns on the skin of her thigh with his rough thumb. Then he moved his hand up, up, to the juncture of her thighs. A place that had gone all moist and hot as Cerian melted under his masterful touch.

When he touched the delicate skin between her legs, Cerian gasped and clamped her thighs together over his hand.

He pulled his mouth from her breast and spoke against her lips. "No, Cerian, darling, don't be afraid, open for me."

His voice was intoxicating, mesmerizing. She slowly widened her knees.

"That's it," he breathed against her mouth. "You feel so good."

He stroked her once, twice, and she shuddered, wrapping her arms tightly around his neck and pressing her forehead against his. His mouth returned to hers and his tongue stroked inside, calming her, relaxing her, telling her without words that he was going to make her feel amazing. And she knew it was true. Every single touch Oliver had given her since he'd brushed her ankle had been better than the one before.

One finger entered her, slid inside so soft, so gentle. She shuddered against him. His other hand wrapped around her back, cradling her against him and then his thumb found the little nub between her legs and he stroked her gently.

"Oh, God, Oliver."

He kissed her then, deeply, all the while using his finger to stoke the fire that was building inside of her. His rough thumb kept up its pressure against her softest spot and when he began rubbing her in tiny little circles, Cerian gasped.

"Oliver, no!"

"Shh," he whispered against her mouth. "Just let go."

Let go? Could she let go? She took a deep breath, let her head fall back, kept herself anchored to him by the arms she had wrapped around his strong neck. His finger moved inside her, and she shuddered. His thumb rasped against her, once, twice, three times. She cried out his name, just before shudders racked her entire body and she sobbed against his chest.

Oliver's breathing was labored, heavy. His forehead was slicked with sweat and his entire body shook. He kissed her again, deeply. Cerian's limbs felt languorous. In her entire life, she'd never imagined anything like . . . that.

He pulled her skirts back down her knees and helped her right her gown, fastening the buttons in the back. Then he pulled her off the cabinet and set her gently on the ground. He hugged her close for just a moment before Cerian, suddenly more frightened than she'd ever been, pulled away from him.

"I must go," she said, making her way past him and grasping the door handle. "Mama will be expecting me for my nap before the ball tonight."

But she knew she wasn't about to get a wink of sleep.

Chapter Sixteen

Oliver glanced across the ballroom. There she was. His stomach dropped. Cerian was laughing at something Sir Gilliam or Lord Esterbrooke had said. Oliver couldn't take it. She looked for all the world as if she was flirting with the two men, standing across the dance floor, looking more beautiful than he'd ever seen her with her dark shining hair catching the light from the candles and a lush violet ball gown hugging her curves. Lord Dashford leaned down and said something near her ear and Oliver's mind exploded with rage.

By God, he was jealous. He'd never been jealous. That unwanted emotion was barely something that had registered with him before. But standing too far away from her, watching her laugh and talk with the two other men, he knew it readily for what it was. Burning, unreasonable jealousy.

Fine. Perhaps he didn't have the right to be jealous. Perhaps he still hadn't had a chance to wrestle with the feelings of desire and longing and confusion that their little interlude in the silver closet earlier had stirred up in him. Perhaps he was about to make a giant ass of himself. But Oliver didn't care anymore.

He marched across the floor toward the little group. Without so much as a by-your-leave, he gave the other men a vicious glare and grabbed Cerian by the hand and dragged her away. "Gentlemen, excuse us," he bit out.

Cerian tugged against his tight hold but he didn't give her the time or opportunity to stop him. Instead, he turned immediately and headed for the nearest door. He dragged her into the corridor, down the long end of the hallway and around the corner. Once he rounded the corner, he opened the door to the silver closet and unceremoniously pulled her inside, shutting the door behind them.

Without saying a word, he struck the flint, and the candle that had caused them both so much grief earlier, burst into flame. Then he turned to face her. She wore a look of shock and outrage on her gorgeous face.

The silver closet. It was too much. The images of what they'd done together here only hours earlier flashed through Cerian's mind like a dirty play. She couldn't stay in here with him. Couldn't even breathe.

She stared him down. "What do you think you're doing, dragging me out of the ballroom like that? The entire room must be agog. We'll be the talk of the house party."

"We're already the talk of the house party," he replied, leaning back against the cabinet, the cabinet where they'd nearly made love, and crossed his arms over his chest. "I wanted to speak with you."

She tossed a hand in the air. "That much is obvious. What do you have to say?"

"Do you really think you'll be happy with someone like Sir Gilliam? Or Esterbrooke?"

Her mouth dropped open and she stared at him as if he'd lost his mind. "What are you talking about?"

"You seemed to be quite cozy with both men in the ballroom just now." A muscle ticked in his jaw.

Cerian pressed a hand against her heaving chest. "Cozy? How dare you? You have the audacity to question *me* when Lady Selina has been chasing after *you* for days?"

"I never seemed as if I was interested, did I?"

If she hadn't been so shocked by his words, she would have slapped him. "I didn't see you turning your eyes away this morning when Lady Kinsey was speaking to you in the breakfast room. And she seemed to be on *full display* at the time."

The muscle in his jaw ticked faster. "I wasn't looking at Lady Kinsey," he ground out through clenched teeth.

"You might have fooled me."

He tossed a hand in the air. "So I'm wrong about you flirting with Lord Esterbrooke? And Gilliam?"

She pressed her hand to the wall to steady herself. "Flirting!"

"Yes, flirting. That's what it looked like from where I was standing."

They hurt, these accusations. They hurt more than she could say. Especially when Oliver was standing there looking so blasted good in his formal black evening wear and acting as if he hated her. It hurt even more because she had feelings for him. Feelings that were stronger than anything she'd ever expected. If she'd doubted them before, their interlude earlier had taught her. She cared for him. Deeply. And here he was accusing her of flirting with those two sops in the ballroom when she had simply been doing her level best not to appear as if anything was out of the ordinary. As if she hadn't just gone and fallen in love with the one most inappropriate person in the entire house party. No, wait, the entire *country*.

Blast it. He would never understand her. He couldn't understand her. He might not have been raised to be a duke. But he was raised in this world. A world of flirting and backstabbing and political alliances formed through marriages. There was nothing in this world for her. She *must* remember that.

She loved him. Fine. Unfortunate, but true. She loved him but she'd sooner trudge all the way back to Wales on foot with no coat or snow boots than admit it to him.

She lowered her voice to a bare whisper. She still couldn't look at him. "My apologies, your grace. But I thought we'd both made it clear that we were done pretending to flirt with each other."

Oliver's head snapped to the side as if he'd been slapped. She might as well have hit him. He would have preferred it actually, would have welcomed the physical pain as opposed to the intangible pain that ripped through his chest at her words. "Pretending to flirt." That's all it had been to her, hadn't it? And here he'd allowed himself to be persuaded that she actually cared for him. Had actually opened herself up to him earlier emotionally and physically because she felt something for him beyond a mutual agreement to use each other to fend off others. Why had she even bothered? It was laughable. She certainly hadn't seemed as if she minded the advances of either Esterbrooke or Gilliam in the ballroom a few minutes ago.

And here he'd acted like a complete fool, dragging her out of there like a lout, wanting an explanation, her attention, something, anything to explain why it made him sick with anger to see her with another man. It was a feeling he found singularly unpleasant and he loathed himself for it.

And why in the hell was she pretending as if she cared about his interactions with Lady Kinsey or Lady Selina? As if he gave a damn about either of those two. Lady

Selina could rip off her gown in the middle of the ballroom and he wouldn't look twice. No. It made no sense why Cerian would even bring it up as if it mattered to her. She was obviously trying to deflect the blame from herself.

He took a long, deep breath. Blast it. The fact was Oliver had never been more scared in his life. His entire adult life. Oh, he'd been a bit frightened of the dark when he was a lad of three or four but he'd quickly forced himself to get over that by experimenting with going into dark rooms time and again and sitting there until the fear passed. He honestly couldn't remember a time when he'd been more scared than he was now. The feelings he had for Cerian were more powerful than any he'd had before for any woman and it scared the hell out of him. This is what he'd always imagined it would feel like when he— damn it all to hell—fell in love. He was completely out of his element.

But here she was, the one woman at the house party who wanted no part of him and his title and she was the one woman he couldn't erase from his memory. Damn it. Life was unfair sometimes.

But the fact remained that Cerian Blake was completely inappropriate for him. She wanted no part of being a duchess and she wanted no part of him either.

He refused to make a fool of himself over a woman who didn't want him.

"You're right, Miss Blake," he said, moving past her and opening the door to the closet. "My apologies. We both agreed we're done with our little distraction. I find I'm also no longer interested in pretending."

Chapter Seventeen

"One of the grooms seems to think there's a madman in here unmercifully punching a bag of hay." Medford appeared on the other side of the stable stall, his hands resting nonchalantly in his pockets.

Oliver barely glanced up from his punching session with the hay bag. He'd ripped off his cravat and tossed it on another pile of hay behind him. His shirt was open at the throat and sweat beaded down his forehead and chest despite the December chill in the stables. He grunted at Medford.

Medford arched a brow. "Seems the groom was right."

Another grunt. Another savage punch to the middle of the bag.

Medford leaned a shoulder against the stall wall. "Care to inform me why you're so angry at a hay bag?"

Oliver wiped at the sweat in his eyes with the back of his forearm, then threw another punch. "Not particularly."

Medford sighed. "Forcing me to guess, are you? Very

well, my guess is this has something to do with one Miss Cerian Blake."

Oliver pulled his next punch and turned to face Lord Perfect, his eyes narrowed.

"I was right, wasn't I?" Medford asked with a smirk.

Oliver rubbed his hand over his eyes and groaned.

"Let me guess a bit more," Medford continued. "You care for the chit, more than you realize, and you don't know what to do about it?"

A savage grunt from Oliver this time. "I suppose you'd never do anything as crass as taking out your frustration on a bag of hay?"

Medford chuckled. "On the contrary, it's better than finding a seedy tavern in London and drinking far too much gin out of an extremely questionable glass."

Oliver furrowed his brow. "Pardon?"

"That's what I did when I found myself inconveniently, unfortunately, undisputedly in love. With a woman who wanted no part of me, I might add."

Oliver shook his head. "Kate?"

Medford nodded. "One and the same."

Oliver felt as if the hay bag had just punched him back. The wind was knocked out of him. He struggled for a breath. "Wait. I'm not . . . I'm not in love."

Medford propped an elbow on the stall wall. "Aren't you? The hay bag begs to differ."

Oliver stared at the bag and then at his bruised fists, and let out a long, slow breath. He rested his hands on his hips and bowed his head. "Damn it."

"Quite right," Medford replied.

"What the hell am I doing?" Oliver breathed.

"From the looks of it, I'd say you're inappropriately taking out your anger on a perfectly innocent bag of hay when what you really should be doing is telling the lady you love her."

Love? The word made Oliver's stomach clench. He kicked at a stray bit of hay with his booted foot. "I can't—We can't—"

"I won't argue that it's not complicated. But I've got faith in you, old chap. You'll figure it out." And with that, Medford strolled out of the stable, whistling as if he hadn't a care in the world.

Oliver stood alone in the silence for a minute. He ruthlessly punched the hay bag five times, six, eight, ten. Then he collapsed against it, completely spent, his eyes closed, his breath coming in ragged pants. What the hell did Medford know about it?

Plenty, his mind replied.

But it wasn't that simple.

Neither was Medford's courtship of Kate.

But Medford wasn't a duke with a name to protect.

No, he was a viscount who owned a printing press and risked his entire reputation and livelihood for Kate.

Damn it. Blast it. Bloody hell. Medford was right.

"Tell the lady you love her," Medford had said. This time Oliver kicked the bag of hay as hard as he could. It was true. He did love Cerian. And she felt something for him too. He knew it. They might not have met under the perfect circumstances, might not have acted appropriately by pretending to be courting, but somewhere along the way, he'd gone and fallen in love with her. His bruised knuckles proved it.

He'd convince her, by God. He had to.

And he wasn't about to waste any more time. He glanced around the stall and swiped up his cravat. He was going to need a bath first, and a new set of clothes.

And a little luck.

Chapter Eighteen

Cerian intended to slap Lady Selina before it was all over. Cerian's fingers were tingling with the urge and that was before that little hoyden had the nerve to put her arm around Oliver's and pull him into the middle of the drawing room.

Following tradition, they had just lit the Yule log in the main room from a lump of charcoal left over from last year's celebration. Everyone was drinking wine and singing a Welsh carol that Cerian's mama had taught them.

"Gather round, everyone," Lady Selina said in a singsong voice. Cerian could barely stand to look at either of them but a quick glance in Oliver's direction at least gave her the comfort that he looked nearly as annoyed by Lady Selina as she was. He did not, however, pull his arm from her grasp, Cerian noted with a bit of ire simmering in her chest.

Where was Mama? It was high time they left this place. The entire week had been a waste as far as Cerian was con-

cerned and even Mama would be able to see reason and realize she wasn't on the verge of getting an offer. Why, after
the snippy words she'd exchanged with Lord Esterbrooke
and Sir Gilliam as soon as she'd returned to the ballroom
earlier, those two suitors were keeping their distance.
Cerian felt nothing but relief. Very well, and a bit of guilt.

And now, whatever asinine game Lady S was up to,
Cerian could be certain it would involve something idiotic and unappealing. Cerian didn't care what Mama said
this time. The woman could be lying across the staircase
demanding she return and Cerian would pick up her
skirts and step over her. Even Mama wouldn't be so crass
as to make a scene on Viscount Medford's main staircase.
Would she?

"It's time for the final game," Lady S said. The look on
Oliver's face remained a mask of stone but Cerian barely
glanced over her shoulder as she made her way toward
the door. Slinking along as unobtrusively as she could so
no one would notice her flight. No. No. She'd just slip away.
Quietly. No fuss. No scene.

"Each gentleman shall be given a bough of mistletoe
and he shall have to present it to the lady most worthy,
the lady he has most enjoyed spending time with, the
lady he might choose to spend time with in the future."
She gave Oliver a sidewise look.

A cacophony of nervous giggles and twitters made
their way around the perimeter of the drawing room and
Cerian rolled her eyes. Why exactly was Lady Selina so
enamored of mistletoe? Why, if she didn't know better,
Cerian would think her family owned a share in a mistletoe farm. But she wasn't about to stay and listen to some
ninny-hammered mistletoe acceptance speeches from a
bunch of ladies she hoped to never see again.

Lady Selina clapped her hands. "The Duke of Markingham shall go first! Won't you please, your grace?"

Cerian closed her eyes. Five simple steps. She was only five simple steps away from the door. She'd nearly made it, by God. But the moment she heard that Oliver was going to go first, she became rooted to the thick Indian rug. She'd expected Lady Selina to save him for last, draw out her own anticipation more, no doubt. Though it stood to reason. No doubt Lady Selina was ensuring that Oliver would pick her first and spare her any potential awkwardness should another potential swain present her with a bough.

It made Cerian's stomach turn. Not enough, however, to cause her to leave the room. Instead she turned on her heel. *Refuse the bough, Oliver,* she mentally begged him. Surely, he would do the right thing and decline to be a part of this idiocy.

Instead she watched with wide eyes as Oliver took the first bough from Lady Selina's only too-eager hands.

Lady Selina had demurely stepped back into the crowd and was smiling prettily, her eyes downcast as if she didn't fully expect Oliver to turn and present her with the bough.

"There is a young lady," Oliver began, "to whom I would like to present this mistletoe."

Cerian ground her teeth. She detested herself for not having left the room and now she had only herself to blame while she was forced to watch Oliver give the mistletoe to Lady Selina or someone equally insipid. "I'm no longer interested in pretending either," he'd said. The words ripped through her heart again as if he'd just uttered them.

She glared at her slippers. Wondering if she could back out of the room without looking up and having to see the spectacle with her own eyes. Could she successfully navigate herself backward toward the door and slip through it without looking? Was she brave enough to attempt it or would she merely end up tripping and making a fool of herself only to look up and see Oliver handing over that stupid branch to Lady Selina? She could just picture the smug look on the younger woman's face now.

A shadow fell across her slippers. Cerian looked up.

She gasped.

There, standing in front of her, offering the bough of mistletoe, was Oliver.

"Miss Blake," he said, his bright blue eyes shining. "Would you do me the honor?"

Cerian's voice caught. Her breathing hitched. She tried to push the word 'yes' past her dry lips but it wouldn't budge. All she could do was stare up at him with wide eyes and dumbly nod.

Lady Selina grasped her throat as if she were choking.

"Your grace?" Lady Kinsey's voice came cutting through the silence that hung in the room.

Oliver half turned as if to hear her better. "Yes, my lady?"

The matron's face was bright red and she looked as if she was on the verge of an apoplectic fit. "Your grace, I believe you've made a mistake, *haven't you*?" The last two words were laced with such venom and innuendo, Cerian wondered at their earlier conversation.

Oliver didn't bother to turn and face the woman. "No, Lady Kinsey. There's been no mistake."

Lady Kinsey's entire body shook with rage. "You choose this *nobody*?"

Oliver spun on his heel to face Lady Kinsey this time. "I'd watch what you say, my lady. You're speaking of my future wife."

Cerian and Lady Selina simultaneously gasped. Lady Kinsey raised a fist. "Your family name won't withstand this! You'll both be outcasts!"

Lord Medford stepped in deftly just then and said, "It appears you're correct, Lady Kinsey. There has, indeed, been a mistake. A grave one, I'm afraid."

Lady Kinsey raised her chin a notch and gave Cerian and Oliver a haughty, triumphant stare. "I thought so," she intoned without actually turning her attention to Lord Medford.

"The mistake was made when you and your daughter were invited to this house party, my lady," Medford said, a completely blank look on his face. "If you'll allow me to escort you to the door, the mistake can be remedied post-haste."

Medford offered an arm. The look of horror on Lady Kinsey's face rivaled the look of triumphant joy that Cerian knew was on her own. She raised her chin a notch this time.

Lady Kinsey savagely gripped her skirts in both hands. "I'll see myself out, Medford," she lashed at him. She quickly marched past all of the gaping mouths in the drawing room and out the door. Lady Selina burst into fake-sounding tears and followed her.

Oliver turned back to Cerian and fell to one knee. Cerian clutched the mistletoe like a lifeline.

"You didn't answer, Miss Blake. Will you be my wife?"

Cerian pulled Oliver to his feet and motioned for him to lean down so she could whisper in his ear. "Is this part of our pretend relationship?"

"No. Why? Would you prefer that?" He grinned.

"No."

"I'm glad you said that because I was hoping you'd agree to be the Duchess of Markingham."

"I don't know how to be a duchess," she said, feeling the eyes of everyone in the drawing room upon them.

"You're in perfect company then because I don't know how to be a duke. We'll learn together."

"What if I trip in front of the queen or use the incorrect form of address when speaking to a baron or something?"

Oliver watched her face, the hint of a smile tugging at

his lips. "God, Cerian. You make me laugh even when I'm proposing marriage to you."

From the corner of her eyes, Cerian saw Mama turning a mottled shade of purple. No doubt the woman was about to have a fit while her daughter took her time saying yes to a proposal from a duke.

Cerian bit her lip. Her foot was tapping in its predictably embarrassing woodpecker-like manner. She couldn't capitulate so easily, however. There were many things to consider. Big, important things. "What about your reputation?" she countered.

"What about it?"

Cerian couldn't seem to get enough air in her lungs. "What about Lady Kinsey's threats?"

Oliver squeezed her hands. "What about the fact that I'm in love with you, Cerian? And I cannot imagine my life without you?" He stood, cupped her cheeks with his hands, and stared deeply into her eyes.

Very well. That did it.

Tears dropped down her cheeks. "Yes. Yes. Yes, I'll marry you, Oliver. Yes!"

A relieved smile spread across his handsome face. He swept her up into his arms and the entire drawing room erupted into a cacophony of cheers.

Moments later, when Oliver let Cerian slide from his arms, she stared up dreamily into his eyes. The entire drawing room was issuing their congratulations to Oliver and best wishes to her. Something brushed against Cerian's ankles and she looked down.

The cat.

This time the cat wore a bit of mistletoe on her head. The sprig was angled jauntily over one pointy ear.

"Medford," Oliver said to his friend who had re-entered the room. "This is the cat I asked you about."

"Yes," Cerian said, looking toward Kate. "What is this cat's name?"

Medford and Kate glanced at each other.

"I have no idea whose cat that is. It certainly doesn't belong to us," Medford replied.

"Whose cat is this?" Kate called out to the assembled guests, turning in a circle to see who would claim the animal.

No reply.

Cerian bit her lip. "She doesn't belong to Lady Kinsey and Lady Selina, does she?"

Medford laughed at that. "Hardly. I can tell you those two ladies have no interest in pets."

Medford called to the butler, "Locke, where did this cat come from?"

The butler shook his head. "Mrs. Hartsmeade has been asking me about this cat all week," he said, referring to Medford's housekeeper. "We assumed she belonged to one of the guests. Mrs. Hartsmeade has been decorating that cat for Christmastide every day. I dare say the animal seems to enjoy it."

They all laughed and Cerian bent down to rub the cat on the head.

"Strange, but the cat doesn't appear to have an owner." Medford shrugged.

Cerian scratched the cat under her little chin while the feline purred contentedly. "Well, she does now. She's our cat."

Oliver glanced down at his affianced bride and smiled. "What do you intend to name her?"

Cerian scooped the cat into her arms. "Why, Merry, of course. With an e and two r's. She was responsible for bringing us together, wasn't she? She'll be a fine cat in a duke's household."

Oliver patted the cat on the head and pulled Cerian

into his arms for another kiss. "I think Merry is the perfect name," he said. "And I think you and I are going to be very happy together."

Cerian nodded, tears in her eyes. "I agree, Oliver. Truly, I do." She smiled at him over the cat's fluffy gray head. "You know, I once thought it was impossible for a duchess to love her duke."

He tugged her hand to his lips and kissed it softly. "Tell me you've changed your mind, my love."

"I have. I absolutely have." She glanced up at the ceiling where a festive bough of mistletoe hung. "And to think it all happened under the mistletoe."

'Tis the season to fall in love...

Don't miss these other delightful holiday e-novellas

Christmas at Seashell Cottage
Donna Alward

The Billionaire Cowboy
Mandy Baxter

Once Upon a Christmas Kiss
Manda Collins

The Mistletoe Effect
Melissa Cutler

A Little Christmas Jingle
Michele Dunaway

Blame It on the Mistletoe
Nicole Michaels

On the Naughty List
Lori Foster, Carly Phillips, Beth Ciotta, Sugar Jamison

From St. Martin's Press